# Worth Saving

A Novel

Michelle M Ryan

# Part One

# Chapter One

*What do these people want from me—God I want out of here...*

*An early spring morning in June 2005, the air in the spacious office was thick with overbearing accolades. Courtney Brooks, freshman pre-med student at the private and prestigious Grayson U, was ready to puke; she smiled instead.*

"You've had an exceptional year, Courtney. Your grades are excellent, and you've finished in the top ten percent of this year's freshmen class. In an institution with our rigorous standards, that's quite an accomplishment. The entire Department of Medicine is proud of you, and you young lady, should be prouder of yourself," Dean Wilkerson said, though he wasn't looking at her and sounded like he was reading from a script.

Nods and murmurs of agreement echoed from the other four School of Medicine faculty members in attendance that morning. Dean Wilkerson, the chair of the department, continued piling it on, as Courtney sat motionless in the massive leather chair, her ankles crossed, and hands clasped in her lap. Her eyes occasionally wandered from his face and intermittent, condescending smile, to the large window over his shoulder; the airplane flying from left to right in the clear blue sky. She wanted to follow it with her mind, to shut out her surroundings. Instead she pulled her gaze from the window, focused on the conversation, and with effort, fixed the smile on her lips that they all expected; her eyes remaining flat.

"We know this is the last week of school, and you'll be heading home for the summer, nevertheless, we want to make you aware of some research opportunities you should consider applying for." This came from Dr. Campbell, the assistant dean, who sat to Courtney's right. Her long, tanned legs were crossed while she sipped coffee from bone china etched with swirling violets.

The office, Courtney surmised, was four times the size of the dorm room she shared with her roommate. This is where the five of them, poised in high-backed burgundy leather chairs, faced the dean who appeared diminutive behind his massive oak desk.

Inside she felt like a panicky imposter, and the leather chair knew it—ready to open at any moment and swallow her whole. Courtney Brooks from St. Joseph, Missouri, didn't belong here, and from the air of stiff cordiality in the room, they all knew it. The conversation was quiet and subdued while in the background, coming from the adjacent meeting room, they heard the clinking of glassware. The aroma of bacon and Belgian waffles lingered in the air, as the food service staff removed the remnants of the lavish breakfast she'd barely touched.

When receiving the call from the dean's secretary, the previous week, informing her of the invitation to breakfast with him and his staff, she'd assumed it included a group of first year, pre-med students, but she'd been the lone honoree.

"We don't often recommend sophomores for these types of projects," this came from Dr. Reynolds, the Vice-chair of the department, who was to her left, "but you've shown such promise, we think you'll benefit from the additional exposure. Of course, it'll involve more work and can in no way affect your regular coursework, but I and the other instructors in the department are confident you can handle it." He pushed his glasses up on the bridge of his nose and nodded to her.

She returned the nod, then gave the faculty administrators the expressions of humility and gratitude they expected, knowing a few more nice words and half-hearted compliments, would bring the ordeal to a merciful end. She hadn't asked for this and wondered, what was their angle anyway? Mary's voice entered her head: "People aren't nice unless they want somethin'". She hated to admit that this time her old grandmother might be right—which is why she dismissed it all: their honors, kind words, and project opportunities—as undoubtedly a means of obtaining some government funding or tax-break; why else were they taking pity on an underprivileged, motherless black girl. It wasn't about them helping her—they were helping themselves.

The facts spoke for themselves, however: Courtney's academic year had been stellar, which was her norm. She'd long been classified as academically gifted and had no memory of earning a grade below an A, ever. The work during this, her first year of college, had been challenging; but being away from home, and her boyfriend Sean, had made applying herself easy. She'd avoided social distractions; he demanded an accounting of every minute she spent outside of class. *God, I miss him so much—I can't wait...*

"We just wanted to take this opportunity to congratulate you again," the Dean said standing, indicating their time had ended. "Enjoy your summer, Courtney, and we look forward to having breakfast with you this time next year and the next."

The professors continued the chorus of compliments as they walked her from the office to the building exit. She smiled and accepted the praise, while at the same time convincing herself it was all meaningless.

"How can I get through to you young women—there are guys *everywhere*," Dr. Curtis, Courtney's biology professor, said the following week during their final conference of the year. Having been her favorite instructor, Courtney had confided in her.

The woman's voice rose with emotion, a product of the frustration she encountered every year, usually with girls. They simply quit. It was more common with students struggling academically, who longed to run home and escape the life of high expectations. Rarely did a student who'd achieved so much and had displayed such promise, as the young woman sitting before her, decide to throw it all away.

The socially awkward Courtney Brooks was a brilliant student. The educator was convinced, another outstanding year at the university would instill in her the confidence she needed to break out of her cocoon. It was their last meeting; her one shot to persuade her to give herself that chance—just one more year.

"So what, Courtney—if you don't mind my getting personal for a minute —the boyfriend wants to settle down and get married—he can't wait for you three more years?" She watched her prized student bite her lower lip, look away, and lapse into a fidgety silence. *The selfish jerk—whoever he is—doesn't even want to marry her.*

The only sound in the room came from the educator—drumming her French manicured nails on her desk. "I've got some advice for you and I want you to listen—carefully," more drumming, more silence. "If you don't, I'm afraid you'll regret it," she paused again while noisy laughter from students in the corridor drifted in. "You've got a free-ride scholarship—coming back next semester won't cost you one red cent. Give it more time. If the relationship is important to him (*and if he's any kind of man*) he should be willing to give you that. If he's not, you're smart, beautiful and better off without him. Maybe after another year, he'll be ready to commit. My God, girl!" She stood up and raised both arms, appealing to the heavens. "Don't give in so darned easy, you're worth more than that, your future is worth more..."

Courtney listened and watched the animated, fortyish blond continue to make her impassioned plea and knew what Dr. Curtis was saying made sense for a normal person who had people who loved and supported them. She, on the other hand, had a dead mother and no father. Her boyfriend was her life; every day she stayed at Grayson; he was with someone else. She was in danger of losing everything and couldn't risk one more year.

She'd had brains all her life and would become a doctor no matter what; who cares who pays for her education or where she graduates from? A doctor is a doctor. She didn't owe anyone anything. So what if the scholarship was valuable; they can give it to someone else who wants it.

*People talk a good game but none of them really give a darn*, is what Mary had taught her. She was sorry to disappoint the well-intentioned advisors who misunderstood her choice, but Courtney had to do what was best for her.

# Chapter Two

"What do you mean you're not going back?" Carmen shouted at her younger sister over the blaring television. She was standing near the front door, refusing to sit anywhere in Mary's filthy house. The place had layers of dust caked everywhere, and smelled like a combination of cigarette smoke, mildew, and body odor. Every piece of furniture was ancient and falling apart, as was Mary.

While in the area, she'd stopped in to say hello to her sister, just home from college, but had been slapped in the face by the girl's casually relayed announcement. "Courtney, you have a full scholarship and you've made a 4.0 your first year. What the hell is wrong with you? Why are you doing this—can you tell me that? There must be a reason. Were you bullied—discriminated against? We can get legal counsel and have that situation fixed." She stomped into the living room and grabbed the remote control from the coffee table, switching off the television in the middle of Mary's favorite talk show. "Old woman, did you have something to do with this?" She said, hand on her hip, standing over and snarling at her grandmother reclining on the rundown sofa.

Mary, a frail woman of barely 95 lbs., squinted up at Carmen with chronically bloodshot eyes. Her skin color was caramel-brown with a yellowish tinge that matched the whites of her eyes. She'd been an alcoholic for as long as Carmen, who was now twenty-eight, could remember.

"She ain't told me nothin'," Mary said, glaring and waiting for Carmen to turn the television back on. "I don't know how *she* knows she's welcome back in here." She reached for the glass of brown liquid ever present on the coffee table, beside the lit cigarette in the ashtray.

"I don't have to ask you anything, old woman; *you* don't have a choice." Courtney rolled her eyes at them both before strutting, in her Daisy Duke cut offs and low-cut red tank top, into the kitchen.

"Where are you going?  We're not finished talking about this.  Do you know how much that scholarship you're throwing away is worth?  It's one of the top schools in the country.  I'm not going to stand by and let you do something so stupid!" Carmen tracked behind her.

"Why not?  Standing by and doing nothing is what you do best—isn't it?  Why change now?" She spoke with her back turned while rummaging through the cabinet

Carmen threw up her hands.  "So– it's my fault you're making a dumb decision?  Probably to be closer to your so-called boyfriend.  I bet that's it," she tapped her foot.  "Know what?  I run into him with some girl almost every weekend.  If he's the reason you're throwing away your future, I'm telling you now—you're wasting your life."

"And you're wasting my time!  Goodbye." Courtney flicked the back of her hand, then poured cereal and milk into a large bowl, pretending Carmen wasn't there.  She'd been home two weeks and decided to tell her family about her plans for the next school year.  Disagreement from her advisers at Grayson she'd expected but was clueless as to why Carmen was so outraged.  Probably thought she'd try to move in with her; she'd choke before asking her for anything.  Carmen and Mary had nothing to worry about from her—she had other plans.

*How can she not see what she's giving up?* Carmen stood in the kitchen, arms folded, tapping her foot, grappling for an answer to avert the disaster. *Maybe drug her, drive her back to Grayson, and dump her there until she gets some sense into her head. Kidnapping? Really? a bit much.* Courtney was young, dumb, thought she was in love, and was legally old enough to screw up her own life. Should be against the law but wasn't. Like herself, she hadn't had any real guidance or parenting. In Carmen's view, Mary, who'd raised them both, had always been worthless.

She sighed, retreated from the kitchen, retrieved her purse, and stormed out of the house without another word to either of them. Stepping out onto the porch, sagging from rotting wood, and walking the short path to her minivan parked at the curb, she wondered, was Courtney really giving up everything to return to this? Or did she truly believe that auburn-haired, hazel-eyed Romeo was going to whisk her away?

A sense of mourning descended upon her, like leaving the hospital room of a dying relative. *The girl has such potential and it means nothing to her; now she's going to learn the hard way. Is this about her being in love—or is she doing it to spite me?* Carmen covered her eyes with her hand and lingered a few minutes before starting the vehicle.

She then maneuvered slowly down the narrow street, passing old and boarded up homes, her mind reflecting on why Courtney had such resentment toward her. It's true that once married and settled into her own life she'd allowed her sister to remain in Mary's care, though doubts as to her grandmother's fitness to be a guardian nagged at her. The choice hadn't been entirely selfish, however; Courtney had given Mary a reason to keep living, after the death of her only child. But Courtney had paid the price; Mary had been verbally and emotionally abusive. Carmen now knew she should've done things differently.

Instead she watched and waited. The anonymous calls she'd placed to child protective services always brought them around to her doorstep; social workers trying to guilt her into taking custody. Why didn't they guilt Mary into treatment? *She owed us; our mother's death was her fault! She should've learned her lesson and gotten herself straight. Courtney was her responsibility—not mine —why should I have stepped in and let that witch off the hook? What has she ever done for me?* Meanwhile the chip on Courtney's shoulder grew with each passing year.

She activated her right blinker and merged onto the highway. *She acts like I owe her an apology for her rotten childhood—but where's my apology? I had to survive two addicts and a baby—nobody felt sorry for me...*

Sitting in the kitchen long after Carmen had gone, Courtney tried to shrug off her sister's words and the outrage that resulted. The two of them had never been close, but things had been better—until that day.

"What the hell are you talking about—you're coming back to live here?" Mary said, when she emerged from the kitchen.

Courtney paused and shot her a sideways look, "Since when do you care?"

"Don't you talk to me like that; this is still my house, darn it.  I guess you don't have a brain in that fool head of yours; don't matter what your grade reports say.  Just a piece of paper, far as I'm concerned," she sipped from her glass.  "—leaving that place to come back here.  I always told you you were nothing; now you're proving it."

"You raised me!  So, what does that make you?"

Mary cackled, and blood rushed to Courtney's cheeks.  "I'm just an old drunk, even I have sense enough to know that; but what are you, huh?"  She sipped again and pointed at her, mockingly.

Courtney turned and stormed down the narrow hallway, retreating to her bedroom.

"Darn fool, that's what, and you don't even know it," is what she heard before slamming her bedroom door so hard the wall shook.

She plopped down on her bed, trembling and staring at nothing in the darkened room, replaying the scenes with her family.  *God—I hate them so much. I wish they were both dead.*

For as long as she could remember, Mary's drunken belittling had been part of her daily life; but the old woman had softened when she'd left for college. Her visits home had been almost pleasant.  But now she was back, for the time being anyway; Mary had reverted to her nasty self.  *If she knows what's best for her, she'd better leave me alone; I'm not going to put up with her anymore!*

Then there was Carmen, who could've stepped in and raised her, but chose not to. Instead, she dragged herself and the brats over for visits, as if she was a prison inmate, or animal at the zoo. Yes, she'd scoop her up for occasional sleepovers. The recollection of which caused Courtney to squeeze her eyes tight; she'd tried so very hard to be perfect, so her sister would want her. But was never good enough; Carmen always took her back to Mary. Eventually she refused to leave.

On one level, she understood; Carmen had her own scars from a hellish childhood, worse than her own. This, however, made her apathy even more unforgivable; she knew what it was like being raised in an environment marred by addiction.

As an adult herself, she accepted that Carmen, and the rest of them who'd remained on the sidelines, viewed her as a burden. Her sister had her own children—a boy and a girl, to love and nurture. Courtney didn't fit in, which meant her childhood could be sacrificed. She wasn't worth saving.

What if…her mother had lived? Hazy memories of Deirdra floated in her mind: warm, smiling, holding and kissing her…her sixth birthday…then she was gone.

According to Carmen, Deirdra was too high and frequently absent to care for either of her children; Mary, unable to cope with her daughter, retreated into a bottle. The burden of survival fell to her, a ten-year-old, who was denied her childhood. She never let any of them forget it.

She often complained about how child protective services would make welfare calls, but since Mary was always home—though drunk–they never did anything. As far as they were concerned, the children had a roof—the house Mary had inherited, and resources—a combination of Social Security, WIC, food stamps, and child support from absentee fathers. They were the fortunate ones. What Carmen knew and they failed to see was—Deirdra squandered every dime to support her habit.

Then Deirdra didn't come home, and her body was found. Relatives on her father's side whisked sixteen-year-old Carmen away. Courtney, at six, was neither their blood, nor their problem. A host of Mary's family members showed up suddenly; then after the funeral, disappeared just as fast. Based upon the horrid way Mary talked about them, Courtney couldn't blame them.

After that, she'd spend the next few years waiting—for the knock on the door or the phone call, telling her it was time to go to her new home with Carmen, who'd promised to come and get her as soon as she could. Mary told her it wouldn't happen. *Nobody wants a crackhead's child, not even me. You need to realize that now. Nobody's coming for you.* She was right.

Courtney's eyes welled up thinking about Carmen's early visits and promises. She was expectant when Carmen graduated high school, then got a job, then got married, then moved several times, into progressively larger homes. She dreamed of her new bedroom; and each time her sister moved into a new place, stood ready to pack up her things. When she asked her, though, she always had an excuse for why it wasn't the right time and would start talking about Mary getting into alcohol treatment, as if that had anything to do with her.

Then Carmen had her first child, a little boy, who claimed Courtney's room; a year later, she had a little girl. Courtney refused to have anything to do with either child, barely acknowledging their existence. Carmen's husband Patrick thought something was off with the moody adolescent, anyway, and didn't want his kids around her.

In the end, Mary had been right: none of them wanted her. At least the old woman had been honest enough to say so.


Hours later, she was still brooding in the dark, unable to quell the rage that boiled like a cauldron inside her. They were going to see the last of her— soon. It couldn't happen soon enough. They weren't the reason she'd come back to this hell hole, so who cared what they thought. Sean was all she cared about; as soon as they made their move, she'd disappear from their lives forever.

Clutching her phone, she stood and paced beside her bed in the dark, then dialed, holding the device away from her ear as it rang. After four rings, she dropped onto the bed, knowing what was coming next. "This is Sean; leave a message." It was the fifth time she'd tried that day.


Angela McNair nearly dropped the glass pitcher of sweet tea she was carrying. "I'm sorry, Courtney, but I'm sure I misheard what you just said." She stood frozen. "You're not quitting—"

Courtney shook her head, "No, of course not." They were in Angela's kitchen; Courtney having dropped by out of the blue to say hello.  She exhaled and was in the process of filling two glasses.  "I'm just leaving Grayson, that's all."

Her breath halted as she allowed the pitcher to momentarily slip out of her grip onto the granite countertop, spilling some of the tea.

"Courtney, why would you consider such a thing?"

The girl shrugged, "I miss—"

Angela lifted a hand and closed her eyes, "Don't say it."

"I mean, Sean and I—"

Angela opened her eyes and squinted at the girl who was bewildered by her reaction.

"It's just that Grayson is so far away."

"That's why you have semester breaks."

"We want to be together more than that."

"Of course you do, and there's busses, and cars, and something called Skype.  If you need help getting home for a quick visit, just ask.  If money is the issue, I'll do what I can; not every week, you understand."

Courtney shook her head.

Angela sighed and finished pouring the tea, then went to the sink and retrieved a damp towel to wipe up what had splashed on the counter. She resumed the conversation, but from a different angle.  "It's very sweet—you and my son think you're so in love, but you don't make life-altering decisions like this because you miss each other.  Your future is at stake."  Courtney returned a dull stare that conveyed she was speaking Chinese.

She sighed again.  "Do you want me to make you something to eat?"  Courtney declined and Angela turned away, staring out of the kitchen window, though there was nothing on that side of the house to look at.

"My son thinks this is a good idea?"  She said, still with her back turned.

"Yes, it was his—" Courtney sputtered.  Angela balled her fists.

"Go ahead and finish; or do I finish it for you?  It was his idea, wasn't it?"  She was walking a tightrope; boyfriend's mommas aren't supposed to involve themselves in their son's relationships.  Much to Sean's angst, however, she and Courtney had always had a bond.

"Not completely," Courtney whined.  "He's just encouraging me to do what I want."

Angela spun around.  "Don't you mean what He wants?"

Courtney set her jaw and glared.  "We both want the same thing," she said, a firmness in her voice.

Angela nodded and studied her; the girl's expression softened under the scrutiny.  "Courtney, you need to give this more thought.

"We've already—"

"I'm not talking to we; I'm talking to you.  A woman needs to know how to think for herself."  Courtney frowned and Angela knew she'd gotten through.  It was a start.  "What does your family think of all this?"

"They really don't care, but my sister's putting on a big act like she does. I see right through it."

"You shouldn't dismiss her, especially if she's telling you right."  This comment ignited a fire in Courtney's eyes Angela had never seen.  "Sometimes a person's motives, or what you think they are, are less important than the wisdom they're trying to share.  Young people need to learn to listen."

"She has nothing to say I want to hear."

"Hmph," Angela folded her arms.  She knew better than to ask what that grandmother of hers thought.  Just thinking about the first time she met that woman spiked her blood pressure.

It was toward the middle of Sean and Courtney's senior year, and she'd become suspicious about where her son had been spending so much of his time. When she asked him, he always said he was at Courtney's.

She'd met the pretty, shy girl a few times and wondered what his fascination with her could be; she barely opened her mouth.  As time went on, she needed to know just what the two of them did every evening after school up until his curfew.  She tried to think positive but knew her son.

His grades were improving, so they were doing homework; and she'd driven by Courtney's house a few evenings and saw his car there, so he wasn't lying.  Hearing from them that the grandmother never left the house, caused her to question how much mischief they could get into.  She still decided to drop by one evening unexpectedly.

"Mrs.—"

"Hadley," the older woman said with a voice that sounded like gravel filled her throat.

Angela stood in the middle of the living room, which was swept and tidy, but the furniture in it was filthy; what she called thrift store rejects. The only sound she heard in the vicinity was the blaring television. Strange, given that two teenagers were in the house somewhere. The older woman, after having let her in, slunk back to her dirty couch. There was a glass of brown liquid on the worn coffee table beside it.

That glass told Angela McNair all she needed to know about the sickly-looking woman and spurred flashbacks of her ex-husband Jimmy McNair, who'd made alcoholism his career. Her mouth became twisted; she couldn't stand drunks, especially Jimmy.

"Excuse me. I don't mean to bother you any further, but where is my son? You did say he was here."

Mary coughed, "If that red boy belongs to you, he's here. You need to put a leash on him."

Angela's breath caught in her throat. " Hold on, Miss Hanson, or whatever you call yourself," she said, her voice rising. "I know my son is no saint,

but these girls have a little something to do with that. Now, where are they?"

Mary sipped her glass, a smirk emerging on her trembling lips. She motioned her head toward a door to the left of the kitchen.

Angela saw the light appeared to be off. "Sean, get out here right now!" She roared, loudly enough to wake the entire block.

She heard movement, then "Oh crap!" as the light clicked on. After a few minutes of scrambling, the door opened and her tall handsome son slid out, his hazel eyes wide, his curly light brown hair matted, his shirt half on and unbuttoned. He was carrying his shoes in one hand and his school backpack in the other.

Angela turned toward Mary, "I'm sorry, Miss Hadley, but why have you been allowing this to go on? My son will go home if you tell him to." Mary grunted in reply.

She wheeled around to her son and clenched her teeth. "What made you think it's okay to use this woman's house as a free hotel—like she's not even here?"

"We were just doing homework," he shrugged as he walked around his mother and sat down at the table to put his shoes on.

Courtney, wearing wrinkled clothes turned inside out, had crept into the room at some point but averted Angela's eyes.

"Do you think this is the right way to treat your grandmother?" Angela demanded. Courtney also shrugged. Then Mary joined the conversation.

"That little witch don't care 'bout nothin'. She's preparing for her future livelihood—just like her momma."

Angela's head swung away from the teenagers, and she took a step toward the couch. "Excuse me, Miss," she hissed her voice raised again. "That kind of talk doesn't benefit anybody. Especially these children—"

"This is my house. You don't like how I talk, well nobody invited you here in the first place."

The kids observed the scene as Angela rolled her shoulders back and straightened her tall slim frame.  "You're absolutely right.  And since I don't want to disrespect you in your house, I'm going to leave it now."  She pointed to Courtney, "Go pack a bag and grab your books, this instant."  She turned to Sean, "Go home, pack a bag and drive to your Aunt Tina's.  I don't want to see you any more tonight."

Mary watched absently as Angela removed Courtney from her home that night; she stayed away until after graduation six months later.  Angela had unofficially adopted her, and the girl loved every minute of it.

For Angela, it had been complicated.  Sean resented her interference in his life.  Her two daughters: Jazmine and Krystal, both college students, resented Courtney's presence in their home and in their mother's heart.  'I can't believe you moved some girl he's fooling around with in here.  What do you think they're up to when you're not here?'  As a precaution, she'd sent Sean to stay with her older son Jay, until Courtney decided she wanted to return home.

None of her family understood her motives.  Courtney was a good girl and a good student who deserved better than to live amidst alcoholism and verbal abuse.  Angela may have stepped over the line but couldn't help it.  Her marriage to Jimmy, had taught her first-hand what living with an addict was like.

Her reasons were also personal: she enjoyed having the girl around.  Courtney appreciated the smallest attention, and as a single mom of four, she found it refreshing to have a kid in the house who didn't take everything she did for them for granted.

"Grayson University is a rare opportunity, Courtney; you've got to value

rare opportunities in life. Once they're gone, they almost never come back."
Courtney exhaled loudly and rolled her eyes up to the ceiling. This broke the dam
on Angela's patience; she clenched her teeth and leaned in to force the girl to look
her in the eye, raising her voice. "You won't listen to your sister—well, you're
going to listen to me–"

Before she could finish, the kitchen door swung open, and there was her
son. His long hair was pulled into a wild ponytail; he was wearing dark shades
and bright colored Beats headphones. Angela couldn't remember the last time
she'd seen him, even though they occupied the same house, but she knew one
thing: he hadn't slept at home the previous night, and Courtney, his supposed
girlfriend, had no clue where he'd been.

"There you are," he murmured to Courtney; he wasn't smiling.

"I left you a message and sent you a text telling you I was coming over
here."

Sean's look shifted from her to his mother, who shot him a side glance,
while loading the dishwasher. "I'm getting ready to leave the house. I need you
to –"

"Mow the lawn, yeah I know," he said. Courtney jumped from the stool
and threw her arms around his neck. He pulled her to him and kissed her.

"I was telling your mom, I'm leaving Grayson," she said, gazing up at
him.

"Really," his eyes darted up in time to see his mother ease out of the
kitchen. "What did she have to say about it?" Angela paused, when out of their
view.

"Nothing much."

Angela continued to her bedroom; by the time she was ready to leave the house, a half hour later, the lawn hadn't been mowed and the teenagers had vanished.

# Chapter Three

"Is everything all right at home, Courtney?" Ms. Green, the guidance counselor of Heather High School said, just as other school administrators had asked her over the years. Courtney was always at school on time, her paperwork always in order; usually completed by her. Still, occasionally, they asked questions.

"Anything you tell me will be treated in the strictest confidence. It's hard to ignore how under-developed your social and interpersonal skills are. You're a junior in high-school, it's time for you to come out of that shell… unless there's something going on in your life causing you to retreat there," she paused, looking intently at Courtney, who stared down at the table. "You're old enough to know what abuse is, Courtney. Would you say your home environment is an abusive one? I've tried to contact your grandmother, what's her name —" she glanced in the folder, "—Mrs. Hadley, but I can't get her to answer or return my calls."

Mary didn't pick up the phone, didn't attend school conferences, and had never once met any of Courtney's teachers. Carmen had attempted to fill that role; but Courtney, as she grew older, resisted her sister's involvement.

"I'm not abused," Courtney said, hearing Mary's words in her ear. "…you go telling some sob story and bring those people into my house again; when they go, you might as well take yourself out the door with 'em. If livin' here is so horrible, find someplace else…"

"Maybe not physically," Ms. Green said. "What about verbally? Does someone in your home make you feel bad about yourself? Is that why you rarely speak?" "—Whoever you are—whatever agency you work for, you can take this bastard whenever you want. I didn't give birth to her. She was dumped on me…"

The sequence was the same: some well-intentioned school official or neighbor would contact the authorities, who'd then show up at Mary's door, or sometimes Courtney's school. They'd ask questions, take notes, make recommendations—or threats. Mary ignored them, and they'd walk away without taking any action. Proving Mary to be right in every instance: Nobody really cared about her.

Courtney shrugged and stared at her notebook. Why should I tell these people anything; where will they be when Mary puts me out on the street…

Now, at sixteen, Courtney had grown accustomed to individuals who came in and out of her life, professing concern for her well-being. She concluded most were simply talking to make themselves feel good. Disappointment had taught her to depend only on herself.

"Do you have any other family or friends you spend time with; anyone else your age?" Ms. Green said, trying to bring the mind-wandering teen back into the conversation.

Courtney heard her, but only shrugged again, hearing Mary's words. "Nobody gives a darn about you –including me; least I admit it."

Ms. Green noticed Courtney becoming more withdrawn as she sat across from her. During that school year, she felt the two of them had forged a tenuous connection; the girl seemed to trust her. That could change in an instant if she pressed too hard; she left her questions unanswered and changed the subject. "Did you have the chance to peruse any of the college catalogs I loaned you?"

Later that same night, after finishing her homework, Courtney browsed through the college catalogs again.  The glossy pages showed pictures of happy, studious young people in bright, carefree surroundings; she wondered if she could ever be one of them.


"Where were you last night?"  Courtney said, as they made a quick getaway from Angela's; Sean, as usual, dodging his lawn-mowing chores.  He pretended not to hear her until she asked him again.

"Work." He killed the engine of his Jeep, having pulled into a space at Crescent Lake, a park in their neighborhood.

She sucked her teeth and turned to stare out of the passenger side window.

"I suppose you called my job."

"They said you had the day off."

"If I say I'm working, it doesn't have to mean the restaurant."

"So where was it you were working, or should I ask who?"

"I don't like your tone—"

"I don't like when you lie to me, then act like I'm stupid." Sean said nothing, but she could feel his eyes on her; she avoided them, wanting him to get the message.  Something about the way he looked at her, always melted the mountain of her anger into rubble.  Staying mad was impossible, no matter what he did.  She sighed then, opening the car door, stepped out and sauntered to a nearby picnic table.  Within seconds he was beside her.

"This isn't how I want things to be," she said dragging her feet in circles on the ground.  They sat silently as laughter and playful screams emanated from the playground.  It was a warm Saturday afternoon in May, and the park was teaming with visitors.

"I know.  I don't either."

She cut her eyes at him, "Then why?" The words came out sounding whinier than she intended.

He shrugged.  "I just got caught up in some crap.  Too much alcohol, with the wrong people.  It's really not what you think."

"You always say that."

After a lengthy silence, he inched his body as close to hers as possible, while she pretended not to notice.  He buried his face in the crook of her neck and whispered. "I'm sorry."

"I want things to be different.  You say you want me here.  I want you to act like it," she said, while he planted tiny kisses along the back of her neck, her jawline, traveling up the side of her face.

"I do and I will.  I promise."


He's coming over here again; doesn't he have work to do?

Ms. Green had helped Courtney land a part-time job at a department store in the mall, the summer before senior year, hoping it would improve her social skills.  The girl was trying; but this boy, who she recognized from school, kept pushing himself in her face.  He was tall with a bronze complexion and light-colored eyes that drew attention to his handsome face.

She kept her gaze lowered onto the counter where she was stocking blouses.  They'd never interacted at school; but after seeing her at work, he became determined to engage her in conversation.  His attempts usually failed but he was relentless.  Today she decided to mumble something to get him to go away.  When he heard it, he smiled.

"That wasn't so painful, was it?  I'm Sean, by the way, and we're going to be friends."

She glanced up in time to see him wink, then stride away and was reminded of one of Mary's favorite sayings –something about friends being unnecessary.

A few months later:  "An occasion to celebrate.  Congratulations on this important milestone in your life," Sean lifted his glass of soda; Courtney, grinning, lifted hers also.  "You have no choice but to remember me forever; a person always remembers their first date."  When they placed their glasses on the table, he became silent, appearing to be studying its contents.  They were occupying a booth at Burger Haven Diner, after having seen a Harry Potter movie.

Since the summer department store job, they'd gone from being work friends, to school friends, to close friends.  Then he'd asked her out.

"Where's your mother?"  He blurted, without looking at her.  Their friendship grew, because he navigated her boundaries and didn't get too personal until now.

"Um…dead—when I was six."

"I'm sorry."

Courtney shrugged and looked out of the window.

"My life at home is all female; my mom and my two sisters. My older brother is married and gone, and the only time I see my dad is if I feel like going down to Blackjack's Lounge on 5th and Fulton. He's there sucking it down day and night."

"My grandmother downs a bottle every few days herself," Courtney said, playing with her fries.

He sighed, "Yeah? Wow—what a thing to have in common." The two of them ate somberly, pondering the realities they were born into they couldn't change; words were needless.


"I think I've decided on Grayson University," Courtney told Ms. Green just before Thanksgiving break of senior year. She'd narrowed her selection down to two choices: Grayson, one of the most prestigious and expensive schools in the country, which was 200 miles away from her hometown of St. Joseph, or Stanford, which was 1500 miles away. Because she'd scored exceptionally high on her entrance exams, scholarship money was rolling in.

"Great choice, and congratulations. Keep your head on straight (and don't get pregnant before you leave town) and you're going to be a great success. What does your boyfriend think about your choice?"

Courtney blushed. "I don't have a boyfriend."

The counselor's eyebrows raised. From the start of that school year, the romance between Sean McNair and Courtney had been the buzz around the school. The girl who didn't talk came out of nowhere and snatched up the boy everybody wanted—to the chagrin and dismay of at least half a dozen of his other love interests.  Ms. Green worried about that situation every time she'd see the two of them, arm in arm, walking through the halls.

"Me and Sean –" Courtney said, as though reading her mind, "—are just friends.  It's kind of complicated."  She stood and grabbed her books to head to her next class.

Ms. Green took a good look at her; she bore no resemblance to the girl she'd counseled the year before.  The old Courtney had looked the same everyday: long thick hair pulled back into a ponytail, her petite frame buried beneath a shapeless sweatshirt and blue jeans.  This girl's hair was straightened, curled and draping around her shoulders.  She wore light makeup on her cocoa brown skin and stylish, figure flattering outfits.

"No, it's actually very simple," she said, walking Courtney to the door. "Sean has more on his mind than friendship, and so do you."  The teen smiled at the counselor as if she were from Mars; Ms. Green sighed and shook her head. "Watch yourself," was all she could say as Courtney darted down the hall.  From her doorway, she spotted that wild hair McNair boy waiting patiently at her locker.


"Nobody wants a crackhead's child –you need to learn that now.  When you finish high school, the clock starts.  I'm done with you like everybody else. Find a place to live and something to do with yourself.  If you think you're smart enough for college –you'd better be smart enough to find somebody to pay for it ..."

It was another dreary evening at home with her grandmother.  Courtney sat at the rickety dining room table, books open, doing her homework, while Mary babbled on; repeating chapter and verse of the same speech over and over, every time they were in the same room.  The girl blocked her out easily enough; could recite word for word everything Mary said.  Why does she bother?  What does she think she's accomplishing?

When Courtney started working at the department store and exerting her independence, Mary's bad attitude became toxic; she didn't like the transformation in the teen's appearance and demeanor.  Also, the girl had stopped fearing her threats of abandonment; unaware Mary was living in fear that she would leave and never return.

Courtney took the hate at face value, accepting her grandmother's unwarranted disdain of her.  She'd had enough of people professing to care about her, then do nothing; namely her sister Carmen and 'father' Earl Brooks.  She could almost respect Mary's brutal honesty.

Earl was listed as her biological father on her birth certificate but was with her mother only long enough to discover his pretty wife preferred the drugs purchased with his steady paycheck, over him.  He'd been long gone by the time Courtney appeared, but since Deirdra's death, paid child support anyway.

Mary said it gave those people a chance to feel good about themselves; helping an orphan, but that was all she was to them.  He and his wife, Natalie, had always been kind to her: gifts at Christmas and on her birthday, but that was where it ended.  She was never embraced as a member of their family.

Slamming her books closed, and kicking the chair against the table, she'd finally had enough of Mary's babbling; she gathered her belongings to finish her homework in her room, hoping the noise would shut Mary up; but she kept up her rambling. 'That mother of yours—you're just like her. She never ca...”

When she got to her room, she kicked the door closed knowing Mary would have plenty to say about that too.

When I leave for college, Mary and Carmen can pretend like I'm dead, because I WILL be to them, and likewise. Earl can stop sending his pity checks and keep his money in his pocket. We can all stop pretending.


Sean slouched at his desk in the rear of the classroom of first period English composition, yawned, then peered at Courtney, who was bright-eyed and alert, a couple rows away. What is it about her? She's cute, but not really my type. But right now, she owned him, which was funny given there was nothing physical going on between them. He was struggling with how far he wanted their relationship to go. She was so innocent—it would be too easy. If not me, then who? was the question that kept popping into his brain.

He knew of wolves in that school ready to pounce on her the minute he turned his back, and they didn't care who got hurt. So, he latched onto her every movement and was probably leading her on in the process. But until he figured out what he wanted, no other male in that school was getting near her.

The teacher stood in front of the room, signaling for the rowdy class to settle down and pull out their homework. He slid down further in his chair. He hadn't completed his assignment and didn't want to be called on. He alternated between sneaking looks at Facebook on his phone and watching her.

“Sean, I don't see you writing. Are you finished with your paragraph already?  If so, why not share it with the class." Mr. Klein, the English instructor said, pointing to a writing prompt on the whiteboard.

He sat up straight; and pulling out his pen and notebook, pretended to write.

"I'm scared to ask where your mind is, but it needs to be here—in this class." The teacher rapped the whiteboard with his wooden pointer.

There were snickers around the room; but when Courtney met his gaze and flashed him a smile that was both amused and sympathetic, he felt a surge of warmth go through him; the teacher, along with the rest of the class, faded away.

"I'm failing that class, badly," he told her later that day.  "Klein said if I miss another assignment, he's going to call my mother and tell her I might not graduate."  They were driving away from the school; Sean was giving her a ride to work.

"It's not that hard.  You're not trying."

"I hate writing.  I can't even think of anything to write about most of the time.  Why don't you write my papers for me, since you love it so much?"

Courtney sighed, and shook her head, then they lapsed into an awkward silence during the rest of the drive.  Despite their school displays of a romantic couple, when not in school, they were rarely alone.  Now she was all nerves, wanting him to like her, but feeling like she didn't know how to be interesting.

"Why don't you tutor me?  If it's so easy," he blurted while stopped at a red light.

"I guess," she said with a shrug, a ripple of excitement trickling down her spine.

"How about tomorrow.  I don't have to work.  I'll come by your house."

She agreed, as she did with everything he suggested, although she hated for him to come into her house again.  The first time, a month prior, had been a disaster.

"That's the bum you're following behind?  Hope he takes care of you when I put you out," Mary went on with that for at least a week.

It was useless explaining to her, she and Sean were friends.  She wasn't pregnant; they weren't even really dating.

"Meet me at the back door, so we avoid your grandmother.  The last time I came in, she looked like she wanted to murder me."  Courtney nodded with relief.  "I'll be there around 6:30. Pretend like you're taking out the trash and sneak me in.  We'll go to your room and I'll sneak out, when she's asleep."

Courtney agreed, but wondered, why don't we just meet at the library?

# Chapter Four

"The bottom line is this—you two are not adults and there will be no more of this foolishness.  If you and Sean are going to do homework after school, it will be done in the library or here in this house—fully dressed.  Do I make myself clear?"

"I told you we weren't doing anything in Courtney's room.  I just fell asleep; that's all.  Why are all involved in our business?"

"You're both under 21, you have no business."

While Sean bantered with his mother, Courtney gave Angela her full attention, realizing that up until now, no one had bothered to talk to her about how she should conduct herself as a young woman.  Sean's mother, a virtual stranger, had also offered her a place to stay for as long as she wanted, something her own blood had been unwilling to do.

"I'm sick of her telling me what to do," Sean said a month later, when he and Courtney were eating lunch in the school cafeteria.  "Why can't she be like other mothers and mind her own business?"

Courtney shrugged and pretended like she was studying her hamburger.

"Why don't you speak up?  She's doing all of this for you.  Tell her thanks but no thanks.  You've let her adopt you, but I don't want any more sisters.  Don't you think it's time for you to go home?  I know it's not that great, but –" he said, leaning across the table.

"Is it so wrong that she cares about me?  Nobody else has –"

He scowled and stood, "What's your problem?  This is supposed to be you and me.  Is it my fault you don't have a mother?  What are you doing, using me so you can share mine?"  His words stabbed and tears streamed down her face as she watched him storm out of the cafeteria.  She left school, telling the nurse she was sick.

He apologized to her that same night, for the way he'd spoken to her, but not for what he'd said.  Failing to get through to Courtney, he then started in on his mother.

"Why do you let her stay here so much?  She's here for days at a time," Sean said, while they were home having dinner.  It was a night when Courtney was at work or she would've been joining them.  "What if I'm tired of her?  You just took over my life; you didn't stop to think about me."

It was approaching Spring, and graduation and prom were the talk of school.  Sean was feeling obligated to date Courtney but had grown tired of her.  Because of his mother's interference, however, he had no choice but to take her to the prom.

Angela laid her fork down gently and cleared her throat.  "I'm sorry.  I really am sorry that you are so selfish you can't see beyond your petty little relationship.  Break up with her if you're tired of her—I don't care.  Courtney has no mother and problems at home, and I'm going to continue to help her, because that's what I do; no one is obligating you.  Yes, I poked my nose where maybe it didn't belong, but that girl has been cheated her whole life.  She's a good student about to go off to college.  The least I can do is to help make her last few months something to cherish.  You're absolutely right, whatever happens between the two of you is your business."

"What about my life, huh?  Seems you care more about her than me."

Angela picked up her fork and resumed eating.

He stood up and threw his fork on the table, "I'm done marching to your tune.  Just because she does whatever you tell her to, doesn't mean I have to go along with this.  Matter of fact, since you're so busy running things, maybe I'm not even necessary.  How about you hire somebody to take her to the prom."  He dumped his mostly untouched meal into the trash, while sulking.

"Watch your mouth, boy," was all she said.  He was frustrated with her, and …maybe he had a right to be.

Now, a year later, Sean still thought of those days; how he resented his mother then and now because of her influence over Courtney.

"What did my mom have to say?"

He and Courtney were back at his house sprawled on the couch in the basement family room, watching a movie.  A box of pizza, bag of chips, and cans of soda were on the coffee table in front of them.

"About what?"

"You know about what, your changing schools."

"I told you, nothing."

"You can speak freely; she's not here.  You act like you're scared of her or something."

"Why are you questioning me?  If you don't believe me, ask her."

Sean sat up and looked at her.  "Cut the crap; she had something to say.  She always has something to say."

"Okay, so she told me I should think about it some more.  She's concerned that I'm doing it to please you, instead of thinking about my own future."

"See, I knew it, there she goes again," he cried, crushing the empty soda can he was holding.

Courtney sat quietly.

"So, what did you say?"

"I don't remember.  You came in and interrupted us, but I think I told her I'd think about it."

"Are you?"  She was silent.  "Are you going to answer me?"  He stood and peered down at her.

She began wringing her hands and when she spoke her voice shook,

"Grayson's a great school and I love it there.  How can I not think about what I'm giving up?"

"Because I need you here."

"If that's really true –"

"What do you mean if – you don't believe me?"

She shrugged.  "I want to – so bad.  You mean everything to me.  If you really mean it, nothing else would matter.  If you would just promise me--"

He stood, "How many times and how many ways do you want me to say I want you here?  Do you want me to sign in blood — will that be good enough?  I'm not perfect; you and I know that.  I've never been perfect, but that's never had anything to do with us."

She felt a web being spun around her.  "I need some air," she darted up the basement stairs, and out to the rear deck.  Sitting down on the steps, she gazed into the distance at the sunset, feeling she was watching her bright future fade away, like the remnants of that day.

"If you go back, that's going to be it for us," he said.  She hadn't heard him come outside, but he was now standing behind her.  "I can't do this another year.  I mean, if that school means more to you than me, I can handle that."

She closed her eyes, trying to imagine her life without him. They'd broken up once the previous summer – or rather he'd dumped her after graduation. She'd been unable to sleep or eat for a month afterward, clueless as to what she'd done wrong.  Then he reappeared, with flowers and apologies, but no explanation except to blame it on his mother's interference.

*Why should I have to choose?  Is this what people mean when they say love means sacrifice?*

She heard the door close behind her; he'd gone back into the house. Loving him wasn't easy, but if things could be right, she knew they could be happy.  If she left him, they'd never have that chance.  The backyard was now enveloped in darkness.  So was she.

*Tomorrow is a new day.*  She inhaled deeply, determined to move ahead to her new life, as if it were the dawning of a new day, putting everything into her relationship with Sean and her education. She'd be the woman he wanted her to be —whatever it took, she'd be perfect so everything else in her life would turn out that way.

# Part Two

# Chapter Five

The deadline to register for sophomore year at Grayson passed.  A couple of Courtney's faculty advisors called and left voicemails, which she ignored.  She applied for and received a scholarship to the pre-med program at City Metropolitan University.  Earl Brooks stopped speaking to her; probably had something to do with the rebuke she gave him when he'd tried to offer 'fatherly' advice.  He wasn't her father anyway.

Once school started, she barely survived two months living under the same roof with Mary.  Her grandmother expected her to be the child she was used to bullying.  Courtney had evolved and wasn't having it.

They argued as Mary demanded Courtney be her caregiver, replacing the home health aides Carmen had procured for her from county social services, during her year away at school.  Courtney, working and attending school full-time, felt she'd spent enough of her life catering to Mary.  Neither were willing to compromise.

She found a tiny studio apartment that was cheap and available, and with Carmen co-signing the lease, she moved in.  Mary stopped speaking to her, and verbally thrashed the aides instead.

It wasn't what she'd envisioned, as she'd hoped to get a place with Sean, but life with Mary was unbearable and he was dragging his feet.  As soon as Courtney was settled, though, he made himself comfortable, which irritated Carmen thoroughly.  It came to a head, during a bitter argument where she pointed out to Courtney his name wasn't on the lease, hers was.  The sisters stopped speaking after that.

By the end of that first semester, Courtney's premonition had become her reality.  She was estranged from all of those whom she'd called her family.

*It's just nerves,* Courtney told herself, standing in her bathroom and staring at the results of the white test stick.  It was mid-Spring semester and she'd been too sick to stay in class that morning.  She grabbed a few of the pregnancy tests from the student health center, hopped on the bus and rushed home.  The blue cross on the indicator told her she was wrong.  She tried to say the words in her head—*I'm pregn...preg—nant...me...pregnant....* It was unreal, unexpected, and.... unwanted.  She scooped up the remnants of all the tests—she'd taken three –and decided she was going to take her time to consider her options.  She was only at about four or five weeks—she had time—if Sean didn't find out.

He'd be thrilled with the news; it was what he'd wanted.  As soon as first sophomore semester was over, he began prodding her about having a baby.  She refused to entertain the idea while still in college; was unsure if she'd ever want children.  A baby before she even started medical school, was unthinkable.  Then her birth control pills started disappearing.  She always kept them in the same place; but somehow, they turned up missing.  A few days later they'd reappear, causing her to lose track of the days she'd missed.  She'd been too slow to realize Sean was the culprit.

She phoned her gynecologist the minute she'd caught on to his antics and made an appointment to get an IUD, which would be her little secret.  Her doctor's office assured her she could come in immediately following her next menstrual period; that never came. Now this.

"What's wrong with you?  How could you be so stupid!"  She yelled at her reflection in the mirror, then sunk down on the bathroom floor, holding her head in her hands, befuddled as to how she'd get herself out of this new hole Sean had put her in.


"Why are you sleeping so much?"  Sean said to Courtney, noticing she fell asleep everywhere they went: the movies, his mother's house, even on short car trips; and she was irritable, crying about everything.  Even now she was on the sofa, open textbooks strewn about, and he'd awakened her.  She hadn't even heard him when he came in.

She sat up and stretched without answering him.  It'd been four weeks since she'd discovered her pregnancy, during which time she'd taken more home tests—as if expecting a different result as time went on.  Then finally went to the doctor both to confirm her condition and inquire about a termination.  The doctor's office assured her the procedure could be scheduled immediately.  She was ready to move forward, but reluctant to proceed until she knew he was okay with it.

"Are you sick or something?  Is that why you've been so cranky lately?"  He moved her books to the used coffee table, clearing a seat beside her on the futon.

"I'm pregnant—eight weeks," she was relieved to finally get it out.

He blinked like he hadn't understood, then broke out in a huge grin. "Really, we're having a…a…" He'd almost forgotten he'd told her it was what he wanted—then. *What was it—two, three months ago?* He sat back on the couch, rubbing his chin. She was uninterested so he stopped thinking about it. He'd played a little hide and seek with the pills, but never thought anything would come of that. Now this—he didn't know how to feel.

"Not if you don't want to," Courtney said, sitting up anxiously as she detected reluctance in his demeanor. *Maybe…*

"Abortion? Forget it. I want my baby," Sean said, then saw her sink back on the couch. "Don't you?"

She nodded limply, "I'll be starting my junior year, and the baby would be due right in the middle. School is the most important thing to me. How am I going to manage with a baby?"

"We'll manage," he said, putting his arm around her waist and drawing her close to him. "How hard can it be? You buy Pampers, give it a bottle, and get a babysitter. We're both working, and my mom will help. It'll work out; you'll see," he assured her.

Courtney knew he meant it and forced a smile to make him happy.

"It's a boy, I know it. We'll name him after me," he said. "My mom won't be so happy; better keep it quiet for a while. She'll be thrilled once she gets used to the idea, especially when the baby gets here."

Courtney watched him babbling about the baby and knew her options

were gone.  There'd be no abortion, unless she did it behind his back and told him

it was a miscarriage.  She wished she hadn't told him at all, feeling like

everything—her whole life, was being taken from her; a tightness gripped her like

a vice on the inside.


"What are you doing getting pregnant?" Angela yelled at Courtney and

Sean.  They'd made their announcement earlier that evening at a family barbecue

at the home of one of Sean's uncles, then slipped out before Angela could corner

them.  She tracked them down, however, and summoned them to her house.  They

knew they'd have to face her eventually.

"He hid my pills," Courtney whined.

"So what—there's a word in the English language spelled 'N-O'.  What's

wrong with you—both of you?"

"It's only a baby, you're acting like we committed a crime," Sean said,

shrugging and sauntering to the refrigerator.

"Look who's talking," Angela said, coming up behind him, then slamming

the refrigerator door closed in his face. "It *is* a crime because you—" she poked his

chest,"-are not going to stay with her and a baby."  She turned to Courtney.  "I

hope you're ready to raise this one by yourself, 'cause I'm telling you now, when

things get tough, *he* won't be there."

The words struck Courtney like blows to her gut.  She dashed to the bathroom, hyperventilating.  Sean and Angela assumed it was sickness from pregnancy.

When she calmed her breathing and returned to the kitchen, Angela was in the same stance as before.

"Sean says a termination is out of the question?"

"Ma, I already told you –" he said.

"Shut up.  I want to hear it from her."

Courtney nodded and looked away, ready to do what Angela told her to do, even if it meant defying Sean.  If Angela said they should terminate, and she convinced him then--

"I wish you two hadn't put yourself in this predicament," Angela said, as she sighed and dropped into a chair at the kitchen table.  "But I believe having the baby is the right thing to do—not the easiest but the right thing.  I don't believe in abortion—don't believe in erasing a life, to make your life easier."  Courtney's heart sank and the dark hole in the pit of her stomach enlarged.  "You'll pay the price one way or the other.  I'm not pleased about this, but I'll help you out the best I can, and believe me you're going to need it," she said.  Courtney felt it odd, she was talking only to her, and not Sean.  "I raised all four of mine alone for the most part; it will be hard but doable."

"But I'm not alone," Courtney said. "Sean—"

Angela snorted and raised a hand to silence her.  "Save it – before it's all said and done, alone is what you'll be."

"What!  What do you know about taking care of a baby, or being a mother?" Carmen cried into the phone.  Her kids, Kyle and Andrea looked up from their video game to see what was wrong.  She ducked out of the kitchen into the living room.  "Courtney, girl you need to re-think your plan."  Hearing silence on the other end, Carmen knew it was already too late; she sighed.  How long had it been since they'd talked...at least a couple months?  No wonder she hadn't heard from her.  "How far along are you?"

"Five months, and it's a little boy.  Sean is thrilled."

"Sure he is," Carmen grumbled.  "How are you going to manage?  You're already working full-time and going to school, now you're going to be caring for a baby--"

"We'll be fine," she said.  "As long as we can afford Pampers, milk and a babysitter--"

"Oh really?" Carmen said with a snicker.  "Who's bit of wisdom is that—his?  Girl, can't you think for yourself anymore?"  Again, there were crickets on the other end, and Carmen decided it best to end their call.  She cleared her throat, "Well, um –take care of yourself, and let me know if you need anything."

"Well, I was ho—" The line went dead.  *So much for sharing this time with my family,* she thought.  If Carmen was reacting this way, Earl and Natalie would be worse; they rarely spoke, as it is.  She'd told Mary when she'd gone to check on her, but her grandmother didn't care about anything except her next drink. *Babies are supposed to be bundles of joy, where the hell is my joy?*

Sean sat in his car in the school parking lot on the late autumn night, trying to decide where to go. He preferred to go home – he was beat from a full shift at work and two classes back to back but feared running into his mother. He was tired of her lecturing him about how he was treating Courtney. He knew how he was treating Courtney; he didn't know what to do about Courtney.

"This whole baby thing is unreal, man. I know I said I wanted this but then—"

"Now that it's happening, it ain't what you thought — huh?" his brother Jay said, handing him a Heineken. "Don't tell Angela." It was the week prior. His brother had called him to hang out and watch football on television.

"All Courtney does is sulk and look at me, like I've beat her or something. Just because she's pregnant, do I owe her my life? She acts like I'm supposed to be there 24-7."

"When is the last time you seen or talked to her? I mean, she's doing this for you, and you act like, she's supposed to call you when it's over."

Sean slammed the bottle down, "You've been talking to Angela; that's why you invited me over here in the first place."

Jay nodded. "She asked me to talk to you, yes. You know she's partial to

Courtney and doesn't want her to be hurt any more than necessary. You're sounding pretty insensitive, about the mother of your unborn child."

Sean shook his head slowly and studied the bottle. "I like her; she's a nice person, and she's so crazy about me—"

"That she'll do anything, even have a baby for you. Did she even want a baby?"

Sean blinked, then looked away and shrugged. "I guess. She never said otherwise; and when she had the chance, she didn't do anything about it…"

He started his Jeep and drove from the parking lot, having decided to crash at his brother's house. On a busy weeknight, Jay would be too occupied with his own family to bother about lecturing him.


"Thank you, these are really nice," Courtney said to Angela, after barely glancing at the new baby outfits she'd bought for her. It was a Tuesday evening, and Angela had picked Courtney up from work so they could have dinner together and discuss baby preparations.

"Would you please smile, and act like you're happy about your new son, who'll be here in ten more weeks. You look like you've been told you have six months to live," Angela snatched the clothes from the young woman's listless hands. "And for God's sake, don't act like this on Saturday." Angela was hosting a baby shower for her at her house. Courtney swallowed hard, and her bottom lip quivered as she tried to speak, but nothing came out.

Angela sighed, "Look, I know my son hasn't been all that attentive, but you're bringing a new life into the world. It's time you switched your focus onto little Bryce. He's going to need all of you and more. Sean comes second."

Courtney's demeanor switched from gloom to fury in a millisecond; she hadn't sacrificed her life for a baby. She'd done it for Sean.

The excitement of the new baby, however, had worn off on him, which had left her emotionally deflated. Her only consolation with the whole event, had been that it made him happy. In her mind, his happiness would translate into their growing closer. That hadn't materialized. The more pregnant she became, the less time he made for her. She whined, cried and complained to no avail. This baby may have been his idea, but Sean had distanced himself from her and it…

"Hello, Courtney—are you listening?" Angela was waving a hand in her face; she hadn't noticed she was still talking. "I know it's not fair, but that's how life is for women. We carry the babies and we're the primary caregivers. You're going to have to wake up. Baby Bryce is going to need you to be all there, not half there and half wondering what his dad is doing."

*I've done everything he's asked and every time I look around, I'm in this alone…*

Angela stopped talking to the air, seeing in Courtney's face, her body was there on the couch, but her mind had left the building.

The baby shower, the following weekend, was well attended by Sean's family.  They were cordial to Courtney, having become accustomed to her being around, though they didn't know her very well.  They were there to support Sean, and he made an appearance, acting the part of a new daddy.  Carmen made a brief appearance, and a couple of Courtney's coworkers also stopped by.

To please Angela, Courtney put on the happy new mommy face and pulled it off, even though she and Sean were barely speaking.  They'd had a bitter argument the night before about the same old conflict: he was MIA — she was too clingy.  After they'd opened the gifts, and everyone had eaten, he slipped out, leaving her stranded.  Nina, Jay's wife took her, and the baby shower gifts, home.  After that day, she stopped calling him.

The two of them spent the next few weeks coexisting.  He'd show up at her apartment at varied times.  Sometimes she was there; other times she wasn't.  They'd stopped arguing.  The bigger her belly became, the less energy she exerted.  She longed for the pregnancy to be over but had no clue what life with a baby would be like.  All she could do was plan around it.

If the baby came on the due date, it would give her three weeks to prepare for the next semester, then three more weeks before she had to return to work.  She'd then have to stagger her class and work schedule around childcare.  Sean had assured her he'd help but resisted any firm commitment and hadn't even told her what his class schedule would be.

Then one day, when she was thirty-four weeks along, maneuvering around her studio apartment that seemed to be constricting itself around her belly, a knock at the door jolted her.  She moved slowly to peek through the peep hole and saw a woman on the other side.

"Oh," she said, startled when Courtney opened the door, "...is... Sean here?" Her eyes were fixed on the other woman's swollen stomach.

"No, who are you?" Courtney stared wide eyed at the tall, pretty, and very slim woman who was asking for her man. *This isn't happening....*

"Okay, well... thanks anyway," the woman stammered backing away, nearly bumping into the wall. "Are you a relative of his, by chance?"

"You could say that. I'm his girlfriend, and this is our baby. What is that to YOU?"

"Nothing at all," she replied, throwing up a hand. "In fact, forget I stopped by," and down the hall she dashed.

Courtney lumbered to the window and watched her walk to her car; then Sean drove up. She wanted to open the window to hear the conversation but was glued to her spot. The girl, whoever she was, was cursing at Sean while pointing to the window. Courtney moved out of view when Sean looked up. A few minutes passed before the girl's car sped noisily out of the parking lot. Sean headed for the building; she darted into the bathroom.

*What am I going to do?* She thought as she sat on the toilet, shaking and unable to catch her breath. She heard Sean in the apartment but stayed where she was, crying quietly, wishing the baby rolling around in her belly would disappear. She longed to disappear too.

He didn't call out to her.  She opened the medicine cabinet to retrieve the Pepto Bismol to calm her stomach, and her eyes landed on a nearly full bottle of oxycodone capsules, prescribed to him a while back.  She grasped the bottle in her hand; and as she did so, her body stopped shaking and her breathing slowed to normal.  Closing her eyes, she waited, wondering what he was going to do. Eventually she heard his footsteps; then the front door closed.  When certain he was gone, she slipped out of the bathroom, tucking the pills away in her purse.

# Chapter Six

Angela cooed and beamed at the sleeping newborn boy she held.  He had a cinnamon brown complexion, a round face and head full of bronzed hair, nearly the color of his skin.  Sean stood over his mother, gazing at his son.  Neither spoke to Courtney, who they assumed was asleep a few feet away.

"His name is Sean Bryce McNair," he said, responding to her question.

"And *you* stayed in the delivery room through it all?" Angela chuckled.

"Yeah," he said, rubbing the stubble on his face.  "Man –I don't think I ever want to do that again.  It wasn't pretty."

It was the week before Christmas, and Courtney's water broke as soon as she'd gotten home from work.  Inspite of their recent arguments, he'd been right where he was supposed to be that night.  In fact, he'd been spending most nights with her since that girl, Kellie, had come to the apartment looking for him that day.  Guilt over that episode, combined with Courtney not speaking to him, caused him to swallow his pride and make up with her.

Courtney listened to their conversation, while pretending to be asleep to avoid talking about anything: the labor, delivery and especially the baby.  He'd arrived healthy.  For her, it was time to move on.

Their exchange continued, centered entirely around the baby—not a word about her.  She wondered if she was now even necessary in Sean's view.  *Why do they all act like I'm supposed to be so happy?*

She had yet to get a good look at her baby; she'd held him briefly then gave him to the nurse, complaining she was tired. And she was. She needed a minute to breathe; he'd been dictating her life for nine long months. She wanted a break. They'd been trying to persuade her to breastfeed, but she refused to consider it. That would give him even more control of her life than he already had.

"Miss Brooks, baby Sean is hungry," the cheerful nurse said, a few hours after Angela and Sean had gone. Courtney kept her eyes closed, hoping she'd take the baby and go away. Instead, she waited patiently for her to sit up in the bed, then deposited the tiny bundle into her arms. She felt like she was being forced to get acquainted with the squirming little tyrant, who was now screaming at the top of his lungs.

"Here's his formula," the nurse said, handing her the warm bottle. Courtney jabbed the nipple at his lips; but instead of sucking it, he screamed louder.

"Take your time, Mom," the nurse said. "He's not a doll; feeding time is when the two of you are going to get acquainted."

Courtney drew him closer, so that his cheek rested on her breast; this calmed him. Then when she touched the rubber nipple to his lips, they parted, and he started to suck. When he opened his eyes and looked up at her, she saw they were hazel, like Sean's. She then took a long look at the rest of him. Other than Sean's hair and eyes, his features were hers-- his nose, lips, chin, and complexion.

It all made a unique combination, and she decided he was the cutest baby boy ever born. *Maybe I can do this...Maybe it won't be so bad. He is so sweet.*

The remaining twelve hours of her hospital stay were like a crash course in baby care. Most of what the nurses told her, was a review from her prenatal classes; but when dealing with the real thing, it all seemed unfamiliar. Bathing, changing diapers, wound care for his naval, circumcision, shots, doctors' appointments, preventing SIDS, danger signs to look for, what to do and what not to do. By the time Sean showed up to take them home, her head was swimming; she longed to escape.

By the baby's three-month check-up, the following Spring, Courtney was critically behind in her schoolwork. Sean, who'd often promised to babysit, was never around; on the times when he did show up, he acted as though he was doing her a favor by watching the baby, then hounded her to return at exact times. She flew into rages, starting loud arguments to make him feel guilty. He repaid her by staying away.

*This is so unfair, it's not supposed to be like this,* she'd think as she was forced to pack a diaper bag and Bryce, to go to the library. All the promises Sean had made during her pregnancy flashing through her mind one by one; their agreed upon commitment to her education, recognition of the demands involved in studying medicine, and sacrifice — mutual sacrifice. *What happened to all of that?* She asked herself, all the while knowing she had to accept her reality; her scholarship for senior year was in jeopardy.

"So, what if I've backed out of watching Bryce a couple times. I watch him enough," Sean said to his mother. "I'm tired of her. All she does is sit around and blame me because she's not getting her schoolwork done."

Angela sighed and looked at her son, stretched out on a couch in her family room without a care in the world, while Courtney was calling around looking for a babysitter so she could meet with classmates to work on a project. She tried to avoid taking sides in the young couple's affairs; but after having raised her children alone, found herself empathizing with Courtney. Anytime she attempted to plead Courtney's cause to Sean, however, he accused her of favoring her over him, like he'd always accused her of favoring his sisters. To make matters worse, he'd moved back home with her full-time, running out on the situation he'd created. What was she supposed to do—kick him out? She'd promised he could live at home if he stayed in school and kept up his grades; he'd held to his end of the bargain. It wasn't her place to tell him to go back and shack up with Courtney.

Angela felt bad for the girl, however—she hadn't even had the sense to demand a wedding ring after everything she'd given up. Not that she would've gotten one from Sean. But by demanding nothing, that's exactly what Courtney had received: nothing, plus a baby. Angela left the room and went upstairs shaking her head. Who did Sean think was going to step in and clean up the mess he was making?

Dear Miss Brooks, the purpose of this letter is to inform you that your academic progress in the Spring semester did not meet the minimal requirements under the terms of your scholarship... We ask that you please accept this correspondence as a tool to help you in making whatever changes necessary... If our office can be of assistance to you in any way, please do not hesitate...

It was July, and she was supposed to be preparing for senior year and Spring graduation. But Courtney had received the letter which she held and read it repeatedly. It was no surprise; she'd had an awful semester--failing one course and scoring grades below scholarship requirements in two others. She was still maintaining her GPA – barely. The one class she'd succeeded in she'd only managed a shaky "B". She now needed to re-take the course she'd failed, at her own expense.

She wanted to drop down to part-time student for a while, to pull herself together; but that would mean falling below her course load requirement and losing her scholarship altogether. Another semester like this one, and that would happen anyway. She'd heard the scholarship board was lenient, especially for women in her field of study; if necessary, she could appeal to them for more time. She wasn't motivated to make any promises, however. The semester had been hard for her to navigate with a baby, full-time job, and minimal help, but not impossible. She wasn't fighting very hard.

Her focus was nonexistent. She was skipping classes, squandering time, sleeping, pacing and staring into space, knowing she should be studying. Having a baby was a financial challenge, and Sean didn't pay her much child support, but she had other resources. There was childcare assistance, WIC and food stamp assistance; plus, she was on the list for a housing subsidy, which could come through at any time and reduce the amount of rent she was paying. If she and

Sean were married, she wouldn't qualify for any of that. Marriage was still what she wanted, and it's what he'd made clear she wasn't going to get.

*'I'm not ready and just because we have a baby doesn't mean I'm going to be pressured,'* is what he'd told her, when she made mention of how he'd moved out of the apartment without even telling her.

More and more frequently, she reflected on her decision to leave Grayson. A simple 'no' back then and everything would be different. Now the word 'no' was not an option in her life. She couldn't tell Bryce 'no' she wasn't going to feed him or hold him when he woke up in the middle of the night, or just when he wanted to be held; or 'no' she wasn't going to drag him with her when all she wanted was a soda from a convenience store. If she told Sean 'no' to anything, she could forget about seeing him for at least a week. Sean was free, however. He could tell her 'no' to anything, anytime he wanted. From what his sisters said, she was the only female in town he was saying 'no' to these days.

"Because I hear you have a girlfriend."

Sheila, the newest waitress at Le Chateau, had been working there for only a week, but had been warned about Sean, the handsome waiter. The way she'd heard it, he had more than good looks, there was a girlfriend and a baby somewhere. Still, he didn't seem to think there was any harm in throwing himself at any female he found attractive, whenever he felt like it.

"What does that matter?" He said. "She and I have no secrets. She can date anyone she wants, and so can I."

"Oh yeah? You two have that kind of understanding?" She quipped, twisting her mouth to let him know she'd heard that one before. Guys always had an understanding; it was one-sided, and the other party was never informed.

"When I meet her, I'll ask her about it," Sheila said, elbowing past him, to get to her waiting table.

Sean laughed and watched her walk. *Oh well...,* he told himself while evaluating her from behind. He'd only been mildly interested anyway—she was okay but couldn't touch Courtney in the looks department. He was all charm and no action most of the time, anyway, just wanting to see how far his looks would get him. He had to admit – he did well, but was only having a little fun, because these days, Courtney was no fun at all.


"I'm on my way over there. Do you need anything?" Sean asked Courtney, later that evening.

She exhaled loudly. "What makes you think I want you to come over? This isn't your vacation home."

"Sorry," he cleared his throat. "I want to see you. Can I come over, please?" Having a conversation with Courtney was like walking in a mine field. He couldn't do or say anything that satisfied her but had to spend at least a few nights a week at her place, or she'd really make his life miserable. What was behind her anger, he knew, was his having moved back into his mother's house;

but he had to.  He loved his baby boy but wasn't ready to play daddy all the time and wasn't interested in being a husband at all.  He knew that was the outcome she expected, but he'd always had doubts as to whether Courtney was the woman for him.


Then in the middle of the Fall semester, that had just begun, Courtney marched into the registrar's office and withdrew from all her classes.  Nine months from graduation, she couldn't go on.  She thought it would lift a burden from her shoulders, but she felt worse.


"He's just a baby.  You can't blame him because you dropped out of school.  That was your choice.  Get a grip!" Sean yelled.

"Take your baby and get out of here!  I don't want him, and I don't want you.  Since you think it's so easy, raise him yourself!" Courtney screamed back.

"What kind of monster are you?  I guess I should expect as much, considering who raised you.  You're becoming just like her.  I'm not going to let you treat my son like she treated you.  That's what's wrong with you!"

"Just get out.  I'll pack up the rest of his things and drop them off at your house!"

They'd been screaming back and forth for more than an hour when there came the inevitable knock at the door.

Sean snatched the door open and nearly walked over the apartment manager, Mr. Simmons, a small elderly man.  He'd grown accustomed to coming upstairs about once a month and threatening to call the police, which usually ended their arguments.  It seemed like they waited for him to come and referee.

"Yeah-yeah, I know, man," Sean said.  "I'm leaving and taking my baby. You won't have any more noise out of us," he said, more for Courtney's benefit. Mr. Simmons shot Courtney a dirty look before turning and heading back down the hallway.

Courtney watched from her apartment window as Sean put the baby in the car and drove away.


"You didn't tell me he was visiting this weekend," Angela exclaimed, delighted to see her grandbaby.  "Come here, Bryce.  Why aren't you asleep?"  She cooed.  "Grandma's got you the cutest Halloween costume.  Tomorrow we're gonna try it on."

"Because his mother's a screaming idiot.  And he's not visiting; she put us both out," Sean said.

Angela started to laugh, until her son flashed her a grave look, causing her to suppress it.  "Give her some time; she'll be okay in the morning."

"She blames him and me for everything that's gone wrong in her life. Nobody told her to drop out of school and lose her scholarship.  How's she gonna blame a baby for that?"

"She's upset with herself.  You kids think everything's supposed to be easy; when it's not, you don't know how to handle it.  She has some growing up to do—and so do you."

"Me?"

"Don't give me that.  You help her when you feel like it, chase other women when you don't.  Do you think she's a fool?  She only had him to make you happy.  It wasn't very smart of her, but what's done is done.  You two are going to have to work it out."


Courtney sat frozen on the couch for a long time, replaying in her mind what had just happened, what she'd done.  Bryce was gone, and she wouldn't have to take him back.  Sean was the one stuck now.  *Wonder how he's going to feel about that,* she thought.  Getting free was so easy, why hadn't she done it before now?  She could go back and start rebuilding her life without Sean and without Bryce.  Then, after she became a doctor, she'd go back for Bryce and bring him home and be the mommy he deserved—not the mess she was now.

Suddenly, she put her hand over her mouth to stifle a scream.  It was all wrong.  She was a mess with Bryce; she'd be worse without him.  What kind of mother was she anyway, giving her baby away without a fight?  Sean was right about her; she was a monster.  Wasn't a mother supposed to love her baby effortlessly and infinitely more than she even loved herself?  *Why don't I feel that way?  Do I even love myself?*

She couldn't answer those questions but did know she didn't like herself much at that moment; felt like the worst person in the world and didn't want to feel that way anymore. She wanted peace; wanted to be the person who could achieve her dreams and not feel badly about it. She was a mother; however, her dreams didn't matter anymore. She didn't matter anymore.

She was tired — tired and wanted a way out. She wondered if her mother had felt that way; if it was that feeling driving the addiction that ended her life. It was an awful, sick, dark feeling in the pit of her stomach, that was always there, had always been there since she was a little girl; but she could ignore it then. It was screaming now, and it was unbearable. She needed peace. *Maybe if I get drunk like Mary or high like Deirdra it'll go away.*

She remembered the pills. A couple painkillers would make her feel better, or at least make her sleep; a few more and who knows. She walked to her bedroom and fished the bottle out of her purse where it had been for nearly a year. It went with her everywhere, she never thought to remove it as she switched from one purse to another. Now she placed it on her dresser and stared at it from where she sat on her bed.

When she awoke the next morning, she was fully clothed lying at the foot of the bed. The untouched pill bottle was still on the dresser. Her face stung from dried tears she'd shed in her sleep. She remembered crying but didn't recall falling asleep.

What she'd intended to do with the pills, when she took them from her purse, was unclear. She hadn't done it. It was a new day, and her baby was gone.

She covered her face with her hands, *Oh God, --what have I done!*  She hurriedly showered and dressed.


"What do you want?" Sean scowled, answering the door.  It was barely seven a.m., and he wasn't in the mood for Courtney's hysterics.

"I don't want to argue, I just came for my baby," she said, her voice trembling.

"You're not getting him.  You said you didn't want him for the last time.  Now you got your wish.  I'm sick of your BS.  I'll raise my son, and we don't need you.  He's probably better off without your craziness anyway.  If you want to see him, go to court and get visitation rights."

"I don't have to go to court.  I have full custody.  If I want to, I can make *you* go to court," she retorted, voice rising.

"We'll see about that after I tell them how you abandoned him," he said, voice rising to surmount hers.

"That's a lie!"  She screamed, while Sean laughed at her.  With teeth clenched, she lunged at him, causing the door to hit the wall.  He laughed harder as he grabbed her wrists, his strength restraining her.

"What the hell is wrong with you two?" Angela, still in her pajamas, yelled as she entered the room.  "Courtney, you stop it this instant and Sean stop provoking her!  I swear that baby in there has more sense than the two of you fools put together—and you're supposed to raise him.  Who's gonna raise you?"

"I came to get my baby," Courtney whimpered.  "He won't give him to me.  Said he was gonna report me and say I abandoned him."

"Why should she get him back?  She said she doesn't want him," Sean folded his arms, glaring at her.

"Who do you expect to raise him?  I'm done raising children.  I refuse to be one of those grandmothers starting all over again," Angela told Sean, then turned to Courtney.  "I'm letting the two of you know, in case you get any ideas, I'm not raising your baby.  You're going to have to figure it out."  The kitchen was silent as Sean and Courtney stood facing but avoided looking at each other.

"I'm going to say this last thing.  It's time you two get your priorities in order.  If your relationship isn't working out, move on, but stop fighting over this baby.  It's not fair to him, or to me.  I'm going back to bed."

"Can I have Bryce?"  Courtney said.

"You cannot.  I'll call you when I'm ready for you to take him.  You and Sean need to talk like you have some sense, then *you* need to go home and get some sleep.  You look terrible," she said leaving the room.

Courtney dropped into a chair at the kitchen table and fumbled with the saltshaker, periodically wiping tears from her eyes while Sean leaned on the kitchen counter and stared out the window.

"She's right," Courtney said in a low voice after about fifteen minutes.

Sean snorted, "According to you, she's always right."

"I don't need your sarcasm," she rolled her eyes.

"What are you saying?"

"I'm not happy and I don't want to do this anymore."

"Are you talking about us?"

"Yes...us," she choked back sobs.

"Just because Angela says—"

"It's over and probably has been for a while. It's time we face it."

"It's not time for me to face anything. The only problem with us is you."

"That's why you're screwing half the town? Because of me?"

"What are you talking about?" he spun around, from the window. His surprise was real. He'd had a fling or two and knew he'd been close to being caught, but she hadn't said anything. He'd convinced himself she either didn't know or didn't care.

"You really think I'm stupid," she said, shaking her head,

He turned away from her again, leaned on the counter and covered his face with his hands. After all his years of vacillation, when it came to his relationship with her, he saw his options closing in; there was nothing he could say to keep her, that he hadn't said before—except...*you could say you'll marry her — it's what she wants—what this is all about....*

"I'm going home. Come get your things —preferably when I'm not there —leave the key," she ordered, no longer crying. Even though her heart was broken, and she was disappointed, the idea of finally moving on felt right.

He didn't respond as he watched her walk out the kitchen door.

Courtney went home, slept as Angela suggested, and was at peace. She now saw how much energy she'd spent, trying to hang on to a person who didn't want to be held on to. Later, as she neatly boxed up his belongings: razor, toothbrush, a few shirts, shoes, and a bathrobe, she still wasn't crying. *I guess it'll hit me later,* she surmised, but suspected the reason it felt right is because it was.

"Sean, aren't you going to work tonight?" Angela asked, seeing him sprawled on the floor in his bedroom.

"No, I'm sick," he moaned. He'd been laying in the same spot most of the day and hadn't eaten, bathed, nor had he paid much attention to his son.

"Sick?" she said, walking over and feeling his forehead. "You don't feel sick." She then remembered the commotion earlier that morning. *Did the girl listen to me for once?* "Did you and Courtney break up or something?"

"She did what you told her to—as always. Why couldn't you stay out of it—we would've worked it out without your help."

"You were arguing in my house. If you didn't want me in it, you should've left and took your baby with you."

He rolled over and turned away, letting her know he was done with the conversation. Angela, snickering, left the room. She couldn't win with any of her kids, they all blamed her for something—everything—that was wrong in their lives.

"Bryce, you're going home to your mommy tomorrow," she said to the baby while he sat in the high-chair and spat food back at her. She decided she wasn't going to contact Courtney but would let Sean take care of returning him to his mother.


"Hi," Courtney said, opening the door to let Sean into the apartment. He was carrying Bryce who was asleep in his arms. "I'll take him—"

"He's asleep. I'll put him in his crib," Sean brushed past her. She'd wanted it to be a quick exchange at the door to minimize the awkwardness of their new situation, but he was now back in the bedroom. She took a deep breath, closed the door and waited for him to return to the living room.

When he did return and saw her still standing at the door, he frowned. "Why are you standing there?  Are you putting me out?"  After brooding the whole prior day, he concluded the best way to deal with her talk of a breakup was to pretend it never happened.

"No, I just –"

"Can't I stay for a minute?  I promise I won't take up much of your time." He started toward the sofa but stopped in his tracks when spotting the box packed with his belongings.

"You've got my stuff packed up?" he said, voice rising.  "I guess you meant what you said yesterday.  You want me out of your life."  She started to speak, but Sean snatched up the box and stormed out of the apartment.  He neglected to leave the key.

# Chapter Seven

"You've been requested by Table three," Sheila said to Sean; he nodded. He knew who Table three was. She always sat at that table, ran up a large bill, and tipped him well. It was going to be a good night.

"Hey, Miss Yolanda, how's it going?" Sean greeted the flawlessly groomed woman who now dined at the restaurant at least three times a week. She was older than he was – he couldn't tell by how much, was below average as far as her looks, but she liked him and showed it. While Yolanda Brown was in Le Chateau, Sean treated her like she was Miss Black America. She liked that also.

"Hey, gorgeous. Look at him, girls; isn't he a prince?" Yolanda said to her party of all females. Sean flashed a smile as his eyes roved around the table. A few of Yolanda's guests were hot, but he knew he had to restrain himself. When Yolanda Brown was in the house, it was always about her.

"Thank you, ladies, for the compliment." He bowed his head slightly then signaled the bartender and within seconds, Yolanda was served her Lemon Drop Martini without having to order it. Her party was impressed; they were supposed to be. "Now what can I get for the rest of you lovely ladies?"

Yolanda Marguerite Brown was the only child of the most prominent African American businessman in the city. She was rich, unambitious, and liked to live well. More importantly, she liked people to see her living well. She was socially active and accumulated many friends, most of whom she disliked, and who disliked her. But in her world, knowing people was important and image was everything

Sean's job was to make certain she and her party were well taken care of.

Will, the owner of the restaurant, assured him that when Yolanda was in the restaurant, he could pull in as many other wait-staff as needed to serve her table, or tables.  When Yolanda was happy with the service, there was a healthy tip for everybody, and she'd bring more customers back on her next visit.

Sean also liked when Yolanda came in; it signaled an easy night for him. Her parties tended to hang around until closing, and at some point, she'd request he sit down and have a drink with them.  This was always acceptable to Will. *Whatever she wants—just keep her coming back..."*

It had been four months since Courtney had dumped him; during the first month, he'd begged incessantly for her to change her mind.  To his surprise she held firm, waiting for the marriage proposal, that he just couldn't muster.  He wanted her back but wasn't willing to string her along —he had zero desire to marry her.  Understanding they'd reached an impasse, they parted ways.

He hated that she wasn't his but stayed hopeful; he kept tabs on her personal life enough to know he hadn't been replaced.  There was no guy hanging around when he went to pick up or drop off his son, but then she wasn't all that attractive these days; beautiful as ever, but her attitude…


"No, I'm not interested," Courtney spat walking away from Michael, a guy who'd just recently started working at the store.  He'd been trying to take her out from the moment he'd walked through the door.  It was Friday night, and she had an empty apartment to go home to, but that was her business.

"Why not?  And don't give me that baby excuse again.  I heard you telling Shelley he's with his dad this weekend."

How many times and how many ways did she have to explain to these guys just because she wasn't in a relationship, didn't mean she wanted to be tied up with them. She'd spent years living her life around Sean and wasn't going to make that mistake again. "My free time belongs to me, that's why," she snarled.

He stepped back, "Alright, Miss Courtney, if that's what you prefer. I'll leave you alone." She sniffed and moved to her cash register as a line began to form. *Why are so many people shopping on a Friday night?* Her usual sour mood, worsened.


She'd survived her breakup with Sean, but the after effect had been brutal. All she saw when she opened her eyes, looked in the mirror and looked at the world, is the fool she was and still is. Whatever made her think he loved her— so much that she framed her life around him, and what he wanted? Now he was gone, content to live his life—having the baby every other weekend, with her out of the picture entirely. Yeah, he was always seeking an opportunity to hook up. There was only one hook up she had in mind: the legal kind.

The disappointment was deep. She'd refused to settle for Sean's crumbs, so he let her go without a fight. It felt like a knife to her gut, that kept twisting, even as she tried to move on with her life.

She needed to re-do her senior year of college but hadn't registered; couldn't fathom homework and studying on top of self-pity and single motherhood.

Bryce was growing, walking and talking, and everybody loved him; secretly she wondered if she did. She was his caretaker, nothing more, and when they were home alone, that's how she treated him. After work though, alone in her apartment that April evening, she sat sulking in front of the television screen, looking at her son's empty bed. *When was the last time I smiled at my son...when was the last time I smiled?*


"Sean, I think I've overdone it tonight. What'd you have him put in my drink anyway?" Yolanda giggled. It was a Friday night, and his shift had ended hours before, but when Yolanda strolled in without a reservation, it was understood he couldn't leave. He'd even had to cancel a date.

"It was made the way we always make it for you, Miss Yolanda," he said. "I can't help that you had five of them. But who's counting."

"Five! My check only says three."

"We don't charge you for everything and you know it," he smirked.

"Baby, you're so good to me. Why don't you drive me home," she cooed, laying her head, with its ten-pound weave, on his shoulder.

He gently slid out of his chair and shifted her into an upright sitting position. "Let me tell Will. I'll drop you off and take a cab back to my car."

Once he'd clocked out for the night, Sean escorted Yolanda to her car, wondering if she was really intoxicated or play acting. He'd seen her down more alcohol than she'd consumed that night with no problem, but maybe on those occasions someone else had been driving.

When they reached Yolanda's car, Sean's heart skipped at the sight of the bright red Lexus convertible. Despite the cool early Spring night, he would've loved to drive with the top down.

"Nice car," he murmured, trying to sound casual; his voice cracked a bit.

"Like it? I just got it last week. This is my baby," she then leaned down and kissed the car, nearly falling over. Sean caught her, then opened the door and helped her in.

He slid into the driver's seat, and in moments the mirrors and seats began adjusting themselves. There was no ignition key, only a button that, when he pressed it, started the engine; maybe it was an engine. To him, it sounded so smooth it was difficult to tell; then the dashboard spoke. *You are currently at Le Chateau, where is your next destination?*

"Home," Yolanda answered from the back seat, and a map appeared on the dashboard. Music—Kem's vocals drifted from the sound system. ♪*...When Love calls...*♪

*Make a right turn in 200 feet onto Park Road...*

Sean reveled in the automobile's handling and sound system, while Yolanda dozed, stretched out on the back seat. The GPS guided him to the Regency Hills gated community and to an elegant townhome that appeared to him to be more than three times the size of his mother's house.

"You live here alone?" He received no answer; she was asleep. He kept the car running while he walked to the passenger side door and opened it, wondering just how he was going to get her up the front stairs and into the house.

"Yolanda," he said gently, as he held the car door open. He had to resist the temptation to laugh out loud as she struggled to sit up. Her hair was a bird nest on top of her head, her clothes were twisted and wrinkled, and she didn't appear to know what planet she was on. *If her groupies could see her now.*

"Huh?" she stirred.

"You're home. Can you get out of the car yourself, or do you need help?"

"I don't need any help," she squinted at him, as if trying to remember who he was. Scooting herself closer to the door, a smile lit up her face.

"Oh Sean," she said, smoothing her hair down and straightening her clothes. "I must look a mess."

"Don't worry about it." He helped her out of the car. "Nice house; you live here alone?"

"It's a little small compared to what I'm used to," she mumbled, fishing her keys from her purse, "but I liked the layout, so I bought it. I've been here about three years now. Do me a favor and put the car in the garage." She gave him the keypad code.

Once inside the house, Sean's eyes lit up. The décor was like nothing he'd ever seen, part Asian, part African and some contemporary. "Did you decorate this?"

"No, I have a decorator who re-does it every year," she said, trying to sober up. "I get bored easily, but I think I'll keep this for a while. I've been receiving a lot of compliments. Look, I'm going to my room. There's a kitchen and bar downstairs. I keep both well stocked, so you're welcome to hang out and help yourself."

He went downstairs and found, in addition to the bar, a complete home entertainment suite with a theater, game consoles, and billiards room. An adjacent room held a lounge with stereo surround sound, massage chairs, a sauna and Jacuzzi, plus a connecting door to the gym. He grabbed a beer, some chips, then powered up the Xbox 360 game system.  When Yolanda appeared an hour later, he

realized he'd forgotten about her, and that he had his own home to go to.

"Sorry I got carried away.  I didn't mean to over-stay my welcome," he

apologized, turning off the game console.

*This gets 'em every time,* Yolanda thought.  Her friends call her

downstairs recreation center the 'man trap'; husbands and boyfriends often got lost

down there; the girls having to drag them out.  "No, go ahead and enjoy.  I

appreciate you're getting me home safely.  Make yourself comfortable.  You don't

need to rush off, unless there's somebody you need to get home to..."

He laughed at her inference.  "No there isn't, as a matter of fact," he then

took a sip of his beer.

"Let me freshen that for you," Yolanda purred, "I hate warm beer..."

"Good morning, Sean," he heard a woman say, and opened his eyes to see

Yolanda standing over him dressed in what appeared to be work-out attire two

sizes too tight, and simultaneously was holding a lit cigarette.

"Hey," he stretched, realizing the game controller was sitting in his lap,

three empty beer bottles and a plate of half eaten hot wings were on the tray beside

him.  *I spent the night in a woman's house and all I did was eat, drink and play

video games.* " He laughed out loud at himself.

"What's so funny?"

"I was wondering: did you take advantage of me last night?  Is that what

was on your mind when you lured me here?"  He was so tickled with his joke, he continued laughing while Yolanda smirked and folded her arms.

She'd never noticed how immature he was, but then realized she didn't know much about him at all. "Renate's upstairs making breakfast. What can I tell her to make for you?

"You have a mai –"

"Shh! Don't let her hear you call her that. Renate is my assistant. She cooks, cleans, shops and runs my life. I can't live without her. Now if you like, you can shower upstairs. I asked Renate to run to the store this morning and buy you some clean clothes to throw on; hope I got the size right. After your shower, your breakfast will be ready."

"Thanks."

"No, thank YOU. I haven't had such a handsome house guest in a long time," she sauntered up the stairs. Sean noticed that although she appeared dressed to workout, she'd ignored her well-equipped gym.

When he emerged from the shower, dressed in the sweat suit he'd been provided, he walked down the hall. following the smoky aroma of bacon and sat at the kitchen counter. "Hello, I'm sorry I forgot your name," Sean said to the tall brown skinned woman busy in the kitchen.

"Good mornin' to you. I'm Renate," the woman replied in a West Indian accent. She then paused mid-step to give him a head to toe once-over and whistled, "*Mahn*, she tell no lies –you are a looker."

"Thank you," he smiled, blushing slightly.

"Hope you have a hearty appetite. She tell me to make sure I feed you good," Renate then placed a plate and silverware in front of him and produced platters of food. "Here's eggs, bacon, pancakes, home fries, and grits wit' cheese. Here's the remote for the television and help yourself to coffee and juice over there. Now I'm off; spendin' de day wit' mah grahnkids."

Sean looked at the spread and scratched his head. He now knew why Yolanda was so unpleasantly plump.

After he'd eaten, while sipping juice and watching the news, Yolanda appeared again. Her house was so big and comfortable that when she disappeared, he forgot about her.

"I guess it's time for me to take you back to your car, if you're ready to go."

"Yeah, I'd better," he said reluctantly, feeling like he was leaving a vacation to go back to the real world. "I have some homework to do, and I've got to work tonight."

"Well, stay a little longer at least. I have a gym with a sauna downstairs. You can give me some work-out tips. I need to lose a couple pounds."

"Stop drinking so much," he suggested, as he checked his phone. There was no point in letting her deceive herself. If she kept eating and drinking like she did, working out would be a waste of time.

"You're not the first person to tell me that," she said. Then his cell phone rang.

"Hey Angela," he said into the phone.

His mother knew, when he answered the phone using her first name, he was with a woman.

"You could've let somebody know you weren't coming home last night," she scolded.

"You know I would've, but it wasn't planned.  I –"

"Spare me the details, please," she cut him off.  "I just called to tell you I have your baby.  He's not going home until tomorrow, but I'm having my hair done and I need you to come and take him for a while."

"I'll be there within the hour," he said, then ended the call.  "I've gotta go."

"Who's Angela?" Yolanda said.

"Is that *any* of your business, Miss Yolanda Brown?"  He grinned, while Yolanda tapped her manicured nail tips on the counter waiting for an answer.  "If you must know, my mother.  I've got to go home and babysit my son," he answered, unsure as to why he was giving her an explanation.

Yolanda wanted to ask more questions, like where was his son's mother, but realized she didn't know this boy, and wasn't sure she'd get to know him. Sometimes her hunger to know everybody else's business got the best of her.

*I'm gonna miss you,* Sean thought, referring to Yolanda's car which she let him drive, back to the restaurant.  He was almost too embarrassed for her to see his car, but quickly got over it.  *One day, I'll have one of these, and a couple others,* he thought.

"Thank you, you were a most gracious hostess," he said, holding the driver's side door open for her.

"Why don't we get together?  Sometime this week," she said.  *He's already spent the night in my house and was a perfect gentleman.  A guy who's good-looking and trustworthy isn't so easy to find these days.*

Sean gave her his cell-phone number, but didn't request hers, figuring Yolanda liked to be the one in control.

When he got into the driver's seat and started his car, he missed Yolanda's car even more.  He drove home wondering how long it would take until he could afford a car like that.  If he continued living with his mother, not that long; but she had his bags packed for the day after graduation.  There was no way she'd let him drive a high-end automobile and live in her house.  He was going to have to be patient, dream big, and… play the lotto?


"Courtney, what's wrong?  Tell me, please?  I'm trying so hard to get to know you, but you keep shutting down on me," Jordan pleaded with her, as he cut the engine, after parking the car.

"I don't know what you're talking about.  Can we just go in, please?  I'm hungry," Courtney said, sitting in the passenger side, but staring straight ahead.

Jordan and Courtney had been seeing each other for three months, but he couldn't figure out why their relationship hadn't moved beyond the cordial stage.

"I'm sorry if I'm boring you, but I was hoping our relation—friendship means more to you than food."

They sat in the car, silent but tense, on the busy downtown street.  It had been a hot and humid August day, and she was ready to go inside to the air conditioning, but as had become the norm, Jordan wanted to talk about them—or really –about her.  She clenched her jaw.  What was going on inside her head was none of his business.

She sucked her teeth and shook her head.  "You did call and invite me to dinner. I didn't think I was going to be ambushed in the process."

"Ambushed," he frowned. "Is that what you call communication: ambushed?"

"What do you want from me? We go out occasionally and we have a nice time—don't we?"

He leaned back, "How do you feel about me? I'm a man, I have feelings. I'd like to know."

She shrugged.

"Really, I'm leaving that much of an impression."

She put her hands over her face, "I don't know what this is about, but I can only be honest—not sure what you want me to say."

"I guess I was hoping that you and I could be closer than a couple dates, and an occasional sleepover."

She shrugged again, "I don't know."

"Are you still in love with him? I've seen the way he still looks at you, and the way he looks at me. Is he the problem; am I wasting my time?"

She'd enjoyed the jealousy on Sean's face, when he ran into Jordan the first time; he'd been calling her regularly since then. Sean's renewed interest in her, however, wasn't preventing her from getting close to Jordan. She was doing that all by herself.

He tapped the key on the steering wheel for a few minutes, before silently exiting the car, and going over the passenger side and guiding her out safely. They had a quiet cordial dinner that evening, but it was their last date.

Sometime later, when he'd called to say they wouldn't be seeing each other again, she was flippant, thinking it was just his way of trying to draw her out. But then she didn't hear from him again and regretted those last words. He'd been so sweet to her, treating her better than Sean ever had. She wanted to call him and apologize for—what? Because he'd been right about her: she felt nothing.

"I called you last night after midnight. Where were you?" Sean interrogated Courtney two weeks later. He was at her door, holding their son, a piercing stare fixated on her.

She sighed, accustomed to brushing off his advances. "None of your business. Thanks for bringing Bryce home," she reached for the sleeping toddler. He walked past her and laid him down in the playpen in the living room.

When he turned to her again, his tone was softer. "You know, I realize it's been almost a year, and you've moved on, but I'm still not happy we're not together. This isn't what I wanted then. and it's not what I want now. I'd do anything if we could go back to how things were." As he spoke, he took tenuous steps toward her.

Watching his movements, hearing his words, he hadn't said he loved or missed her; she saw nothing compelling about going *back to how things were.*

"I hear you're seeing somebody," she said.

"Yeah, and so are you. I see a lot of people, what does that have to do with anything?"

"Like you said, it's been almost a year, and I don't want to go back to the way things were. Remember it was a little one sided. I figure if you're not going to marry me, I might as well keep my free—"

"Here we go again. I've told you I'm not ready, and you're not going to force me. I don't care how long you refuse to see me."

She nodded, "Understood. Goodnight."

Instead of walking to the door, he flopped down on her couch and sulked, while she remained standing. She scooped up Bryce, took him back to the room, and put him to bed. When she returned, a half hour later, Sean was still in the same spot and brooding.

"I don't know why you're still here –"

"Because I miss you...I can't stand this," he said half whispering, half whining.

For the first time, in a long time, she felt an ache stirring inside her, she'd thought was dead. "I miss you too, but we don't want the same things. I can't –" she heard her voice break as she spoke, the pitch sounded strained.

He heard it too, and rose to his feet, grabbing her hand, gently pulling her limp frame to himself. The nearer to him she came, the more she felt the progress she'd made getting free from him evaporating. He put his arms around her waist and pulled her down on the couch next to him, wrapping himself around her. She didn't move to embrace him; didn't push him away. Closing her eyes, she leaned back on the couch. When they kissed; the battle was over.

She clung to him, while they made love. They remained in the same spot until Bryce began crying a couple hours later. As she went to Bryce's crib, she hit herself on the forehead – they hadn't used any protection. Emergency contraception was something she'd heard vaguely about and made a mental note to call her doctor first thing the next morning.

# Chapter Eight

"Being rich has its benefits," Yolanda said at dinner, "but it's not as great as people think. I can buy cars, and clothes and houses, but I can only use one thing at a time. The rest of the stuff just sits –sits and collects dust. Till I get sick of looking at it and buy something else."

Sean watched her. When she pulled out a cigarette, he lit it for her. She was on her fifth Lemon Drop and was starting to slur her speech, lapsing into her poor little rich girl diatribe. When she was drunk, she was boring, but trying to tell her not to drink so much was futile.

They'd been seeing each other once or twice a week for six months, and Sean was unsure why. He found her physically unattractive, and their sex life was nothing to write home about. He liked her when she was sober, or wasn't power tripping, but that was rare. He loved her stuff, however—all of it, and Yolanda was generous; he especially enjoyed when she treated him to impromptu shopping trips. His most serious emotional attachment, however, was with her candy apple red Lexus convertible.

"Baby, you're so good to me. I'm so glad we met," she cooed with a tipsy giggle.

"So am I, Yolanda," he replied. "Are you ready for some coffee?" He wasn't about to let her get sloppy drunk. His job was to take care of her and make sure she was always together—sometimes inspite of her. Usually he was patient, but tonight, he was anxious to wrap up their date and drop her off. He had to be subtle about it, however, Yolanda liked to think the lives of everyone she interacted with revolved around her, and normally he didn't mind indulging her.

Tonight, Courtney was waiting for him; he couldn't wait to get to her place.

"No, I don't want coffee. Not yet. Have another drink, baby. You know I don't like to drink alone. What's your hurry anyway?"

"No hurry, Yolanda," Sean said, ordering himself a soft drink. He spent the evening attending to her, while checking his watch when she wasn't looking, thankful he still had his key to Courtney's place.

Three hours later, when he tried to use his key, he found Courtney had chained the door, making certain he couldn't slip into bed beside her. He'd tried to call her and got no answer. He dialed again repeatedly until she picked up.

"What?" Courtney barked.

"Let me in, babe."

"I chained the door for a reason. You were supposed to be here at 8:00. It's after midnight. Go home."

"I'm sorry I'm so late, baby. Let me in. I'll make it up to you. Please."

"What do you think this is? Go make your booty call somewhere else!" she then hung up.

He walked out of her apartment building and climbed into his car, wondering why women always made things more complicated than they had to be.


"What now?"

"Wow, is that how you answer the phone first thing in the morning?" Sean laughed.

"What do you want, Sean. I'm angry with you for standing me up last night," Courtney said.

"Yeah, I know.  Again, I'm sorry."  She noticed there was no explanation.  "Get dressed.  I'll pick you up in a half hour and take you to brunch."

"Are you bringing Bryce?"

"He's hanging out with Mom today.  It'll just be us.  Do you accept, or are you going to make me beg?"

"I'll be ready," she mumbled, not wanting to reveal how thrilled she was he was taking her out for once.  Since they'd started seeing each other again, they rarely went anywhere together, with or without Bryce –his excuse always being schoolwork or his job.

When they arrived at the restaurant, on that early November day, Courtney found herself distracted by Sean's clothes.  He wore the standard urban attire: jeans, t-shirt, sneakers, but Courtney knew from working in retail, the cost of the clothes on his back could've paid her rent and fed her and Bryce for a month.  *Are his waiter tips that good these days?*

Then the restaurant itself.  It was called the Acorn Loft, and was bright and colorful, not the type of place he'd pick; the kind of venue a woman would go for.  She loved it and wondered how he'd found out about it—or who he'd been there with.  She filed her observations away, however, determined to enjoy the outing.

The two mimosas took her past her alcohol tolerance, and they returned to her apartment, spending a blissful rest of the day in bed.  When the evening came, Sean had to shower and leave with some vague explanation.  This had become their all-too-familiar routine.

In the month since they'd started seeing each other again, he was all sweetness and love when around, but he was also evasive. She'd been waiting to hear what his plan was for them, since he'd claimed to want her back in his life so desperately. So far, however, she had no firm place in his life, and it was also obvious –he was in a relationship with someone else.

"Who is she?" Courtney demanded, sitting up in bed watching him. "You might as well tell me; not like I care."

"I don't know what you're talking about. I've got some stuff to do, that's all."

He pecked her forehead and hurried out. Yolanda had reservations at one of the most exclusive restaurants in the city and had warned him not to be late. He drove away from Courtney's place humming and smiling to himself. He'd spent the whole day with her, and she was still pissed. *Maybe I'll send her flowers next week,* he thought as he drove down the road trying to decide what he'd wear to dinner.


"I have to go, baby," Sean said again a couple weeks later. He'd only spent half the night with Courtney this time. She hadn't checked the clock but could tell from the windows it was still dark outside. Sean, however, was showered, dressed, and sitting on Courtney's side of the bed. He bent down and kissed her passionately. "I love you. Do you love me?"

She rolled over and turned her back to him, feeling like she was having an affair with a married man.

"I'll call you later," he promised, leaving the room.

Their relationship was ruled by the cellphone Sean never put down or stopped looking at.  On one of the rare times when she was able to peek at it, she saw three entries repeatedly:  YOL-home, YOL-cell, YOL-offc.  She was dying to know who the hell was Y O L!

When she glanced at the clock on her nightstand and it read four a.m.  She cursed out loud and threw her pillow against the wall.

On top of everything else, her period was late —very late.  So late, she was scared to even walk down the home pregnancy test aisle of the drugstore fearing the boxes would fly off the shelves.  Every day, she kept hoping to see a spot of something, reminding herself her period had become erratic since she'd had the baby.  That was true—but not this erratic.

*Maybe it's just stress*, she told herself as she exited the shower, but recalled having the same conversation with herself two years prior.  The result of that stress was now running around her room eating dry Cheerios.  Could she be that unlucky?  To get pregnant the one time she didn't take precautions, considering all the times she had?

She groaned out loud, then heard a crash and Bryce crying for her.  What a great start to her day...


"Okay, Courtney, you can get dressed now.  Meet me in my office when you're done," Dr. Michaels instructed, after the pelvic exam.  Courtney already knew what the doctor was going to tell her and knew what her response would be.

"Okay, m'dear, your blood work is back, and yes, you are pregnant.  Looks to be about eight or more weeks.  From the expression on your face, this isn't what you want to hear."

"No.  Can you take care of it?"

"You mean a termination?  That's an option.  If you want to pursue it, there are some things we're required by law to do—education and counseling.  As soon as that's completed, we can place you on the schedule, to receive the pill."

"Can we get it all done today," Courtney's breath was coming so fast, she was hyperventilating.  "I need this to be over and done with."

"Courtney, please calm down."  Dr. Michaels wouldn't continue until she'd composed herself.  "Now, we can't do anything today, but we can get you started.  First, here's a pamphlet giving you full details of the process..."


"Courtney, how've you been?"  Sean's sister Jazmine asked while they were at Angela's house on Thanksgiving.  Neither of Sean's sisters liked her much, so she was suspicious when they were friendly towards her.

"I'm alright."

"I'm surprised you're still dealing with my brother, considering Yolanda Brown has taken over."

"I'm not dealing with him.  We broke up a while ago," she said, trying to conceal her ignorance of the identity of Sean's new woman.

"Then why are you here?"

"Sean invited me, and it's where I've spent Thanksgiving the last five years.  Old habits, and your mother's cooking –you know," Courtney flashed a carefree grin, but quickly escaped the living room as soon as Jazmine's head was turned.  On the way to the kitchen she spotted Sean on the phone, again.  Seems he'd gotten a call every fifteen minutes since she'd been there. Now that she knew

the woman's name, which sounded vaguely familiar, she decided to spend the time

before dinner safely in the kitchen with Angela, free from talk of Sean's girlfriend.

The savory aroma of the turkey, just out of the oven, filled the house,

mixed with the sweetness of the pecan crusted candied yams still baking.

"You've put on some weight, haven't you?"

"A little. I'm going to start working out next week, but today I'm going to

eat my fill of your dinner," Courtney said. Angela loved when people raved about

her cooking, and the compliment turned attention away from her expanding

waistline. If anyone could detect pregnancy, Angela McNair could. It was the last

thing she wanted.

Once dinner started, the evening's comedy began at Sean's expense. His

girlfriend called his cell phone every fifteen minutes; his family teased him

mercilessly. Even Courtney was embarrassed for him, as he couldn't take a bite of

his meal without the phone to his ear. He avoided her, while she marveled at the

scene. He would never have tolerated that kind of badgering from her, but then

she noticed the new and weighty gold chain hanging from his neck.

"Girl let me tell you, Yolanda Brown looks like Bullwinkle with a Diana

Ross hair weave," Krystal said, when Sean left the room. The entire dining room

exploded in laughter. Upon his return, they quieted down, but some were still

smirking.

He ignored the snickering. "I've got to leave –" he said to Courtney.

"Bye," she looked past him. Even though she hadn't driven herself,

Angela would make sure she got home. "I'm going to stick around for a while."

He shoved his hands into his pockets and rocked back on his heels.

"Better go, the boss is waitin'!" Nina, his sister-in-law yelled from the hallway, which spawned more laughter.

Sean kissed Bryce who was sitting in Courtney's lap, and walked out of the house without saying goodbye.

Courtney then sat and listened while his family ripped Yolanda Brown apart piece by piece. She learned from them; Yolanda was the wealthy daughter of businessman Oscar 'Ronnie' Brown. She was older than Sean, nearer to thirty, and Sean's family considered her a snob, who never stopped bragging about where she'd been or what she had. They also implied she was bullying Sean, or may even be drugging him, but Courtney knew him better than that. He'd weighed the cost of the situation and was making a willing trade-off. Regardless of what Courtney or anyone in his family thought about his choice of Yolanda Brown, she suited him.


Sean let himself into Courtney's place the following Monday, after not having spoken to her since the Thanksgiving Day debacle. She wasn't due to be home from work for a couple hours, so he kicked off his shoes and stretched out on her bed. He needed a break from Yolanda but didn't want to go home; his mother was giving him the silent treatment. He hoped enough time had passed since Thursday and Courtney missed him enough not to bring up any of the events of that day.

The whole thing had been unreal. Yolanda had intentionally embarrassed him because she believed that day, she was supposed to be introduced to his family as his new woman.

"If I'm the most important woman in your life, why is it you've invited your ex to your mother's house instead of me?" Yolanda demanded, a couple days before Thanksgiving.

"I didn't invite her; she goes every year.  She and my moth –"

"It's time for a change.  When I'm in a man's life, I will not be pushed to the side," Yolanda said.  He was sitting in an armchair while she hovered, pointing a nail at him.

"No one's pushing you anywhere.  It's just dinner," he attempted to look around her to the television.

"Un-invite her.  I mean it.  She might as well get used to it anyway."

"You need to get used to the fact that she's a part of my life.  We have a son and we still see each oth –"

"I don't care.  Tell her there's been a permanent change of plans."

Sean didn't answer her, but the flash of anger in his eyes let her know she wasn't getting her way—this time.

"Get out and leave my car keys.  Drive that wreck of yours for a change," she folded her arms. while tapping her foot.

When Yolanda called him on Thanksgiving Day, Sean assumed she'd had a change of heart; that wasn't the case.  She'd decided, if he wasn't going to invite her, she was going to make her presence felt anyway—and she had.

They'd had a huge fight Thanksgiving night, but she made up with him the next day, the way she always did—by taking him shopping.  He now sported a nice rock on his left earlobe, to replace what Yolanda called *the speck of glitter* he'd bought for himself.  She'd also made it clear –she'd be spending Christmas Day with him and his family—not Courtney, and there'd be no debate about it.

Sean didn't know how he was going to tell Courtney, or what he was going to do to soften the double blow; he and Yolanda would be flying to New York for New Year's Eve.  It occurred to him to take the second earring of the set, and have it made into something for Courtney, but that seemed like such a low thing to do.  But then he was juggling two women at once.

He rolled over on his side, and a glossy pamphlet sitting on the nightstand caught his eye.  He picked it up –and found it featured two women on the cover, one with a lab coat and stethoscope.  It was entitled "A Woman's Agonizing Choice".  He swung his legs onto the floor and sat upright, swallowing hard as he opened and discovered abortion literature.  *What?*  He asked himself. As he turned the page, a pink sheet of paper fluttered onto the floor.  He picked it up and saw Courtney's medical chart label at the top.  She had an appointment for Wednesday morning, two days away; the diagnosis: *Incidental Pregnancy*.

He closed the pamphlet and put it back in its place on the nightstand.  *In two days, it'll be over,* he thought.  *She's made up her mind, no point in... She's pregnant...carrying my baby...another baby....* The absolute last thing he needed was another baby.  *Leave it alone...it's her decision...her choice—isn't that what the law says?  Stay out of it, man...let it be.*  But he couldn't.  When he saw another baby, he saw Bryce, the only real love of his life.  His baby: innocent, trusting, loving, needing protection, how could he sit by and let Bryce's brother or sister be destroyed? for what?  Because he couldn't commit to one woman—yet.  Courtney was the only woman for him; deep down he knew that—didn't he?  He just wasn't ready now.

He wasn't sure how long he'd sat there; but when Courtney walked into the bedroom, he was holding the brochure and appointment slip.

"What are you doing here!" She yelled and snatched the brochure from his hand, while Bryce ran around the room, then jumped up on the bed to greet him.

"Hey, man. I missed you," he said, unable to bring himself to look at or speak to Courtney. He was trying to pull together one lucid thought, but everything in his brain was scrambled. After about fifteen minutes he put Bryce in his playpen with his sippy cup.

"I came to see you," he said quietly. Courtney was sitting on the opposite side of the bed with her back to him, still wearing her coat. "You asked me what I was doing here."

"Oh," she replied, without turning around.

"You're pregnant?" An opening suddenly appeared to him in his mind, "Is it… mine?" He blurted.

"No."

He exhaled loudly through his teeth and shook his head. "Stop lying."

She removed her coat and hung it in the closet. "It's all arranged. You don't have to worry about it."

He wanted to leave it there, but the child was his and he was going to have his say regardless of what she did. "I don't like the idea of my baby being butchered by some doctor. It just seems like we can do better…"

"Get over it…"

"Why?  What have I done so wrong that makes that right?"

"We're not together.  You're with her and I'm—"

"And the baby has to pay for that?"

"I'm not talking about this anymore.  You're twisting everything.  It's a medical procedure, nothing more."

"Like bunion surgery huh?  When's the last time a bunion had a heartbeat?"

Courtney approached Sean and poked him in the chest.  "When did you get so high and mighty, huh?  You whore!" she flicked the bauble in his earlobe.

"This isn't about me.  Yeah, I might me a whore, but my baby doesn't deserve to die because of it."

"And who's going to raise this baby, while you're on your righteous crusade, huh?  You and Yolanda Brown—your mother.  It won't be me!"

"You know what Courtney," he said, shaking off her reference to Yolanda, a subject they'd had yet to confront.  "Accidents happen, and this was one of them.  You don't have an innocent killed because you screwed up; you deal with it.  That's all I'm trying to say.  Sure, I admit, it would be easier; but I'll never completely forget about that baby that didn't make it."

Her mind suddenly shut down, clouded with the pain she'd been navigating the past few months, and she could find no rebuttal to his arguments. She crumbled onto the bed; but when Sean moved to comfort her, she pushed him away.  "Who asked you to come here?"  She sobbed.

He left her alone, picked up Bryce and went into the living room.  He sat on the sofa and played with his son all the while, trying to think about what he'd do next.  How far would he go to fight a battle with her, over the life of a child even he had to admit, he wasn't ready for.

He reached in his pocket and switched off his cellphone. Yolanda would be trying to track him down, and he didn't feel like lying to her about his whereabouts.  There was no way he'd involve her in this situation; it wasn't any of her business.

Bryce started to cry, and Sean, noticing the time, realized he must've missed his dinner.  He started to walk to the bedroom and tell Courtney, then had second thoughts.  It wouldn't serve his case for the new baby, if he wasn't willing to make a plate of food for the first one.  He went to the refrigerator, trying to look for the types of things his mother fed Bryce, and was relieved to find a plate of food already prepared.  When Courtney came out of the bedroom, Bryce was in the highchair eating cheerfully.

"Ha Mommy, ha Mommy ha," he waved.

Inspite of her red puffy eyes and tear streaked face, she smiled.  Sean then walked up and put his arms around her.

"Are you feeling better?"  He said, and she shrugged.  He began to stroke her back and massage her neck; she relaxed to his touch.  He then lightly kissed the spot just below her ear –that usually got him whatever he wanted.  "I'll run you a hot bubble bath.  Then I'll give you a massage the way I did when you were pregnant with Bryce..."  He was thinking on his feet, figuring if he could make her happy to be pregnant, she might not be so quick to run to the abortion doctor.  It was his only hope since he had no intention of marrying her –yet.  He didn't even plan on giving up Yolanda—yet.  He had to do his best to make things okay between them just the way they were right now.

"Nice seeing you again, son," Ronnie Brown, Yolanda's father greeted Sean, while shaking his hand firmly.

"Thank you, sir. It's nice to be here." Yolanda beamed euphorically at the two of them.

*For a poor boy, Sean knows how to handle himself,* she thought. She couldn't say the same about herself all the time –she sometimes drank too much, always talked too much, and had come to rely upon him to cue her when she'd gone too far. What he lacked in social status, he more than compensated in looks, manners and charm. She was working with him on other areas, such as how to dress, and proper social etiquette. He moved easily among her friends, laughed at the right times, and didn't give away too much information about his background. Most of her crowd figured he was a poor nobody from nowhere, but he knew how to blend in without making it obvious. Sean was great to have around, and there was never any conflict between the two of them about who was in charge—she was. Yolanda was starting to think she just might want to keep him...

"Baby, this is Mr. Harrington Hilliard. I call him Uncle Harry. He's one of daddy's oldest friends."

"No, unh-uh, he's the one who's old," the man quipped, and he and Yolanda laughed as if he'd told the funniest joke that ever was. Sean followed suit.

"You're so bad, Uncle Harry. Anyway, I think I told you he's the President of Hilliard Enterprises," Yolanda said, cuing Sean.

"Oh, yes. I'm honored to meet you, sir. I'm Sean McNair. Yolanda's told me many great things about your organization," Sean hoped the older man wouldn't ask for specifics; even if he did, Yolanda had his back. The two of them had become adept at working the crowds at her various social functions. They'd gotten plenty of practice as Yolanda's calendar was always full, and he was happy to go along for the ride. In the time they'd been dating, he'd met every mayor in their locality and had been to dinner at the Governor's mansion. He'd also met several celebrities and people who knew people who knew people. She'd introduced him to a world he never thought he'd be a part of –wasn't sure even now if he wanted to be, but he was having fun just the same.

"Sean's an engineering student, Uncle Harry. He'll be finishing up at the Technical Institute in June and is looking for the right internship opportunity. Aren't you, Sweetie?" He hadn't been looking for an internship, but Yolanda had been bugging him about quitting the restaurant. A waiter boyfriend didn't fit her image.

"Hmmm. We can always use a sharp intern—they don't cost us much. Hold on a second." He lifted his hand to get the attention of a younger man across the room, who was at his side within seconds.

"This is Ross, my Managing Director of Operations. Ross, this here is Yolie's friend… what was your name?"

"Sean, sir."

"Yes, Sean. And he's looking for an internship. Do we have any more spots?"

"Of course, sir," Ross said, and handed Sean his business card. "Give me a call at this number on Monday morning, and we'll schedule a time for you to come in."

"Thank you, I will."


Sean's meeting with Ross occurred within an hour of his calling him the following Monday morning, which was a stroke in his favor. By being ready on short notice, Ross had no opportunity to blow him off.

"So, you're dating Yolanda Brown, and think that will earn you a position within Hilliard, huh?" The shorter man queried stepping into Sean's path, as soon as he'd crossed the threshold of his office.

"No sir," Sean said, nodding reverently, then meeting Ross's penetrating stare.

"Good. Because it won't. I'm only talking to you because the boss said so. He has no input as to whether you stay or go. Your pretty boy looks might get you by with Miss Yolanda, but they don't mean anything around here. Do we understand each other?"

"Yes sir." Sean stood up straight as if poised for a military examination.

"Good. So far you have the right attitude. Take a seat and tell me about your background."

The interview lasted all morning, as Sean was given a thorough tour of all the operational areas, and his grilling continued over lunch. Despite what the director had said, it was obvious the job was his from the moment he'd stepped onto the premises. Ross dragged out the process, trying to wear him down, and find a reason to reject him. When that failed, he was processed through human resources that same day.  He stopped at the restaurant on his way home to quit his

job; the new position started the following morning.


Three days before Christmas, Sean appeared at Courtney's door, carrying

ten elaborately wrapped boxes and three bags of gifts, all of which were for her.

His new job paid well; and on top of being able to help with her bills, he was able

to give her the type of Christmas she'd never had.

Courtney giggled like a little girl; she'd never received more than two or

three Christmas gifts at once.

"You can't open anything until Christmas, except this.  I want you to open

this now," he said handing her a small box obviously containing jewelry.  It was

the size that usually held earrings—or a ring.  She held it for a moment telling

herself to temper her expectations.  This *was* Sean after all.

It contained a pair of diamond earrings that sparkled brilliantly –like the

one in Sean's ear.  In fact. as she studied them a little closer, she guessed that the

two of them together could make one of his.  She slammed closed the box and

handed it to him.

"That's pretty tacky: re-gifting Yolanda's baubles."

"That's not what I did," Sean lied, "I got a new job.  How else do you

think I could afford all of this?  I also paid your rent and the babysitter this

month," he added, wondering what the hell she had to be mad about.  The stone

itself was worth a fortune, but the money he paid to get it cut and put into earrings

set him back also.  Even though he had a new job, he was still broke, from all the

money he'd spent on her.  But if she kept the baby –and so far, she had –it was worth it.  Besides, he never had to spend a dime on Yolanda, ever.

Courtney relaxed but still sensed something wasn't right.  "Why'd you bring this stuff over here so early?"

He took a deep breath, "Because I, uh, probably won't see you on Christmas Day."

She let the words sink in.  It didn't make sense; where was she supposed to be on Christmas?  Then it came to her:  it was where she wasn't supposed to be that mattered.

"I have a friend coming over to my mom's, and she's going to be my guest.  I mean, it's not my house and you're more than welcome to be there; but I don't think you'll be comfortable."

*Why does he avoid saying her name, like half the town doesn't know he's Yolanda's boy toy?*  "You're the one who'll be uncomfortable, especially if our little secret gets out," she said throwing the unopened gift boxes onto the floor.

"That has nothing to do with it.  If people find out you're pregnant, so what," he replied and meant it.  If it got out, he'd feign ignorance.  So, what if people suspected he was the daddy?  It was nobody's business.  Courtney alone knew the truth; if she decided to put their business in the streets, that was on her.

"After the holidays, then what?  Are you going to give me an assigned time when I'm able to visit your mother, or am I banned from her house because of your girlfriend?"

"Don't be an idiot.  Who am I to keep you from going wherever you want to go?  You're making too much of this.  I'm doing this for your sake.  I've made a mess, I know; but things will sort themselves out.  In the meantime –"

"In the meantime, I'm supposed to be happy when you throw a few of Yolanda's crumbs my way.  No, thank you.  That's not for me."

"What the hell is your beef now?  I spent my whole paycheck to buy this stuff for you, and all you can do is complain about a situation that's out of my hands."

*Can he really think I'll go along with this?  Am I that pathetic?*  She looked back at him –and in that moment saw the things she'd always made excuses for.  Where was the enchantment, she'd attached to him –those qualities that made her love being near him?  He was a worm in expensive clothes, fidgeting nervously, trying to convince her something was wrong with her.  Even now, he expected her to live her life around him and his rich girlfriend but made no place in his world to work on their relationship.  *I can live without this.  Matter of fact, Yolanda Brown is welcome to him.*

She considered giving back the gifts he'd brought her, but decided she deserved them—even the earrings.

"I hope you have a Merry Christmas, Happy New Year and a wonderful life in your new relationship."

"I'm not in a new relationship.  Yes, I'm seeing someone, but that has no effect on us –"

"Yes, it does. I don't want to see you anymore –"

"There you go with the drama again!"  Sean interrupted and, rising, threw up his arms.  "Always playing the victim.  We've never had chains on each other, you've always been free to do as you pleased, you just happened to get pregnant, that's all.  I've never held you down, so what's with this *release me from my bondage crap.* You stuck with me because you wanted to; stop trying to blame me for that."

Courtney absorbed the blows and grew more determined: even if she stayed pregnant –she didn't have to stay with him.

"I think you should leave now," she half whispered.

He sat down, realizing he'd hurt her feelings again. He wished he could get her to appreciate the trouble he'd gone through in carefully crafting the lie he'd told Yolanda just so he could be there. He'd gotten the whole night free to spend with her, and she was intent on ruining everything.

"Courtney, I'm trying –I'm doing my best. I want you to be happy, about us, about the baby—"

"You want me to have the baby. I guess I'm going to. You don't have to worry about that. Go and enjoy your life, without trying to fit me in it. It's not working for me."

He knew when she spoke in that flat, lifeless tone, conversation was over. His romantic plans for that evening were postponed indefinitely; he and Yolanda were leaving town after Christmas to spend New Year's Eve in New York City. It was easier to leave things as Courtney wanted them for the time being.

"Have it your way," he retorted walking to the door. "When you tell my mother how bad I've treated you, remember I didn't leave you, you pushed me out."

Tears rolled down her cheeks as she closed door behind him, speaking out loud. "You haven't given me much choice, have you?"

On Christmas Day, after a brief conversation with Angela, Courtney packed up groceries and took them over Mary's house and began cooking

Christmas dinner.

"You coulda told somebody you were planning on coming over here,

girl," Mary said, with a hint of a smile on her lips.  "What happened to that pretty

boyfriend of yours and his family you're so in love with?"

"We broke up," Courtney said, while chopping onions, trying her best to

make stuffing the way Angela did.

"Ha!  He finally dumped you, huh?"

"Yeah.  Guess you can say that.  He's got a new girlfriend," Courtney

continued, adding the onions to the celery and butter in the skillet.  The pungent

odor pierced the air in the house.

"I told you he was no good—didn't I?  I guess I didn't raise you with no

sense, did I?"

"Nope.  And I'm pregnant."  The smoke rose from the skillet as she

stirred the contents, waiting for Mary's reaction.

"Girl, you sure are a dummy," Mary shook her head.  "Start bringing my

great-grand-baby to see me more often.  They don't *own* him, you know."

"Yes, ma'am, I sure will."

"Another baby.  Um umh umh!" she shook her head again, then took a sip

from her glass as Courtney chuckled.  At that moment, she preferred Mary's

company; there'd be no lecture, or even sympathy –Mary was Mary.


"Thank you for being so gracious.  The food smells delicious," Yolanda

said to Angela as they greeted at the door on Christmas day.  The younger woman grinned from ear to ear, a little too hard for a little too long.  Her nostrils were bombarded by the heavy odor of what she guessed were collard greens probably swimming in fat, she also caught the scent of a salty ham.

It had occurred to Yolanda, on the drive to the house, that since she'd been successful in getting herself invited to dinner, she'd now have to endure an afternoon in a crowded house, with Sean's family.  They were probably nice people, but they had little appreciation for her conversation or her world.

Yolanda stayed planted on the living room couch and insisted Sean stay at her side as she made small talk.  To his family, Sean appeared like a man in prison, his behavior completely out of character.  Yolanda allowed him a few moments leave to play with his son Bryce, who'd spent the previous night with Angela.  The toddler, who'd just turned two, was too busy playing with his cousins and new toys to notice.

"Come downstairs to have a beer and watch the game," his brother, Jay, urged later after dinner.  Sean turned to Yolanda; but she spoke first.

"Baby stay with me.  It's Christmas, you can watch the game anytime."
She whined; he sat.
Angela  , positioned adjacent to her, felt her eyes widen.  Sean's sisters laughed hysterically before their mother shot them a steely glare that sent them from the room.

Yolanda was oblivious, and once she'd warmed up to her surroundings, shared her knowledge of restaurants—none of them had ever been to, art shows she'd attended, and the famous artists and decorators she knew personally.  She even offered to send one of her friends to Angela's house to help *update* her décor.

Sean winced as his mother politely concealed her offense. The younger woman stuck her foot in her mouth repeatedly, but then pulled out Christmas gifts – a diamond pendant for Angela, and $100 gift cards for each of Sean's siblings and any other household represented.  All was immediately forgiven.

"His taste in women is improving," Jazmine commented to Nina, Jay's wife, as she pocketed the gift card.  Nina scowled at her.

"Girl shut up.  Money can't buy everything," she rolled her eyes at how the family had suddenly warmed up to the woman they'd been castigating for months.

Once the gifts were delivered, Yolanda was ready to leave.  She been unimpressed with Angela's downhome cooking and recommended her to a caterer friend who specialized in low-fat, low-salt cuisine.

"That's very sweet of you, but I enjoy doing my own cooking," Angela said at the door as Yolanda and Sean were leaving, a chilly smile on her face. Jazmine and Krystal laughed again; this time Yolanda noticed.

"Did I say something wrong?"  She asked Sean, as soon as they were in the car.

"Don't pay any attention to them," he shrugged.

They spent the rest of the evening at the house of one of Yolanda's friends, where he smiled at the right times, made suitable conversation, and kept Yolanda from making a spectacle of herself.  When they got back to her house, he dropped her off, telling her he needed to go home and help his mother with Bryce. To his relief she declined to question him and let him borrow her car.

While he drove home, he wondered how he'd let Yolanda bully him into spending the day with her instead of Courtney.  It had been a mistake.  Yolanda didn't mix well with his family, and the two hours she'd been at his house had been an embarrassment he'd be hearing about for the rest of his life.  His family never forgot anything.

Then there was the way he'd betrayed Courtney; he wished he could take that back also.  Of course, she'd forgive him.  He'd give it time, but she'd take him back.  Time was on his side.  Courtney was pregnant and –how long could he and Yolanda last anyway?  Dating her had its perks but –she wasn't even his type...

# Chapter Nine

"I saw you and that woman. Who do you think you're fooling with, Sean?"

"Yolanda. I don't know what you're talking about. She was flirting with me." He was sitting on the bed in their hotel room, rubbing his temples. He'd gotten friendly with a female down in the hotel bar and Yolanda had slipped his mind –until she busted him and dragged him out of there by his ear. Their New Year's trip to New York had been filled with one argument after another. He was tired of her.

"If I would've come downstairs five minutes later, the two of you would've been up in her room. You can play those games with your *department store princess* back home, but this is me. I'm not stupid."

"I apologize. I have a weakness for *attractive* women. I promise to work on that."

The fallen expression on Yolanda's face told him he'd hit the bullseye; and as far as he was concerned, she deserved it. She needed to be knocked down to earth from time to time.

"What does that mean, Sean?"

"Nothing, baby," he said kissing her cheek, then went into the sitting room of their suite at the Waldorf to watch television. She had little more to say to him until later, during dinner at a restaurant near the airport.

"I've been giving some thought about us, and where our relationship is going, and I think you should too. I mean, it's a new year. How far do we want to take this?"

"Okay, Yolanda, I'll give it some thought," he stated, while eating a salad.

"I've told you I'm no fool, nor am I naive. I know you're still involved with your son's mother, and I've stayed out of that until now. But moving forward I think you need to make a decision."

"Well, I don't agree," he threw his napkin into his salad plate and signaled the waiter for another drink.

Riddled with guilt, he wasn't about to let Yolanda tell him how to run his relationship with Courtney, like she tried to run everything else in his life. He was already trying to figure out how he'd fix things with her. They'd had no contact since their last argument, except when he'd slipped away from Yolanda and drunkenly called her at midnight on New Year's Eve.

"Happy New Year."

"It will be," was Courtney's answer before she hung up.

Sean sipped another Jack Daniels and grimaced while Yolanda preached.

"...we're a good team, you and I, but there's no place for her. I don't expect you to be perfect, but I also don't feel comfortable knowing you're still involved with a woman you have so much time invested in. Obviously, there's a problem, or the two of you would be happily married by now, and you and I would've never happened. Maybe you need somebody like me to come along and help you cut the strings of the comfortable and familiar."

"And maybe you need to mind your business and get out of mine," he growled.

"If your *business* means more to you than me—than us, maybe I'll leave you to it."

*She's threatening me,* he thought, anger rising. There was no way any female was going to call the shots in his life, he didn't care how much money she spent on him –or if she was pregnant –or even if she was his mother.

"That works for me," he said, lifting his glass. "Happy New Year, *Miss Yolanda Brown.*"

They didn't speak on the flight back home. When they arrived at Yolanda's house, Sean walked her to the door, opened it for her, and bid a curt goodnight.

He threw his suitcase into the back of his old Jeep and left her gated-community, certain it was for the last time. He drove home full of anger and adrenaline at the thought of how Yolanda had tried to pull rank on him. Last time he'd looked, he was still a man; she wasn't going to turn him into some punk. He needed to prove, if only to himself, he was still his own man—that Yolanda hadn't taken over, and he just hadn't accepted it yet.

He came to the intersection of Garden Blvd –Courtney's street—a little past 12:30 in the morning, wondering if she'd let him in. He went through the light, then abruptly made a U-turn, heading down her street—*all she can do is say no...*

Courtney was still awake. She hadn't been sleeping well lately and wondered why she wasn't happier yet. It had been two whole weeks. She'd done the right thing; she'd cut Sean lose. If a person does the right thing, weren't they supposed to get the right result? Wasn't he supposed to realize he was going to lose her for good, then hurry and end things with Yolanda, and run back to her?

Every time she closed her eyes, she dreamed that dream –a phone call, or Sean appearing at the door, telling her he realized what was important; that she and his children meant everything to him, and nothing would get in the way again. When she woke up, the reality was he and Yolanda were living it up in New York City; he'd even called her on New Year's Eve to gloat. She was alone, hurting, and pregnant. She didn't want Sean if he didn't want her; at the same time, she didn't want to hurt so badly either.

She knew single mothers who'd survived being abandoned and had pressed on. They'd gotten beyond the hurt and did what they needed to do. It could be done, but Courtney doubted *she* could do it—somehow, she'd end up like her mother, who'd failed miserably. Wiping her tears, she heard a knock at the door.

She didn't bother checking the keyhole, figuring it was her neighbor Vicki, whose phone was shut off. She'd been coming over the last few nights about the same time to call her married boyfriend. She and Courtney weren't exactly friends but were near the same age and tended to confide in each other about their relationship struggles. She called Courtney crazy for breaking up with Sean.

"Swallow that pride. I know it's rough to go from *the* woman to *the other* woman but look at it this way. She's the one who has to worry about what he does, not you. You say he's paying your bills too? Girl, treat that man good every time he shows up, even if it's only once a month."

Courtney opened the door and froze when she saw Sean standing there. His face was unshaven, and he looked haggard. She guessed he'd just gotten off the plane.

"It's almost one a.m.  Bryce is asleep," Courtney said, starting to close the

door; but he put his hand out to keep it open.

"I didn't come to see Bryce," he said, pausing to look at her.  "You

always come to the door like that?"  He smiled.  After a weekend of looking at

Yolanda, his eyes were enjoying a treat.  Her long hair was draping her shoulders,

and she was wearing a camisole which was straining against her full breasts; her

belly was poking out over the pair of drawstring pajama pants.  There weren't

many women who could look so sexy without trying.

She looked down, then folded her arms, "I thought you were my

neighbor.  It's late.  What do you want?"

"You," Sean said.

Courtney rolled her eyes and shook her head but didn't tell him to leave.

When she moved to close the door, it was too late; he'd edged in sideways, leaving

her standing there as he dropped his bag and walked back to her bedroom.  She

closed her eyes, then the door, leaning her back against it.  *I did the right thing and

now he's here... I need him...  I can't get any more pregnant, and I'm already

hurt.*"  She decided then, Vicki had a point; Sean was Yolanda's problem now, not

hers; the trouble was –she didn't want him anymore.


"Are you punishing me or something?"  Sean said the next morning, after

she'd refused him.  "How long am I going to be in the doghouse?"

"You're not in the doghouse.  I told you I'm through with us and I meant

it.  It doesn't matter what time of night you show up here."  She expected him to go storming out of her place, never to be heard from again; but he stayed.

In fact, he stayed for three days –swore he was finished with Yolanda and once he'd saved enough money, he and Courtney would get a place together—that was the first night. She kept her distance; however, and the longer he stayed, the surlier he became; his promises failed to have the effect on her he desired. By the third day he was ready to leave but stayed only because she told him there was nothing for him to come back to. He wanted to get angry with her but was forced to admit she had every right to treat him as she had.

She happened to be sitting in the rocking chair at the window, putting Bryce to sleep, when a long black Mercedes pulled into the parking lot. She laid Bryce down and started packing up Sean's belongings.

"What are you doing?" Sean, who was laying on the bed watching television, said just before they both heard the knock at the door.

"It's for you." She walked into the bathroom and scooped up his toiletries.

He grabbed his shirt as he went to the door. When he looked through the peephole and saw it was Yolanda, he decided to keep the shirt off.

"We need to talk," Yolanda said, as soon as Sean opened the door. As if she knew he'd be the one to answer.

"Talk," he said.

"Not in this dump," she said, cringing as she looked around. "Get dressed. I'll be in the car."

Sean took a quick glance in the apartment. Courtney was nowhere to be found. When he turned back to the hallway, Yolanda was heading to the stairs.

Courtney had Sean's packed bag, jacket and shoes waiting for him when he walked back to the bedroom.

"You in a hurry to get rid of me? I don't need all that –I'll be right back."

"Don't bother."

"Whatever, Courtney," Sean sighed, as he snatched the bag, and left.

"Did you have your fun and get her out of your system? Because I'm not going to tolerate this crap ever again," Yolanda threatened, while they were sitting in a secluded section of Arthur's Place, a downtown restaurant. She was, of course, having a drink.

"I thought we understood each other. We were through, remember?"

"Don't be childish, Sean. That's not what you want. Don't tell me you enjoyed being cooped up in that roach motel with your *baby momma* for three days," she sniffed. "Then there's the matter of your new job. One word from me to Uncle Harry, and they won't even let you on the premises."

He started to get angry but changed his mind. What good would it do anyway? She had him where she wanted him because she was right: life with Courtney wasn't what he wanted after having enjoyed the fringe benefits of being with her. Courtney's coldness toward him hadn't helped. After dinner and drinks, they left the restaurant reunited as a couple.

"Leave your car there, baby," Yolanda said, not wanting to risk an ugly scene by having him return to Courtney's to retrieve his Jeep.  Not that she couldn't handle the *Department Store Diva but* didn't want Sean having any second thoughts.  "It's about time you stop driving that wreck anyway.  I've got three cars, why don't you start using one of them."

Sean drove Yolanda's car back to her house in silence, wondering if he even knew who he was anymore.  Seems everything he said he wouldn't do, he did.  At the same time, both Courtney and Yolanda seemed able to predict and intercept his every move.  He felt like he was stumbling around in circles.  *How did Courtney know I wouldn't be back?*

Sean and Yolanda talked things through, and *they* decided he'd move out of his mother's house and in with her.  Then he took the liberty of asking her for a *loan.*  It was the first time he'd done so since they'd been dating.  She gave him a healthy roll of bills from her safe, which she didn't count, but he had a feeling she knew what was there.  The next day, he skipped his morning classes and stopped by Courtney's apartment rental office, the babysitter, and the cell phone company to pay her bills for a few months.  He also left her some cash and the keys to his Jeep in an envelope he slid under her door.

When Courtney came home from work later that day, she opened the apartment door, and while carrying her sleeping son, her foot landed on the package.

She picked up the envelope, which wasn't addressed, and opened it, finding cash –quite a bit of it—Sean's car keys, and no explanation.

*Hush money?* Was she being paid to keep quiet about her pregnancy? She doubted it, Sean had never told her not to tell; she was too embarrassed anyway. No –this was the *kiss off*—where else would he get so much cash, if it wasn't from *her*? Courtney was being dumped with an old car and cash. She wondered if it was Yolanda's idea.

"I'm sorry Courtney," the doctor said, after reading her lab and sonogram results the following week. "You don't have to raise this child, but you will have to carry it. You're too far along. Have you considered adoption?"

The doctor handed Courtney some adoption agency brochures, and she thanked her quietly as she left the office, doubting she'd have gone through with the abortion even if it had been an option. At least now it wasn't a choice. She'd stalled for a month, knowing as the weeks went by, her option to terminate was slipping away. It'd taken her that long to face the reality Sean was gone for good—she'd played hard to get, and still lost. Yolanda claimed him and he'd drifted off into a life of ease. He didn't even have to drive his old used car anymore, which is why he'd left it with her—*his old used* woman.

"Sean, I'm 28 years old. I'm ready to get married, and you're the one I want to marry."

The champagne Sean had been sipping suddenly went down the wrong pipe, and he erupted into a coughing fit.

Yolanda's eyes became two narrow slits, as she watched him choking. "Are you okay?" she asked disingenuously, grabbing her champagne flute for a sip, waiting for his cough to subside.

"You shouldn't have sprung that on me," he sputtered, loosening the top button of his shirt.

"I was speaking my mind.  You know I don't believe in playing games and subtlety isn't my strong point."

Sean took a deep breath, "Well...I—uh—I don't think—"

"What don't you think?  You live in my house, drive my cars, we shop, travel together, and *you* don't have to spend a dime.  Just what is it you want out of our relationship anyway?  When you move in with a woman, it's a serious step.  You seem to have no complaints about the accommodations, so what's the problem?"

Yolanda was standing directly in front of him, flat footed, hands on her hips, winding up for a fight, while Sean sat with his head bowed, waiting for it to be over.  He felt as though a cinder block had been dropped on his head.  She'd never hinted at an interest in marriage; but when Yolanda wanted something, she knew how to get it.  *I should have seen this coming.*  With Yolanda everything had a cost and eventually she'd expect him to pay up.  Now the dilemma was how the *hell* he was going to get out of it?  He wasn't marrying her.  If he married anybody, it should be the woman having his babies, and he didn't want to marry her either – yet.

Yolanda's tirade lasted about an hour.  She then went to moping and, finally, resorted to the silent treatment.  When Sean didn't make any moves to appease her demands, she dropped them, much to his relief.  They were in Las Vegas, staying at Caesar's Palace; and he preferred to go down to the casino and gamble, not stay penned up in the hotel suite arguing.  It was Valentine's Day, and

if he'd known what she'd had on her mind, he would've never agreed to the trip in

the first place.

> *Happy Valentine's Day, Baby, and I'm sorry I haven't been in contact. I've been confused about some things, and I need some time.  I hope you and the baby are well, and I hope the money I've sent helps, although I know it can't make up for the way I've hurt you.  I know it's hard for you to believe me, but I do love you, and I miss you.  Please accept these small tokens of my love, and no matter what don't allow anger or bitterness to keep us from having a future together.*

> *Sincerely, Sean*

Courtney stared at the vase of two dozen long stemmed roses, and the box

holding a diamond engagement ring—of all things.  *He's crazy,* she thought, then

trashed the roses with the crystal vase.  No one was keeping them from having a

future together but him; his letter made it seem like he was deployed in Iraq or

something, but she'd heard he and his woman were in Vegas!

She also threw the ring into the trash, then changed her mind and

retrieved it.  *No point throwing away a good diamond.  Yolanda probably paid a*

*lot of money for it.  Maybe I'll give it to somebody*, she laughed at the thought of

Sean seeing Mary wearing it on her pinky.


"Come on, baby, let's go shopping.  Vegas has the best stores in the

world," Yolanda urged, pulling Sean onto his feet.

"Okay." He tried to sound enthused, but had been up all night in the

casino, and they'd just had a large breakfast.  All he wanted to do was sleep the

rest of the day and hit the casino that night.

To his surprise, the first place Yolanda dragged him wasn't a mall, it was to an automobile dealership—a Jaguar showroom, to be exact.

"I've always wanted one of these," Yolanda exclaimed. "I've never owned a Jag. Want to test drive this one?" They were standing beside a sparkling XKR convertible in silver. Sean's eyes were fixed; he was nearly panting.

The hovering salesman heard his cue and alertly opened the driver's side door for him.

They were in that dealership for three hours. Sean saw what Yolanda was doing and tried to remain aloof, stand his ground, and hold on to his principles; but when she and the salesman started discussing custom options on the new vehicle, he crumbled.

Once the purchase order was signed, with Sean listed as the owner, and the date of the delivery to their home location was set, Yolanda stroked Sean's thigh. "You happy, baby?" She said softly.

Sean was sweaty and exhausted, not only from lack of sleep, but from the train wreck he'd been through. She was no match for him; he realized then, she never had been. He sat back in the chair, closed his eyes, and saw a vision of himself driving around town in that car—his car, and it made everything else worth it.

"Yeah," he said, starting to smile. "Where to now?"

"The jewelry store, of course," Yolanda giggled.

The next day they boarded the plane home, Sean with the brochures about his new car, and Yolanda with the new diamond engagement ring he'd given her – which she'd purchased. The diamond was a size modest enough to look as though he could've bought it.

The flight home was two hours long; and the closer the plane got; the worse Sean was starting to feel about himself. How was he going to tell his family he was marrying *Yolanda?* His mother was cordial to her but didn't like her much; the rest of them hated her. In fact, he and Yolanda were the running family joke and the topic of most of the gossip these days. Their engagement was going to be like giving raw meat to a pack of hungry lions. To top it off, he didn't want to marry her; but it seemed a small price to pay for what he really wanted –a car he could never afford to buy for himself for another twenty years, especially given the amount of child support he'd soon be paying.

He nearly groaned out loud when he thought about child support –it turned his mind to Courtney. What was he going to tell her? Especially after the card and roses he'd just sent. He cringed when he remembered the ring he'd sent her, like the one Yolanda was now wearing. *What am I doing*? He groaned to himself again as the pilot announced they were preparing for landing.

When they arrived home, Sean was edgy while Yolanda chattered about everything he didn't want to hear about. If she noticed his discomfort, she made no mention of it. She was stuck on one topic: the engagement, and it was making him queasy. Engagement parties, news releases, and then she hit him with the topic of setting the date.

"Let's give it some time?" he said, nearly whining. "We just got engaged. How about next Valentine's Day?"

"No, Sean," Yolanda said unsmiling. "It's going to be this year, and I think June 12th is time enough."

"Why ask me, if what I say doesn't matter?" he retorted, grabbing his keys and jacket. It was as good an excuse as any to escape for a while.

"Where are you going? I wanted us to call Daddy and Mother and tell them the news," Yolanda called out as he exited her room.

"Later," he said, heading down the stairs and to the door. He drove around town for over an hour, getting up the nerve to face Courtney; he owed it to her to tell her now, before the engagement became public knowledge.

"I'm outside. Can I come up?" Sean said, calling from the parking lot of Courtney's building.

"What do you want?" Courtney said.

"We need to talk. It's important."

When she opened the door to let him in, she noticed he was nervous and wouldn't look her in the eye, instead, he glanced quickly at her protruding belly, then looked around the room.

"How have you been?"

Courtney answered stiffly. They hadn't spoken in about six weeks, since the night Yolanda came and retrieved him.

"It looks nice in here," he said, noticing she'd bought new furniture. He squirmed uncomfortably when she closed the door behind him. "I see you've used some of the money—"

"Yes," she said, cutting him off. "Have a seat."

Sean sat down on the couch. He leaned forward, elbows on his knees, and studied his hands. She sat in an armchair across from him, watching and waiting for him to speak.

"You said you needed to talk..." He seemed to have forgotten what he'd come to say.

"Yeah...I do," he said, then swallowed hard. "I don't know how to say this. I don't want you to get the wrong idea..." He paused and rubbed his forehead like he had a headache. "It's just that I've gotten myself into something... and I don't know how to get out. So...to make a long story short –I'm engaged," he then exhaled, seemingly for the first time since he'd walked into the apartment.

Courtney didn't know exactly what she was supposed to do, or how she was supposed to feel about what he'd said. She'd been so wounded by the pregnancy and his staying with Yolanda, it felt like her pain reservoir was full, she couldn't absorb anything else.

"That's pretty humiliating," she mumbled, showing no other emotion.

"I'm sorry, Courtney, really. I didn't want things to be this way. If I could take back everything that's happened in the last six months, I would; but I can't. Now I'm in a corner and I've got to do some things I don't feel right about; but if you just trust me, I'll make everything alright in the end."

Courtney snorted and looked up. *How does he think he can make this alright?*

"I swear to you, this doesn't have anything to do with –anything really. Except that it's what she wants—"

"And *she* gets what she wants," Courtney said, regretting saying it as soon as it escaped her lips. It sounded jealous and pathetic.

He looked down at his hands while he thought about her words. Finally, he answered. "Yes, she does. I admit it. Just makes things easier that way—for now." They sat silently, with the tension in the room so thick Courtney didn't feel like she could move if she wanted to. What she wondered was why he was still there. He hadn't moved, except that he'd stopped staring at his hands and was now leaning back, staring at the ceiling.

"Thank you for telling me to my face. It's a bitter pill, I admit, but at least I don't have to hear it in the street. I hope you'll be happy," she said, as the tears started forming. Then she was angry with herself as she'd hoped to hold them back until he'd gone. "I don't want to be rude," she said, as she wiped her face. "But will you leave now?"

Sean finally looked at her and she appeared weak, fragile and in pain; and add to that her belly, and he felt like he deserved to be *beat with a switch*—as his mother would say. *Man, you'd do this to her for a car...a car?* he asked himself and knew the answer. The question now was how he'd find a way to make it work for them both.

"I can't leave, Courtney—not until I know you understand—I'm sorry – *understand* isn't the right word. I need to know you'll be patient with me, even if you don't understand. This has nothing to do with our children or...or us really. I know it's wrong, but if you'll just trust me. It doesn't mean I care for her more than you, or she's more important to me. In fact, I need you now more than ever." At some point while he was talking, he'd gotten up from the couch, and was now on his knees at her feet. "Don't leave me, please."

She didn't answer him. What he was saying sounded insane. "What are you talking about? I haven't seen you in weeks. How can I leave you when you've already left me?" she insisted, pushing him away as he went to wrap his arms around her waist.

"I never left you," Sean said, "I stayed away because you wanted me to." What he'd left out was Yolanda had also been watching his every move.

Her tears stopped abruptly, as sadness changed to anger. "Go home, Sean. I'll see you in child support court in August."

"I can't leave. Not until I know you forgive me" he pleaded, reaching for her again. "I'm an ass, but I do love you and I'm smart enough to know I can't live without you. This doesn't mean anything—please believe me." He was now holding her, his face buried in her belly; she felt foolish.

*This is ludicrous,* she thought. *Yolanda will probably be knocking on the door any minute.* Once that image flashed in her mind, she relaxed. *Why should I care? Let her come and get the man she's going to marry.* She wrapped her arms around his shoulders and ran her fingers through his hair. He then stood and pulled her to her feet.

"Do you forgive me?" He prodded, whispering in her ear, then kissed the side of her face and her neck. "Huh?" he asked again as his lips moved to her face, then to her lips.

"Sure, Sean, whatever you want," she said. Anything to get rid of him. He made a move to try to seduce her, but she told him she was cramping. Still, he wouldn't leave.

*He makes me sick!* Yolanda fumed. It was one o'clock in the morning, and she was parked across the street from the *department store diva's* apartment building, glaring at her other vehicle, the one Sean drove. It had been parked there for hours, there were no lights on in Courtney's place, and he'd turned off his phone.  It was her third trip there that night; each time she saw her car, she became angrier.  "You don't acknowledge a whore your man sleeps with, *especially* when you're planning to marry him" was one of her mother's nuggets of wisdom; having been married four times, *she* should know.

It's not that Yolanda expected Sean to be an angel; they hadn't known each other all that long and he'd had an active life before they met.  Old habits are hard to break.  But she'd told him she refused to be a part of any triangles and meant it.  She uttered curses out loud. then started her car to go home, making up her mind Courtney Brooks would need to be dealt with.


"The next few months, this wedding business and everything leading up to it will be overblown, overdone, over the top," Sean said to Courtney, while lying beside her, rubbing her belly and nuzzling her shoulder.  "I promise I'll make it up to you when it's all over, after the baby gets here," he propped himself up on his elbow.  "What are we having anyway?"

"They say it's a girl," she replied, having found out the day before; he was the first person she'd told.

Sean laughed, "A daughter.  That means I'm really finished having kids. I'm gonna get it fixed soon as this one shows up healthy."

She turned and looked at him.  "You can't do that; your wife will probably want kids."

"She won't have any with me.  I promise you that," Sean said.  He was now so scared of getting Yolanda pregnant, it was affecting their sex life, although she hadn't seemed to notice.

"That's not fair."

"When have I ever cared about being fair?  I'm not being fair to you.  I know that." Just then he got a glimpse at the time and cringed.  He was going to have hell to pay when he got home—if he still had a home.  He couldn't get up and leave Courtney, however, until he got it across to her his feelings for her were the same, even if he was marrying someone else.

"If I asked you to come meet up with me sometime, would you?"

"No," Courtney replied, ready for him to leave –she was tired of his silly conversation.

"Then I'm just going to have to find a way to get you a house, soon."

"You do that, Sean," Courtney placated, while yawning and rolling over. *Some marriage—he hasn't even tied the knot yet and he's planning how he's going to cheat.  Yolanda's money must've affected his brain,* she thought, before falling asleep.

Sean slid out of bed, as soon as he knew she was asleep.  Once he got into his car, he decided against going home.  Instead, he quietly slipped into his mother's house, raided her refrigerator, and fell asleep in the family room, while thinking up the lie he'd tell Yolanda the following day.  Odds are she knew where he'd been –Yolanda knew everything, but he wasn't going to admit to anything he didn't have to...


"Daddeee......, Daddeee, appo!  Eat sum appo, Daddeee!"

Sean awakened to his son shoving apple slices between his lips.  There was also something wet dripping onto the couch.  The toddler had tried to get him to drink milk from his sippy cup and had missed his mouth.  There were drops of milk splattered over the side of his face.

"Thank you, Bryce," Sean said, yawning and sitting up on the couch, while taking an apple slice from him.

"We'cum," Bryce replied, pleased with himself.

"You're such a good boy to feed your daddy." Sean heard Angela's voice behind him.

"Thanks, mom.  You stood there and watched him do this."

"I thought it was cute.  I told him to wake you up, and he decided to feed you.  What're you doing here anyway?  I thought you were out of town."

"Got back last night," he said, while turning on his cell phone.

"And why are you here?  Did y'all have a disagreement?"

Before he answered, his cell phone rang.  "Hey," he said into it.

"What do you mean 'hey'?  I've been trying to reach you all night.  Where are you?"

"I'm at my mother's.  I was hangin' out at Jay's pretty late, so I came over here to see my son," he said.  "Sorry I didn't call."

*Does he really think I don't know where he was?*  Yolanda thought, and the phone line was silent while she quelled her anger.  She cleared her throat and continued, "Tell your mother I said hello—"

"Mom, Yolanda says hi," he said, turning the phone in his mother's direction so Yolanda could hear her voice clearly.

"Sean, I'll see you when you get home," Yolanda said, then hung up without a goodbye.  Something in her tone let him know he was in for it.

He immediately dialed his brother. "Hey man, what's up?"

"Nothin', player. Hear you're a high roller these days. Win anything in Vegas?"

"Naw,"

"Least you didn't lose your own money," Jay laughed, while Sean was silent. He was tired of comments like that coming from his family, but knew that was mild, compared to what was coming.

"Look, you're my alibi for last night; cover for me if you're asked."

"Yeah, whatever," Jay sighed.

"And don't say nothin' to your wife," Sean said. Nina might hate Yolanda; but if she got wind of a cover-up, they'd be best girlfriends—for a day, anyway.

"Man, I don't care what you do; but why do you have to use my name all the time?"

"'Cause, Mom won't go along,"

"You got that right," Angela chimed in, and he realized she'd been listening to everything. "Are you going to spend time with your son this weekend? Since you've got time to be everywhere else?"

"Yeah, I'll take him with me," Sean said, without moving from the couch.

"And you didn't answer me—why are you here?"

Sean rolled over onto his back and swallowed hard without looking at his mother.

"It's that bad, huh? I told you not to move in with her in the first place –" He took a deep breath and wondered if he'd be able to get the next part out. "I'm," he said, then closed his eyes and covered his head with his hands. "I'm getting married—in June,"

"Boy, have you lost your mind?"

"Yeah... I guess I have. She's laid down the law—it's what she wants and I—"

"You need to say no. You're not ready. You can't even be faithful living together. What's your marriage going to be like?"

"I don't know. She doesn't care—"

Angela stared at him for a few moments while her mind tried to put things together. "There's more to this. Since when are you such a wimp? You're not that in love—I don't believe it. There's something you're not telling me. And what about poor Courtney? You're going to tell her, aren't you?"

"She already knows," he answered sitting up now, still partially covering his face.

Angela dropped the glass she was holding onto the floor, and it shattered. "That's where you were last night." She shook her head, wondering what was wrong with her son and who raised him. Every day his personal life was becoming a bigger mess, one he seemed unwilling to clean up. "You agree to marry one woman, then you go and sleep with another one—"

"That's none of your business," he roared standing abruptly, pulling his keys from his pocket. "Is Bryce's bag packed? I've got to go."

"Pack it yourself," she said, then picked up the toddler. "Bye-bye, Bryce. Ma-ma loves you." She hugged and kissed him goodbye before walking out of the kitchen, ignoring his father. He heard her slam her bedroom door a few minutes later.

Sean swept up the broken glass she'd left on the floor, before leaving the house with Bryce. He got into his car, irritated by his mother's overreaction to his latest development. What he was doing was questionable, but what was *she* so fired up about?

He carried the half-asleep toddler into the townhouse. Once inside, he was met by the spicy aroma of Caribbean food being cooked, which meant Renate was there. Yolanda didn't boil water if she didn't have to. Bryce must've sensed Renate's presence also, because he stirred from his sleep and started looking in the direction of the kitchen. The toddler knew when Renate was around, there'd be treats for him.

"Dere's my little mahn," Renata said clapping; Bryce wriggled, ready for Sean to put him down.

"Why are you here on a Sunday?" Sean asked.

"I don't know," Renate said, and sucked her teeth. "She decide we need to start gettin' organized for sometin' but she don' tell me what. Watch yourself, she in one *hell* of a mood!"

Sean walked slowly up the stairs, and found Yolanda in her office, sitting at her computer.

"Hi," he said, bending down to kiss her. The look she gave him, caused him to change his mind. He turned without a word and walked into their bedroom. She rose from the desk and trailed him, closing the bedroom door behind her. With the door closed she didn't say a word, as she stood across the room staring at him, arms crossed.

*She knows,* he thought and wondered what she was going to do about it. The fact that he'd gotten into the house, and his clothes were still in the closet was a good sign. She was furious, but how much so was hard to say.

"I brought Bryce, he's downstairs," Sean said, to break the silence, as he changed into his workout clothes.

"Do you want to tell me again where you were last night?" Yolanda said.

He sighed. "No, I don't think I do." He walked away from her and into the closet to retrieve his sneakers. When he turned around, she was blocking his path. "You apparently know where I spent some of my time last night. So, drop it," he said and walked around her.

"Drop it? Drop it! Who the hell do you think you're talking to? Look at me! Now!" She screamed at the top of her lungs.

"What?"

"You sleep with that department store whore and lie to me—and you tell me to '*Drop it*'".

"If you mean my son's mother, yeah, I went to see her. I thought I should be the one to tell her the *happy news,*" he sneered, then sat on the bed to put on his sneakers. "She was upset about it –"

"And you stayed to comfort her—laying down, I suppose."

Sean didn't understand women and didn't understand why she insisted on having this conversation. It made it too easy to get himself into more trouble. "No, a couple times we were standing up."

Yolanda shrieked and raised her hand to strike him, but he caught it before she made contact. He restrained her as she struggled to hit him, and finally grabbed both of her arms and pulled her face up to his, forcing her to look

at him, as she tried to turn away. "You got what you want," he panted. "What

does what I did last night matter?" he said, before releasing her.

"Get out of my room. I'm not sleeping in the same bed with you after

you've been with her. Sleep in the guest room with your baby."

"Anything else?"

"Yes. If I find out you've been with her again, your little toy will be

staying at the dealership."

Sean walked out of the bedroom without responding. When he went

downstairs to check on Bryce, Renate gave him a sympathetic look.

"You okay?" she said.

"Never better," he winked.

"You devil, you," Renate laughed, shaking her head, "She don' know

what she get-tin'".


"Courtney, I know you've been getting my messages. I don't know what's

wrong with you, but I—we need to talk. Call me. My work number is..."

Sean had been calling her twice a day for the last three weeks, but she

refused to return or answer his calls. He was desperate to know what was going

on in her head but didn't dare go to her apartment to see her. He didn't put it past

Yolanda to have him followed. He could always catch Courtney at work, or the

babysitter's house, but needed his contact with her kept at a low profile, which was

hard these days since he'd gotten his new car. Everyone knew when he arrived

anywhere.

Which was another reason he wanted to speak with Courtney—to explain to her about the car, to counter the negative things she may have heard.  He needed to reassure her it wasn't what it seemed.  He'd rehearsed his pitch a hundred times, but she wasn't allowing him the opportunity to use it.

He re-dialed her number.  "Have it your way.  I'll stop bothering you.  When news of your pregnancy gets out, you can play the victim.  I'm guessing that's what this is all about anyway," he slammed the receiver of his desk phone down loudly.

Courtney listened to Sean's message, then turned off the phone.  She wasn't angry with him, even when she'd heard about the new sports car *sugar mommy gave him for being a good boy*.  She didn't care – about anything.  She spent her life these days in the same place where he'd left her—in bed, a dark mist having settled over her life, and each day she felt it growing darker.  She felt like a robot went to work, picked Bryce up from the sitter, came home, ate dinner, and went to bed.  It occurred to her something was wrong, that maybe she needed help.  Then she'd remember one of Mary's favorite sayings: *If you're stupid, you're stupid; there ain't no help for you..."*  That's how she felt: like there was no way out of the depths she'd sunk to.

"I confess, I've passed by your apartment a few times and wanted to stop in and check on you," Carmen said.  They were sitting across the table from each other having lunch at Foragers Seafood restaurant.  It was Courtney's twenty second birthday.  "Seems every time I drive into the parking lot, his Jeep is there.  I'm sorry, I shouldn't feel the way I do about him, but I can't help it.  If I run face to face into that boy, they might have to arrest me."

Courtney covered her eyes and laughed, for the first time in a while, at the visual. "He's not there. He left that Jeep because he doesn't need it anymore – seems she's bought him a new sports car. The last time I seen him was in February when he came to tell me about his engagement."

"His what? To that rich woman? Does she know about…" Carmen looked down at her sister's belly.

Courtney shrugged. "Not as far as I know; not my place to tell her."

"You're too nice for me. You need to break up his cozy little setup."

"If I thought it would—but it won't. She's come to my house to get him before." Carmen scowled at her, and she waved both her hands. "Not what you think—there was nothing going on, I swear. I don't even want him anymore. Besides his looks, I don't know what possessed me. What am I doing having another baby by him?"

"Well," Carmen observed, as they watched Bryce, who'd gotten bored with sitting and was walking around the small restaurant making friends at the other tables. "You've gotta give it to him: he makes pretty babies."


"That son of yours is a hot mess, Miss Angie," Martha the babysitter said, as the two women sat having a cup of coffee. Martha Burruss was one on Angela's oldest friends and had watched her children when they were young. "This little cutie is going to be just like him. Look at those eyes."

Bryce knew by her tone she was talking about him and broke into smile before running to the other side of the room to grab a toy.

"His daddy sits here every other day, pretending like he's visiting me, waiting for her to show up.  I guess he finally figured out, she won't come near this place while that car of his is parked in front of my house."

"Who –Sean?  What's he waiting for Courtney for?  He claims he's getting married to his girlfriend."

Martha's eyebrows raised, "Oh…really?"

Angela abruptly set down the coffee cup.  "What does that mean—?"

"—not sure I should say anything.  It's not like anybody has said anything to me but –"

"Spit it out.  You're dying to, I can see it in your face.  You don't fool me for a second."

"Well –that girls gained some *weight* up front."  The two women locked eyes for a second and Miss Martha nodded.

"No!" Angela exclaimed.

"She ain't said a thing to me, and if she wants me to hold a spot for her new baby, she'd better say something soon –but I *know* what I see."  The other woman said, clearing the coffee cups and saucers from the table.

"Come on, Bryce, baby," Angela said grabbing his diaper and weekend bags.  "We're going to visit your mommy."


Courtney had stopped by the Chinese carryout on her way home from work and was now sitting in bed nibbling shrimp lo Mein and egg rolls.  She never had much of an appetite lately but made herself eat at least one large meal a day.

When she heard the knock on the door, she cursed under her breath.  When she got closer and heard Bryce crying, anger rose in her.  Since she wouldn't talk to Sean, he was using her baby as an excuse to come and see her.

She ripped open the door, only to find herself standing face to face with Angela,

who was startled by the way the door had suddenly flown open.

"Oh!"

"Hey, Miss Angie. I'm sorry, I thought you were—"

"Let me guess," Angela said, then took a step back to get a good look at

the younger woman. Yes, Courtney was pregnant; by her estimation about six

months along, and Angela had no doubt who the father was. While she stood in

the hallway, Bryce cried and reached for her to pick him up and take him out of

there; he probably had enough of his mother and being confined in the playpen all

week.

Courtney stood at the door fidgeting.

"Can we come in?" Angela asked, causing Bryce to wail even louder.

Courtney stepped aside.

"Your furniture looks nice," Angela said, looking around briefly before

sitting down on the loveseat. She tried to sit Bryce beside her; but he immediately

climbed into her lap, taking no chances she'd leave without him.

"Thanks," Courtney said, still standing. "You want some—"

"I want to know why you didn't tell me you're pregnant. We've always

had a good relationship, better than me and my own daughters. You and I have

always been able to talk. How could you keep this from me?"

Courtney looked down at her hands as she spoke, "It just didn't have

anything to do with you. If I would've told you, you would've felt obligated to get

involved—fix things. It's your nature, and there's nothing here you can fix."

"What do you mean?  That's my grandbaby, isn't it?"

Courtney shrugged, then looked away.

"Answer me, Courtney.  That's my son's child, isn't it?"

"I don't know."

"Stop lying to me.  Of course, you know."  She glared at the younger woman, who refused to meet her gaze.  "Courtney, if you don't talk to me, what am I supposed to do about this?"

"I'm trying to tell you there's nothing for you to do," Courtney said, then began sobbing, "I'm not in high school, and I'm not your child –"

"But you're carrying my blood—"

"It doesn't matter; this baby's going to be adopted.  You'll never see it."  Angela fell silent.  Courtney felt relief after telling the lie, Angela would have to leave her alone.  When she looked up into the older woman's face, however, it was crestfallen.

After a few minutes of silence, Angela stood up and sighed.  "Come on, Bryce, let's go bye-bye."  When she got to the door, she opened it and then turned around.  "I'm going to call my son, and the three of us are going to sit down and talk this through.  You'd better answer your phone, or I'll come over here and get you.  Do you hear me, little girl?"

"Yes, ma'am." Courtney said, then walked them downstairs to the front door.  When she watched Angela drive away with Bryce, she felt better—lighter.  There was something about having Angela involved that made her feel everything would be alright.

"Get over here now," Angela said to Sean, later that evening.  She could hear crowd noise in the background but didn't care.  He would have to leave whatever high fallutin' event he was attending with his high fallutin- fiancée.  What she needed to talk to him about was more important.

"What?  I just can't—"

"You can and you will," Angela commanded, then hung up.

Sean looked down at the phone, aware of what his mother was calling about; he'd been expecting it for weeks—the baby was out of the bag.  What surprised him was how the news had remained a secret for so long.  He started to think of an excuse to give Yolanda for leaving, but then changed his mind.  It was time his mother got it through her head she didn't run his life.  He strolled back to the table of Yolanda's stuck-up friends, determined he wasn't going to leave the boring charity affair she'd dragged him to, to hear one of his mother's self-righteous lectures.  He'd face her when he felt like it.


"Hey, Ma, I'm here." Sean called out the next morning, wondering where his son was.  They'd previously arranged for him to pick up Bryce that morning so he could keep him the rest of the weekend.

"'It's about time you showed up," Angela quipped, walking into the kitchen.

"Yeah, well, I couldn't get away.  Where's Bryce?"  He poured himself a cup of coffee.

"I took him over to Nina's this morning so we wouldn't be interrupted.  You can go over there and get him, after we talk."

He pretended to be concentrating on stirring cream into his coffee, waiting for Angela to get to the point.

She went to the other side of the counter directly across from him and folded her arms, "Just what the hell are you doing?" She glared at him.

He looked up at her and chuckled nervously, "What's it look like?"

"Don't get cute with me. I saw Courtney yesterday."

He returned to his cup. "So?"

"So? Are you trying to tell me you don't know she's pregnant?"

"She and I don't talk."

Angela noticed he wasn't surprised and hadn't answered the question.

"You're not the father?"

He shrugged, "What did she tell you?"

"She didn't tell me anything—said it didn't matter 'cause she's putting the baby up for adoption."

The cup slipped out of his hand, spilling coffee all over the counter, with some splashing on his clothes.

"Yes, she's putting the baby up for adoption," Angela repeated slowly, watching her fair-skinned son turn a darker shade of red with each word.

"I don't want her giving my baby away," he whined, knowing legally Courtney could do whatever she wanted to. "Didn't you talk to her?"

"She won't talk to me. I'm telling you right now, I'll adopt that baby, but one of you *idiots* is going to raise it. I suggest you call her now," Angela said, while wiping up the coffee he'd spilled.

Sean went to the phone and dialed. Courtney picked up on the first ring.

"It's me. I'm at my mother's. Can you come over so we can talk?"

"Yeah," Courtney said, then hung up.  She knocked lightly on the kitchen door within ten minutes.

Angela opened it solemnly, "Thank you for coming.  I know you didn't have to."

Courtney and Sean's eyes clashed briefly as she entered the kitchen.  He then turned away from her back to another cup of coffee; she took a seat at the kitchen table as far from him as possible while still in the same room.

"Want something, Courtney?"  Angela said, and Sean stole a look at her. She was pale, hadn't gained much weight, except for the basketball that had replaced her belly, and she looked sad.  Seeing her made him angry—this was all unnecessary.  He'd tried to make her happy, wanted them to be together, at least when he could manage it; but she'd pushed him away, preferring to be miserable as she was now.

"No, thank you," she replied, and the room became silent as a morgue. "Let me get this over with now," she cleared her throat.  "I lied about the adoption. I haven't decided completely against it, but –"

"Why did you do that to me?"  Angela said.  "I didn't get a wink of sleep all night."

"You were questioning me, and I didn't feel like you should've expected me to speak for *him*—"

"All you had to do was tell me—"

"If he didn't tell you, why should I?"  Courtney said, and Angela nodded. Both women then turned to Sean.

"Why are you looking at me?  I didn't plan this," he said, throwing up his hands. Then pointed at Courtney, "She was going to have an abortion—had it scheduled and everything, I talked her out of it. Don't I deserve some credit for that?"

"Yeah, then you go and move in with another woman," Angela said. Sean grimaced and went back to his coffee.

To Angela, it was all making sense now—Yolanda, the wedding, everything. He hadn't been swept away by the wealthy woman at all. He was scared to death of his looming responsibilities and was choosing to run away. Yolanda, with all her money and toys, seemed like as safe a place to run as any. Just so he wouldn't have to grow up, be a man, and raise his family.

"Bet she didn't tell you I've paid all of her bills since December," he said, glaring at Courtney. "She won't even pick up the phone when I call to see about her—"

"Not everyone can be bought—" Angela chided, and Sean jumped to his feet.

"What the hell's that supposed to mean, Ma?" he growled, walking towards her. He'd endured the snickers and sneers of his family members on a regular basis. They called him names –gigolo, gold digger—and laughed at him whenever they saw him step out of his car; *payment from Yolanda Brown for services rendered.* He never expected to hear that type of comment from his mother. She sounded just like them.

Courtney had never seen Sean so angry with his mother. She wanted to diffuse the situation but realized calling any attention to herself would aggravate it more.

"Break your engagement, give back the stuff, quit the job she got you—if necessary, and RAISE YOUR KIDS!" Angela glared up at him through clenched teeth as he towered over her.

"No," he retorted, pointing his finger at her. "Mind your business. This has nothing to do with you."

Angela stepped back from him and sniffed, "Hmm, does your fiancée know about you're impending fatherhood?"

"It's none of her business either, and don't you tell her."

"I won't be at that wedding. Do you understand me? I'll tell you another thing: you're not ready for marriage. It's going to be a disaster."

"Thanks for your support, Ma," he said, before grabbing his keys and darting out of the house, slamming the door behind him.

He drove around a couple hours to cool off before going to his brother's to collect Bryce. He couldn't talk to Jay about what had happened, as he'd take their mother's side. Besides, she was probably right.

But the wedding was an eternity away; and if he left things as they were, with he and his mother not speaking, Yolanda would start asking questions. Angela was unrelenting when she thought she was right, and she knew she was right about this. He then made a decision.

It took a week of convincing, cajoling and conniving, but Yolanda agreed to an elopement. Sean confessed to her how the grand affair planned for June was overwhelming him, prompting him to have second thoughts. Her compliance came with one caveat, however: They would go through with a formal ceremony in June, the scale of which would be toned down. Once he assented to this, they were married at the courthouse the following Friday.

After tying the knot, they flew to a resort in Mexico for a short honeymoon. When they returned, Yolanda, the happiest of brides, continued with the wedding-turned-reception plans. Sean, on the other hand, began drinking to oblivion until he passed out every night.

*Is this how my dad got started?* He wondered, lounging in the game room, sprawled on the sofa, with the bottle of his favorite tequila nearly drained, *drinking to get over some woman who refused to follow along with the game plan?* He determined at that moment he wasn't going to let a woman—any woman—turn him into what his father had become. It was Courtney's fault he'd ended up where he was; and since it was his last night drinking, he decided to tell her so.

"Congratulations," Courtney said, answering the phone on the first ring.

"Now you decide to pick up the phone," he said, slurring his words.

"Are you happy?"

"This isn't what I wanted. If you hadn't left me, it would've never happened; this is your fault."

Before she could ask how his marriage was her fault, he hung up. She laid back on her bed in the darkened room, stared at the ceiling and asked herself what the crazy conversation meant. Then she wondered what was going to happen to her.

"Courtney, I don't mean to pry in your business," Sylvia, her manager at the department store, said from behind her desk, in the cramped office at the rear of the stock room. "But you haven't said a word and you're obviously pregnant. I have a department to run and need to plan for your absence. When are you due?"

"Sorry, Sylvia...the end of July.  I know I should've told you but I just..."
Courtney, standing in front of the cluttered desk shrugged, then her lip started
quivering and she was sobbing.

"Oh, don't do that," Sylvia rushed to her side.  "Come here and sit
down—it's okay, baby.  I'm sorry things aren't working out between you and the
dad, but it's going to be alright.  Children are an inheritance from the Lord, no
matter what the circumstance, you have to remember that."

Courtney nodded and sat silently.  She respected Sylvia and suspected the
woman, who was about her sister's age, knew a thing or two about life.  Now she
had her ear and wanted to confide in her about the fear that felt like it was burying
her; she needed to talk to someone now.

"I…" she started to say, then the phone on Sylvia's desk rang; at the same
time, she was being paged overhead.

Sylvia stood, leaned over, and patted Courtney's shoulder.  "I've got to
go, but if you want to talk later, call me on my cellphone.  I'm usually home by
six."  Sylvia then fled from the office and into the chaos that was an everyday
occurrence somewhere in the department store.  She made a mental note to call
Courtney later that evening, if she didn't hear from her; she did call, several times.
Courtney never picked up.


"I think we should, Sean," Yolanda said, dragging him by the hand while
marching toward Andover's Department store, where Courtney worked.

He was in a panic.  Unless he was lucky, Courtney, along with her big
belly, was standing behind the cosmetics counter at that very moment.

"It's not a good idea. If you want to invite her, it should be handled differently. I'll—"

Yolanda stopped and turned toward him slowly.

"—tell my mother to invite her. Not this way; not while she's at work. It lacks class," he said, feeling sweat breaking out in his armpits—next it would be his forehead. He wanted to sprint for the door.

"It's going to be done this way. The two of us will give Courtney a personal invitation to our wedding. It's the least we can do," she cajoled, yanking him along as she talked, "coming to her job, I think, will alleviate some of the awkwardness of the situation. Then we can all start to move on. Let's go."

He felt his heart pounding in his throat. Courtney was nearly eight months pregnant. He'd be homeless after his wife saw that. Once again Yolanda had caught him off guard; ordinarily, she'd rather die than shop in this mall, which she complained was too working class. He'd assumed if his secret got back to her it would be through gossip, which was easy to deny any knowledge of. Visual evidence was different. How was he supposed to feign ignorance with Courtney glaring at him, her belly in his face?

He knew where Courtney was stationed and spotted her, as soon as they entered the store. While his wife was searching her out, Sean made eye contact, hoping she and her belly would clear out in a hurry.

"There she is," Yolanda said, gripping his arm tighter, pulling him in Courtney's direction, while he dawdled, groaning inwardly. When they got closer, Yolanda put a smile on her face and relaxed. Her walk up to the fragrance counter was slow and leisurely, as if they were out for a stroll with no destination in mind.

Courtney saw Sean's desperation from clear across the store. His eyes were pleading *disappear, please... please...* For a moment, she'd thought about skipping into the stockroom; but pride and anger prevented her from doing so. She didn't want Yolanda to think she was hiding from her; she also didn't want to be the one to inform her of the pregnancy. *If that weasel of a husband hasn't told her, she won't find out from me!* Sliding over a few inches caused her to be shielded by the cash register from the chest down. This is where she was positioned as the grinning bride and panicked groom approached. She took a deep breath and steadied herself.

"Courtney, hello."

She looked back at the woman and tried to speak and sound just as cheerful, but only managed to mouth a greeting and nod. She and Yolanda's eyes became locked for a moment, before she shifted her glance to Sean, who looked ready to collapse.

"I guess you know, I'm Yolanda. We've never formally met, but I have met your adorable son. He and I have become great friends."

Sean watched with awe as Courtney's face brightened into a genuine smile and her posture relaxed. There was something about women when they talked about children that could diffuse any situation.

"He talks about you all the time," Courtney said, and it was true. She found herself conflicted on whether to be jealous of this woman who on top of taking Sean, had captured her son's heart, or be appreciative she treated him well.

"I wanted to thank you personally for allowing him to share in our wedding next weekend. It's very kind of you, under the circumstances."

The smile on Courtney's face froze. "You're welcome, but he is Sean's son also. I don't think it'd be fair for me to be that selfish."

"Well, I think it's gracious of you..." the other woman continued.

*She's good...*Courtney thought, admiring how skillfully Yolanda was putting her at ease, saying all the right things in just the right way. She then got a glimpse at how Sean ended up with her. She was a charmer—like him. *Did he teach her, or was it the other way around?*

"Anyway," Yolanda extended her hand. When Courtney placed a hand in hers, she squeezed it in a sisterly way. "It's nice to finally meet you; and since it looks like we're a family now, I hope you'll accept our personal invitation to the wedding on Saturday."

Courtney almost laughed out loud. She felt tempted to tell her '*Trust me—you don't want me, in my condition, showing up at your wedding*'. Instead, she chose to be diplomatic. "Thank you both for the gesture. But this is still difficult for me. I hope you understand—"

"Of course, we do," Yolanda said, patting her hand. "Tell you what, we'll keep your place reserved, in hopes you'll change your mind. Even if it's at the last minute. We'd love for you to be there."

As they turned to leave the store, a relieved Sean shot Courtney a look which she returned with a smirk.

"You had nothing to worry about. I know how to be civil," Yolanda chided, once they were out of the store. She then looked around the mall and cringed. "Let's get out of here."

*What if I do show up-- just to see him squirm*, she thought smiling, while taking her break in the staff lounge. Sean's discomfort in the store that day would be nothing compared to what he'd experience if she were to come waddling into the middle of his party. His wife would demand some answers.

All it would accomplish, however, is to show the world what she already knew—she was the cast off, and Yolanda the bride. No matter how badly she embarrassed Sean, that fact wouldn't change.


"Courtney?"

"Krystal," Courtney said, biting her bottom lip, "how have you been?" She usually brought her meals to work and avoided the mall food court. It seems however, she'd picked the wrong day to venture out. Krystal had seen enough of her, in that brief instant, to know why Courtney had gone underground.

"Okay but...look at you."

"Yeah, I've grown a bit since the last time you saw me," Courtney said, rubbing her belly. There was no pretending it wasn't there.

"Does my brother—"

"This has nothing to do with him."

"Oh—oh really," Krystal said. "Well, look, you go sit down over there. I'll bring your food. What do you want?"

She told her, then took a seat at one of the tables, all the while, trying to think if Krystal had ever been nice to her before.

While in the fast food line, Krystal slipped on her Bluetooth and speed dialed her sister. "Jaz, I'm at the mall and, girl, you won't believe *this*. Guess who

I just ran into and she's pregnant as she can be..."

She brought Courtney's food, and talked to her about everything in the world as if they were old girlfriends.  "Will I see you on Saturday?" she inquired, just as Courtney stood to return to work.

"No—but I did receive a personal invite."

"Well, if you're invited you've got to come."

"I'm happy for them but—no..."

"Girl—please.  You might as well go and remind my brother what he gave up.  I'll hook you up: clothes, hair, and make-up.  By the way, does Mrs. Moneybags know about...?"  Krystal nodded toward Courtney's stomach.

"Why should she?  I told you it's not his." Courtney said, while Krystal pursed her lips.

"If that's your story—I'll go along.  But even pregnant you'll look better than her on her best day.  How about it—I'll pick you up and we won't stay long. I'm only going to keep my mother off my case.  You know I can't stand my baby brother or his wife."

"I'll think about it—"

"Give me your number.  I'm going shopping for your dress and shoes right now. I'll bring them over to your place Saturday morning, and I'll get Jaz to come over and start working on your hair.  Trust me, this is going to be fun," Krystal talked fast without taking a breath, or letting Courtney answer.  "And don't tell Momma.  Let her be surprised."

Courtney watched stunned as Krystal flitted off in the direction of the maternity store.  Sean's oldest sister was usually moody and sarcastic and had always treated her like she was an airhead.  It had been a while, but had she

changed that much?  She needed some advice from Angela—who was the one

person Krystal asked her not to tell.  It was just a wedding after all, and she did

want to be there, if only to be nosy.  She'd be a fly on the wall, and nobody would

have to know…

"Be careful; don't smear your make-up.  Are you sure you can walk in

those heels?" Jazmine grilled Courtney, who was in the back seat of the car trying

to feel as glamorous as she'd been made up to look.  Her hair seemed to be pinned

up a mile high, with dramatic ringlets framing her modestly made up face.  Eye

catching gold, beaded earrings dangled from her earlobes and matched the beaded,

strapless and cleavage baring, evening gown form fitted to her slim, pregnant

frame.  She also wore gold high-heeled pumps, which were a challenge to walk in,

but she didn't complain since Krystal and Jazmine seemed to think they were vital

to her look.

The attention made to her appearance had distracted her from the reality

of what she was doing, until they'd pulled into the parking lot of the Milford

Estate, where the wedding was taking place.  *Oh God, am I really doing this—

crashing his wedding?*  Yes, she was invited; but had the bride known she was

pregnant, that invitation wouldn't have been extended.  Now here she was, and

there'd be no blending into the background which had been her intention.

She'd allowed them to talk her into a complete glamour makeover—a

gaudy presentation from head to toe designed to turn heads.

Once they entered the building, Courtney was awed by the beauty of the old restored mansion, with its dark wood paneled walls, large heavy crystal chandeliers, and brightly colored floral displays throughout.  All she'd heard about the Milford Estates, up until then, was of its popularity for society events; and looking around, she could see why.

As they moved through the halls, her confidence increased; and by the time they'd reached the Terrace ballroom, she'd convinced herself she could make it through the evening, if Krystal kept her word and they wouldn't stay long.  She was also prepared to slip out and into a taxi, if necessary.

Upon entering the ballroom, the lighting was dim with elegant candelabras on each table.  There was a subdued hum of the large crowd, milling about having drinks and hors d'oeuvres.  Courtney could see the large bridal party assembled in a reception line that was coming to an end, on the other side of the room.

Krystal had insisted upon arriving late; said she had no stomach for the mock ceremony or her gold-digger brother.  The only reason she attended at all was because it was a free party paid for by Yolanda; not for any sentiment she held towards Sean.  But tonight, it was all good and she was all smiles because she'd stumbled onto a grenade that was going to blow the whole phony affair to pieces: the ex-girlfriend and the secret baby.  She was just waiting for the right time...

## Chapter Ten

*What is she doing here?*  Sean thought, seeing Courtney enter the ballroom, flanked on each side by his sisters, her pregnancy accentuated in a tight-fitting gown.  His throat became constricted; and as soon as the photographer was finished, he ran to the bar.  Jay followed him.

"You okay?" his brother said, "Most guys have that look before the wedding, not after."

"I'm in big trouble, man," Sean hissed.  When he saw Yolanda, a tight smile on her lips, heading in his direction, his heart rate spiked.

"He wants to take some pictures in the lobby around the fountain," she snapped, grabbing Sean's arm firmly, without waiting for a response.

Courtney was busy with the hors d'oeuvres, while Krystal and Jazmine grabbed flutes of champagne from the waiters working the crowd.  Shortly after the reception line dispersed Courtney heard, "Mommy!"  Bryce had found her and had, at the same time, loudly informed the curious onlookers who she was.  She forgot about being self-conscious, however, when she saw how cute he looked in the black tuxedo with a red carnation in the lapel.  He climbed up in a chair and threw his arms around her.  "You look pretty!!"  He said, then started tugging at his bow tie.

"Bryce, you have to take some more pictures, while you still look nice," Angela coaxed, bringing a cookie to ensure his cooperation.  She paused briefly and gave Courtney a puzzled frown.  "I'll talk to you when I come back," she said before carrying the toddler off in another direction.

Jay looked across the room, searching for his wife, then spotted a woman in white, standing near her. As he focused in on the woman's familiar face, his eyes widened. "Oh, my Lord."

"Courtney, is that you?" Nina's mouth hung open, as she took in the front view of her.

"Hey, Nina," Courtney said, as they embraced.

"Wow, it's been a long time, and you've been keeping secrets," Nina observed, stepping back and patting her belly.

"Yeah well, you know. Not something I wanted to publicize."

"Is it...?" Nina made a sideways motion with her head in the direction of the bridal party table.

"Of course not."

"Uh-huh-well, anyway, you look wonderful. Pregnancy agrees with you and looks like you're finished with him—that's got to be a good thing." Then noting there was no ring on Courtney's finger, and she was there alone, she wondered if she'd done any better this time. Then again, Nina didn't quite believe Courtney's denial anyway.

Once in the lobby, Sean looked around for the photographer; but Yolanda led him past the fountain to a secluded corridor, away from the ballroom.

"She's pregnant," Yolanda hissed as loud as she could, while still whispering.

"Who?" Sean asked, wishing he'd grabbed his drink.

"You know who!  Your son's mother.  Why didn't you tell me!  And is it yours?"

"Courtney?  Is that who you're talking about?  She's not even here.  You must have her confused with some other pregnant woman."

"Don't play with me," she gritted her teeth.  "Answer my question."

"If it's true, I didn't know, and I—I doubt—"

"You doubt!"  She struck him in the chest so hard he hit the wall.

He shrugged, and she left him there, muttering curses and threats under her breath.

Nina and Courtney continued to make small talk, mostly about Bryce and Nina's daughters, when a photographer interrupted them.

"Excuse me, Ladies, can I take your picture?" he inquired.  Nina stepped away, while he snapped shots of Courtney, as if she was part of the wedding party.

"My name is John, by the way," he said, "and if you don't mind me saying so, you're very attractive.  Have you done any modeling?"

Courtney smiled at the line she'd heard since high school, while John continued snapping pictures of her, as if Yolanda wasn't the one paying him.

"You're not wearing a ring.  Are you married, or hooked up with?"  He nodded toward her belly.

"Neither," Courtney replied, smiling like she was more interested in him than she was.  She then saw a frowning Angela heading in her direction.

"Would you mind posing for some shots by the fountain outside?"

"Why not," Courtney said, seizing the opportunity to avoid Angela and her scolding.

While he snapped pictures, Courtney got a good look at him. He was a handsome man probably in his late thirties, judging by the amount of gray in his short-cropped hair. As she posed, she thought about what it would have been like meeting someone like him, had things been different.

Sean remained in the darkened hallway for a few minutes, steeling himself for the impending doom. He knew it was his own fault; he should have done things differently: should have told Yolanda about the pregnancy months ago. It seemed as though keeping quiet about it was working for him, but all he'd done was set himself up for the disaster that was playing out before his eyes, and if his sisters had anything to do with it—the rest of the world.

His thoughts were interrupted by a woman's—Courtney's—laughter coming from the lobby. *I'm about to be lynched. What is she so happy about? Does she even have a clue...?"*

When he stepped out into the lobby, he found Courtney having her own personal photo shoot with one of Yolanda's photographers.

Sean quietly walked up behind him. "I'm not trying to get in the way, man, but aren't you being paid to—?"

"Yeah—okay man," John said. "Courtney, give me a call?" He then headed back into the ballroom.

Sean scanned the lobby quickly, then gave Courtney a stern look before heading into the same secluded corridor Yolanda had dragged him to. This time he found an empty supply closet. He opened the door and waited for Courtney, who eventually realized he'd expected her to follow him. As she walked toward him, she thought how picture perfect he looked in his black tuxedo, starched white shirt and white bow tie, his hair and mustache groomed to perfection. It was how she dreamed he'd look for their wedding.

"What is this—revenge?" He asked, once she'd joined him.

"I was invited, remember?"

"You come in here with Krystal and Jaz—of all people. Whose idea was it for you to be made up like some pregnant Barbie doll? Theirs I bet? Did you stop to think why? I mean, it's not like they've ever liked you much."

She had thought about what their motives might have been, but in the end, decided it didn't matter. They didn't know anything, so what could *they* do to her.

"They've got something planned for me and it involves you—"

"They don't know anything."

"God, Courtney!" He cried, raising his hands, his face contorted. "Are there *any* brains in that pretty head of yours? What difference does it make what they *know*? Appearance is everything and you're pregnant. Regardless of what they know or what you say, before this night is over, everybody in here will know that child is mine."

She stared at him, taking in what he'd said, knowing it was true—feeling foolish and naive. They would've spread the gossip about the baby even if she hadn't been there; she'd been brought along as visual proof.

He watched the confidence and gaiety disappear from her stance; she became a frightened child before his eyes, and he was sorry, again, for being the cause. "I deserve everything I get for all of this, and I can handle it. But I hate seeing you being used. I've caused you enough pain."

Courtney's eyes filled with tears. When Sean tried to touch her shoulder, she pulled away.

"You have every reason to hate me, but I beg you to get in a cab and leave, now. I don't know what's going to happen, but at least you won't be caught up in it." Sean fished bills from his pocket and pressed them in her hand. "Here's money for the fare."

He left her in that closet and headed to the ballroom feeling like scum. The only people who should've felt worse were his sisters, but he knew they wouldn't. If it meant exposing his dirt, they'd sacrifice anything or anybody.

"Are you okay, Miss?" one of the mansion staff asked Courtney. She didn't know how long she'd stayed in that dark corridor.

She walked away without answering, wiping tears with the back of her hand. Her makeup was probably a mess, but it didn't matter because she was getting out of there. She turned down the hallway leading to the exit, then remembered Bryce. She needed to tell Angela she was leaving. She tried to call, but Angela's cellphone was turned off. She turned and headed back towards the ballroom.

Before entering, she stood behind the partition, looking to see where Sean's sisters were, to assess if she could go in without them seeing her. The lighting was dim, and everyone was seated as dinner was being served. She saw Jazmine looking around periodically, probably for her; but when the waiter served her plate, she was occupied. Courtney slipped in and took a seat near the door.

The waiter immediately appeared with a salad, and the baby gave her a few stern kicks in her ribs to let her know *she* was hungry.  Concealed from view, for the moment, Courtney couldn't pass up the meal.  After the salad, came hot rolls and soup.  The main course was filet mignon wrapped in bacon, with jumbo shrimp, grilled vegetables and seasoned rice.  She enjoyed the food so much she forgot her urgency to leave.  After a couple bites of the dessert, Raspberry White Chocolate Cheesecake, she returned to reality and knew it was time, during the sappy speeches, to make her escape.  She was planning to ask one of the waiters to get Angela's attention for her, but then heard Bryce screaming and giving somebody a hard time.  She instinctively rose and went to him, dismissing her need to conceal herself; she was on her way out the door anyway.  Whatever Krystal and Jazmine had planned, they'd have to do it once she was gone.

"There you are.  I thought you'd gotten some sense in your head and left," Angela said as Courtney approached.

"I'm leaving now.  I just came to get Bryce," Courtney said,

"How are you getting home?"

"Cab," she replied quickly, then headed for the door.  She tried to get out as fast as possible; but Bryce started crying, refusing to walk, and the stupid heels she was wearing slowed her down.  When she heard Krystal's voice over the microphone she didn't stop or look up.

"I just want to congratulate Sean and Yolanda.  My brother and I have had an interesting relationship over the years, but he knows I love him.  And I also want to take this opportunity to welcome Yolanda to our family."  She paused as everyone drank to the toast.  "Incidentally, I also have another announcement—not sure if Sean has told everyone, but he has a new baby on the way.  What is it Courtney, in about eight weeks?"

There was an uncomfortable silence and some snickers, as all eyes shifted to Courtney who was trying with every inch of her life to leave the ballroom.

"It's a joke, everybody!  Gotcha, Sean.  Cheers, everybody," Krystal proclaimed raising her glass in a toast while laughing hysterically.  There was an uneasy roar of laughter in the room by the time Courtney reached the door.

"That was just wrong!" the DJ said.  "What would we do without our family, huh?" Loud dance music then started playing.  Once in the hallway, Courtney took off her heels, picked up her son and left the party behind her.

*Why do my kids have to act like fools—all of them?*  Angela thought. Once the crowd became occupied with the party, she stormed out of the ballroom, searching for Courtney who she caught just as she and a screaming Bryce were climbing into a cab.

"Courtney, wait," Angela said.

Courtney's face was wet with tears, and the sight of her with the screaming baby made Angela feel obligated to do something.

"Let me take you home."

Courtney shook her head.

"Then let me take Bryce.  He can stay the night with me.  I'm leaving now anyway."

Courtney didn't protest. Bryce did—but only mildly.  Once his mother was gone, Angela sat down in the lobby and quieted him.

She stood up to leave just as her daughters, who were also departing, entered the lobby.

"That was a nice little show you put on.  Don't you have any regard for me while you're making a spectacle of yourselves?"

"You're just mad, 'cause I exposed your little coverup," Krystal slurred from too much champagne.  "You knew all about it, didn't you?  And there you are—covering for him as always.  It's about time everybody sees what a snake he is, even if you don't."

"It wasn't my business to tell—and it wasn't yours.  They've been married for two months. Whatever her husband is or isn't, it's up to her to find out and deal with."

"You hypocrite—" Krystal hissed, stepping closer to her mother, "you make me sick."

"Shut up, Krystal.  You've had too much to drink.  Watch how you talk to your mother and give me the car keys," Jazmine ordered.

Krystal handed Jazmine the keys while still scowling at her mother.

"Sorry, Mom.  We were so caught up in what we were doing, we didn't think," Jazmine said, kissing her mother's cheek but Angela turned away.

"Don't apologize to her.  We just told the truth." Krystal said, and continued fussing all the way to the car.


"We're taking off man," Jay said, patting his brother on the back.  He noticed Sean was tense and distracted, but Jay had nothing to say to make him feel better.  He'd have to ride this one out by himself.

"Yeah, okay. Thanks for staying." Sean said, figuring the rest of his family left early in a general show of disapproval over Krystal's *joke*. They all knew the truth when they heard it.

All the while Yolanda Brown McNair was a simmering, smiling, dancing volcano. He was thankful there were no sharp knives around, as she would've stuck one in his gut, in between one of their "happy couple" video moments. It was amazing a person could be so angry and conceal it from everybody but him and Ronnie, her father.

Once Jay was gone, and he'd put on enough of a show for Yolanda's guests, Sean retreated from the crowd, into the adjoining restaurant. He purchased a pack of cigarettes, sat down at the bar; and once he was sure no one from the wedding party was there, closed his eyes and rubbed his temples. *Why'd I do this?* Knowing he'd had hundreds of opportunities to avoid what had happened that night. But it seemed the longer no one knew, the easier it was to simply keep it to himself. How could he have known Jazmine and Krystal would find out at the worst possible time? Now he was dead. Yolanda could deal with the baby, but not the public humiliation. He was going to pay for this night for a long time.

"So, is it congratulations?"

Sean turned to see his father-in-law smirking at him. "You did get married, didn't you?"

He rolled his eyes and went back to his drink. The two men had a cordial relationship. The older man didn't trust him, and Sean knew it. He figured he wasn't with Yolanda out of love, but it wasn't money either. Sean had no qualms about signing a prenuptial agreement guaranteeing him virtually nothing upon their split.  Ronnie wondered if the handsome man was gay, and using Yolanda as

a front, but now knew that wasn't the case.  Sean would soon be a father to two

kids by one woman.  Yolanda was his parachute: He was bailing out of that

relationship.

"Couple months ago.  You know that," Sean said staring into his glass.

Ronnie took the seat next to Sean, ordered a drink, and pulled out a cigar.

"So, then the other thing—the joke.  Was it?"

Sean shrugged.

"Did she know?"

Sean cleared his throat but didn't speak.

Ronnie laughed.  "Boy, you got a death wish—don't you?  If I were you,

I'd leave town for about a week and let her cool off."  Ronnie had raised Yolanda

and knew the tantrums she was capable of.  He wouldn't wish that experience on

anybody –even this pretty boy who probably deserved it.

"No, I'll deal with it.  I guess it's about time..."

"Suit yourself, my young brother," Ronnie said, then drained his glass

and left.

Sean went back to the ballroom, danced more, posed for more pictures

and waited for his sentencing.


Courtney paid the cab driver with money wet with tears and trudged,

sobbing, up the stairs.  She'd never felt so used in her life, but it was worse than

that.  It was everything, all of it.  Everything had always been wrong, and every

day just got worse.  She'd never be able to make it any better, and her daughter was going to be her all over again.  It was going to start over, the nightmare that had been her life.  She'd had her chances, thinking back to Grayson, but she blew them.  Who's to say if she'd made a different choice the outcome wouldn't have been a disaster of another kind?  She couldn't do it—couldn't make it.  Mary was right about her: she wasn't worth much and never would be.

She found herself on her knees, in her living room.  She couldn't go on another day with that empty feeling.  She was dead inside...the only part of her alive was the baby she was carrying.  *I can't carry anymore...any longer...I can't do it.  It's too hard.  Who cares anyway—who do I have—who needs me?*  She couldn't answer any of those questions and needed to escape the pain.  There'd be no sleep, because she didn't want to wake up, see herself tomorrow, and know what a fool she'd been.  She'd do anything to escape how she felt.  *Would alcohol take it away?*  She then remembered the pills.


"YOU LYING BASTARD!  I'LL SEE YOU DEAD!"  Yolanda screamed from the back of the rented limo.  She then launched a champagne bottle which grazed Sean's head, and followed with each of the two glasses.  The bottle hit the panel that separated them from the limo driver, shattering it.

"Mrs. McNair!" the limo driver exclaimed, brushing glass from his hair.

"Shut up and drive.  Whatever I break, I'll pay for!"

The driver looked at Sean woefully, then pulled away from the curb.

"How long did you know?"

"I didn't know—I swear.  I'm still not sure."

"Is that why we eloped?  You really thought being married would keep me from dumping you?  How stupid do you think I am?  We're through.  I'm putting your belongings out as soon as I get to my house.  You don't live there anymore.  I don't care where you go, back to your knocked up cosmetic queen for all I care.  Have a nice life in that rat hole with her and your babies!"

"Look, if I wanted to be with her—"

"I don't want to hear any more of your lies.  I have grounds for an annulment and I'm getting one," Yolanda said, then turned away and stared out of the window as the limo drove through town.  She'd planned the social event of the year, but it had been turned into *Madea's Family Reunion* by Sean's low-class family.  She'd thought twice about even inviting them, but in the end what could she do?  Just shows what happens when you marry beneath your class.

Sean thought about pleading his case, but figured he'd told enough lies for one night.  Besides, he had his doubts about what his wife had said—*an annulment*—and risk being the talk of the town? He'd stake his life against it.  Once she calmed down, she'd do what Yolanda does: put a positive face on the situation, tell her friends as little as possible, and nothing would change—except his life wouldn't get any easier.  On the whole things, hadn't turned out as bad as they could have.

Courtney fished the bottle of painkillers from her purse and opened it.  There were only about ten or twelve capsules in the bottle, and she wondered if that would be enough to do the job.  She wanted to sleep, to enter oblivion, but couldn't face the thought of waking up again.  Her resolve started to falter, but she reminded herself of what her tomorrows had in store and knew she had to get out, get off the boat and disappear.  She couldn't face it.  She was going to spare her daughter the pain, before she drew a breath, before she could become her.  That's what Deirdra should've done for her.

She was then wracked with violent spasms and muffled her screams with a pillow.  Her last moments on earth—she was going to die.  Why didn't she have peace?  She grabbed the pill bottle and swallowed half of them, got up from the floor onto the bed and waited for death to take her.

*What am I supposed to think about?*  She decided she'd think about her life, as short and as misguided as it had been.  *An abortion, that's what it was...*She then decided to focus on the good things, and there was only one: her baby.  She started to cry again, *how can I leave him?*  But he had a father, and a grandmother who loved him.  *Will he understand?*  She asked herself, panic rising in her.  It wasn't fair—she was being unfair—she was cheating him like Deirdra cheated her.  She owed Bryce better than that.  But it was too late, she was starting to experience blurred vision and drowsiness.  She managed to grasp the phone and pressed speed dial...

"Hello?"  Carmen answered.

"I'm in trouble—took some pills.  Help me!"  Courtney whimpered, before passing out.

"What? Courtney, hello?  are you there?  Answer me.  OH MY GOD!"

# Part Three

# Chapter Eleven

Sean's cell phone rang, and he stirred with a moan. As much as he'd had to drink it was amazing, he'd woken up at all.

"Hmm," he mumbled.

"Sean, wake up." It was his mother on the line. "I need you to watch Bryce for me."

"What—what time is it?"

"It's two a.m. Sean, wake up! Something's happened." She could tell by his voice he was drunk. Now what was she going to do?

"I can't watch nobody, Ma. I'll get him tomorrow."

"Sean. Courtney's in the hospital. I need to see if she's okay."

"What? Did she have the baby?" He said, struggling to gather his thoughts.

"No... her sister said she took some pills."

"What? Why the hell did she do that? What about the baby? I'm on my way," he said, struggling to stand while at the same time feeling around for his car keys.

"You can't drive like that. Stay where you are. I'll take Bryce to—"

"Bring my son here. I'll be sober by the time you get here. Oh wait. I'm not at home. I'm at the Hilton Inn on Gilford Highway. Yolanda kicked me out."

"What?"

"She's pissed about Krystal's *joke*."

"She should be pissed about more than that," Angela said, as she hung up the phone.

"Courtney, I know you can hear me. You didn't take that many pills, and they've pumped your stomach. You're alright, so open your eyes and talk," the nurse demanded, but Courtney's eyes remained closed. She'd awakened to the reality she was still alive—not only had she screwed up her life, she couldn't even get suicide right. So now, as painful as being alive was, she'd just as soon stay that way. That didn't mean she had to talk about it.

"You try," she heard the nurse say. Then Courtney heard Carmen's voice from across the room.

"If Courtney doesn't want to talk, she won't –it's simple as that. When she was a little girl after our mother died, she went more than a year without talking to anybody." Courtney was startled and nearly opened her eyes. She had no recollection of that memory.

"Okay. Suit yourself, Miss Brooks. But if you don't start talking soon, they're going to hold you in the psych ward. You don't want that, do you?"

Courtney didn't respond, not even with a blink. Then she heard the door open and guessed it was the nurse exiting. She heard light footsteps move closer to the bed and Carmen sigh heavily.

"What have they done to you?" She said, not really asking a question. "And why didn't you tell me you were feeling so down? Was I so hard on you that you thought it better to kill yourself than ask for help? If so, I'm sorry—I didn't mean it. I just wanted things to be better for you, and you were doing so well until..."

Just then the door swung open and a frazzled Angela entered.

"Carmen. Thank you for calling."

"Since she's closer to your family than she is to ours, I thought I'd better let you know," Carmen said, trying to be courteous, although she knew for certain Angela's too handsome son had a hand in what happened that night.

"How is she doing?  Is she asleep?"

"Doubt it.  She's just not talking to anyone right now.  They think the baby's fine, just drugged."

"Really?" Angela frowned then went to the side of the bed.  "Courtney, are you awake?  Why aren't you talking?"

Carmen let out a breath.  "Do you know what happened?  Why she'd do such a thing?"

Just then a tall young man, apparently the doctor, entered the room and stood by Courtney's bed.

"Miss Brooks.  Miss Brooks, answer me, please.  You're not asleep or drugged and you can hear me.  I need you to answer." He then whispered something to the nurse, who turned to Carmen and Angela.

"Ladies, we'll need you to step outside, please."

They both nodded and walked out of the room.  When they were in the hallway, a few feet from the door, Angela answered Carmen.  "I saw her last night and she'd had a pretty bad experience.  But I never expected her to do anything like this.  I don't know if you heard but my son was recently married."

"She told me he was engaged."

"It's been a few months now, but the reception was held last night, and when Courtney turned up there, it escalated into a huge embarrassment for her."

"You mean nobody knew about the baby?"

"It wasn't common knowledge—not before last night."

"Why, that little worm!  Excuse me, Miss Angie," Carmen said, stepping away, trying to calm the anger she felt towards a boy who'd done nothing but ruin her sister's life since the moment she'd met him.  Had he been there, Carmen knew she would've punched him.

"I'm not happy about it, and I'm blue in the face from all the times I've told the two of them to put the brakes on their relationship.  Seems the more I've talked, the more involved they became.  Now it's gotten to be too much for them."

"But *he* ain't pregnant, is he?" Carmen growled.

"I'm not defending him, and I don't expect you to understand where I'm coming from, but he is my son.  He's as selfish as they come, but he didn't want this."

"Then where is he?"

"Miss Brooks.  We need a urine sample; and since you are able, you'll need to get up and use the bathroom," the doctor said.  She remained still with her eyes closed.

"Okay, Miss Brooks, I'll put it to you this way: You either go to the bathroom, or we'll have to catheterize you, which involves a small tube being placed in your—"

She opened her eyes and sat upright in the bed.

"That's better.  You're going to be here for the night.  You'll have an evaluation scheduled first thing in the morning; and depending on the outcome, you could possibly go home."

The prospect of going home and resuming her misery, made her feel instantly sick.

"Would you like me to tell your visitors to come back tomorrow?" The doctor offered and she nodded.

"I'll do that. The bathroom is over there, and make sure you use the receptacle."

When the doctor exited the room, Angela and Carmen approached him.

"She's fine—physically, anyway; but doesn't want any company right now. She'll be speaking with a counselor in the morning, and if they think she's out of danger to herself, she'll be released. Then she'll need someone to take her home."


"Good morning, Courtney. My name's Kate Fitzgerald, and I'm a psychologist who's been asked to come in and talk with you. How are you feeling this morning?"

*That's a good question.* she thought. She'd been sitting in a chair in the corner of the hospital room for hours, and hadn't slept, reliving in her mind every stupid thing she'd done in her life, right up until that night—which she concluded was probably the dumbest thing yet. What she couldn't figure out was if it was dumb because she'd tried to kill herself or because she'd failed. Then about four a.m., the baby started kicking —hard— which meant there was still hope.

"Okay," Kate said. "Either you didn't like my question, or don't have an answer. That's perfectly fine. But you will need to talk to me. Can we start with last night?"

Courtney's body stiffened, and she turned to look out of the window.

"Courtney, can you answer me, please. Are you going to work with me? If not, I'll leave you alone; but you'll have to stay here until we do talk."

"Yeah, okay," Courtney complied with a hoarse whisper.

"That's better. Thank you." Kate said. "You took some pills last night. The medics assumed they weren't prescribed to you. Is that correct?"

"Yes."

"It says here they were painkillers. Were you in physical pain? Is that why you took them?"

"No."

"Were you trying to harm yourself?"

Courtney was silent. Sobs wanted to gush out, but they were caught in her throat.

"It's okay if you need to express your emotions," the woman placed a hand on Courtney's shoulder. "This is certainly the time and place to do it."

As Courtney's tears began to flow, Kate made notes in her chart, then poured a glass of water and set it on the tray beside her.

"Was there something traumatic that happened last night that made you want to harm yourself? Or is this something you've been thinking about for a while?"

"A little of both, I guess," she whispered, while wiping her eyes with the back of her hand.

"Thank you for your honesty," Kate said, "alright, so that was last night. Today's a new day. How do you feel about things now? Are you over last night's crisis, or do you still feel like you're in the middle of it?"

Courtney stared out the window, "I don't know where I am, and I haven't for a long time."

"Do you want to die?"

"No ...I just don't want to be me anymore." And with that the dam of sobs broke, loud, convulsive and in full force. Kate didn't stop her but stroked her back and soothed her, until she was composed again.

"Okay, Courtney. In my brief assessment, I'd say you're significantly depressed. Without knowing anything about your family history, my guess is you've been depressed for a long time. You've learned to live with it, hide it, ignore it, but it's been there. If you weren't pregnant, I'd treat you with anti-depressants and counseling; but we can't give you any drugs, until you deliver and aren't breastfeeding." She then perused over Courtney's demographic data.

"It says here you have another child—a two-year-old." Courtney nodded. "I need to make a decision here of what would be best for you and your family, but I need you to help me. Do you want to go home now, put this episode behind you, and seek care on a voluntary basis?"

Courtney swallowed a lump in her throat. "It's been hard for me. I don't want to go back..." she whispered, then started to whimper.

"Shh, it's okay. That tells me what I need to know. If I can get you into a facility, for a week or so, so we can start to chip away at some of the things bothering you, would you be agreeable to that?"

Courtney nodded, and Kate saw an expression of relief wash over the young woman's face.

For Courtney the idea of hiding away anywhere, seemed like heaven; she would've stayed barricaded in that dingy hospital room if it meant she wouldn't have to go home.

"Okay, I'll place you on a three-day hold, which will give me time to find the right facility.  A social worker will be coming in to talk with you about making provisions for your son's care while you're in the hospital."  Kate rose to leave, then took Courtney's hand and squeezed it.  "You've made a good choice.  It takes courage to ask for help when you need it.  You're going to be fine."

When Kate left, Courtney was relaxed enough to get some sleep.  She was going away, where none of her problems or her past would find her and maybe she'd never have to come back...


"Pastor, if you and Miss Elise could stop by and look in on her, I'd be so grateful.  She's a sweet girl, just a little confused.  And I'm afraid things have been so crazy at work; I haven't taken the time to talk with her like I should have."

Pastor Ricardo Douglas was a busy man.  Serving his large congregation was a job bigger than he was; hospital visits to people who weren't church members was something he'd assigned to his pastoral staff years ago.  But Sophia Harris was a person who was faithful to everything he asked her to do, and rarely asked for anything in return.  If she made a request of him, then it meant something to her; he decided to honor it himself.

"Sure, I will.  It just happens we're going to be at that hospital today anyway.  Elise's sister had surgery," he explained

"Hey, Miss Alice," Pastor Douglas said to the nurse sitting behind the desk in the hospital maternity ward, doing paperwork.

"Hello there Pastor Rick, it's been a while," Alice smiled.

"Can you help me? I'm looking for a Miss Brooks. I was told she's on this floor."

"There she is," Nurse Alice pointed, shaking her head. "Over there in that corner, staring out the window. She sure could use *you* right now. She's been sitting there for hours, only gets up to use the bathroom; and as pregnant as she is, she barely eats."

He walked slowly to where Courtney was sitting. Sophia hadn't told him much. The girl was pregnant; the father wasn't with her, and a day earlier, she'd tried to kill herself. He prayed silently as he approached, asking the Lord to give him the words to help her see past her pain.

"Miss Brooks?" he approached cautiously, standing a few feet away from her. Her mind seemed so far away; he didn't want to startle her.

She turned toward him hazily. "Is it time to go?" she asked.

He ignored the question and held out his hand. "I'm Pastor Rick Douglas. Sophia Harris—I think she's your boss at the department store, asked me and my wife to come and look in on you."

"Oh," Courtney said, then turned back to the window.

He grabbed a chair that was close by and sat down across from her. She was a pretty girl, but there was something strange about her demeanor. He'd seen enough people going through emotional turmoil, to see the signs. She had to be in her late teens or early twenties, but the way she was acting was childlike, so that's how he decided to engage with her.

"What do you see out the window?" he said.

"I don't know" she shrugged.

"Do you want to go outside?  Me and my wife will walk with you if you'd like?"

Courtney shrugged again, but now the man was getting more of her attention.

"I'm going away and I don't think I'm coming back.  I hope Bryce doesn't hate me.  I can't stay here anymore."

"Who's Bryce?" he said, assuming he was the baby's father.

"My baby.  I didn't want him, not at first.  Now I'm going to leave him, but at least he has a daddy.  Not like me, I don't have anybody, really."

Just then Elise Douglas, Rick's wife, found them.

"Hi, how are you?  My name is Elise," she said introducing herself.  The look her husband gave her let her know she should approach Courtney carefully.

Courtney didn't respond to the introduction, as her mind was focused on her tale of woe.

"Do you think he'll forget me?  I don't remember much about my mother."

"Of course, he won't forget you, and you'll be back with him soon.  Elise, this is Courtney," he said, as he surrendered his seat to his wife and went to find another chair.

"You're a pretty lady, Courtney.  When is the baby due?"

Again, she didn't answer Elise, but started looking around for the pastor, as if she'd formed an attachment to him, in that short amount of time.

"Sophia tells me good things about you, Courtney. She's looking forward to your returning to work," Pastor Douglas said, as he sat down again.

"I'm not going back. I'm going away. I'm giving Bryce to Sean."

"You're going to be better soon, then you'll get Bryce and go back to work. Maybe you'll get a new job or—"

"I can't go back." Courtney insisted as she started to weep. "I've messed up everything so bad. I just want to go away."

"Everybody messes up, Courtney," Pastor Douglas said in a low voice, almost a whisper, while Elise stroked her shoulder.

"None of us would be here if we quit when we mess up," Elise added.

Just then Kate Fitzgerald walked up to them. "Hi. I'm sorry to interrupt," she whispered. "Are you Courtney's parents?"

"No, I'm Pastor Douglas, and this is my wife; we're just here to help."

"That's great. She's going through a tough time right now. Thank you for your support," Kate then turned to Courtney, who she noticed had become more withdrawn and confused as the day progressed. "Courtney, you'll be leaving here tomorrow. We'll have to go to family court briefly to take care of the custody matter with your son; then you'll check in at Meadowfield Behavioral Center." It didn't appear that Courtney understood a word of what Kate said to her. The doctor smiled helplessly at the Douglases. "I don't think she'll make the hearing tomorrow. It looks like I'm going to have to have her transported to the facility directly. I was hoping a chance to see her son would get the idea out of her head that she's leaving him for good."

"What time is the hearing?" Elise asked, and Ricardo knew why he loved his wife. She had a big heart for everyone she met.

"It's at 9:30.

"I'm not busy in the morning. Why don't I meet you here and help with her," Elise offered.

"That would be great," Kate sighed with relief.

"Actually, we'll both help," Ricardo added. He *was* busy in the morning; he was every morning, but the Lord was talking to him clearly—about this girl.


"I guess you'd better come by so we can talk..." Yolanda said, to Sean's surprise. It had been three days since she'd kicked him out of the house. He'd expected to be banished by her highness for at least a week.

"Just so you know, I have Bryce for a while."

"You have Bryce—why?"

"His mother's sick. He could be with me for at least two weeks, or longer. We have a temporary custody hearing tomorrow."

"What? Is she having complications?"

"Yeah...You could say that..." Sean said, clearing his throat.

"What? Is she in early labor?"

"She's having some problems...emotional..."

"Oh..." Yolanda said, speechless for the moment as her mind worked through the details. "Check out of that dive and bring him here now," she ordered, before hanging up in Sean's ear. There—she was reuniting with Sean, temporarily, for the sake of the baby. She and Sean had plenty of time to work through the details of their split. In the meantime, why should Courtney's precious little boy suffer in some hotel, because his mother's a psycho and his father's a moron?

Yolanda then paced around her massive bedroom, trying to get a handle on the mess she was in. Her head was telling her to cut her losses and cut Sean loose—wouldn't that keep her social circle chuckling for a while. *I should've known better,* she groaned inwardly. She'd moved too fast, determined to have who she wanted, without knowing much about him. Maybe she'd spent too much time looking at him and not enough time seeing who he was, confident she could handle whatever skeletons came poking out of his closet. And she could. But how much more embarrassment would it cost her?


Carmen waited patiently in the lobby of the Meadowview clinic with Courtney's packed suitcases. She'd skipped court to avoid being dumped with her sister's baby. Unlike Courtney, she wasn't going to allow Sean to escape his responsibility. If his overbearing mother chose to step in, that was her business. *Let pretty boy and his momma do their part, since this is their fault,* Carmen thought as she saw two cars approach. She recognized Courtney's doctor Kate in the first automobile, but noticed Courtney wasn't riding with her. Her sister was huddled in the back seat of the car following Kate, and there was a couple in the front seat whom Carmen didn't recognize.

When the man stepped out of the vehicle, however, Carmen noted he had a familiar face. She assumed he was a family member they'd lost touch with over the years but couldn't imagine who.

"Carmen, how are you today?" Kate greeted her. "Sorry we're late. Courtney became kind of emotional when she saw her son, but she's calmed down some."

The woman who was with the driver of the car was helping Courtney out of the back seat. The driver joined Carmen and Kate in front of the entrance.

"Hello, I'm Rick Douglas. You must be Courtney's sister," he said, offering his hand.

Carmen shook his hand with a slight frown. "I'm sorry to stare, but your face looks awfully familiar. I thought you might have been a member of our family."

"Well, we are all one family in Christ," he smiled. "No, I just met your sister yesterday. But I must say your face is familiar to me also. This is my wife, Elise." Elise didn't look up as she was busy talking to Courtney, who seemed to be in another world. Rick took the bags from Carmen, and Kate guided him to Courtney's room.

Carmen tried to talk to her sister, but she was unresponsive. It seemed to take everything she had to put one foot in front of the other, while Elise coaxed and urged her on. Carmen's heart broke seeing her sister so lifeless; and by the time they reached her room, she struggled to hold back tears.

"Don't worry," Kate assured her. "It's not as bad as it looks. She's zoning out, giving herself a break. She'll come back when she's able."

Once Courtney got into the hospital room, she felt instantly safe and secure, oblivious to the people and conversation taking place around her. There was something about the décor that soothed her and made her feel she could relax. There was a single window with sheer yellow floral curtains that overlooked a garden, blooming with a variety of flowers. It reminded her of the child's bedroom she never had, yet had imagined, a room she would want to have for her daughter.  Ignoring everyone, she laid down, curled up on the bed, and was asleep within minutes.

Kate smiled.  "That's what she needs more than anything right now.  She hasn't slept well in the last few days.  Once she's rested, I'm sure she'll be able to focus better."


"Spit it out—you blame me for what has happened to her," Sean said, to his mother as she was loading her dishwasher.  He was seated at the kitchen counter, playing Solitaire, having stopped by her house on his way home from work.  Anticipating a generous dose of recrimination and finger pointing, he decided to give her the opportunity to get it out of her system.

"Would you like something to eat?"  She said, without looking up at him.

He'd been ready for a fight, but her calm deflated him.  He threw the cards that were in his hand onto the counter and covered his face.  "What if she doesn't get better?  What am I going to do?  I don't want to raise my kids.  She's supposed to do that."

While his eyes were covered, Angela looked at him and grimaced, *only my son could make a statement like that and think it makes sense.*

"Courtney's doctor says this was a long time in the making.  It wasn't just one thing or one person.  She lost her mother at an early age, was raised by that crazy drunk; it's no wonder she has some problems, but we all have problems.  I didn't have the best childhood; and as hard as I tried, neither did you.  The only thing I can say to you is, the next time you decide to play games with a woman's head, maybe you'll be more careful."

"So," Sean surmised, looking around the large bright reception area with its comfortable seating and private zones designed for family visits. "This is what it looks like inside a crazy house. How does it feel to be an inmate?" He was smiling at Courtney but studying her at the same time. She had a calmness about her that made him feel it was okay to joke with her. Although she didn't smile at his attempt at humor, he could tell she wasn't bothered by it either. It was her first visit with Bryce since she was admitted ten days before, and Sean was amazed at how different she looked—nothing close to the pale wreck she'd been on that day. "Seriously, how are you? I've been worried."

"Better. Learning how to deal with things. It's kind of like being taught how to look at life a different way."

"Yeah. How many ways can you see 'Sean is a bastard'?"

He smiled again, but Courtney swallowed hard and shifted her look away. Her doctor had been lecturing her for a week about personal responsibility—but at that moment she was apt to agree with him.

He then stopped smiling and looked down at the floor, wishing they were somewhere more private as he had an urge to drop to his knees, bury his head in her lap, and listen to the baby's heartbeat. Anything to make her smile at him again. "I never wanted anything bad to happen to you; you know that, don't you?" he pleaded. "I just didn't think. Maybe I would've done things differently if—"

"I had my chances to make better choices and I didn't. Now I need to make the best of things the way they are," she shrugged, looking down and stroking Bryce's hair, as he slept in her lap.

He let her words sink in as he watched her trying to be tough, pretending he no longer mattered in her life. Her face had gotten round, her body rounder. He couldn't believe he was going to be a father again, and that he was married to somebody else. Where had his brain been vacationing when he'd made those moves?

"I'm out of here in a couple days. Are you going to let me have Bryce back?" She inquired, knowing if Sean wanted custody of Bryce, he could make a strong case against her.

He nodded, concealing the relief he felt at knowing he'd have his freedom back. He liked having his son around but wasn't ready to be Mr. Mom. Although Yolanda spent a fortune buying Bryce whatever she thought he wanted, she did *not* babysit.

Courtney checked the clock on the wall; it was nearing the time for her afternoon group session. She motioned for Sean to take Bryce.

"I've got to go as well," he said, as he stood, then leaned over to kiss her; but she shifted out of his range and lifted Bryce instead. Neither of them said goodbye, as he carried their son out of the hospital reception area.

She then got up and walked to the window where she could watch them drive away. She wondered what Sean was thinking, wondered if he understood she wasn't interested in his patronizing displays of affection. She'd have to live with the fact that she'd tried to commit suicide because of him but knew he wasn't her cure.

"Sean called me to see if it was okay for him to visit you," Kate said later, during their afternoon therapy session. "He seems to genuinely care about you—maybe not in the way you want him to. We all have different needs, and his gorgeous set of hazel eyes doesn't mean he's the one for you. Doesn't matter how many babies you two make together. He and the rich wife may be well suited to each other. There's a reason why he married her and not you. It could just be the money, but it could be other things as well."

Kate's words sounded callous to Courtney, who stared back at her with a clenched jaw. She wanted a villain: Sean or Yolanda or Mary or somebody. Kate wasn't giving her one. It had been the theme for the entire week: things are what they are. Deal with it.

Her therapy sessions the rest of that week didn't get any easier, but after fourteen days Courtney was discharged. Kate told her she'd made good progress. She felt like a big, fat, pregnant mess. But she was ready to return to the real world; grateful that after what she'd attempted to do to herself, she and her baby were still alive to have that option.


"Can I move back in?" Courtney asked Mary who shrugged. "I'm too pregnant to go apartment hunting, and I don't think I have a job anymore anyway."

"Do what you want to do. You're going to anyway," Mary mumbled, then took a sip from her glass. "You're not asking me; you're telling me. But let's get one thing straight: He's *not* part of the deal."

"What are you talking about? He's married and rich—"

"That don't mean jack; and if you don't know it, you ain't learned nothin'."

When Courtney gave Rick Douglas the address of her grandmother's house, he realized he knew the area well. He'd grown up in that part of town, and his mother still owned a house in the same neighborhood. Still, there was something familiar about the house number.

When he parked in front of the house, he knew why it seemed familiar. At one time in his life, he'd been a regular visitor at that house. *Deirdra,* he mouthed the name, catching himself before he said it out loud, because his wife was seated next to him; he wasn't ready to answer any questions about her.

"I know this house," he said, then the pieces came together. How he and Carmen knew each other, and why Courtney's face seemed familiar to him, even though they'd never met. She looked like Deirdra, much more so than Carmen did. Then his stomach dropped when he remembered Deirdra's mother Mary. Back in the day she was a witch and hated his guts. Maybe she'd mellowed with time.

"Is something wrong?" Elise said to him, wondering why they were still sitting in the car.

"No, not really. Just another one of those ghosts from the past," Rick sighed.

Elise sighed also, but inwardly as she thought, *not another one.* Her husband had a checkered past, which included drugs, using and selling, jail, pimping, living homeless on the street, and a few scattered kids. She didn't hold any of that against him. By the time they'd met, all of that was behind him and she was proud of the man he was today.  At the same time, there was always some skeleton peeping around the corner.  In the fifteen years they'd been married, they'd encountered their share.  It'd slowed down, but she never knew when something or someone else from his past life would show up.  Looks like today was their day.

"Is there something I should know before we go in?"

"Her name was Deirdra Hadley, she's dead now, and I'll tell you the rest later," he said, as he stepped out of the car.

*Great, another old girlfriend,* Elise thought as she started up the concrete steps to the screened porch.

Courtney greeted them at the door cheerfully.  "Thanks for coming," she said, talking quickly.  "I'm not sure if you can help me, but I don't know who else to ask.  Since you know people in your church that do this kind of work—"

"What did you say your mother's name was?"  Rick asked, having heard little of what Courtney had said.  He was studying her face, the way she held her mouth when she talked; *after all these years...*

"Deirdra –" Courtney started, noticing him staring at her strangely.

"Hadley?"  He finished, and she nodded.

He took a deep breath, "Small world.  I knew her.  I grew up just a few blocks from here; in fact; she and I grew up together.  You look like her."

"Yeah?  You're right—small world," Courtney wanted to talk to him more about what he remembered about her mother, but then she didn't know many people who had good things to say about her.

Suddenly Mary stirred on the couch, after having been napping.  She took one look at Pastor Rick and snarled. "I can't believe it, 'bout time you showed up."

Rick, who assumed the alcohol had finally gotten the best of the old woman smiled. "Hi Miss Mary, do you remember me?"

"I know who you are, Ricky Douglas. I'd know you anywhere. I hear you became a preacher. Once a pimp, always a pimp," she quipped.

"Mary!" Courtney cried, "How can you be so rude? Pastor Rick and Miss Elise have been helping me."

Mary sat up on the couch just enough to freshen her drink. She ignored all three of them.

"I'm sorry," Courtney said.

"You don't have anything to be sorry about," Rick assured her. "This goes way back, before you were born. If you knew a little about me back then, you'd agree her hostility is understandable."


"Hello, Miss Mary, can we talk?" Pastor Rick said. He'd stopped over at a time when he knew Courtney wasn't there. She and Elise were at her apartment packing up.

There was something about their conversation the previous week that bothered him—things Mary had said that didn't make sense, but he couldn't pass them off as old age, or senility. Despite the drink, the old woman seemed to be as sharp and as mean as she was two decades earlier. There was some meaning behind the comments she'd made during their last meeting; he needed to clear the air and let her have her say, without the girl around.

"What do you want now?" She snapped as he walked into the house.

"I was curious about some things you said the other day; I thought we should talk privately, without Courtney around. She doesn't need to be burdened by our past."

"Funny you care about that now. Where you been all these years? Parading yourself as some preacher. Now you got everybody thinkin' you're some good Samaritan, when all you're doing is taking care of what you left behind 22 years ago. They might be impressed—but I ain't. I know what you really are."

"Are you trying to say that she's—"

"Don't act like you didn't know. Where were you livin' 22 years ago— right upstairs, a crackhead like her. Nobody else would take you in, so she dragged you in here. She got pregnant and you disappeared."

Rick sat down slowly while Mary's accusation registered. She was saying he was Courtney's biological father. It was certainly possible; he had a couple other children near her age—that he knew about. And in those days, Mary was right, he was a crackhead, and his life was out of control. But she was omitting an important detail: Deirdra was a prostitute. That's how they paid for their high. He should know since he was the one who put her out on the street in the first place.

"Miss Mary, I'm sorry about what happened to Deirdra. I really am. She was beautiful, and she loved me; but one day she started loving drugs more. When I got out of jail, I came back for her—tried to help her, but she wouldn't have nothing to do with me."

"That's your fault!"

"And she didn't tell me about a baby.  Matter of fact, I was at the funeral and neither did you."

"You didn't deserve her!"  Mary said, trying to shout but all she managed was a croak.  "You'd taken all I had; you weren't getting her."

Rick stood up.  "Thank you for your time, Miss Mary.  I can't say I'm her father, but it's possible.  I beg your forgiveness for the hurt I've caused you and your family in the past, and I know I can't make up for your loss.  But I hope in time—"

"Words.  Nothin' but words.  They don't mean nothin'.  You took everything and now you came back for her.  I'm surprised you're letting her, and your grandbabies move in here with me.  No, I don't forgive you.  I will never forgive you."


"Sean, I'd love to take your money," Tracy, the secretary at Courtney's apartment building, told him.  She loved tenants that paid on time, and he paid cash months in advance despite not living there.  He'd be missed even if Courtney wasn't.  "But I think you should speak with Courtney.  She gave us her 30-day notice last week."

"Really?"  He put the money back in his pocket.  "Thanks for the info."

"No problem.  I think she's upstairs packing now."

Sean nodded as he left the office, not sure if he should talk with Courtney or not.  His mother had threatened his life if he upset her, or even approached her, so he'd kept his distance.  But he was tired of all the people who'd suddenly shown up in her life, who she was listening to; tired of being shut out.

He debated with himself for a moment and decided to go upstairs to feel

her out.  If she seemed to be disturbed, he'd leave.

"It's open," she called from the kitchen, hearing the knock at the door.

No one came to her apartment usually but Vicki, her neighbor, so she was stunned

to see Sean closing the door behind him.  He was wearing a charcoal gray suit that

must've been custom tailored—it didn't even wrinkle as he moved.  She then

looked down at her fat body sitting on the dirty floor and knew they didn't live in

the same world.  She also knew she didn't have to feel bad about that anymore.  He

lived in Yolanda's world and was happy there.  Still, she couldn't take her eyes off

him.

"I hope it's okay.  I was downstairs paying your rent, and Tracy said—"

"I can't stand this place anymore.  You look nice in that suit, by the way."

He was caught off guard by the compliment and Courtney saw him blush.

"Why didn't you tell me you wanted to move?  I would've found you a place.  I've

been saving up for a while just for that purpose," he said, taking small steps

toward where she was packing up dishes in the kitchen.

"I need to stop depending on you."

"Of course, you should depend on me.  We have a so-" he stopped and

corrected himself, "children.  I'm responsible for their welfare."

"It's your job to take care of your kids, not me.  I need to start depending

more on myself."

"You're depending on a bunch of strangers who hold your hand and make

you feel good about yourself," he said, then regretted the way it sounded.  "Don't

misunderstand me; I'm not knocking anybody.  You've had a hard time, and you're coping the best way you know how.  But what do they know about you, or us?"

"There is no us.  I guess that's the point," Courtney said, struggling to get up from the floor, until he reached out and helped her to her feet.  Once she was on her feet, he held onto her arm, until she shook it off and turned her back to him.  She hoped he'd do what he often did when she said things he didn't like: walk out and leave.

While her words hung in the air, he moved toward her, until he was behind her; she pretended not to notice.  He wrapped his arms around her belly, nuzzled the back of her neck with his face, and then whispered, "You can save that talk for your therapist.  I know the truth and so do you.  When everyone is gone—Yolanda, your preacher friend, everyone—there will always be us: you, me and our kids."  He then turned her around to face him.  She didn't look him in the eye but allowed him to wrap his arms around her tight, while she buried her face in his chest, surprised he still had that effect on her.  "Where are you moving, anyway?"

"Back to Mary's," she said, breaking out of his embrace.

"Oh God no," he moaned.  "You know she hates me.  How am I going to see my baby?  Besides, that place is a rathole."

"I'm having the house fixed up—with your money.  The painters are there now."

"Whose great idea is this? The pastor's, I suppose."

"It was my idea, but I did get some help from him."

Sean looked at his watch.  His lunch break was ending, and he needed to get back to the office.  He grabbed her and stunned her with a long and lingering kiss, that she allowed.  He then pulled some business cards from his pocket.

"Here's how you can reach me.  Leave a message anytime day or night.  If it's urgent, ask for June; she'll find me."

Courtney stood at the window and watched him drive away, the old feelings she'd had for him resurfacing.  Then the baby inside her gave her a few swift kicks in her ribs, bringing her back to reality.  She spent the rest of the afternoon angry with herself for getting carried away—again.  *What was it—the way he looked in that suit, the sound of his voice?*  Why had she turned to jelly at the sight of him?

*You're too hard on yourself,* Kate would've told her.  *You can't turn off five years of emotion because you want to—doesn't matter how many wives he has.  Give it some time and understand you might slip up occasionally...*Courtney was tired of slipping up.


Yolanda parked her car in the lot of Courtney's building, silenced the engine, then extracted a tube of bright red lipstick to match her bright red nails and the black and red tailored business suit.  She was dressed for war.

She knocked on the door firmly; she'd called ahead, and Courtney was expecting her.

"Hello, Courtney.  Is this a good time?"

"I suppose," Courtney shrugged.

The two women stood facing each other in the hallway.  Yolanda appraising her in a way Courtney found intimidating but did her best to conceal it.

"As I said on the phone, I was hoping we could talk," Yolanda said, "Can you spare a few minutes?"

Courtney silently stepped back and opened the door so Yolanda could enter.

"Have a seat if you can find one," she offered, referring to the disarray across her living room. Yolanda remained standing.

"You're moving, I see?" she said, hoping it was out of the country. "I wanted to talk with you earlier, but I understand you were sick. Are you better?"

Courtney nodded as she cleared a space and lowered herself onto the couch. Sitting wasn't a simple task at 37 weeks pregnant. She then dragged over the box she'd been working on, while waiting for Yolanda to spit out what she'd come to say.

"I'll get to the point. I'd like to know if it is your claim that my husband is the father of your baby."

"I'm not comfortable answering that question. I think you should ask him," Courtney replied.

"I have, and he says he's not sure. So now I'm asking you."

Courtney felt like she'd been punched in the stomach but stiffened so as not to give Yolanda any indication she'd gotten to her.

"That's personal information between me and the child's father, and he knows who he is. If Sean is uncertain of anything, he's more than welcome to ask me."

"Why should we believe you?" Yolanda charged. "I mean, a chick will say anything after she's been dumped."

She was jolted by Yolanda's sudden change in tone, then realized the meeting had nothing to do with her child's paternity.

"Well," Yolanda said, brushing her clothes with both hands as if debris had been dropping from the ceiling. She then dug into her over-sized purse and handed Courtney a card. "If you have anything to tell me, call me. If Sean is the father, we want to help you. We'll relocate you and your children anywhere you want to go so you can have a fresh start—but the offer won't last forever." She gave Courtney a hard stare before walking to the door. Courtney followed her slowly. Before turning the knob, however, Yolanda spun around. "From now on, you deal with me—not my husband. I'll make sure he gets any messages. If I find out you've been contacting him, my offer is rescinded."

A barrage of curses hit Courtney's brain all at once; but before she'd gotten any of them out, Yolanda was gone, having closed the door in her face.

The best she could do was grab a glass vase that was nearby, hurling it at the door.

Yolanda, who was down the hall stopped and giggled when she heard the crash. She then opened her compact, freshened her lipstick, and smiled at her reflection. She exited the building humming a song she'd heard on the radio that morning.

Courtney made an emergency call to her therapist's office and was seen later that afternoon.


"Courtney, I don't know what you want me to say. You know he's a bit morally challenged; why are you surprised that, once again, he's not telling the truth?"

Courtney sat slumped in a chair, her eyes red and her face streaked with tears.  She had balled-up tissues in both hands and on the floor, with a box resting

in her lap.

"You know what I think?  You and Yolanda are making things easy for

him.  She's going to fix everything by paying you off, while you swoon every

time, he looks your way.  You can't blame him for playing both sides.  You girls

are letting him get away with it."

Courtney sat and sulked while letting Kate's words sink in.  It was her

hour, so she took her time.  Kate left her alone and went back to her desk, waiting

until she was ready to talk.

"God, he's so two-faced!   But I should know that by now; he's going to

do and say what's easiest for him.  To her and to me."

Kate half shrugged and watched her.

Courtney put her hands over her eyes and leaned back in the chair.  "Am I

ever going to get a clue?"

"If you want to.  Some women don't and stay caught up in the same cycle.

You don't have to fall into that trap; but if you do, you can't blame him.  Now, isn't

it about time you had that baby?"

# Chapter Twelve

"Hey, Mom."

"Your daughter's here, born about an hour ago."

"Thank you," Sean replied curtly, letting Angela know he couldn't talk freely.

"She's healthy—nearly 8 pounds and 21 inches long.  They're both doing well...  Angela heard a muffled "thanks" before the line went dead.


"She's a feisty one," the nurse said, lifting one of the babies whose complexion was so fair she could've been white.  Sean could see through the nursery window; however, she was a miniature version of himself; he couldn't see any of Courtney's features in her at all.

"She's on her way to Mom's room for a feeding," the nurse said.  "It's Room 1247 around the corner if you'd like to meet us there."

Sean knocked lightly on Courtney's door, but received no response. When he entered the room, he found her asleep, snoring quietly.  He sat on the side of the hospital bed, smoothed down her hair, which was all over the pillow, and kissed her mouth until she stirred.

"Hey," she said, in a raspy voice.

"She's beautiful."

"Because she looks like you?" Courtney stretched while yawning, as the door opened, and the nurse rolled the bassinet into the room.

Sean reached in and scooped up the little replica of himself: his ears, his nose, and his lips.  The shape of her eyes was Courtney's but her eye color, like Bryce's, was his.

"I'm going to have a lot of explaining to do, thanks to you," he cooed, grinning at the squirming baby, who unable to wait any longer to nurse, screamed back at him.

"What's her name?" he asked, handing her to Courtney.

"Cori Angelia," she said, as she opened her hospital gown and placed the infant to her breast in the way the nurse had taught her.  Sean played with the baby's feet while she nursed.

"I've got to go," he said, after a few minutes.  He'd been hoping to see the baby once more before he left, but she didn't appear to be coming up for air anytime soon.  "Have Angela call me if you need a ride home from the hospital. I'll try to get away."

*Who asked you?*  she thought but decided, since he was being nice, she'd play along.  After all, it was their daughter's birthday.

"Is there anything you need?"

"Sign her birth certificate," she said, pointing to a folder sitting on a shelf beside the bed.

He looked in that direction, but hesitated.

"Is there a problem?" Courtney demanded, watching him, her lips tightening and eyes narrowing as she spoke.  "There's no reason to wait for a DNA test—is there?"

Sean rubbed the back of his neck and thought about it a few more seconds before picking up the paper. He stared at it a minute longer before he completed the information and signed it. He wasn't sure if sweat was visible on his face, but he *was* sweating, even if only in his mind. He was admitting, in writing, to lying to his wife. If he refused to sign the birth certificate, however, it would be worse – Courtney would be done with him forever. She'd forgive how he'd treated her in the past but failing to acknowledge their baby was another thing entirely.

"Her name is McNair—not Brooks. I guess that was an oversight," he said, nearly throwing the paper back on the shelf.

Courtney waved her hand, "Pay the child support, call her whatever you want."

As he exited the hospital, he wondered how he was going to maneuver through this one. Yolanda would be waiting for a blood test that wasn't going to happen. Just how many lies could he tell? Maybe it was time for him to stop lying and take the fallout. That was always an option...


Yolanda watched Sean for weeks and waited for him to say something, about Courtney Brooks, about the baby, anything; but he hadn't. She then started making calls to his family members—who, in her view, were nothing but a bunch of gossips anyway. Surely, she'd find out something from them. But they didn't like her. Neither of Sean's sisters, nor Nina his sister-in-law, would tell her anything. It was possible they didn't know, but Yolanda knew who did.

"Hi, Mom," Yolanda said, as Angela opened the door. "These are for you." She presented her with a bouquet of rare flowers, exquisitely arranged. It was obvious they hadn't been picked up at the supermarket.

*She wants something,* Angela thought, certain she knew what. "They're beautiful. What did I do to deserve such a gift?" She turned away from Yolanda to search for the right spot for the bouquet.

"It's just to say thank you for the support you've given me and Sean during our brief marriage and the wedding and everything. I appreciate you being here for us. I know you and Sean don't always agree on things and it's not easy for you. You must feel like you're being placed in the middle of things you shouldn't be—"

"Sometimes, yes," Angela nodded slowly.

"Like for instance the night of the wedding, when Courtney showed up. I know Krystal *said* she was joking, about the baby. But Sean didn't dismiss it as a joke. In fact, he's admitted to me that there's a possibility—"

"If you're asking what I think you're asking, Yolanda, you know I can't get involved in that."

Yolanda stopped talking and allowed a heavy silence to fill the room.

Angela then exhaled loudly, angry with her son for the chaos she was now confronted with. "Yolanda, you're my daughter-in-law, and if that husband of yours won't fill you in, I guess I'll have to. I won't guarantee I can answer all your questions but ask if you must."

"Has the baby been born?"

"She's three weeks old yesterday."

Yolanda's eyebrows raised.

"Courtney and I are close, as you know.  I was there at the birth.  That's about all I can tell you, Yolanda."

"Does Sean—"

"Yolanda, please."

Yolanda skillfully changed the subject, then tried to approach it again from a few more angles before finally giving up and going home.

Once she got there, she thought about what she should do next. Courtney's baby had been born.  Sean almost certainly knew about it and hadn't bothered to inform her.  What about the paternity test? What else was he keeping from her?


"Baby let me find you a place.  I didn't think you were planning on staying here forever," Sean said to Courtney.  Cori was asleep in the bassinet beside the couch; and Courtney was sitting in Sean's lap, her arms draped around his neck.

"I'll think about it," she said, knowing his promises were talk and their new lunch-time romance would be coming to an end soon enough.  She wondered how it had started up in the first place; it was the last thing she needed.  Having him show up every day to see her felt so good, she lacked the strength to end it, but knew Yolanda would.

"I can't keep coming over here.  Your grandmother's going to stick a knife in my back one of these days," he said, then checked his watch and patted her thigh.  "I've got to go back to work but think about what I've said.  Tomorrow, tell me when you want to move."

She nodded, smiled, and walked Sean to the door, giving him a long passionate goodbye kiss, as if she was seeing him for the last time, certain one of these days she would be. It was all innocent enough.  There wasn't much trouble she could get into, during his short lunch breaks.  Still she felt ashamed and longed to talk about her feelings but knew what everyone would tell her: the same thing she was telling herself.


"I hear Courtney Brooks has had her baby," Yolanda said, taking a seat across from Sean at the dining room table.  It had been elegantly set with linen, candles, crystal, her best china, and his favorite meal prepared by Renate —prime rib, rosemary garlic potatoes with almond green beans.

"Yeah?" he said, not looking up from his tablet.

"So, when is the blood test?"

"Soon, I guess," he shrugged.

"Why are you so nonchalant about this?  I'd think you'd want to know."

Sean then slammed his fork down on the table.  "What difference does it make?  She's mine or she's not.  Either way, it has nothing to do with you."

"So, it's a girl, is it?" she said.  Sean picked up his fork and pretended to be too engrossed in his meal to respond.  After a lengthy silence Yolanda continued.  "This situation does involve me.  What does she have to say about it?"

"If you mean Courtney, I've told you we don't talk."

"That's funny—what's this?" She reached under the placemat for papers which she threw down on the table in front of him. "I pulled your cell phone records.  Two calls to her in the last two weeks, and you talked for quite a while.

Are you sure the topic of the baby didn't happen to come up?"

Sean moved his chair away from the table.  "I don't appreciate—"

"And I don't appreciate liars.  Are you going to tell me what's going on?"

Sean stop moving and exhaled deeply, "There's nothing else to tell.  I've

talked to her.  I believe the child is mine.  We're waiting for the test results."

"Why haven't you told me any of this?"

"Why didn't you tell me about your little payoff offer?  Seems I'm not the

only one keeping secrets."  Courtney had told him about that a few weeks back,

and he'd been waiting for the right time to use it.

"I did that for us," Yolanda claimed, rising from her seat.

"Oh, really," he snorted.

She walked to where he sat and stood over him, while he stared straight

ahead.  "I'm done playing games with you.  You will *not* contact her again, until

paternity of that child is established, is that understood?"  She then pushed his left

shoulder and he turned to face her.  "And by the way, I've been wondering why

I'm unable to reach you during your lunch hour every day."  He looked away from

her, and she could see he was holding his breath.  She allowed the question to

hang in the air before continuing "Whatever is going on, it stops now or I'm

through with you.  This time I'm not bluffing!"


When Sean didn't appear at Courtney's the following day, it was the first

time in a month.  Instead of being hurt or angry, she took it as an opportunity to

catch her breath—a reality check.  Thinking clearly had been hard for her when he was coming around.  She spent that day into the evening contemplating her future and building up the strength to tell him to stay away—and mean it.  That proved unnecessary.

"I, uh, can't come visit my daughter anymore," he said, over the phone on the second day of his absence, "—for a while."

Courtney almost laughed but remained silent, as she tried to think of something to say.  "Goodbye, Sean," is what she settled on; before he could reply, she hung up.


"I'd like to see little Cori," Elise told Courtney, who'd called her as soon as she'd hung up from Sean.  "Why don't you come to church tonight?  We have a guest speaker, but service shouldn't run too late."

Rick and Elise had stepped back from Courtney's life since the baby had been born.  In fact, they'd only visited once; they didn't want her to feel obligated to them because they'd helped her.

"I'm tired of struggling and ending up in the same place.  I want a better life.  I don't even want Sean anymore; he's so weak and spineless.  I'm tired—I need help.  I guess I need God," Courtney told Elise in the car, on route to church.  Bryce chattered to himself, while the baby slept in the back seat of the car on that August evening.  Courtney let her tears spill as she spoke.

Elise listened and felt the pain in Courtney's voice.  While the young woman talked, Elise prayed and asked God to give her the strength she needed.

"You know, if I can stop beating myself up, maybe, if there is a God, He can put me back together."

# Chapter Thirteen

"...God doesn't care about where you've been or what you've done. He *cares* about what you do now...right at this moment...while He's talking to you....while He's tugging at your heartstrings...while He's trying to make you see and comprehend just how much He loves you." The woman speaker stepped away from the podium, nodded, then pointed to the congregation while pivoting from side to side. "You—with the messed-up past...the baggage... and *all* those mistakes—yeah you. That's who He's talking to—you. What are you going to do with the future He's offering? You can be free...you can be whole...you can be whatever He created you to be..."

*Why does this seem so personal?* Courtney thought, looking around to assure herself she wasn't alone in the large, densely crowded building. She'd been to church before, and it had always reminded her of school: the group assembles, half listens to the lecture, then class is dismissed. But not tonight.

*What's wrong with me?* She'd been crying from the moment she'd sat down, and feared she was on the verge of another emotional breakdown amidst a room full of strangers. She had no control. Something about the woman's voice, what she was saying, the story she was telling—it was about her. "*And Hagar, while crying in the wilderness alone with her child, called the name of the Lord who spoke to her You are the God who sees...*

The doubts she'd carried around her whole life were answered in that one statement—she felt it. *Whoever He is—He sees me...* She was filled with a hope so bright, it took her over. It made her weak and unable to speak, but happy. She felt tears but didn't want to move from where she was; felt someone take the baby from her arms while she melted under the weight of whatever it was that had surrounded her. She knew one thing: it was God and she was free, and everything would be right for her from that moment on. She was being claimed by love—a real love, and there was nothing else like it....

"You heard what you needed from God this evening didn't you?" Elise affirmed, after the service was over, placing an arm around her shoulders.

"He's real and He saved me—He's saved my life. I—"

Elise laughed gently, stroked her back, then handed her a box of tissues.

"Keep hearing Him and trust Him; He'll never lead you astray."

Courtney and her children rode in the back seat of the car as Pastor Rick drove them home. She felt happy and loved for the first time in her life and marveled at a God, whose very existence she'd doubted, loved her enough to value her, more than she valued herself. God loved her; and Elise and Rick, who God placed in her life, loved her also.

In the weeks that followed, her mind was often filled with questions and doubts about her encounter with God, she couldn't answer with any logic or reasoning: *How do I know I'm 'saved'? What does that even mean? How do I know it was God who spoke to me? Could it have been my imagination?* She posed some of her questions to Pastor Rick but found his answers more confusing. Ultimately, she made up her mind to believe what she knew inside and wait for her brain to catch up; somehow there was an ironclad certainty, deep within her, she couldn't explain. She decided to trust what she'd believed was God and let Him lead the way. Anything was better than where she'd been.

"This came for you," Angela said, slipping Sean a piece of certified mail while Yolanda was out of the room.  She'd invited the couple to her house that Saturday morning for breakfast, figuring Sean, tired of his mother's lectures, wouldn't have shown up otherwise.

He glanced at the slip of paper, saw that the sender was the County Child Welfare Division and slipped it into his pocket—he'd been expecting it.  Still, he was irritated Courtney had chosen that route instead of a more private arrangement. But then maybe this was what he needed to conclude the cliffhanger he'd created; he could openly acknowledge his daughter and wrap up the pile of lies he'd told his wife into one convenient bundle.  Keeping the date of the upcoming hearing to himself until after it was over, he'd then give Yolanda his version of events.  From there, life could proceed as normal.

However, Yolanda found the certified letter while going through his pockets a few days later and demanded answers.

"It has nothing to do with you," Sean said, as his wife trailed him around the house, swatting him with the envelope every time she spoke.

"That mental case is dragging you into court, ordering you to take care of her baby.  You say you don't even know if the kid is yours.  Seems you and your family feel sorry for her, because she's got two kids and a mental problem, but I don't.  If she didn't want the kids, she should've aborted them.  Until I see the test results, I'll be in court with you."

*Where could I get a fake lab report?* he thought, once he'd finally escaped to the downstairs man cave. He dismissed it quickly, knowing it wouldn't fly. His best route would be to go upstairs and tell Yolanda everything. He knew however, he'd never admit anything to her; she'd turned him into enough of a punk –her money, her toys, her demands. Yolanda claimed to want to know the truth, but the truth was a flashing neon sign—obvious to everyone. He'd been seeing her and Courtney at the same time, one he got pregnant, the other he married. Yolanda was playing dumb simply to drag a humiliating confession out of him— one more thing she could use to control him. He wasn't going to do it. He grabbed a beer and settled back on the couch, resting his feet on the coffee table. He'd catch hell but was determined to play the game as long as Yolanda did.

By the morning of the court date, Sean had less resolve. Yolanda was determined to accompany him, despite his pleading with her to stay out of it. He thought of stepping out of the shower and having that talk with her—admitting everything, so they wouldn't go through the charade, but he dismissed it. She was going out of her way to make a big deal out of a normal situation. People hook up, and things happen. It should be no surprise to her there are remnants of his past life hanging around. Now he was about to find out just what she was going to do about it.

"You okay, man?" Asked a well-dressed man who was washing his hands in the sink of the men's room at the county courthouse.

"I don't know," Sean said, shaking his head.  From the moment he and his wife had entered the building and he'd spied Courtney seated across the room, he'd started feeling dizzy and his head was pounding.

"Child support court?"  The man asked.

Sean nodded, grimacing.

"Man, you know you made that baby.  Grit your teeth and write that check," the man chuckled.

"My wife ain't gonna be so understanding, man," Sean covered his eyes with wet paper towels.

"What's done is done, my brother.  If you need a good lawyer, here's my card."  As Sean read the card, *"Ronald Wiley, Esq. Protecting the rights of Men amidst Divorce,"* Sean laughed heartily.  The attorney smiled along with him and patted him on the back.  "Good luck," he said, as he left.


Courtney was astonished at how calm she felt, having to face Sean and his wife at the child support proceedings.  Over the weeks since she'd last seen Sean, she'd rarely thought about him.  Her faith had become her focus; and unlike Sean, God had been there for her.

Sean looked as good as ever, however; in fact; he and his wife looked good together: well-dressed, well-groomed and rich, in the middle of the county office building filled with poor people like her seeking assistance.  Yolanda bore the sour facial expression of someone sitting on a pile of garbage.

"Brooks, McNair," the clerk announced from the hearing room.

Courtney entered first and took a seat on the far side. When the McNairs walked in, Yolanda attempted to sit in between Sean and Courtney, but the bailiff prohibited it.

With his wife to his immediate right and Courtney seated a few feet to his left, Sean was starting to feel sick all over again.

For Courtney, this was her second go-round in child support court; she knew what to expect—it was all routine. She was hopeful, however, of a sizable raise, given that Sean had recently graduated from college and was rumored to have landed a high-paying job.

The magistrate entered the hearing room; and this time it was a woman, African American and in her late forties. Courtney thought her attractive and, seeing her in such a prestigious position, reminded her of her own dreams that had been put on hold indefinitely. *There's still time for me,*

"Good morning. I'm Judge Young. We're here to establish child support for Cori Brooks McNair. Miss Brooks, I have a financial statement on file for you. Is it current?" Courtney handed her some papers.

"This looks like part of a social service application. You currently have no income; is that correct?" Yolanda snorted. The magistrate glanced in her direction, then back to Courtney who acknowledged the fact.

"Mr. McNair, I'm showing you have a son Sean Bryce McNair, who you are already supporting. Is your financial statement current?"

Sean answered hoarsely, then produced paperwork Yolanda hadn't seen before. She was also confused about the order of the hearing. There was nothing said about establishing paternity. Where were the results of the DNA test?

"Mr. McNair, your income has increased substantially since your son was born. He is due an increase, and your support for your daughter will be substantially more. You'll need to pay at least half of the arrears today, the remainder in ten business days," the magistrate instructed.

Sean nodded, and the magistrate turned to give instructions and paperwork to her assistant seated to her right.

Courtney felt relief that everything was moving smoothly and was anxious to see the final support amount she'd be receiving so she could start getting things in order in her life. Her thoughts had moved on to apartment hunting when Yolanda's voice cut through the silence.

"Judge Young, is it?" Yolanda said. Out of the corner of her eye, Courtney could see Sean loosening his tie. "Has paternity been established?"

The magistrate ignored question as she spoke with the clerk.

"Excuse me," Yolanda said louder, her red-lacquered lips stretched into what could be interpreted as a smile. "I've asked a question. Where are the test results?"

"Mrs. McNair, *is it?*" Judge Young responded. "You're not a party in this case, so I can't entertain any questions you may have—"

"I'm speaking for my husband. We want to know about the DNA te—"

"Mr. McNair," the magistrate said, before Yolanda could finish. "would you like a reading of the transcript of this case?"

The room was quiet, and all eyes were on Sean's except for Courtney's. She'd turned her head to the wall away from him, waiting to hear what he was going to say.

Sean knew if he said no, he was guilty, if he said yes, he was guilty. He realized the easiest thing would've been to skip the hearing completely and let the law come and get him. That would've been too risky, however—what if they came to his job. *Just get it over with man.*

Sean shook his head, but the magistrate waited for an audible answer. "No, that won't be necessary." Sean's voice cracked like an adolescent, and the magistrate stifled an urge to grin.

"Mr. McNair, I'm holding a copy of the child's birth certificate, with what appears to be your signature, dated on the child's date of birth. Is this valid?"

"Yes, it is," Sean said; and Courtney could see him mopping sweat from his forehead.

"Are you disputing paternity in this case? If you have doubts, express them now. If you request the test later, and it turns out to be negative, there will be no refunds. For the record, Mr. McNair, do you understand what I've just told you?" Judge Young persisted.

"Yes, Judge," Sean replied, looking straight ahead, his face reddening by the second.

"Do you still decline the paternity test?"

"I decline the test. She is my child."

"Thank you, Mr. McNair, for not wasting the court's time," the magistrate said with a smile and a nod.

There was thick silence along with the rustling of papers until suddenly the door slammed—so loudly it sounded like an explosion. Yolanda had exited.

Courtney turned and glared at Sean in disgust before rolling her eyes away from him.

When it was over with, Sean had agreed to pay Courtney nearly double his legal requirement.  The magistrate cautioned him against it, warning him he'd have a difficult time trying to get a reduction if he changed his mind later; he barely listened.  After scribbling his signature on the agreement, he snatched his copy and bolted from the room, leaving Courtney alone with Ms. Hayes the court clerk.

"Are you okay?" Ms. Hayes asked, while typing the paperwork into the court computer system.

"He's an idiot," Courtney said.

"Yeah?" the older woman paused from her typing.  "That's for her to worry about, isn't it?"

The clerk studied the young girl, who'd made her life into a huge uphill battle.  She saw hundreds like her during an average month and often longed to take some of them aside to encourage them or give words of wisdom.

"Did you know he was married?" Ms. Hayes inquired softly.

"They're newlyweds," Courtney snorted.


"Let me get this straight...there's been no paternity test and you were there at the birth—"

"I saw her the day she was born.  And no, a test would've been a waste of time.  She's mine and I've always known that.  I didn't mean for you to find out this way.  Things just got out of hand, and I didn't know how to—"

"You lying bum," Yolanda said, through clenched teeth.  "You let me think—"

"You *thought* what you wanted to, Yolanda," Sean said louder than he should have.  They were still in the county office building, standing near the elevators trying not to broadcast their argument to the world.  By the way onlookers were smirking at them, however, they weren't succeeding.  Sean was relieved—at least Courtney wasn't watching; that would've been more humiliating.  "I need some air," he stated, and with Yolanda in mid-sentence, ducked into the stairwell.  They were on the sixth floor; he decided the walk down would do him some good, if only to allow him to escape his wife for a moment.  Yolanda's stiletto heels prevented her from chasing him down the staircase.


"You have it pretty good, as far as I can see," Ms. Hayes said.  "You're young, beautiful, and *not* married to him."

Courtney laughed, but the older woman was serious.

"Let me tell you something, Miss Brooks.  I don't know you, but I can read people and situations.  She's got herself a pretty man who likes pretty women.  She's going to be spending her time trying to keep track of him.  She should learn from your experience—that won't work."

Courtney sighed and nodded, thinking about all the time she'd spent worrying about who Sean was with.

"I'm going to give you a word of advice as an older and wiser woman: Keep out of his life and his messed-up marriage.  He didn't think twice about giving you double the court-required child support.  Now, he could be a nice guy who wants the best for his children; but in my experience, most men aren't that generous out of love for their children or kindness of their heart. My guess is, he's trying to keep a foot in the door; you need to make up in your mind you're moving on...."

Courtney listened intently to this woman who didn't know a thing about her giving her the same advice as everyone else, including her therapist. *Why do they all keep saying the same thing?* She asked herself. She didn't see it. Sure, he'd said some things and made advances; but when it came down to it, Yolanda had him hog-tied and handcuffed; when she was around, he barely acknowledged Courtney's existence. Why was everyone so certain that was going to change?

"Your children are a beautiful gift. Enjoy them every minute, despite what their father does. They grow up fast," Ms. Hayes said, as she walked Courtney to the door.


"After Daddy's party this weekend, I want you gone. Don't tell anyone at the party that we're breaking up. Start packing and Monday morning get out. I don't care where you go, but I've had it with you," Yolanda growled as they drove away from the courthouse.

"Whatever you want, Yolanda," Sean said, driving the car while looking straight ahead. He was certain he had nothing to worry about. If she'd wanted him to move out, she would've put him out that day—that hour. In fact, she wouldn't have allowed him in her car; she would've given him cab fare, then had his belongings shipped to his mother's house. Having him hang around a weekend meant she was giving herself an excuse to keep him around for good.

He smiled to himself, knowing he wouldn't be moving out of her house until *he* was ready to go.

# Chapter Fourteen

"I'd like to see my daughter this weekend...if it's alright with you."

Yolanda was expecting as much and had been mulling over how she was going to handle it. Since that day in court, Sean had transformed himself into the perfect husband, perfect friend, perfect companion, everything a woman could ask for. He'd made it crystal clear since that day—he was all about her. Things had been so good, in fact, she hadn't wanted to bring up unpleasant topics. Now it was time to face reality, however, time to deal with Courtney Brooks.

Instead of answering him, she climbed out of the Jacuzzi and wrapped herself in a towel. It was a late Saturday morning—nearly noon; they'd enjoyed a lavish breakfast in bed and spent the rest of the morning making love. She now knew why she'd been privileged to have so much of his attention on a Saturday morning: He was softening her up. She walked out of the bathroom into the bedroom. Sean hopped out of the tub and followed her.

"Are you going to give me an answer?"

"I can't keep you from your children," she said, while getting dressed, but it is time we have a talk about—what's the term—the elephant in the room."

Sean sat on the bed, waiting to hear what was coming next.

"Courtney Brooks," Yolanda said, then stopped what she was doing and folded her arms.

"There's nothin—"

"You've told me the same thing for a year. Since then I've had to drag you out of her bed, monitor your cell phone log to see if you've called her, and oh yeah, there's that new baby. Don't tell me there's nothing between you. Admit it

to me, admit it to yourself, there is *something,* and we need to deal with it."
Yolanda exhaled loudly as Sean did his best to look befuddled. "Sean, I'm not
blind or stupid. She has a pretty face, empty head, curves in all the right places,
and apparently doesn't know how to say no. I don't see what the fascination is, but
then I'm not a man."

Sean turned away and started throwing on his clothes. He opened the
bedroom door, intending to walk out, but paused, realizing this issue wasn't
disappearing. If he was going to see his children, Yolanda would have to be
involved, and he would have to throw her a few crumbs to satisfy her womanly
*need to know.*

He closed the bedroom door, and Yolanda resumed talking to his back;
he hadn't yet turned to face her. "I want to know what your plans are as far as
she's concerned. I don't share men; I get rid of them. Until we understand each
other, you are not going to see your baby—or her mother."

Sean turned, then dropped down heavily into a chair beside the bed.
"Okay. Yolanda... the truth is, when I met you, I wasn't over her yet; but things
with Courtney and me have never worked. I've been struggling with the loss of
that relationship, and I still have feelings for her, but I'm not going to jeopardize
what you and I have. I swear to God it's over...

Courtney parked her car in front of Angela's house the following Friday
evening, feeling as though she were playing a role in a bad reality show. This was
Cori's coming out party, her formal introduction to her family, which was
wonderful; but Sean and his wife were also going to be present. The three of them

hadn't collided since court, and Courtney had no idea what to expect.

"It's going to be civil.  I can't promise Yolanda will be all that friendly; she's either overly nice, or a complete witch.  You never know what you'll get with her.  Since none of our family cares for her, she probably won't say much." Angela explained, over the phone the week before, while informing Courtney of her plans for the family get-together.

"It's time we get everything out in the open, so the tongues can stop wagging."


"Here she is, everybody! Meet Cori Angelia McNair—twelve weeks old today," Angela announced, as soon as Courtney walked through the door.  Cori was a big hit—Sean's family loved babies, especially their own.

"She's beautiful," Jazmine complimented Courtney.  "And I'm not just saying it because she looks more like me than you."  They laughed at the truth in the statement, as Jazmine and Sean could've been twins.

"Courtney, as it turns out, I was right," Krystal exclaimed, bursting into the room.  "I don't know why you just didn't come out with it back then.  All the stress of trying to protect that jerk of a brother of mine is probably what made you sick."

"You were sick?"  Nina, who was stirring a boiling pot of collard greens, frowned.

"You mean you didn't hear?  She was in the nut house for a couple weeks," Krystal said, while munching on a deviled egg.

"Thanks for your sensitivity, Krystal," Courtney scowled.

She cleared out of the kitchen and went into the living room where she could be alone.  Moments later she heard people entering the house from the kitchen door.  The show was about to begin.  Mr. and Mrs. McNair had arrived.  Courtney took deep breaths, practiced her smile, then dragged herself into the family room to join the others.

No one noticed her slip in as she took in the scene.  Sean was holding Cori, and Yolanda was all smiles holding Bryce.  *They look like such a happy family,* Courtney thought at the instant Sean caught her watching.  After things settled down, she tried to behave normally, but felt like she was being watched and whispered about.  Piling up a plate of food, she retreated upstairs to Angela's bedroom.

When Cori started wailing, a while later, demanding to be nursed, it was Yolanda who insisted upon taking the infant up to her mother.

"Mommy, she's not very happy," said Yolanda, cooing and handing the screaming baby to Courtney.

She thanked her, then positioned the baby to her breast.  When she looked up, Yolanda was sitting on the bed, watching her.

"I think you and I should talk," she said. "I hope you didn't feel it necessary to hide out up here because of us."

"It was all a little much for me.  I needed to get away."

Yolanda nodded, "It's an awkward situation.  It's awkward for me also.  But we're going to have to live with it." She rose and walked to the doorway.  After quickly scanning the hallway for eavesdroppers, she closed the door.  "After all, you and Sean have children together, and I'm not going anywhere."  She paused to see if Courtney would react to her statement, then continued. "I'm wondering if there are things the three of us need to iron out so we can move forward."

"No, Yolanda. There's nothing to discuss," Courtney said, without looking up.

"You and Sean have been talking since the baby was born, and I'm wondering if there's something I should know—maybe some expectations you have of him?"


Sean, who'd watched Yolanda walk up the stairs with the baby, knew she was going to confront Courtney. While his family was occupied eating dinner, he tiptoed up the stairs after her. The conversation was about him, and he needed to know what was being said. He couldn't sit back and allow Yolanda to hit him between the eyes with it later, when they got home. If Courtney chose to, she could make his life difficult. He'd said some things, and made some promises, in personal conversations they'd shared. It would be her word against his, but he'd still be placed in an uncomfortable situation at home. If forced to, he'd resort to lying, crying, and apologizing, to wriggle out of trouble, but needed to be prepared. Easing down the hallway, he placed an ear near the closed door.

"Sean has admitted to me he's had difficulty cutting ties with you. Has it been the same for you?"

"No," Courtney said. "Sean has made it difficult for me. I didn't try to hang on to him as much as he was determined to hang on to me."

Yolanda's eyebrows raised. "Are you saying your feelings for him have changed? You no longer want a relationship with my husband?"

Sean decided it was a good time to interrupt, before some things came out that were none of her business. He knocked on the door, and after getting no response, opened it and poked his head in. Neither woman seemed concerned about his presence; Yolanda was focused on Courtney and her answer. He quietly stepped into the room, closed the door, and attempted to make eye contact with Courtney before she spoke. She, however, was looking down at the baby.

"No...I can't say that," Courtney said.

"You're still in love with my husband?"

"Yolanda, this isn't nec—" Sean started to say, but Yolanda's glance at him, over her shoulder, was two daggers, and she raised a hand to silence him.

"I have a right to ask some simple questions, and that's what I intend to do, Sweetie."

Sean stepped forward; but before he could disagree, Courtney spoke. "You have the right to an answer," she said, then paused and bit her lip. She hadn't thought about her feelings for Sean since God had entered her life, and the reality of what she felt was forming in her mind as she prepared to speak about it. "I've learned some things about myself since my emotional breakdown and one thing I've learned is my feelings for Sean have never been about love. I thought I needed him. Now that he's chosen you, I can admit I'm hurt he didn't try harder at our relationship...I'm still attracted to him, and... I'm jealous he married you and not me."

The room was still as Yolanda's eyes narrowed, and she drummed her nails on the wooden dresser she leaned against, "What do you plan to do about that?"

"I plan to get over it.  I don't love your husband and have no interest in interfering in your marriage."

Yolanda exhaled and nodded as she straightened, "If that's the truth, we'll be just fine," she stated, then turned and walked past Sean, leaving him and Courtney alone in the bedroom.

He knew if he stayed too long, Yolanda would question him all the way home about what was said.  He was stung by Courtney's responses but suspected she was giving him a little payback.

"Those were some interesting comments you made," he sneered.  "Good thing neither of us believe them."  When Courtney opened her mouth to speak, he held up his hand.  "Forget it.  Can Bryce come with us?"

She nodded.  Sean took the sleeping baby from her arms, kissed her forehead and handed her back.  He then started to exit the room but stopped before he got to the door, put his hands in his pockets and turned.

"Sorry," he cleared his throat.  "I imagine this has been a rough night for you.  Are you okay?"

She took a deep breath, knowing the hard part—the encounter she'd been dreading—was finally over.  She smiled more to herself than at him.  "I'm great, and it all gets better from here."

## Chapter Fifteen

"How are things going on your new job?" Yolanda asked Courtney, during Sean's weekly parenting visit.

She smiled as she told Yolanda about one of the projects she was working on. The two women talked in the kitchen, as Courtney prepared dinner. Sean stayed in the living room, playing with the baby. The scene had become the norm in the last three months. An observer, ignorant of their history, would have assumed the women to be girlfriends.

The baby was a healthy and fussy six months old, and Bryce was three. Courtney was proud of the way the three adults had managed their new family dynamic.

She'd started a job at the hospital laboratory and was looking forward to resuming school to finish her undergrad degree, her sights still on medical school. With the days of lamenting her failed relationship with Sean now over, she was able to move on with her life.

Becoming acclimated to the ostentatious Yolanda Brown McNair was another accomplishment entirely, but she had no choice. If Sean wanted to visit the baby once a week, it meant Yolanda would be visiting as well. Courtney found her easy enough to get along with. Ask the right questions and then shut up—she'd take it from there. Mrs. McNair loved talking about herself.

Having the opportunity to observe the two of them together, Courtney thought them an interesting pair. On the surface they seemed ill matched; but after a closer look, she believed she got the connection. Yolanda was comfortably in the driver's seat, while all Sean had to do was sit back and respond when called upon. Seeing how her former flame cowered to his wife was enough to douse any lingering torch she carried for him. Spineless was not attractive.

In time, Yolanda stopped tagging along every week, seemingly satisfied there was nothing between Sean and Courtney for her to be worried about. She was right.

He'd tried to get something started up again, seeing as things had 'quieted down' as he put it; but the young single mother had her hands full with two children and wasn't interested. As attractive as he still was to her, his life was too complicated, and she wanted no part of it.

Unable to get anywhere with Courtney, he stopped making time for the weekly parenting visits also, opting instead to visit Cori at the babysitter's house on the Fridays when he'd pick up Bryce for the weekend.

It was then Courtney realized Sean was really and finally out of her life.


"We still need to run some tests, but so far things don't look good. Who is your grandmother's physician?" The doctor asked Courtney. He was a tall man with pale gray eyes that stared back at her, neither expecting nor interested in receiving an answer to his question.

"I don't know that she has one."

"She appears to be a heavy drinker. How long has that been the case?"

"As long as I can remember."

His eyebrows raised slightly. "Hasn't anyone in your family tried to intervene into her destructive behavior? She's not that old of a woman, but her addiction to alcohol has done irreparable harm to her body."

Courtney's face grew hot as she looked back at the man who was pointing an accusatory finger at her, knowing he didn't care. "There was only me, and she's not the type of person you can tell what to do."

The doctor sighed loudly and wrote some things down on his clipboard. "She's dehydrated, malnourished, and anemic—probably caused by some gastrointestinal bleeding. Her coloring suggests significant cirrhosis and enlargement of her liver, but we'll have to do further tests to assess the extent of that. She has high blood sugar readings and low blood pressure. That's for starters. Do you want me to go on?"

"I get the point," Courtney rolled her eyes.

"Too bad somebody didn't a few years ago," he jibed, as he moved to the door. "She's in bad shape. I can't give you a guarantee she'll get any better. I guess that'll be up to her."

Courtney didn't look up as she heard the door of the small meeting room close quietly. She'd been working at the hospital nearly a year but was still amazed at how some doctors talked to people however they liked.

At the same time, her body froze at his words. For him to say it was up to Mary as to whether she'd survive was like writing her obituary. The old woman had nothing she'd wanted to live for in more than a decade; she kept breathing simply because she knew how to.

She looked in on Mary in her hospital room before returning to work in the lab, which was located across the hospital campus. As she walked briskly, she checked messages on her cell phone and discovered she had three from June,

Sean's assistant.

*Sean and this darn party,* she muttered to herself, wanting to stop in the middle of the sidewalk and scream. *Don't they have any real work to do at an engineering firm?* June had called her every day that week because Sean had delegated to her the job of throwing Cori a huge and ridiculous birthday party. No detail overlooked; no expense spared—for a one-year old. The whole affair annoyed Courtney, especially considering Mary's illness. She was curious as to what Yolanda thought about it.

Sean's marriage had gone through plenty of challenges in the last few months, and thankfully she hadn't been involved in any of it. From what Courtney could tell, he was doing well in his career, and this seemed to be causing some of their problems.

She noticed he'd stopped driving the luxury sports car Yolanda had used to entice him into marriage in the first place, purchasing for himself a more modest luxury SUV. *I gave it back,* was what he told Courtney when she inquired what happened to the Jag. Also, from the gossip she heard from his sisters, he spent a good amount of time these days out of the house, sometimes because Yolanda made him leave, other times he just didn't go home. They told her the latest scoop every chance they got, assuming she'd be turning cartwheels; but she didn't care.

"June don't apologize to Courtney. None of this is coming out of her pocket. Cori is my daughter, and I'll go overboard if I want to," Sean said to the older woman standing in front of his dark cherrywood desk. She nodded, then left his office, closing the door behind her.

He'd fared well in his career at the Redmond Engineering firm, having been there just over a year. *Sometimes it just pays to be me,* he thought, knowing much of what he'd achieved on the job had been luck and charm, not always effort. He'd worked hard, but there were people who'd been with the firm for many years who'd worked harder and hadn't moved up as fast as he had. Mindy, his boss, was only a few years his senior and had risen quickly herself—maybe in the same manner. Which would account for the way she threw money and perks at him as if he'd earned them.

"We've been married over a year. I'm ready to start a family."

"Not this again," Sean moaned, while covering his head with a pillow, hoping to end the conversation before it started.

"You're not going to do that to me again. Look at me now and explain to me why we can't have our own baby. I'm tired of playing part-time mommy to Courtney's kids. I want my own."

It was early Sunday morning, and Yolanda had awakened him to announce she was ovulating and had stopped taking the pill. He told her he'd taken a vow of celibacy until she came to her senses. They'd been arguing about the same topic for months, but this is the first time she'd tried to ambush him with sex.

"I don't want any more kids, Yolanda." he said, climbing out of bed and grabbing his pants. "I'm sorry, we should've talked about this before we got married. I would've told you then."

"*You* don't want any more kids. Well, what about me?" She said, sitting up. He continued getting dressed in silence. "That's not good enough, and it's not fair. Of course, *you* didn't mention it before we got married; you had a baby on the way at the time, didn't you?"

"Let's not re-hash—" he said, shoving his wallet and keys into his pockets.

"Where do you think you're going? You're going to stay here and we're going to talk about this. I don't care if you've got your babies. What am I supposed to do?"

"Like I said. I'm sorry." Sean then darted from the room while Yolanda screeched out a stream of expletives. He chuckled to himself as he jogged down the stairs; he'd never known a woman who could curse like her.


"All this for a birthday she'll never remember," Angela murmured to Courtney as the two of them watched the spectacle of Cori's first birthday party. Sean had reserved the kiddie section of an amusement park and had hired clowns, magicians, and other performers for the children. He'd also brought in caterers to set up a barbecue pavilion with a full bar for the adult guests. Yolanda was the only guest taking advantage of the bar, at that moment, and was on her way to being pickled by lunchtime.

"Courtney, come over here," Yolanda said loudly; and as Angela rolled her eyes in disgust, Courtney obliged. "Well, look at you Courtney—the pretty, smart one. Did Sean ever tell you I used to call you the department store diva?" Yolanda snorted, looking like she was about to laugh uproariously. Then her demeanor changed. "You've got the babies—all I have is *him*."

She stared at Yolanda, perplexed as to how to react to such a statement. Then a man, who Courtney had been unaware was present, spoke from the rear of the pavilion.

"Nice to meet you, Courtney." She turned to see a tall man, with grayish hair, smiling and walking toward her; she recognized him as Yolanda's illustrious father, Ronnie Brown. In addition to Yolanda's boasting, Courtney often heard his name mentioned in the local news. "Don't mind my daughter," he said, extending his hand. "She and the hubby are having a little disagreement." He held her hand loosely while locking her in his gaze. "Bernard, I think you should drive my daughter home, before she becomes more impossible." He still held Courtney's hand, until she gently slid it from his grasp.

"I'm paying for this affair and I'm staying. I don't care how *impossible* I get," Yolanda countered.

Courtney watched as Ronnie motioned to the man, who looked like a bodyguard, and whispered something to him. Feeling out of place, she started to back away to look for Angela.

"Where are you going, Courtney? We were just getting acquainted," Ronnie said, and the way he smiled at her made her blush.

"I'd better go find my children."

"Hurry back."

Before she could tell herself not to, she flashed a smile and nearly collided with a waiter carrying a tray of drinks.

She laughed at herself as she flounced away from the older man, who she was certain was still watching her.

Sean, who seemed to have invited the entire city, carried Cori around the park, riding rides, with a photographer in tow.  At some point during the afternoon, a thin, gorgeous brunette appeared and was strolling with them, while playing with Cori as if she'd seen her before.

"There you are," Sean said, as she approached.  "Mindy, this is Courtney.  Mindy is my boss."

"Sean has brought Cori into the office a couple times.  She's really adorable," Mindy said.

Courtney shook hands with Mindy, then left them as they switched to workplace conversation.  She was nearly run over by Yolanda.

"He's screwing her," she declared to Courtney, loud enough for others to hear.  "He tells me I'm imagining things, but I *know* what I'm talking about."

## **Chapter Sixteen**

"Miss Brooks, you'll need to prepare. Your grandmother is too weak to fight off the infection, and we've also found spots on her lungs."

Courtney swallowed hard but wasn't surprised by what the doctor was telling her. Mary had been in and out of the hospital for the past year, and each time a different organ was quitting on her. Now she had pneumonia, on top of everything else, and was too weak and stubborn to fight it off. Mary was going to die because she didn't believe she had a reason to live.

"Mary, we need to talk. Can you hear me?" Courtney said, now sitting at her bedside, looking at her. She'd lost even more weight, if that were possible, and hadn't eaten any solid food in weeks. They were giving her oxygen to help her breathe, against her own wishes.

"Yeah," she hissed, barely above a whisper.

"The doctors say you might not make it. I wish I could lie and say you're getting better, but you've always been straight with me; I figure I should do the same."

Mary, with the oxygen mask over her face, simply nodded.

"I guess you need to tell me what you want, since we've never talked about this." It never occurred to her Mary would die one day. She seemed too ornery to succumb to anything.

Mary motioned for Courtney to move the oxygen mask. Before she complied, she called the nurse.

"It'll be okay for a few minutes," the nurse said, as she removed it.

"First of all," Mary started, then was stopped by a coughing fit. Courtney offered her a cup of water, which she waved off; then continued. "Don't have no phony funeral, not in a church, not anywhere. And if you have that so-called pastor of yours eulogize me, I'll jump right up out of the casket. Do you hear me, girl?" Her voice was weak, but her tone was harsh as ever. "There's a folder in my room with all the insurance information. I want to be buried next to my baby, Deirdra."

*Where is that?* Courtney started to ask but decided she shouldn't prolong the conversation. She'd have to find it herself but thought it odd all the same; she didn't remember ever visiting her mother's grave.

"There's a list of people I want you to notify, once I'm gone. Don't contact them until then. I don't want to look at none of them; they can see me once I'm dead."

"Mary!"

"Shut up and listen. I'm getting tired. Have a wake with music; I left a list of songs I want. There's a small policy that's yours, but the house ain't," she managed say, before starting to cough again. The attack was more violent and prolonged than the one before, so Courtney called the nurse. Once they got Mary settled and sedated again, Courtney went home. The kids were staying with Carmen that night, which is one of the three places she crashed on a regular basis since Mary became ill. Wherever her kids were, was where she usually spent the night, except when they were with Sean.

She decided to stop by her house and look for Mary's papers, before joining her kids. They were tucked away in the back of Mary's bedroom closet in a plain brown accordion file, which also contained old pictures, obituaries, and Deirdra's report cards.  There were also old Mother's Day cards she and Deirdra had given her; Courtney was shocked Mary cared enough to keep any of it; the old woman didn't seem to have a sentimental bone in her body.  Even when it came to Deirdra, she expressed more anger than grief.

Then she found a plain manila envelope; within it was Mary's living will and her last wishes, dated over a decade ago.  *She's been waiting to die all this time.*  Courtney thought.  *She's gonna be pissed if this time is a false alarm.*

She found the list of contact names, none of them Courtney recognized except for Darla Harrison and James Olson, Mary's siblings.  Courtney knew she'd either met or talked to each of them during her childhood, but only once or twice.

She then found a burial and a life insurance policy for $60,000, which had been updated recently as it listed her and Bryce as the beneficiaries.  A sealed white envelope with the word Deirdra written on it in Mary's scraggly handwriting lined the bottom of a battered cardboard shoebox.  Courtney opened it and found some Polaroid photographs she'd never seen of her mother wearing an afro in some, a jheri curl in others.  There were pictures from Deirdra's prom and high school graduation—her in a cap and gown standing beside a smiling Mary, who looked like a real person back then, not the shadow Courtney had grown up with.  Then there were other photos, some ripped in two.  Deirdra was draped all over a man—who wasn't Earl Brooks.

The man was handsome, even in those dark, shiny photos; and Deirdra was hanging on tight, nearly smothering him.  Whoever the man was, her mother was in love.  Courtney studied his face because it looked familiar.  The smile, the shape of his head, she imagined him older, without the afro and facial hair. She stood up suddenly and put the photos under a stronger light. The man became Pastor Rick—she was certain of it. *Wow, he said he knew my mother. That was an understatement.*


"Mr. Ricky. Yes, I told you I remembered him. He practically lived with us," Carmen said, when Courtney showed her the photos. "But don't believe these pictures—he and Deirdra fought like crazy people. The cops were always at our house because of them."

"Was I around then?"

"This was all before you were born. Mr. Ricky was in and out of our house for years. Mary couldn't stand him, even back then; but Deirdra got whatever she wanted. Then he disappeared for good, and you came along."

"Where did Earl fit in?"

"She married him, during one of those other times Ricky was gone— maybe he was in jail or something—I don't know. But when Ricky came back around looking for her, she left Earl high and dry. Once she and Ricky had broken up for good, Deirdra's life really went in the gutter. He was probably the last man she was ever crazy about. After that, there were dozens of Mr. Rickys in and out of our house, and Mary did nothing about it. It was a terrible life for me; I was about twelve or thirteen taking care of you and never knew what man would be walking around our house at any given time."

"He's never said anything. There were hints about his past life in some of his sermons but—" Courtney trailed off shaking her head.

"Do you blame him?  If you lived that kind of life, with somebody's momma, would you tell them?"

*What an awful way to die,* Courtney thought to herself while she sat by Mary's bedside.  The old woman had wanted to talk, so she'd had the oxygen mask removed, and was now listening to a chorus of who Mary hated, and who'd done what to her.  Most of the people she talked about were unknown to Courtney, except one.

"I can't stand that Ricky Douglas—that dog—calls his self a preacher.  He got her hooked on that stuff.  Why was I gonna let him take you? Huh? Why should I?  You were all I had left; I wasn't gonna just let *him* take you!"

Courtney had difficulty following her.  The sadness of the waning moments of the old woman's tragic life caused her to sit back in her chair and start to sob.

"Don't go and start that," Mary moaned.  "Move these pillows and help me sit up," she ordered; Courtney sniffed back her tears and did what she was told, then picked up her purse and started to leave.

"Where the hell do you think you're going?  Pour me some water."

Courtney again complied with her request and held the glass while she drank out of it.  When Mary was done, she sat down and waited.

Mary looked down and seemed to be focused on her loud and labored breathing.  After watching for a few minutes, Courtney thought it best to replace the oxygen mask and let her get some rest, but she wanted to talk.

"I wasn't a good parent to you; I know that.  Not what you deserved, anyway.  I didn't mean to be that way...just happened.  I promised myself I'd stop drinkin' and do better; but then the years rolled by, and next thing I knew you were grown, and it was too late to make up the time."  She started coughing then and grasped for the oxygen mask.  Courtney gave it to her, and she inhaled deeply for a few minutes, then moved it to continue.

"I don't expect you to understand, completely.  But you're a mother now," she shrugged.  "...so maybe.  She was my everything: Deirdra."  Her voice then broke, and she came as close to tears as Courtney had ever seen her.  "Her father died in Vietnam, and she was all I had left of him.  My family complained about me spoiling her, and I did, I admit that but...  She was mine and was doing so good.  She got pregnant in high school and had a baby, but that was okay.  She got a good job at the bank and was working on buyin' herself a house.  Then that no good, smooth-talking Ricky Douglas, came along, and she wouldn't go to work no more—she wanted to lay up with him.  He didn't have a pot to piss in, his family wouldn't have nothing to do with him, and she didn't care.  I told her he was on something, but she wouldn't listen to me.  Found out why, cause she was messin' with them drugs too.  The two of them would be in my house all day while I was at work, then go out every night.  She did anything to make money for him.  Then he gets locked up, gets himself straight, and leaves her a mess.  You're all I have left of her.  If he knew about you, he and that uppity mother of his would've come and scooped you up so fast—probably wouldn't even let me see you.  I know it.  I kept up Deirdra's lie, because I knew I wouldn't have to worry about Earl Brooks. Deirdra had done him so wrong, he could barely stand to look at you."

Courtney stared at her, still unsure of what Pastor Rick's mother had to do with anything. She assumed Mary's illness was doing the talking.

"I'm tellin' you all this to say I wanted to love you; I just didn't have much to give. But you got what I could; I swear to that. You're a good girl—and I hated to see that boy messin' over you. It reminded me of that scoundrel Ricky Douglas all over again. But you were smart—smarter than Deirdra. You have your kids and picked yourself up. Proud of you," she coughed.

Courtney got up to embrace her, which was too much intimacy for Mary, who flinched and backed away.

"I was hard on you. I wasn't nice and said things I didn't mean. But when Deirdra left me, I didn't know how to love anymore or be nice. I didn't deserve you, and I'll go to my grave knowing I cheated you—but I did what I could. I was selfish; but God, if he exists, will judge me. I'm askin' you not to." By that time, the effort of drawing each breath was excruciating, and Mary slumped back on the pillows, seemingly satisfied—as if she'd said all she needed to say.

She suddenly sprung forward, before Courtney had the chance to reposition the oxygen mask. "Come to find out that snake knew about you all along. How else could he have showed up out of the thin air when you got sick?"

*God*, Courtney answered in her mind; the only reason he came to see her in the hospital—the only reason they'd met at all was because of her former boss Sophia.

Mary pointed to the oxygen mask and laid back on the pillows as Courtney helped put it in place. She then closed her eyes, and Courtney slipped out of the room.

Her kids happened to be staying with the Douglases that evening.  The conversation with Mary had made her angry and confused, feeling like she'd been wronged in so many ways, without any way of getting back what was stolen from her.  Who was going to give her a mother, and who could make up for the love she'd missed in her childhood?  When she arrived at their door, her anguish was evident.

"Courtney, I'm sorry—is she gone?" Elise asked as she let her in.

"She's hanging in there."

"Then what's—"

"I need to speak with Pastor Rick. Is he here?" She was clutching the manila envelope.

"He's in his office.  Go on in.  The kids are asleep.  When you're finished, your room is ready." Elise knew what Courtney was going to speak with her husband about: Mary had made a deathbed revelation; Rick also had been expecting it.

Courtney walked slowly to the office, and when she got there found the door open and Pastor Rick sitting behind the large mahogany desk talking on the phone.

"Yes, well, you need to keep praying.  If you want God to change the situation, arguing isn't going to do it... uh huh... Yes, I know.  Yes but...but..." He looked up to see Courtney standing in the doorway and motioned her in.

She stepped into the room and headed toward the red leather couch, situated across from the fireplace.  She loved to sit there when she came into his office; they talked—about everything.  He'd been a good friend, big brother and mentor to her.  At a time when she'd badly needed a positive male relationship in her life, he'd treated her like she was family.  She thought of him and Elise as family and had believed God had created something special around them.  Now she had doubts as to his motives and if it was ever about her.  Was the kindness he'd shown motivated by guilt?  What was she to him anyway?  Did he care for her at all?

"I'm not going to give up.  I'm going to keep on praying, and I hope you will too.  I know it sounds cliché, but the truth is it's not your battle anyway.  In fact, you might be in the way.  Alright, then, sir, I've got to go.  My daughter is paying me a visit."  Courtney bristled at his words, although he often referred to her, and others in their church, as his children; this time it sounded different.

Pastor Rick, having noticed Courtney's strange demeanor and the way she was watching him, was only partially listening to the caller on the other line.  One of the problems of his occupation was he often had the same conversation, but with different people.  This caller never listened to him anyway.

"How are you?"  He asked Courtney, who continued standing in front of his desk.

"I've been better."

"Then your grandmother's—"

"Feisty as ever; she's still here."

"Oh," he said, watching her, wondering what was coming next—what Mary had told her.

"I was going through Mary's things the other night, trying to get her affairs in order, and I found these," she handed him the photographs.

"Oh. No," he said cringing and placing his hand over his eyes, at the sight of the scruffy young man he'd been over twenty years ago. "I don't remember these being taken. I sure thought I was the man back then—bet I was high as a kite."

She was baffled at his lack of surprise, as if her walking into his office and showing him pictures of himself with a woman—her mother draped over him—was an everyday occurrence.

"You and my mother—"

"Yes, off and on for years. Until I went to jail—the last time. Finally got clean. I told you I knew your house well. I used to crash there, in those dark, dark days. I was a mess."

"This was quite a shock—you never—"

"I don't like to live back there. When I tell you, they were dark days— you could never imagine. You don't have many memories of your mother, and I wouldn't have been able to give you any good ones. I can tell you she was wild about me. God only knows why. I guess I should have told you that I'd had a talk with Mary, over a year ago. She seems convinced I'm your biological father and accused me of knowing it and that was the reason I turned up. But I never knew Deirdra had ever had another child. Our meeting was strictly God's plan." He then looked her in the eye, and she was annoyed he wasn't saying more. Just as she was about to ask more questions, her cell phone rang. It was the hospital.

"Miss Brooks, your grandmother's taken a turn; you need to get here as soon as possible," the voice on the other line warned.

"I've got to go back," she whispered to Pastor Rick.

He stood and turned off his desk lamp. "I'll drive you."

When they arrived at the hospital, Carmen was already there. Mary lived long enough to scowl when she saw Pastor Rick in her room. He immediately called another one of the pastors of his church to ask her if she wanted to accept Christ before she died, which she agreed to do, to Courtney's relief—and probably more for her benefit. Mary then abruptly ceased breathing, as if she'd said, *enough is enough.*

"She's gone," Carmen said, once they'd all filed into the hospital hallway. "I've spent my life hating that woman. What am I supposed to do now?"

"Love the Lord," Pastor Rick replied to her... "Hate never accomplished anything anyway—did it?"

"*She* didn't care. That's for sure."

Courtney sat on the bench, feeling numb. Mary hadn't been much of a mother but was all she'd known. Losing her was more difficult than she'd imagined it would be. She was unsure how she'd make it out of the hospital, not to mention through the rest of her life.

"Courtney, are you ready to go?" Pastor Rick said to her softly. She looked back at him as if she didn't recognize him but managed to get to her feet.

Carmen embraced her; she didn't return the gesture, feeling distant. In her mind there was no one who could understand how she felt right then, as isolated and alone as when Sean had left her.

"I know you have a lot of questions," Pastor Rick said, later in the car. "I'll answer them for you as best I can, when you're ready. But let's put all that aside, for now. Once this is over, you and me, we'll talk. I can't promise you'll be happy with the truth, but I can promise I'll be completely honest with you."

While he talked, Courtney stared straight ahead.  When they arrived at the house, she jumped out of the car and walked through the door Elise held open, without looking back.

The next morning when Rick walked into the kitchen, Courtney was feeding her children breakfast.  She stiffened when their eyes met.

Instead of conversing, he played with the kids for a while, then poured himself a cup of coffee.  He sat down next to her at the kitchen table.

"Courtney, you have valid reasons for the way you're feeling.  I just wish I could help.  More importantly, I don't want to make things worse."

Something about the gentleness in his voice caused everything she was using to hold herself together to crumble, and she burst into tears the minute his wife entered the kitchen.

Elise ran to her side, embraced her and whispered.  "I've cleared my schedule and I'm all yours today.  We'll get through this together."


"Mary got angry with me because I sat her down and talked about the way she let Deirdra treat her," Courtney's Aunt Darla said to her while sitting at the dining room table.  She was enchanted by the good-natured woman, a few years older than Mary.  She had no memory of her, but Mary had mentioned her occasionally over the years.  As soon as Courtney contacted her, she rushed to the house and took over the funeral arrangements.  The way she devoted herself to helping Courtney made her wonder how she and Mary could've been related.  Mary never did anything for anybody, and Courtney couldn't remember her ever attending a funeral. "When your mother got on drugs, she was terrible, and Mary let her walk all over her. My sister stopped speaking to me; and when Deirdra died, she wouldn't even say anything to us at the funeral. I've called her about twice a year since, but the last few years she stopped even picking up the phone. I still kept trying."

It had been a mere two days since Mary's death; in that time, Courtney met aunts, uncles and cousins who were all new to her. They filled the usually gloomy house with home-cooked meals, flowers, laughter and good-hearted conversation. Given the reclusive life Mary lived, the outpouring of kindness in response to her death was unexpected, overwhelming and made Courtney feel sadness for herself and anger toward Mary; she'd rejected a decent family so she could stay miserable. It was her grandmother's choice, but she'd been the casualty.

At the same time, neither Aunt Darla, nor her two brothers James and Horace, had a negative word to say about their younger sibling. All were too filled with sorrow at the way she'd pushed them from her life, even depriving them of the opportunity to say goodbye. There was no need for Courtney to disclose the last words Mary spoke regarding her family; sadly, they got the message.

"Look, baby," Darla said, holding and squeezing both of Courtney's hands while looking into her eyes. "Mary was a hard woman, and you might feel like life hasn't been fair to you. I feel a little guilty myself, 'cause quite frankly, we forgot about you. I remember you as a baby: pretty little thing with a head full of hair. Then Mary never brought you to see us; we thought you were gone with your father, like Carmen. There's no point crying about the past. You were born at a bad time. It wasn't your fault, but you paid the price anyway. But God knows why, and He doesn't make mistakes."

Courtney nodded, but abruptly pulled her hands away. She'd heard a lifetime's worth of excuses. Seems every day she heard a new one. *Why don't they all, Pastor Rick included, admit they didn't care.*

"This house belongs to you and your brothers," she said, changing the subject.

"Our father left it to us. In our younger days, we tried to get Mary to sell; we wanted the money. She flatly refused, which didn't make our relationship any better. Now I'm glad she didn't listen to us. This place brings back some good memories. My sister wasn't always like she ended up."

Courtney wanted to ask what they intended to do with the house, but then realized it didn't matter. When the time came, the proceeds from Mary's life insurance policy would be enough to help her buy a house. She was looking forward to the change.

"But *when* is Grandma coming back from God's house?" Bryce asked Courtney for the tenth time, the following evening. Sean had done her a favor, by taking the kids off her hands for a few hours on that weeknight, and now they were home. Carmen, who'd come over to help clean the house, held a hand over her mouth to conceal her laughter.

"Bryce, when people go to live with God in heaven, they don't come back. I told you this yesterday," Courtney reminded him. The four-year-old nodded as if he understood, but his interest shifted instantly to the snack his Aunt Carmen handed to him.

Courtney turned to thank Sean and walk him to the door, but noticed he'd settled himself on the living room couch, remote control in hand, and was channel surfing as if he were at home. *Since when does Yolanda allow him to hang out on his own this time of night?* She frowned as she watched him. Things got stranger when after two hours, he'd given the kids baths, read to them, tucked them into bed, then returned to the couch where he kicked off his shoes and stretched out. Carmen noticed, gave Courtney dirty looks, then hung around well after their work was done, waiting for him to leave.

Finally Courtney, ready to retire for the night, walked to where he was sprawled on the couch and stood over him, her arms folded. "What's going on?"

"I need a favor, "he whispered, so Carmen couldn't hear. "I'm having some problems at home and need a place to stay for a couple days. Since you've got plenty of space, I thought maybe...I won't get in your way."

"Forget it. I'm not taking any crap off your wife," Courtney shook her head.

"It's not like that anymore. When she puts me out, she doesn't come looking for me. She gave up on that a while ago. She won't find me if I don't want to be found."

Courtney rolled her eyes but left him on the couch, knowing she should send him to a hotel; it was way out of line for him to ask her for such a thing. By the time Carmen finally left, however, he was sound asleep, and she was too tired to be bothered.

Mary had a viewing and memorial at the mortuary on Friday morning, after which there was a brief graveside service, followed by a family dinner held in the fellowship hall of the Life in the Word Christian Center, Pastor Douglas's church, later that afternoon. Sean took the entire day off work and stayed by Courtney's side, holding on to the kids for her. Anyone who didn't know thought the four of them a beautiful family. Those who did know watched them closely, their faces wearing the same question: *Where's his wife?*

While at the grave site, Courtney somberly looked upon her mother's grave for the first time. A heaviness enshrouded her, but not for Mary. Mary was where she wanted to be: in the grave. Courtney could only hope she was spending eternity where she wanted to be also, because there was no turning back now. Those around her began making their way to the waiting vehicles; but she stood glued to the spot, grieving the mother and childhood she'd never had.

"As bad as the past has been, the future can be that much better. The past is dead and gone; we don't have to live in it. None of us."

Courtney looked at Pastor Rick, eyes blazing. Who asked him to stand with her at her mother's grave, or try to comfort her? She hated him, at that moment, for so many reasons. "It was easy enough for you to walk away; you were a grown man. Children stay trapped; they don't have that option," Courtney spat, then pushed past him to the waiting limousine.

After dinner was over, several of her family members came over to the house for coffee and dessert. They joked and told family stories; some of them even included Mary and Deirdra. Courtney felt she was peering into a part of her own life she'd been excluded from.  As family members started trickling out, with their promises to keep in touch, she felt a growing since of loss—the life that could never be re-claimed slipping further through her fingers.  Soon she and her children would be alone again.

"What's been up with you today, I mean besides the obvious?"  Sean quizzed her, taking a seat at the table.  He'd found her sitting in the kitchen alone, brooding.  "I've been watching you.  You've been downright rude to your pastor.  What did he do?"

She shook her head and twisted her mouth.  "Oh, I just found out some things that…"

"Like what things?"

"Mary had some old pictures stashed away.  I went through them and found some Polaroids of him and my mother.  He told me he knew her—but not that well."

"And?"

"Mary swore on her deathbed that she's believed all these years he's my father.  I guess that's why she kept his pictures.  She sure couldn't stand him."  Sean raised his eyebrows and shrugged.

"Don't you get it?  I thought he was here for me, but he's not.  According to Mary, he helped me because he feels guilty about leaving Deirdra 23 years ago.  He's trying to make amends for his past; I just happen to be a part of it."

Sean watched as she teared up again and kissed her cheek, just as Carmen walked in.

Courtney's sister shot him a look that had daggers all over it. "Isn't it time for you to go and find your wife?"

"Why? She's not lost," Sean said standing. "Anyway, I've gotta go into the office." He smiled at Carmen as he eased by her. "You have a lovely day."

Carmen scowled at him, then at Courtney, before leaving the kitchen.


"We're going to talk this week, okay?" Pastor Rick said to Courtney at the door, attempting to get her to look at him.

She didn't want to look at or talk to him. Her whole perception of him had changed. Did he think she was supposed to love him or be grateful to him when she knew he simply pitied her? She didn't need his pity. Each time he'd attempted to converse with her during that day, she'd walked away. He and Elise remained at the house with her, however, almost until the last guest had gone home.

"Maybe," Courtney said with a shrug, after embracing Elise, still refusing to make eye contact with him.

Then she was alone. Angela took the kids with her, and Carmen was the last to leave.

At some point during the ordeal, she'd stopped talking to God and everyone else. It was too hard; she was too confused. Everything was bottled up and her confidence in the one person she usually talked to was shaken, because he'd had an affair with her mother before she was born. *Does that have anything to do with me?* She was lost, alone and convinced she'd always be –Mary's legacy.

It was who she'd had raised her to be; and no matter how hard she tried; escape was impossible.  How was she now supposed to raise children who made the right choices and did the right things?

She sat on the couch for hours, curled up in a ball, her mind sinking into the past, replaying every hurtful thing Mary had ever said to her.

The phone rang, jarring her back to the present.  She sat still, letting the call go to voicemail. When she checked the caller ID, it was Sean.  He'd been with her, supporting her, most of that day and it felt good to have him around—too good.  Now he was calling her well after midnight.  A few moments later, there was a knock at her door.

She opened it a few inches and stared at him silently.

"I was just checking on you.  It was a tough day; thought maybe you need some company."

"I'm okay, thanks" she replied, barely above a whisper.

Even with the lights off, he could see the puffiness around her eyes.

He put his hand on the door and pushed it open a little wider.  "I know you've become this strong fortress of a woman, and the last person in the world you need is me—but I *am* here now.  It's not weakness to choose a little company over loneliness, if you have that choice."

She sighed and stood back as Sean walked slowly into the house.  He closed the door, then reached for her.  She buried her face in his chest and sobbed, while he stroked her back, rocking her gently.

When the tears stopped, she stood back.  "I'm sorry about that," she pointed to his wet shirt.

"No problem, I needed a shower anyway," he grinned, while removing his jacket.

Her emotions switched to longing, and he saw it in her eyes. When he reached for her, he covered her mouth with his, and she returned the kiss hungrily.

She heard the warnings in her head, but mentally pressed a mute button, giving herself permission to be selfish like everyone else in her life.

In bed hours later, with Sean dozing next to her, the mute button was gone and the guilt of her failure—with Yolanda's husband of all people—rained down on her. *Now how do I get rid of him? No way I'm getting mixed up with him again...*

He awoke when he felt her stirring, turned on his side and found her laying on her back staring blankly at the ceiling. His own feelings of guilt crept in. He'd taken advantage of her weakened state, and now he was ready to go home. He had nothing to offer and no place in his life for her. Amazing how much you can think you want something until you get it....

He stroked her thigh, yet she was unresponsive to his touch. "Are you okay?"

"Yes."

"Are you angry with me? I guess I shouldn't have come over."

"No."

"What happens now?"

"Nothing."

He sighed before rolling over and checking the clock sitting on the dresser; he wondered if he dared show up at home that time of the morning, would Yolanda give him hell. He decided against trying and dozed off peacefully, relieved about one thing: Courtney had no new expectations of him he'd fail to live up to.


"I've been doing a lot of thinking, since the night your grandmother died," Pastor Rick said, his hands resting, clasped on the table in front of him. He and Courtney were seated facing each other at a restaurant near her job. He'd shown up there unexpectedly at lunch hour. "I've kicked myself, repeatedly, for not saying what I should've said—what you needed me to say. But I must admit I don't know what that is. I've tried to be here for you. Tell me what else you want me to do."

Courtney sat forward in her chair and crossed her arms, "Leave me alone. Live your life and stop using me to try to make amends for your past. I'm not your pet project anymore and I don't need your pity. I appreciate all you've done, and I'll always be grateful, but you haven't fixed anything. The past is still what it is. You're wasting your time."

He sat back and stared at her, nodding slowly, while the waiter placed drinks and a basket of bread on the table. He remained silent for some time.

"You've got it all wrong."

She sucked air through her teeth and shook her head, evading his eyes.

He moved to the seat directly to her right, so she wouldn't miss what he had to say.  Then the waiter appeared to take their order.  Rick ordered for them both while she fumbled with the silverware and the straw in her glass.

Once the waiter left, he observed Courtney's gestures, thinking how ironic it was she was behaving like the Deirdra he remembered.  "I knew your mother most of her life."  That statement drew her attention to him.  "We attended all of the same schools.  I didn't grow up far from where you live.  She was pretty, like you, and I was crazy about her.  We dated some in high school; but then she got hooked up with Kenny Franklin, got pregnant, and that was that.  We didn't meet up again until about ten years after graduation.  Unfortunately, by then, I was in the midst of a drug addiction.  She was working at the bank and was bored with her life.  She became interested in me, I guess, because I was wild.  I think she found me exciting; but to be honest, I was the worst thing that could've happened to her."  The waiter brought their plates, but neither of them looked down.  "Anyway, I was wasting my life doing drugs, living off anyone who'd let me; my family had long since given up on me, and there's Deirdra.  All she wanted to do was take care of me and make me happy.  She'd never done any real drugs until she started hanging out with me and began using cocaine and crack just to keep up with me.  She knew I was only interested in women who lived that kind of life."

"Did you love her?"  Courtney asked.  The question startled him, and he frowned.

"I was a drug addict; my only love was drugs.  I didn't care about anybody, really.  Not even myself."

"She didn't realize that?"

Rick shrugged. "Miss Mary tried to tell her. The more she warned her about me, the less Deirdra listened. That's why I couldn't blame Mary for how she felt about me. Believe me, back then I destroyed many lives; that's what addiction does. That's why I'm so passionate about saving lives now. The thing I pray for every day is that the Lord uses me to heal more lives than I've destroyed. I believe he's granted me that. That's all I've tried to do with you. I don't need to make amends for my past. What have I told you repeatedly? The past is nailed to the cross."

He picked up his silverware and began eating. Courtney watched him for a time, then did the same.

"Anyway, let me finish this sad story. Deirdra eventually was fired from her job at the bank because she stopped going in; work was interfering with her time with me. We lived off her savings for a while, but for addicts that didn't last long. Then she had to find other ways to make money that weren't nine to five, because if she wasn't around, I was likely to find another *friend*, and she wouldn't see me again for weeks. She worked in strip clubs for a while and from there started taking on side jobs, after hours, from some of the club clientele —which paid better. You get what I'm saying."

She nodded. "You're not telling me something I didn't know."

"We lived an awful filthy life, then I got busted for possession. Went to jail for two years and didn't hear a word from Deirdra. I'd try to call her, and neither she nor Mary would accept the charges. Jail turned out to be the best thing for me because I got the drugs out of my system, found God, and cleaned up my life. That was in 1984. Is that the year you were born?"

Courtney nodded.

"I got out of jail and went to find Deirdra, but she wouldn't have anything to do with me. She was as hostile as Mary was. The truth is, I could be your biological father. She gave birth to you while I was in jail, and as you know I have two other children around your age. Given the way Deirdra made a living at the time, there's only one way to know for sure. I guess you need to decide how important it is for you to know."

She stared back at him.

"Will it really make such a difference? Elise and I feel that since the day the Lord brought you into our lives, we've been more than blessed. It just doesn't matter to us who your daddy is. Look, I know I ruined your mother's life. Sure, she had a hand in it; but so did I. When I knew you were her daughter, it was difficult. Remembering her brought back a lot of bad memories of who I used to be. But I was happy also, because God gave me the chance to do good for someone I'd wronged so badly. I think I treat you like you're mine, don't I?"

Courtney nodded. There was no denying he and Elise had become her parents.

"As far as God and I are concerned, you are my daughter; no blood test is going to change that. My wife and I are so proud of who you are and who you're becoming. But whatever you want me to do to prove I'm in your life for as long as I live, I'll do. I've put you in my will, and I'll take a test whenever you decide. I just want you to be happy. I want you to know who you are, to know you have a family and that you're a part of my life."

His words, one after the other, chipped away the wall of resentment she'd built towards him since finding the photos of him and her mother, until she couldn't find that anger anymore.  It was gone.  She covered her face with her hands and took a deep breath.  When she removed them, she found herself smiling, her heart no longer burdened with the strife that comes from pride.

Rick saw her smile and briefly smiled in return.  He then cleared his throat and furrowed his brow.  "Now that we're talking again…what's going on with you and Sean?"

# Chapter Seventeen

"They're separated, and I don't know where he's living," Angela said to Courtney, over the phone. "My concern is I haven't seen my grandbabies in over a month. Please bring them to me and pack their overnight bag."

*Thank you, Lord,* Courtney thought. Sean had been AWOL from his parenting weekends for months, which meant she hadn't had a break. Carmen and the rest of Sean's family were great when she was in a bind but having to beg for childcare was getting old. She'd called Angela only to see if she'd heard from him. The news of his separation, while she believed it inevitable, was a surprise.

*I wonder where he's living,* she thought, grateful he hadn't shown up at her door.

The rest of the details broke and the phone lines heated up weeks later after one of Sean's family members saw in the public record, he was seeking a restraining order against Yolanda. He'd moved in with his boss Mindy and was complaining his estranged wife was stalking them.

After the restraining order was granted, Yolanda chose another method of attack: Sean's career. She marched into the engineering firm where he worked and met with human resources. They in turn alerted the managing partners to the affair between Sean and Mindy. After lengthy meetings, Mindy was given a slap on the wrist; Sean was given the opportunity to resign. They gave him thirty days to find a new job; but Mindy, embarrassed by the revelation of their affair, gave him less time than that to move out of her place.

A month after leaving Yolanda, Sean was out of a job, needed a place to live, and couldn't remember the last time he'd seen his kids.  Then things got worse.


*Why does that guy keep looking over here?*  Sean asked himself, while seated at a stool at one of his favorite happy hour spots.  He wondered if the alcohol was making him paranoid, but he hadn't had much to drink yet—not as much as he planned to.  *He doesn't look gay, but then these days you never know...*It then seemed to him another guy with him was watching him too.  Feeling uncomfortable, he dropped some bills down on the bar and decided to go and drown his sorrows elsewhere.  *Is it my imagination, or did they both get up as soon as I did?*  He headed for the parking lot.

He was about to enter his car when one of the men approached.

"Hey, man, how ya doin'?  Aren't you Mike, used to live over by—"

"Naw, I'm not Mike," he said, noticing too late the other guy had crept up behind him.

When he turned back to the first guy, his eyes widened. "What the—" he said, seeing the fist coming toward his head.  The blow landed on his left temple; then the other man unloaded on his right jaw.  Sean started swinging wildly, until one of them grabbed his arms, restraining him.

"You wife says she wants your pretty face messed up," the first man said, as he punched his nose and mouth repeatedly.  Sean tasted blood.  After a barrage of blows mostly to his face, he heard a woman scream from somewhere in the parking lot.  His assailants let him tumble to the ground, climbed into a waiting vehicle, and sped away.

"Are you okay, sir?" he heard a man ask. "They messed you up pretty good. Did they take anything?"

Sean tried to answer but passed out as he heard more voices around him.


"Hello, I'm looking for Mrs. Angela McNair...Ma'am, this is the Mercy Hospital emergency room. We have Mr. Sean McNair here. It appears he's been a victim of an attack and has asked that we notify you. I wouldn't say he's okay, but his injuries are not life-threatening. He's being treated for some deep lacerations and a fractured nose. He's being sutured now and can leave as soon as the doctor releases him. He'll require transportation. You're welcome."

"Sean, what happened?" Angela exclaimed, as she rushed to his bedside, close to tears seeing his bruised and swollen face.

"Yoyanna," he said, his mouth sounding full of marbles.

"What—Yolanda? She didn't do this," Angela said. "How could she?" Sean laid back on the bed and didn't answer. There was no way she could've understood him had he tried.


While Sean recuperated at Angela's, he had several visitors. Mindy came by to drop off his belongings, retrieve her house key, and to tell him he'd still be paid for the remainder of the thirty days, but no longer had a job. His father-in-law, Ronnie, also came to see him.

"Boy, you sure made a mess of things." he said, studying Sean's wounds. "You're healing up well, though.  My daughter won't be too happy about that."  He then sat down opposite him and shook his head.  "Tell me why—why'd you have to blow everything to hell? —Huh?"

"I wanted to give Yolanda a good reason to divorce me.  I don't want anything from her; I just want to be free.  Figured if she were pissed off enough, she'd go ahead and do it."

Ronnie sat back in the chair and squinted at the younger man.  "Games? Is that what this is all about?  You're playing games.  Damn, boy, I thought you were smarter than that."

He wanted to defend himself –tell the older man about all the games his daughter played—but knew it was better to stay silent.  It didn't pay to offend Ronnie.

"Look, you know I've always liked you; I'm gonna do you *one* favor. Screw it up and you're on your own.  I have a job lined up for you in San Diego, and I suggest you take it.  When you've both had some time and space, you come back and settle things."

"What? California?"  Sean said, sitting up.

"That's what I said and I'm hoping that's far enough.  First, you've got to agree to drop the case against my daughter and disappear.  I need your answer here and now."

"Le-let me--" he stumbled over his words.  He had nothing left where he was, and a fresh start would be nice.  But then he'd let Yolanda off the hook, after she'd tried to have him killed.  The case he'd filed against her wasn't going anywhere anyway.  Ronnie would make sure of that.

"Here and now, Sean," Ronnie demanded, glancing at his watch.  He then stood.  "What's it going to be?"

"Yeah, okay.  I'll take it," Sean threw up his hands.  What choice did he have?

"Smart decision," Ronnie said, and they shook hands.  "Your new employer will be in contact shortly.  You're going to have to move fast, so start packing."

"Did I hear right?  You're moving to California?" Angela said, walking into the den, after Ronnie had gone.

"Yes.  I'm leaving."

Ronnie said things would move fast, and he was right.  The following week, Sean received a new employee packet, complete with his plane ticket.  He had two weeks to report to work.  The executive search department arranged to ship all his belongings, including his vehicle.  When he arrived, he would be provided accommodations at an extended-stay hotel, while corporate relocation services looked for an apartment.  He would walk into this new engineering firm as an executive with a salary considerably more than the job he'd left.  The bottom line was he was being paid off in exchange for quietly disappearing out of Yolanda's life.  He was fine with that.

"I'm sorry about the way things have turned out," Sean said to Courtney, a week before he was scheduled to leave. "I'm hoping you'll let me take you out for an evening, without the kids, as a final goodbye." They were standing near the kitchen door of Angela's house. Courtney was dropping off the kids so they could spend the next few days with their dad before his departure.

"Thanks for the offer, but no. It's not necessary," she said, her face expressionless. She was in no mood to serenade him out of town. Because of his selfish actions, her children would be forced to settle for a long-distance father; he wasn't that good of a short-distance one.

"Please. This is the last chance we'll have to see each other for a while. I'm going to try to get back for Cori's birthday, but I'm not sure I'll be able to," he pleaded, lightly touching her elbow. "I am going to miss you." He'd been hoping for a passionate goodbye, from the one person he believed still loved him. No one else cared one way or the other that he was leaving town.

She turned to him, wanting to yawn. "Unfortunately, I don't go out with married men; and last I checked..." she quipped, then turned toward the door.

"That's just a formality," he said, following her, then holding his hand on the door before she could open it. "Courtney, I know I've messed up, but I want you to think about us. Maybe the four of us can make a fresh start in California. Once my situation is settled."

She tugged the door open and walked through it without turning around. Behind her she heard him say goodbye; then the door closed quietly.

*DING DONG!! pound.... pound.... pound! DING DONG! DING DONG! pound...*

*pound!*

*Who the devil is that?* Courtney said to herself, as she grabbed her robe. Her first thought was Sean after a night of drinking, but he'd been in California for six months.

She turned on the porch light, looked out the window and saw the familiar black Mercedes parked crookedly behind her Nissan, and wanted to scream.

"Yolanda, what are you—" her words were lost at the sight of Mrs. McNair propped up against the door jamb, looking ready to collapse at any moment.  Her hair and clothes were disheveled; she smelled of alcohol and vomit.

"I'm sick.  I can't let anyone see me—" she sobbed, stopping mid-sentence while staggering into Courtney's living room.

Courtney tried to feel compassion for her, but instead was annoyed at being awakened at that time of morning by a drunk.

"What do you want, Yolanda?  You look awful.  It's a wonder you didn't kill yourself and someone else, driving in your condition."

"Stop yelling at me!  Where's your bathroom?  I'm feeling sick."

Courtney pushed her into the bathroom and closed the door.  She planned to call a cab but decided to wait until Yolanda was feeling better.  When she checked on her fifteen minutes later, she was passed out on the floor beside the toilet.

"Why me?" Courtney moaned, and dragged the woman out of the bathroom as best she could, to a spot on the carpet, next to what had been Mary's bed. She placed a blanket over her, a bucket next to her, kept the hallway lights on and went upstairs to her own bed.

"Oh God. My head is hurting so bad, I can't open my eyes. You wouldn't have anything for a hangover, would you?"

"Ibuprofen is the best I can do."

"People who don't drink make me sick," she groaned, while Bryce and Cori stood in front of her staring like she was a television show.

"Do you need me to drive you home or something?" Courtney asked.

"No, just grab my phone out of my purse and call Renate. She'll take care of me."

"You didn't show up with a purse, Yolanda."

"What? You're kidding. My life is in there. Do you mind going and looking in my car?"

"Yes, I mind," Courtney snapped, irritated that Yolanda was ordering her around in her own house.

"Fine, then." She stood up in a huff, but the brisk movement made her dizzy. She straightened herself as much as she could, and became aware of her soiled, crumpled clothes. Instead of risking being seen in such a state, she picked up the phone sitting nearby, and called her assistant.

After hanging up, she sat in the chair, crossing her legs, "What's your problem? Why are you so testy today? Oh, I forgot my husband has left town, hasn't he? You haven't had any."

"You can wait for Renate outside. I didn't invite you over here and I don't have to put up with—"

"Relax. I'm just joking with you. Girl, when I drink too much, it's no telling what I'll do or where I'll end up. I was at this party, and after a few drinks I started feeling bad—about things. Then I left and went to this little out of the way bar I used to frequent; then I came over here cause I needed to talk."

"Talk—to me, why?" Courtney wondered if Yolanda knew about her one night slip up with Sean. The one she'd promised to confess to her—one day.

"I guess I felt you could understand."

"What, because we were dumped by the same man?" Courtney said, taking a seat in a chair at the table. Her kids, still in their pjs, had toys spread all over the dining room and were playing loudly. The noise was tormenting Yolanda's aching head; but she knew if she asked Courtney to tell them to be quiet, she'd get kicked out for real. Still she wondered how Courtney lived with it.

"I wasn't dumped."

"No girlfriend you were kicked to the curb—hard—and for a white woman."

Yolanda grimaced, then started removing her soiled outfit. "Can I have a robe?"

"Can you stop giving orders," Courtney admonished, then crinkled her nose "—fetch me this—fetch me that. Go home!"

The doorbell then rang.  Courtney opened it for Renate, who flashed in carrying an overnight bag.

"I humbly request permission to use your shower," Yolanda mocked, with an exaggerated bow.

Courtney rolled her eyes while Yolanda sauntered to the bathroom.  She emerged wearing a loose-fitting jogging suit and carrying the clothes she'd been wearing in a bundle.

"Can you—" she started to say to Courtney, who glared at her.  "I'll just take these to a Dumpster."

Courtney expected her to leave, but instead she sat down again at the dining room table.  "I'm hungry.  Renate, can you go—"

"What do ya want?"  Renate asked, handing Yolanda her purse.  Yolanda pulled out a crisp fifty-dollar bill.  Renate took the money, the bundle of dirty clothes, and left the house to get Yolanda's breakfast.  She returned in ten minutes with coffee and breakfast for everybody; Courtney noticed Yolanda received no change from the fifty bucks.

"You know what, Yolanda, it's been an interesting visit; but the next time you want to crash somewhere at three in the morning, don't come here.  Now, I don't mean to be rude, but if you don't mind—"

"Spare me. If it'd been my husband making a booty call, everything would've been alright."

Courtney's eyes widened, "Is that why you came over here at three a.m.: To accuse me of your husband, again?"

"I know he was here, when your grandmother died."

Courtney looked back at her silently, determined not to lie. Evading the question was one thing; but if Yolanda was determined to know, she felt it was only right to tell her.

Yolanda saw the admission in her eyes and nodded. "Thank you for clearing that up. You certainly weren't the only one. No, I would say you were way down on that list," she said, her features softening. She dropped down into the chair next to the sofa. "Truth is, I'm so screwed up. I've lost control, Courtney, I mean really lost control. And I don't even understand myself. I need to talk and you're the only person I know—"

"Who came unglued because of a man?"

"It's just that you got yourself back together. I'll be honest, I thought you were pitiful, the way you fell apart. But you picked yourself up, and I don't know if I can."

"Yolanda, I didn't do anything. God put me back together. I'm not perfect. I've messed up, but He hasn't given up on me."

They sat in silence, as Courtney prayed for the right thing to say, to make the conversation about Him and not about Sean, or either of them.

"I've done a lot of things I'm not proud of, and God has forgiven me, and He keeps on doing so. He can do the same for you."

Yolanda exhaled deeply and stood. "Thank you," she said, amazed that after having sessions with her therapist almost daily for weeks, she hadn't found the relief she felt at that moment. There was something about Courtney Brooks, a peace that seemed to be contagious.

"Make sure you talk to God about what you're going through. I promise you'll see things differently."

Yolanda smiled genuinely, something Courtney realized she rarely did. Always so under control, even her facial expressions seemed orchestrated much of the time. "I'm going to do that."

She went to the wall, checked her reflection in the large mirror in the living room, tousled her hair a bit, slid on her oversized designer sunglasses and grabbed her keys. "I need to go. Look Courtney, I'm having a party for my dad's birthday next weekend. Why don't you get a babysitter and come as my guest?"

Courtney raised her eyebrows, "I don't know if I'll fit in –"

"Get off it. With your looks you don't have to fit in. As a matter of fact, why would you want to?"


The next weekend, Courtney found herself walking alone, along a lighted pathway which led to the outdoor pavilion of the Majestic Pearl restaurant; headed to a gathering of people, none of whom she knew or wanted to know. They weren't her type of crowd. Still, it was a beautiful August evening, and she happened to be sporting the perfect outfit; a past Christmas gift from Yolanda she'd never worn. The off the shoulder, form-fitting black and gold cocktail dress—tasteful as well as alluring—had come in handy.

As confident as she was in her appearance, she hated the thought of being around people who would judge her by how expensively she was dressed and if she had any high-profile friends. Yolanda didn't get Courtney's apprehension because she refused to acknowledge how much of a snob she was herself. As she drew closer to the music and noise of the party, she was preparing herself for an evening surrounded by 200 or so wealthy people who were full of themselves.

Two tall manicured hedges framed the entryway onto the patio, and she hid behind one of them while searching the crowd for Yolanda. Unable to locate her, she inched slowly into the entrance.

"Miss Brooks," she heard a man's voice, and turning, saw Yolanda's father smiling brightly and sauntering toward her.

"I was so honored when my daughter told me you'd be attending, but why are you hiding back here?"

He held out his hand, and Courtney accepted it, smiling uncontrollably; his smile was so sincere, he made her feel welcomed. She wondered how he remembered her, as she only recalled meeting him briefly on one other occasion. But then there was the night of Sean's wedding.

"I'm not exactly hiding, Mr. Brown. I'm looking for Yolanda," she said, still smiling coyly. "By the way, Happy Birthday."

"It is now that you're here, and might I say you look exquisite this evening. Why don't we find your table and get you some refreshments? The food is wonderful."

"Really, Mr. Brown, you don't have to—"

"Call me Ronnie," he said, then held out his arm for her. She linked her arm with his and let him lead her through the center of the crowd of party guests, who seemed to step aside for him. "Yes," he said, stopping at a table where she saw her name on a place-card. "You've definitely brightened up this place."

"Why *look* at you. You're making out just fine. To think I was worried about you," Yolanda exclaimed, when she found Courtney a half hour later.

"You don't have to worry about Courtney," Ronnie said, patting her hand, before she could answer. "I'll take good care of her."

"Behave yourself," Yolanda clenched her teeth as she pinched her father's arm. It reminded Courtney of how she warned her children when they misbehaved in public. He responded by laughing, then heading to the bar.


"My daughter says you're in the market for a house," Ronnie said to Courtney, later over dinner. He'd insisted on having her moved to his table, and she was now seated directly across from him, to the disappointment of one of his business guests. "I'm usually privy to some of the best real estate bargains in town. If you're interested, I can have one of my employees get a list of properties for you."

"That would be great. I've started working with an agent. But I really feel like I don't know what I'm doing."

"Just leave it to me. I know people who can steer you in the right direction," he winked, just as Yolanda showed up and whisked her away.

"I'm sorry. I invited you as my guest, then abandoned you. There were so many details I had to tend to. Are you having a good time?"

Courtney nodded. "Your father's very charming."

Yolanda's eyes rolled up; she grumbled something under her breath Courtney couldn't make out, while dragging her to join a group of her friends.

After fifteen minutes, Courtney started looking at her watch and preparing her excuse to leave; then Ronnie found her again and ushered her inside the restaurant to have a drink with him.

"So, tell me about you, Miss Courtney," Ronnie said, taking a sip of what she guessed was cognac. He'd been drinking non-stop during the two hours she'd been at the party, but the alcohol didn't appear to affect him. They were sitting away from the noise, but with a full view of the festivities on the patio.

"I have two kids. I'm a student at State University and a lab assistant at the hospital. End of story."

"And when you're not working and going to school?"

"I'm home with my kids or I'm at my church. What about you?"

"I work all the time. Everything I do, everywhere I go is about work, and even tonight is really work. I've been married twice. If I could commit to a woman the way I've committed to my career, I'd still be married; but that hasn't happened, and I guess it won't."

Courtney sipped her soda silently, when he asked, "Can we have lunch sometime?"

*Absolutely not is* what she thought; but instead of speaking, shrugged her shoulders while stirring the lime around in her glass.

He smiled and studied her. "Are you involved with someone?"

"No."

"Still hung up on my soon to be ex-son-in-law?"

"Who?" She frowned and he laughed.

She was beautiful—but too young; then there was that awkward family connection.  Ronnie knew he should leave her alone.  He also needed to stop drinking, smoking cigars, and cursing; but none of those things had killed him yet.  Suddenly an idea came to him, and he pulled out his cell phone from his dinner jacket.  "Hey Erica, I'm inside at my usual table.  Can you join me, please?  Just for a moment.  Thank you."

Within seconds, a woman was standing at their table.

"Courtney, this is Erica, my executive assistant.  Erica, this is Courtney and we're going to help her find a house."

Erica was a light-skinned, full-figured woman with freckles and large dark eyes that spoke volumes.  Those eyes gave Courtney a quick sweep, from head to toe without blinking; she then turned to Ronnie with a smirk and said, "Yessuh—whatever you say, boss."  Unaffected by her sarcasm, he gave her instructions, then left the table while Erica collected Courtney's contact information.  When he returned, Erica made a show of snapping her purse shut, then folded her arms.  "Is there anything else?" she rolled her eyes and walked away without waiting for an answer.


Three months later, Ronnie called Courtney at work.  "Congratulations, they've accepted your offer.  You're a new homeowner.  You can come over to my office to sign the papers at noon today, and I'll take you out to lunch to celebrate."

It was the third time she'd visited Ronnie's office in the last month, and they'd had lunch together twice. She hadn't planned on seeing him so much, but once he'd volunteered his resources to help her find a house, he'd made himself a part of the bargain. She liked it.

"This is the price you're paying for the house," Ronnie pointed out the numbers as he handed Courtney the sales contract. Even though the details were no surprise to her, the deal being completed so quickly had her dumbstruck, along with the final price, which was less than half of what the house was worth.

"How'd you manage this?"

"The owner needed to get rid of it and owed me some favors. Also, my inspector found some things in the foundation. Nothing you need to worry about, of course; but they gave us bargaining power. He's going to take care of those issues, along with refinishing the floors, replacing the upstairs carpeting, and they're also throwing in some custom window coverings. Overall, you've got one hell of a deal, if I do say so myself."

She shook her head, while still paging through the contract. "I don't know how to thank you."

"Don't give it a thought; this is what I do every day," he said with a wave of his hand, then leaned back in his chair. "On second thought—I'm in need of an escort for Friday night. If you'd do me the honor, I'd be grateful. There's a renowned jazz artist giving a concert which I have VIP tickets for. Promise I'll have you home early."

She put the contract down and folded her arms.  He was smooth and subtle, but they'd had an understanding: there would be no dates.  He'd made it clear he wasn't looking for another wife, and she wasn't in the market for a lover. But as she was starting to learn, agreements didn't matter to him. He did what he wanted—always with charm and finesse.  Which made it difficult for her to refuse.

"Maybe... if I can get a sitter."

"Renate will do it, I assure you; and if it will help, I'll cover the cost."

She bit her lower lip, then threw the contract onto the desk and exhaled loudly.  "Okay, let me know what time and where to meet you."

His desk phone rang at that moment, and he answered it.  He paused the conversation. "Work that out with Erica and—sorry, looks like I have to renege on lunch."

"I guess I'll see you Friday then," Courtney stood to leave.

"I can't wait."  He took a moment to grin and let her know he was watching her walk out of the office before becoming businesslike and returning to his phone call.

As she sat at her desk at work, she couldn't help thinking how weird it was she was going on a date with Sean's father-in-law.  Courtney also wondered what Yolanda would think about it and guessed she wouldn't like it much.  It didn't matter what she or anyone else thought, she concluded, since it was just one night.

# Chapter Eighteen

"Excuse me," Sean said to the flight attendant, a petite Asian woman, who'd noticed him boarding the flight.  As she walked towards him, his eyes scanned her figure before making their way back up to her face.  He then read her name tag, "Margo, I love that name.  My name is Sean, and I have a fear of flying.  I might require special attention, if you're available."  He winked, and she smiled back.

"Thank you for warning me, Sean," she purred, then lightly brushed his hand.  "I'll do what I can."

"I bet you will," he replied as the two of them shared a giggle before Margo went about her duties.

Sean loved San Diego—his job, the weather and the women—definitely the women.  Now he was headed back home for a visit, his first in over a year, for his baby girl's third birthday.  He also had a few legal matters to take care of with his soon to be ex-wife Yolanda.  As the plane taxied from the gate, he placed headphones over his ears and closed his eyes, wondering what Courtney had been up to during the year he'd been away.  He'd intended for the two of them to talk, but that had never happened.  His effort had been minimal, but so had been her interest the few times they'd spoken.  He assumed that, as a single mother, a relationship with him or anyone else would be her last priority.

"There's my handsome baby," Angela exclaimed, clutching Sean so tight it felt like she was going to squeeze the life out of him.  "I've missed you so much."

"It hasn't been that long, Mom," he said, loving her rare display of affection. He'd just walked into the house from the airport; and his mother, clutching her purse, was nudging him to the door again.

"We've got to go. Can you drive? I need to take this food over to Courtney's." She pointed to three densely packed boxes.

"Why is the party at her house, if you're bringing all the food?"

"I'm not bringing *all* the food. Just a few of her favorites. This is her first time entertaining in her new house. Wait till you see it."

While he drove, his mother chatted, bringing him up to speed on everybody except Yolanda and Courtney. He wondered if it was because the two of them were now supposedly friends, and perhaps she'd helped Courtney get a deal on the house. When it came to real estate, Yolanda and her father had inside knowledge of unbelievable deals. He regretted not making some investments of his own during his marriage. In fact, what had he accomplished while married to Yolanda, besides blowing a ton of cash on clothes, jewelry and travel? He was still asking himself that question when his mother directed him to pull into the driveway of Courtney's house.

He looked at the front of the modern brick home and was impressed both by Courtney's choice of a home, and her drive to succeed. The house was in a great neighborhood for his kids. She'd also told him she was in the last semester of her bachelor's degree and would be entering medical school in the fall.

Toting the boxes, he followed his mother around to the back yard where he spotted Nina and Courtney cooking at a large barbecue grill off to one side of the spacious patio. Children dressed in bathing suits were running around everywhere, and there were two above ground swimming pools set up in the rear of the yard.

They mounted the deck stairs and went into the kitchen, where he helped unpack the boxes.  Eventhough he knew most of the adults he'd seen milling about, he felt uneasy and out of place--like he'd entered a world he was no longer part of.  He was expecting an eventful day, particularly when Yolanda and her boyfriend Sam arrived.

Through the open door he heard his son's voice, "He's here, Mommy!  I saw him."

"Hey! How's my man?"  Sean said, stepping out onto the deck.  Courtney blinked with surprise.

"Daddy!"  Bryce screamed, running into Sean's arms.

Courtney smiled and, while he was busy hugging Bryce, she got an eye full of Sean.  He'd cut his light brown hair shorter than she'd ever seen it and had regained the muscular physique he'd let slip while being married to Yolanda.  The tank top he was wearing showed off the California tan that had turned his body a golden shade of bronze.  He looked good—so good, she wanted to keep looking, but stopped herself in case he caught her.  He already believed himself to be the object of her every waking moment.  She then remembered they had a daughter running around somewhere.

"Asia, bring Cori over here," she called to Jay's oldest daughter.

"Cori, look, it's a surprise!  Your dad's here for your birthday," Courtney said.

Cori was wearing a pink metallic one-piece bathing suit, large pink sparkly sunglasses, and a matching plastic tiara.  She looked at Sean hard, and Courtney saw signs of recognition on her face.  It had been a year, which is a lifetime for a three-year old, but she knew him.  He reached for her, but she stood her ground and kept looking.

"Aren't you going to give your dad a hug and kiss?"  Courtney asked.

The preschooler puckered, gave him a kiss and let him hug her for about ten seconds, then ran away to return to the pool with her cousins.  He sighed and scratched his head.

"I swear, she talks about you all the time.  I don't think she's made the connection between you and the guy on the phone."

Sean smiled at her attempt at sparing his feelings.  "This is a really nice house," he said, glancing around.  "When Bryce told me you were moving, I hadn't pictured anything like this.  How did you af—"

Before she could tell Sean to mind his business, his brother Jay emerged from the house.

"Watch out! Here I come!"  He cried out, waddling from the house to the pool.  He was wearing swim trunks, flippers on his feet, a multi-colored clown wig on his head, a red clown nose, and a snorkel sticking from his mouth.  As he neared the pool, the kids screamed as loudly as they could.  When he jumped into the water, causing a huge splash, they screamed even louder.  Crawling beneath the surface, breathing through the snorkel, he saw his brother staring down at him, squinting.

"What's up, man?" Jay greeted him then sat up laughing, while the kids poured and splashed water on him.

"What have they done to you, man?" Sean snickered. He didn't know whether to envy his brother, for knowing how to have a good time, or pity him, for acting like a fool. The kids loved him, no matter what he or anybody else thought.

By the time Yolanda made her grand entrance, Sean had settled in. The two of them maintained a polite but safe distance from each other.

"Daddy...Daddy!" Sean heard Cori call. Surprised, he started walking toward her, only to find she was calling his brother and not him. When she returned to the pool, he marched over to his brother and pulled him aside.

"Why is my daughter calling you Daddy?"

Jay's eyes narrowed. "She spends a lot of time at our house; she's copying what she sees my kids do. Why are you so stupid?" He shoved Sean out of his way.

Sean was planning to confront Courtney, when to his surprise, his father-in-law showed up.

"Hey, man, how are you? Is this your lovely wife? Glad to meet you," Ronnie grinned working the crowd like a politician. He had a way of electrifying any atmosphere—making it feel like the party starts when he arrives and is over the moment he leaves. *What is he doing here?* Sean thought as he observed Cori, who when she spotted Ronnie, stopped what she was doing and ran to him. Instead of jumping into his arms, however, she turned her head up to look at him, as if he were the tallest tree she'd ever seen.

"Happy birthday, Beautiful," he peered down at her. "See that big box over there? It's for you!"

Her fascination with him ended. She ran over to the huge box, which was wrapped with pink metallic paper, big white bows, and had been carried by one of Ronnie's assistants.

"Courtney," Ronnie barked.

Sean watched her stop what she was doing and float to where the older man stood waiting for her. Looking in her face, he'd never seen Courtney so happy to see anybody, including him. *This has got to be some kind of sick joke,* he thought, suddenly feeling ill. He'd have to apologize to Jay; he'd had things figured out all wrong.

"I guess you didn't know about that," Yolanda whispered, suddenly appearing at his side.

"What's going on with them?"

"Not much from what I can tell. They go out occasionally. But she's *crazy* about him." Yolanda found his pained expression amusing and laughed at him while he walked away.

"They did a good job with the counter tops," Ronnie said to Courtney. He hadn't seen the house since she'd moved in, and she was giving him a quick tour.

"The only thing left is some rewiring that needs to be done. Mr. Zack said he'll be here sometime next week."

He turned and gazed down at her. "Are you happy?"

For a moment he looked like he was about to kiss her; but he often looked at her in that way, and never did.  She smiled, "Yes, I am.  Thank you."

He held her gaze for a few moments more before checking his watch. "I've got to go.  Why don't you open her gift from me before I leave?  I want to see how she likes it."

Sean seethed while watching Courtney help his daughter open Ronnie's box.  It contained a motorized miniature pink Escalade.  *Why is her mother accepting that?*

"You okay son?  You seem kind of quiet," Angela commented, after Ronnie and Yolanda were gone.

"Why didn't you tell me about them?"

"You mean Courtney and Yolanda's father?  Far as I know, there's nothing to tell.  She seems a bit infatuated, and he's acting like a sugar daddy, but I think things will straighten themselves out.  She's got a good head on her shoulders."

"And what if they don't?"  Sean frowned at her casual attitude.

Angela shrugged, "People have to live their own lives."


"Who do you think you're talking to, and what are you implying?" Courtney growled at Sean, slamming her front door after he'd walked in.  He'd barely stepped into the house before putting his foot in his mouth, and his mouth in her business.

Sean laughed to himself, *did I really ask her that—and use Angela's term for Ronnie: sugar daddy?* He'd said it, and it was too late to pull the words back and swallow them. While she glared at him, he looked around the house for a sign of his kids.

"I'm waiting, Sean. Explain what you meant."

"Bryce, Cori. It's me!"

"DADDY!" Bryce screamed, and Cori, parroted him. Little feet ran from the rear of the house.

"So, you're not going to answer me, but you had no problem saying what you said."

Bryce ran and jumped into his arms. Cori stopped short, and stood watching her brother, until her dad scooped her up too.

Courtney threw the kids' packed overnight bags at Sean, aiming for his head. He ducked, as they sailed past him, refusing to look at or speak to her.

Heading to the door, he picked up the bags, slung them over his shoulder, then took both children by the hand and walked out.

"Mind your business!" she yelled to the back of his head, as he loaded the kids into his rental car.

Courtney knew it was best he'd ignored her. She was angry enough to hit him for what he'd implied. Just because Ronnie treated her well and she enjoyed it, he, of all people, was implying she was for sale. She wondered, however, if her anger and defensiveness were more of a problem than his insinuations.

"Ronnie," Sean implored, gulping the drink of whiskey his father-in-law had poured him. "Of all the women in this state—why her?"

The older man laughed as he got up from the patio chair and walked towards the pool in his back yard. It was early evening, and the way the setting sun overlooked the manicured grounds of his estate always captivated him. Sean had showed up at his door uninvited, interrupting his enjoyment of the evening; but he knew what was on the young man's mind.

"How do you like your job? I hear you're doing well there."

"It's good. Back to my question—"

"Hear your making quite a reputation for yourself outside of work too. One female at a time," Ronnie said, turning slightly in Sean's direction.

Sean shook his head, "That's an exaggeration."

Ronnie sniffed, then turned back to the sunset.

"There's got to be some law against it, man. I mean, we're practically related."

Ronnie laughed again, then turned away from the pool, "I assume you're talking about Miss Brooks, and my question is why. You don't want her...I just might. Get over it."

Sean shook his head. "That's not right, man. You have to be careful with her, she gets depressed. She tried to—"

"I know," Ronnie nodded, then turned and resumed watching the sunset.

Sean slammed his glass down on the patio table. "Whatever happens is your fault," he stood abruptly. Ronnie half turned and shrugged. Sean stormed out of the yard to the circular driveway where his rental car was parked.

"We're all so proud of your accomplishment. And I believe I speak for all of us when I say, we're happy to have had a part in it," Pastor Rick said, raising a glass of champagne in a toast.

Courtney beamed as she raised her glass, along with the thirty dinner guests who'd gathered at the Glass Slipper restaurant to celebrate her graduation from college earlier that day. Although it had come a few years late, and some things had happened along the way, she'd made it—through this round anyway. Medical school was the next step, a journey she'd begin in the fall.

"I only wish Mary could have lived to see this day," Aunt Darla sighed deeply. Carmen who was sitting next to Courtney nearly choked on her champagne. Courtney nodded solemnly while poking her sister under the table.

The dinner table itself was a large rectangle, adorned with an elaborate sparkling crystal centerpiece that matched a chandelier suspended from the ceiling. Each place-setting was of elegant crystal and fine china. Four waiters were assigned to each side, ready to refill glasses and serve the guests as necessary. The centerpiece was ringed by white and gold flowers, and lit candles. The room had a roaring fireplace in one corner, a huge Christmas tree decorated in white and gold in the other. It had a comfortable feel like one's living room, not at all like a banquet hall.

The lighting in the room was subdued, but Cori still made her way around the dinner table like it was her party; everyone who comprised her world was assembled in one place. Her grandmother Angela, aunts Krystal and Jazmine, Uncle Jay and his wife Nina with their kids, even Sean was there with the date he'd brought with him from San Diego, an attractive woman with serious curves, who Courtney labeled buxom Belinda. Krystal called her Belinda the bimbo.

Ronnie, with Yolanda, and Renate were seated at the opposite end from Courtney, while Pastor Rick and his wife sat to her right next to Carmen, Earl and Natalie. Courtney said little throughout the evening, because she couldn't stop smiling; didn't know if she ever would.  She was grateful—so grateful to have so much to celebrate.  The things she'd gone through before, dropping out of school, her emotional collapse, had made that night even more special.  She couldn't express it, there weren't words; so, she watched her guests mingling, enjoyed the food and festive atmosphere, and continued smiling.

Ronnie's people had planned every detail of the event.  When he'd told her his desire to give her the party, initially she declined.  When he insisted and told her it was her Christmas present, she decided she couldn't argue with that. Besides, she'd worked hard and failed to see the sense in denying herself a reward from someone who was offering.  When Ronnie later assured her the owner of the restaurant was an old friend who'd only charge the wholesale cost of the food, she agreed to accept.

Everywhere she looked Ronnie was watching her, letting her know that although they weren't seated together, she was still close to him.  Their eyes met and they smiled at each other frequently throughout the evening.  She wasn't exactly sure what the smiles were about; but his approval made her feel confident, as did the designer outfit she was sporting, a cream knit three-piece sweater set, with a fur collar; a gift from Yolanda.

"Sean, come over to my house, okay?"  Cori said to her dad, who was too busy watching Ronnie and Courtney to devote his full attention to her.  His daughter had changed in the six months since her birthday party.  For one, she remembered him.  Although she didn't call him Daddy, she knew he belonged to her.  As soon as she saw him that night, she climbed up into his lap, determined to establish ownership.  And like the rest of his family, she turned her nose up when introduced to his date Belinda.

Later, while Courtney was seated in front of the fireplace enjoying coffee and dessert, Sean whispered in her ear.  "I can't believe you're hung up on that old man.  I bet he's the one paying for all of this."

She spun around to face him; but before she spoke, Ronnie stepped in front of him.

"Courtney, come over here a minute.  I'd like to introduce you to my old friend Lawrence, the proprietor of this establishment."  He gave Sean a curt nod, then led her past him.

Sean chewed on his lower lip as he watched them.  He'd figured Courtney and Ronnie would've been long over with by now; but they weren't, and there was nothing he could do about it.

"Mr. Brown, this was very gracious of you," Pastor Rick, who'd been waiting for a chance to speak with Ronnie alone, said to him.  He'd found him, stationed in the rear of the room watching everything.  "Why don't you let me write you a check to reimburse you?  I know what you've told Courtney, but I imagine this evening is quite an expensive one."

"No need, Pastor.  I assure you.  It's been my pleasure," Ronnie gave him the trademark smile and pat on the shoulder, while looking past him.

"I appreciate the thought, but you've done too much already.  I'd feel better if you let me pay.  It'll be just between us."  Rick persisted, and Ronnie's gaze returned to him, no longer good-natured and jovial.  "Just tell me the amount, and you'll have a check before I leave."

Ronnie chuckled.  "Sir, I have no idea what this evening is costing me.  I have people who take care of these things.  But if it means that much to you, here's my card.  Call my assistant Erica on Monday, and she'll give you the figures.  I can assure you; you won't like what she tells you."

Pastor Rick took the business card Ronnie offered him, and the two men glared at each other a few moments.  Ronnie, satisfied he'd had the last word, left Pastor Rick glowering while he went to rejoin the waning party.


"Did I tell you how beautiful you look tonight?"  Ronnie said to Courtney, as he helped her with the silver fox fur coat, he'd given her to wear for the evening.

They were leaving the Mayor's Valentine's charity black tie gala, an event that was so high profile, he'd rented a limo for the evening.  To Courtney it was just another dull party but getting dressed up and being with him made it worth it.

"Did you have a good time tonight?" he asked, as they were seated in the back of the limo.

"Of course," she was conscious he was watching her.

"You know I'm really starting to like you—a great deal," he said.  "These are for you."  The chauffeur handed him a bouquet of long-stemmed white roses.

"Thank you. They're beautiful as always," she said. He often gave her flowers either before or at the end of an evening out; but on this night, there was also a bottle of chilled champagne, even though he knew she rarely drank. When he poured the wine into the two crystal flutes, she stopped him. "None for me, thanks."

"Don, you can start driving," he instructed the chauffeur, who then closed the partition separating them. "I'm hoping tonight will be special. I'd like to make a toast to us," he said, handing her a glass, then lifting his.

"I'm not following you," she put the glass down on the tray.

"You don't like my toast?"

"I don't understand it."

"It's just that. I've been thinking about us: How I'd like us to spend more time together. I'm planning a trip to Europe soon. This place is getting me down. I'd love for you to come with me."

"Europe?" she chuckled "You must've forgotten who you're talking to. I'm not one of your rich friends. I'm a single working mother. I can't even get the time off work."

He put his glass down and looked at her soberly. "I'm asking you to change your life around to be with me. Quit the job. I'll take care of everything. I know you have your sights on medical school, and I'm all for it. When the time comes, we'll work it out so you can pursue your dreams. I'm on the board of a few organizations who award scholarship money. Right now, I'm ready for new scenery, but I don't want it without you."

Courtney's head was spinning. "My kids—"

"Will go to the best schools. They'll have the type of life you've dreamed of for them."

She blinked. It all sounded so good, so perfect; but there was a whole lot to the story he was leaving out.

"You and I both know I have my pick of women I could share my life with. You also have your pick of any number of younger men, but you choose to hang out with me. Have you stopped to ask yourself why?'

Yes, she had. Seeing him had been enjoyable and uncomplicated until now. She shook her head. "The kind of relationship you're suggesting goes against my beliefs."

"Change your beliefs. For me."

Her eyes widened. "What? What makes you think—"

He put down his glass, cupped her face in his palm and touched his lips to hers. His movements were not forceful; and though she was surprised, she could have stopped him. Instead, she kissed him; like she'd been desiring to for a long time.

He then leaned back and picked up his glass, "That's what makes me think. I know how you feel about me, even if you don't."

She slid away from him to the other side of the car and stared out of the window, wondering what had happened to their perfect friendship and why hadn't she seen *this* coming.

"I know I sprung this on you," Ronnie said, "But I had hoped you'd be more pleased with my invitation. Do you need more time to consider it?"

*Invitation—word carefully chosen, not to be confused with proposal. Mistress...kept woman. Is that all he thinks of me?*

"No," she said, thankful she was thinking clearly. "I'm sorry, there are somethings that aren't worth the compromise."

He scoffed. "You're putting *me* in that category."

"Not you personally, just your invitation."

He pressed the intercom button. "Don, we can take Miss Brooks home now."

She continued staring out of the window until the car came to a stop in her driveway. Ronnie wasn't smiling as he helped her out of the car. She walked to her door quickly, unaware he was following her. He reached for her house key; but she waved him off, hoping he'd turn around and leave. He followed her in; and as bad as she wanted him to go, she'd learned you don't tell Ronnie Brown to do anything.

He sat in his usual spot, on the soft Italian leather sofa he'd helped her get a deal on, in the house he'd found for her. She ducked into the kitchen and brewed coffee, another one of their end-of-the-evening routines. She poured the coffee and cream into his cup and pulled out the bottle of brandy she kept in the cabinet for him.

Instead of sitting on the couch beside him and making small talk like she usually did, she kicked off her shoes, listened to phone messages, and called Angela to check on her children. He sat on the couch and sipped his brandy-laced coffee and watched her as if he had nowhere else on earth to go.

"Thank you for a lovely evening," she finally said, knowing if she didn't talk to him, the evening would never be over.  He said nothing.

They sat at opposite sides of the room, facing each other.  Courtney's resolve strengthening with each passing moment.  Maybe she did have feelings for him, and maybe he'd viewed her as an easy target all along.  She didn't want to be his lover, however, didn't want that familiarity between the two of them.  She'd enjoyed their romantic, flirtatious liaison; it'd felt good and didn't require much.  What he wanted now she was unwilling to give—even after all the favors he'd done for her.

Ronnie put the coffee cup down, stood abruptly and walked to the door.

"I guess you'd better take this with you," she said, following him and handing over the fur coat.

"Keep it as a parting gift," he growled without turning around, then stormed from the house, slamming the door.

She paced around her living room for what seemed hours after he'd left and barely slept that night.  She hated knowing she'd disappointed him but was also angry he'd assumed she was an account he'd invested in which entitled him to withdraw *benefits* at will.  She'd shared so much of her life with him.  They'd talked about her past, her commitment to her faith; she thought, even though he wasn't a man of faith himself, he understood her, that he realized she was finished compromising herself in relationships with men.

By the time the morning light shone through her bedroom window, she was thankful to God for keeping her out of the disaster she'd nearly gotten herself into. She'd allowed herself to be distracted by Ronnie Brown's attentions but was grateful she hadn't forgotten about Him.

In the following days, she had all the right words carefully chosen. Ronnie usually called her about twice a week; and the next time he did, she planned to be ready. A full week passed, and she didn't hear from him. Then a courier appeared at her door to retrieve the fur coat he'd referred to as a parting gift. That was the last contact she'd have from him. Yolanda mentioned in passing a few weeks later, her father was vacationing in Italy.

## Chapter Nineteen

"I wish you'd pretend you're having a good time.  I didn't invite you here to be a drag," Yolanda seethed in Courtney's ear, through clenched teeth.

Courtney was about to remind her the only reason she'd come to the party at all was because Yolanda had harassed her.  Before she spoke, however, she spotted Ronnie entering and began searching frantically for a place to hide—preferably near an exit where she could slip out.  He was making the Ronnie entrance: smiles, hugs, handshakes, back slaps, oozing all charm and charisma.  She stood watching him a second too long, however, their eyes clashing before he turned his attention back to his adoring fans.

"I thought you said he was out of town," she hissed at Yolanda.

"So, I was wrong."

It'd been three months since the night they'd parted ways, and Courtney was still feeling the sting.  She wasn't over it yet but didn't want him to know that.

Pulling her shoulders back, she lifted her head, pasted on a smile, and started laughing along with Yolanda's friends, even though she'd missed the joke.

"How have you been, Sweetheart?"  Ronnie suddenly appeared beside her.

When she turned to him, working hard to maintain her smile, she found it a wasted effort.  He wasn't looking at her, nor did he wait for an answer.  He pecked her cheek, then stepped past her to embrace Yolanda.  After making a few jokes, he wished everyone a goodnight and moved on.

Without excusing herself, Courtney headed straight to the ladies' room and collapsed in a chair in the lounge. Within thirty seconds Yolanda was standing over her.

"What did he do?"

"Nothing. I don't feel well. I'll be okay in a minute."

Yolanda glared at her, then decided she didn't want to know what her father did this time. She'd heard a lifetime's worth of Ronnie's girl stories, since the days when he was still married to her mother. When she exited the ladies' room, her father intercepted her.

"Is she okay? Has she said anything about me?"

Yolanda glared, while attempting to walk around him; but he pulled her aside.

"You make me sick. I don't know what happened and I don't care, but you need to fix it. She liked you. Now she's mortified to be in the same building with you."

He inhaled deeply and nodded as Yolanda rolled her eyes and stomped away. He attempted to catch Courtney as she exited the restroom but was waylaid by one of his colleagues. About an hour later, he spotted her on the mezzanine level of the ballroom, tolerating a young man attempting to charm her.

When Ronnie approached, the young man did what he knew was expected: he stood up and quickly bid her goodnight. When Courtney realized the reason he was scampering away, she tried to coax him to stay, but to no avail. She then admitted to herself, Ronnie had been the reason she'd stuck around in the first place.

He sat down in the chair vacated by the young man, while she ignored him.  The scene reminded her of the last night they were together.

He motioned a nearby waiter to refill their drinks, then cleared his throat and turned toward her.  "I didn't handle things well—with us.  I want to try to clean it up if I can," he said, then paused. He believed it appropriate to give the woman he'd wronged time to whine, moan and tell him what a swine he was.  To Courtney's credit, and his relief, she didn't.  "I'm not accustomed to rejection.  It's no excuse, but that's how it is.  If I told you I didn't mean to hurt you, I'd be lying; but it wasn't nice of me.  You're a lovely person and I'm sorry."

"Sorry if I led you on," Courtney responded, while watching partiers on the dance floor.  His weak apology gave her no comfort.  What she longed for was for them to go back to where they were before their disagreement; that was neither possible nor wise.

Ronnie glanced at his watch and stood, "Can I take you home?"  She started to decline, but he lifted his hands.  "I'll behave.  I promise."


"May I come in?"  Ronnie pressed, when they were in front of her door, after a silent and awkward drive to her house.  She didn't look at him or answer, simply left the front door open for him after she'd walked in.  Once inside, she brewed the coffee, without the brandy, which she'd disposed of weeks before. Ronnie, however, produced a flask from his suit pocket.

"I'm going to miss you.  I already do.  I hope you know that," he said as he stirred his coffee, then sat back on the couch and looked at her.  "What did you expect to happen between us anyway?"

She shrugged, then after a brief silence said, "You know, when you said you didn't want another wife, I was good with that. I told you I was done with lovers. You said you understood—"

Ronnie laughed. "That's because I thought I could change your mind. Look Sweetheart," he said, taking her hand in his, "We had a good time, and it's sad things can't stay the same, but it wouldn't be fair to you. You need a man closer to your age who wants to build a life with you. How are you going to find Mr. Right with me hanging around?"

"Who cares about him—if he exists?"

Ronnie shook his head. "Maybe you see me as some father figure. That's not how I see things."

Courtney ran her fingers through her hair as she listened to what he was saying, knowing it was true. He'd been right to end their relationship. They were wasting each other's time.

"Admit it: You would've married me if I'd asked you to," he asserted, pulling on his coat, standing at the door.

She nodded and laughed at herself; he kissed her forehead. Once in his car he backed out of the driveway, satisfied he'd accomplished his mission. *That's why you leave the young ones alone,* he scolded himself, knowing at the same time he wouldn't listen.

# Chapter Twenty

"Good evening.  My name is Alonzo Jeffers; I'm an investigator with the state's attorney's office," the man standing on Courtney's front porch said as he quickly flashed a badge.  "I'm looking for Miss Courtney Brooks."

Courtney stood at the door staring at the man, until he pulled out his identification again, this time handing it to her so she could examine it further. She handed it back but made no effort to invite him into her house.

Jeffers then coughed, "Excuse me, may I—"

"Can you tell me what this is about?"  She said, folding her arms.  She'd had a long day, her kids were having a screaming match in the kitchen, and she had an exam to study for.

"I understand you're a friend of Oscar Brown III."

Courtney exhaled loudly, "Yeah, Ronnie.  So what?"

"The state's attorney's office is investigating some of his business dealings, and your name came up.  Particularly related to a real estate transaction and *other* improprieties."

Courtney frowned, looking through him, as her brain attempted to decipher his words; they made no sense.

He then stood up straighter, his stare boring down on her, while he firmly gripped the handle of his briefcase with both hands.  "It would be in your best interest to speak with me now, *before* you're subpoenaed into court. If you cooperate, voluntarily, you might avoid prison time altogether."

# Part Four

# Chapter Twenty-One

*Prison......he's got me confused with.... I need to straighten this....*
Courtney thought, looking past the man while he was speaking, only catching every other phrase.

".... we'll try to be fair with you, Miss Brooks...consider all of the relevant circumstances....do our best for you and your children." His speech was slow, patient, and confident, as if he knew she had no choice. Finally, he checked his watch. "It's getting late, Miss Brooks. If you let me in, I'll take your statement, and we'll go from there."

"I have nothing to say to you. Good night," she said, ignoring his objections as she closed and locked her door.

"I'm sorry you've made that choice, Miss Brooks. You'll be hearing from us!" She heard his footsteps and the start of a car engine. She didn't begin breathing normally or thinking clearly until sometime after the car had driven away.

She then put her children to bed early and called Yolanda.

"Some guy came over here—an investigator—"

"Yeah, yeah. They've been to see me too," she laughed. "Man, they *are* reaching if they're contacting you. What's he accused of –being a dirty old man? Since when is that against the law?"

"It's not funny," Courtney insisted, even though she was laughing too. The fact that Yolanda was joking made her feel better. "He mentioned my house purchase and—"

"I'll tell Ronnie, but you need to call him, or better yet, go see him. Your phone is probably bugged. He'll tell you what to do. There's nothing to this, I promise you. Every few years, he pisses somebody off and they file a complaint against him. Because of his name, it gets blown out of proportion."

After the discussion with Yolanda, her nerves were settled enough to study for her exam. When she and her children left the house the next morning, however, Alonzo Jeffers and another man, were sitting in a car parked in front of her house, watching her.

She rushed to Ronnie's office on her lunch break.

"Hey, stranger," Erica, Ronnie's assistant greeted, as Courtney entered the outer office. "Go on in. He's expecting you."

Courtney smiled. Ronnie knew how to make a person feel important. He also knew how to cut them to pieces.

"Hey, baby," he smiled from behind his desk when Courtney entered. She noticed the double brandy sitting in front of him—it was barely noon—which was a sign he was having a bad day. "I understand you've had visitors."

She told him of her visit from Alonzo Jeffers and how he insinuated that something was wrong with her home purchase.

"Listen, Sweetheart, everything with your home transaction was by the book. You don't have to worry. Now, as the broker, there may be questions about the price I negotiated; but they'll have to deal with me on that—not you. I've retained a lawyer for you. I want you to call him and give him a statement as soon as possible, then direct any further inquiries from Mr. Jeffers to him."

Courtney sighed.  If Ronnie said it wasn't her problem, she believed it.

He saw her look of relief and his expression became somber.  "I wish I could tell you it all ends here, but these people are on a fishing expedition; depending on how determined they are to dig up some dirt, it could get nasty," he warned.  "I can only help you with the legal part.  Your past association with me makes you a target.  Do you understand?"

She nodded as she stood and left his office, not comprehending why he suddenly became so melodramatic.


"Let me explain something to you, Miss Brooks," Alonzo Jeffers said, calling her at work.  "Just because Mr. Brown has set you up with one of his high-priced attorneys doesn't mean anything.  I work for the State, and as such I'm authorized to contact you whenever and wherever I want.  I received that lame statement you've made through Mr. Brown's attorney and I'm not satisfied.  I'm giving you the opportunity, once again, to give us information on your business dealings with Mr. Brown.  I'd advise you to take advantage of this opportunity.  We're giving the details of this case to the local media in the next few days; if you cooperate, I'll leave your name out of it."

Courtney laughed at him and turned off the phone without giving him a response.  Did he think he was going to intimidate her by telling the press she'd bought her house at a discount?  Why would anyone care about that?

## Chapter Twenty-Two

The title of the front-page article that hit the local newspaper's Sunday edition, read:

"RONNIE'S ANGELS"

It featured pictures and bios of various attractive young women romantically linked to Ronnie Brown; Courtney's picture was the third.  The article insinuated she and others occasionally used their looks and other assets to secure business favors to benefit Ronnie.  In return they received gifts and other benefits from him—in her case a home purchased in an upscale neighborhood for less than half the market value.  It also implied Ronnie was paying her mortgage and possibly her medical school tuition, since there were no records of her paying it herself.  The article also stated her bank accounts were being audited for the source of regular cash deposits.  *Have they never heard of monthly child support?* She threw the newspaper across the room.

She then retrieved it and read the article through multiple times, looking for one piece of evidence that wasn't a groundless insinuation based on hearsay and supposition.  There was nothing except her face plastered on the front page.

*How could somebody write this? Why me?*  She asked herself, noticing Yolanda's picture hadn't made the article at all, although she was mentioned toward the end.

She grabbed her phone and dialed Pastor Rick's cellphone.

He picked up on the first ring, "I saw the article.  Sorry, baby girl.  You don't deserve to be dragged through the dirt like this.  I'm not sure Mr. Brown deserves it either, but at least he's equipped to handle it."

"What am I going to do?"

"Not much you can do, I'm afraid.  There are no real accusations in the piece.  Just quoting of unnamed sources saying what they think happened.  It's the worst kind of journalism, but there's nothing there.  You may have a libel suit against them, but the damage has been done."

Courtney hung up the phone, so angry she couldn't imagine going to church, but realized if she didn't go, she'd sit around all day thinking about the article with its intimations.  She'd never in her life given thought to her reputation or felt a need to protect it.  Now, someone had gone out of their way to attack her character, and she was helpless to do anything about it.


"Miss Brooks let me straighten you out about a few things.  I don't smear anyone.  I merely make certain facts available to people who want to write about them, and I'm afraid there are elements of your life that read like a reality show.  You may think your life is uninteresting, but in the hands of a skilled writer…" his voice trailed off, and there was silence on the line between them.  "Last chance, Miss Brooks.  If three this afternoon doesn't suit you—"

She pressed the button disengaging the call.

The next story was in the mid-week edition.  Still front page, but this time in the lower right-hand corner.


KEEPING IT IN THE FAMILY.

Courtney Brooks, the alleged former lover of businessman Oscar 'Ronnie' Brown (the target of a State investigation into his business dealings), is no stranger to the Brown family.  In fact, Mr. Brown's former son-in-law, Sean J. McNair, is the father of two of her children.  While Miss Brooks' wasn't specifically named in any of the legal filings from the divorce proceedings of Yolanda Brown McNair and her husband, it is widely believed his continued affair with Miss Brooks was the overriding contributor.  While receiving and doing favors as Mr. Brown's lover and business associate, sources say she was carrying on a relationship with his son-in-law at the same time.  Hospital records also indicate a suicide attempt by Miss Brooks and a brief psychiatric stay, rumored to be tied to Mr. McNair's refusal to leave his wife.

It is believed that many of the 'gifts' Miss Brooks received from Mr. Brown were an attempt to appease her, while at the same time save the McNair's marriage, which was eventually dissolved in October of 2010.

Neither Courtney Brooks, Sean McNair, nor Yolanda Brown McNair, were available for comment.

Courtney read the article and wanted to laugh and cry at the same time. Not only was it tawdry and ridiculous, but nothing about it was newsworthy.  It accomplished what the state's attorney's office wanted; however, it embarrassed her.  She felt bad for her children—thankful they were too young to read and know what was being said about her and them.  The truth was bad enough; but the way the facts were twisted in the article cast her in a terrible light, making her appear an immoral and scandalous opportunist.  She wondered if the humiliation was worth it, since she had no information to give anyway.  What harm could be done by meeting with Alonzo Jeffers?

"I wouldn't recommend it, Miss Brooks," Mr. Banks, the lawyer Ronnie had retained for her, advised.  "I know you're in a tough spot, but you can see how these people operate.  They don't care about you, and they don't care about the truth."

When Alonzo Jeffers contacted her again with more veiled threats, she again refused because she had no incentive to cooperate. Her dirt had been painted black and exposed to the world.

The next article appeared mid-week and was on page ten:

"UN-HEAVENLY BEGINNINGS"

The opening of the article focused on Courtney and her late mother Deirdra Brooks, complete with police mug shots; it was no surprise her mother had been arrested a few times. The piece then went into the link between herself, her mother, and local Pastor Ricardo Douglas—listed as Deirdra Brooks' former lover.

The remainder of the article centered on Pastor Douglas and included mug shots from some of his early brushes with the law, making implications about the church finances and a possible crime-money link. There was a subtle suggestion near the conclusion of the article of a possible church connection to Ronnie Brown's investigation; an attempt to justify mentioning Pastor Rick in the article at all.

When she called Pastor Rick, he answered the phone chuckling. "Is that the best they could do? They should've called me. I'd have given them a few good stories for free."

She was relieved he wasn't angry, but at the same time, was heartbroken at what they'd done to her mother's memory. People didn't say many good things about Deirdra Hadley Brooks, but most had the decency to leave her in her grave and let well enough alone.

"Miss Brooks, why did you show up here if you were going to waste my time?  You've told me nothing," Mr. Jeffers yelled at her.  "If you want us to leave you alone, you're going to have to do better than this, and you can get rid of Ronnie Brown's mouthpiece over there."

Courtney realized Mr. Banks had been right.  They knew she had no incriminating information against Ronnie; they didn't have any either.

"Sorry I've wasted your time.  I'll look forward to the next piece in the newspaper," Courtney said standing, as Mr. Banks walked to the door and held it open for her.

"Can we talk without your lawyer for a moment," Mr. Jeffers asked, while Mr. Banks shook his head.

"I'll be right out," she nodded to Mr. Banks.

"Okay, Miss Brooks," Detective Jeffers said in a much softer tone, as he sat down heavily in a chair facing her.  "Sorry we've had to play rough, nothing personal—"

"It's very personal. Save your phony regret."

His mouth tightened.  "We need your help.  We know Mr. Brown is skirting the law but—"

Courtney stared at the man, then smirked and headed for the door.

"Miss Brooks, this isn't funny—" she heard him say, before the door closed behind her.

In the following Sunday edition of the newspaper, it was obvious they'd moved on to a new target.  This time a past associate of Ronnie's, a known thief with no credibility, made some accusations against him.  Still the reporter couldn't help throwing Courtney's name in the article for good measure.

# Chapter Twenty-Three

"Shhh, Cori, it's going to be alright.  The doctor's going to fix it...."
Courtney rocked the four-year-old, trying to console her.  It was three a.m. and they were sitting in the emergency room waiting to be seen.  Cori had been running a fever for most of the day, then woke up with what must've been an excruciating earache, if her nonstop crying was any indication.

"Cori McNair," the ER nurse finally called.

Once back in the examination room, as Courtney feared, her daughter was having nothing to do with doctors or nurses, despite her misery.  She screamed and thrashed to the point Courtney had to help pin her down so they could peer into her ears, down her throat, and take her temperature.  By the time the two nurses left, Cori was too exhausted to cry anymore.

The two of them were practically asleep when Courtney was awakened by a lightly accented male voice.

"Good Morning, Ms. –"

When Courtney's eyes fully opened, she saw a dark brown-skinned man with shoulder length dreadlocks standing in front of her, studying a clipboard.

"—Brooks.  I'm Dr. Michael," he said, as Cori awakened and started to whimper.

"You must be Cori.  What's wrong?"  He said, as he rolled a stool closer to her and sat down.

The examination and lab work took another two hours and revealed Cori had an ear infection and strep throat.  The doctor would release her from the ER only when her fever went down.

While waiting, Courtney used the time to do some informal career research. She knew her specialty would be pediatrics but had yet to decide whether she'd stay with internal medicine or go into something more challenging such as emergency medicine or a surgical specialty. Witnessing the brutal pace in the ER gave her a clue she would steer clear of emergency medicine. Her attention drifted from the buzz of activity happening around her, to Cori's physician, Dr. Michael.

*How does he do it?* She wondered, watching the young man, who appeared perfectly calm. He had physicians barking orders at him one minute, nurses harping at him the next, not to mention complaining patients. None of it showed on his face nor his demeanor, and Courtney was watching him closely for the signs. She had little else to do.

She then caught herself conducting a more personal type of evaluation. In her opinion, Dr. Michael was an attractive man; tall and athletic, with an easy smile. His high cheekbones, and deep dimples, were his most engaging feature, besides the absence of a wedding ring.

A few times, Courtney thought he'd caught her watching him; but when looking in her direction, he appeared to look through her. She had her story prepared if he asked—she was a medical student after all.

"Here are her meds. I've only given you a week's supply; if she's not better in 48 hours or so, call your primary care doctor. Follow up with them anyway in about a week," Dr. Michael said, smiling; Courtney noticed his dimples again. "And how are you doing, after a long night in the ER?"

"Ready for sleep right about now." She stood, preparing to lift Cori and carry her to the car.

"Why don't you go and get your car. I'll have a nurse look after her for a few minutes."

She thanked him and did as he suggested. By the time she pulled her car around to the emergency room entrance, Dr. Michael and a nurse were waiting with Cori, who was groggy and slumped in a wheelchair.

"Thank you. I've got it from here," Courtney said, walking around to the rear passenger door; but Dr. Michael had already opened it and was lifting the child into her booster seat.

After strapping Cori in, Michael closed the car door and he and Courtney stood facing each other.

"Thank you so much—you really didn't have to—"

"No problem," he said smiling and holding her gaze. "Feel free to come back anytime. I hope I'm not offending you by saying it was a pleasure having you as an audience."

She laughed lightly as he followed her to the driver's side, then held the door open while she slid behind the wheel. They were both grinning as she steered her car out of the parking lot.

"Welcome to my class. I'm Dr. Mallard, and this is Physiology of Anatomic Systems—Class 101. Students this term are fortunate because we have two intern assistants helping us: Dr. Greta Voelker,"—a thin blond woman stood and waved at the class—"is a German exchange student, and her specialty is endocrinology. Dr. Michael Adewele—" the doctor stood and faced the class; Courtney recognized him immediately—"comes to us from Nigeria and is currently an intern practicing neurology..."

Courtney felt her heart speed up, when Michael's eyes briefly locked on hers as if he'd spotted her when she'd entered the classroom. ... *tons of people go through the ER; he couldn't possibly remember me...*she told herself, biting her lower lip before turning her attention back to Dr. Mallard's lecture.

Later, when the instructor dismissed the class for a break, Michael caught up with her sitting alone at a table in the student lounge.

"Hello—Miss Brooks, isn't it?" He extended his hand to her. "How's your daughter doing?"

Courtney smiled as she took his hand and nodded when he pointed to the vacant seat across from her.

"What a small world," he surmised. "That night you were in the ER with your daughter, I noticed how interested you were in everything that was going on. I should've guessed you were a medical student, but I thought it was me."

Courtney laughed, "It was a little of both. I kept watching you. Your composure fascinated me. I kept asking myself how can he stand it? I may not know what my specialty will be; but after watching you, I know what it won't be. I don't have your temperament."

Michael put a hand to his heart and feigned a pout. "Is that all it was? Now I *am* disappointed. I was hoping your interest might have been more personal." Before she could come up with a witty retort, he was pulled away by a classmate.

Michael made certain to find her after class, however, to ensure she got to her car safely. "It's late, and this parking lot is too dark in some spots," he said once they'd arrived at her car.

"Are you always so considerate?" She inquired, as he held the car door open for her.

"When it comes to beautiful, soon-to-be doctors like yourself, of course," he said. "Honestly, I've thought about you since that night in the ER, and I'm happy to have the opportunity to see you again."

"Really?"

Michael nodded, "Really. Good night." He then closed the car door. As he watched her exit the parking garage, he hoped he hadn't been too aggressive; he was a busy man and believed in letting women know he's interested in them as soon as he knows it himself. He'd only seen her twice; and besides her beauty and obvious intelligence, he knew nothing about her; but he wanted to get to know her. He'd played his hand and would wait to see if he'd scared her away.


"For those of you looking to specialize in Pediatrics, it will be of great benefit to you if you increase your focus on anatomic development as it relates to..."

Michael's Nigerian accent was melodic, his voice smooth and even. Courtney followed his every move as he delivered the class lecture that evening, admiring his effortless speaking style and the ease with which he presented before the large audience of nearly 300 students his extensive knowledge of the subject matter. For her, it was also an excuse to watch him.

"Great lecture, Doctor," Courtney complimented him after class was over.

"Thank you, Miss Brooks."

She smiled, intending to remind him to address her by her first name; but she liked the way the formality rolled off his tongue.

"I must confess, I'm jealous," he said, following her out of the classroom. "I saw you in Greta's office the other day, but you have yet to schedule any time with me this semester. Is there a reason for that?"

She stopped walking, and turned to him, and bowed her head slightly. "Don't get me wrong. I have every confidence in your abilities; but as a single mom with two kids at home, I must use my time wisely. I think it's best if I work with a woman and not a handsome man who already attracts so much of my attention."

Michael laughed heartily and followed her to an empty table in the student lounge.

"I'll make a deal with you," he offered while taking a seat. "Make an appointment with me, and I guarantee I'll make the most of your time."

Courtney's eyebrows raised. "All business?"

He leaned on the table and looked into her eyes. "No. I'm saying it won't be a waste of time."

She leaned back in her chair, took a paper from her notebook and began fanning herself while looking around the room as if there was a sudden heat wave.

"So, this is where you hang out when not in class. You won't come to see me. I now know where to find you."

Courtney grinned at the familiar accent without bothering to look up from her book. There was no way for her to avoid Michael Adewele. Every time she turned around; there he was. She didn't mind. It had been two weeks since he'd encouraged her to schedule tutoring time, but she'd yet to take him up on it.

"I'd love to chat, but must get back to work," she said, closing the book she'd been reading and placing it into her backpack.

"Fine. I'll meet you here tomorrow—same time. It'll be my treat."

"I'll be here," she quipped, over her shoulder, while walking away. When she exited the building, she could see Michael watching her. His persistence made her laugh on the inside. She enjoyed being pursued—but longed to be captured. *Lord, if he's a waste of time, let me know* she prayed as she entered the lab building and headed to her desk.

"Can I ask you something?" Michael questioned Courtney, while they were in his office. She'd shown up for a tutoring appointment which had lasted for an hour and had been all work as he'd promised. When the hour was up, however, he'd mysteriously discovered his afternoon was free and asked her to hang around to chat. "Did I hear something about some recent news articles about you?"

All humor left Courtney's face, and her body froze in the chair she was seated in. If she could've moved, she would've gotten up and escaped the office without a word. While she struggled to respond, Michael's phone rang, and she found the ability to stand and retrieve her coat.

Michael paused his conversation, "Courtney, don't leave—please."

She did as he asked and once his call ended, they walked silently to her car.

"I'm sorry if I offended you."

"You caught me off guard, that's all.  I thought all of that was forgotten. It was a bad experience.  If you want me to tell you about it, get in," she said, pointing to the passenger side of her car.

Once he was seated, she told him the story behind the articles.

"You know Pastor Rick Douglas" What a coincidence: He was a mentor of mine," Michael said, "I still work with him sometimes in his prison outreach project.  He's a great man of God."

Courtney smiled and nodded, relieved that was his only comment.  He didn't ask any questions about her relationship with Ronnie Brown, or any of the other insinuations in the articles; and she'd told him all of them.

"There was no truth or substance to anything that was written, but that hasn't stopped people from pointing fingers at me," she said.  "Some have stopped speaking to me.  And it's even worse at church.  Seems I'm innocent until proven guilty everywhere but there."

Michael reached for her and wrapped his arms around her.  "You can't worry about that.  You're different.  Everything about you stands out.  You're beautiful, smart; you've set high goals for yourself, and you're achieving them.  A person like you will always have critics, even in church. You'll have to get used to that."

Courtney closed her eyes and allowed herself to rest in Michael's embrace, feeling that maybe she'd found a man who valued her hopes and dreams beyond his own self-centered expectations.

# Chapter Twenty-Four

"Bye, baby, I've got to hang up.  They're paging me in the ER.  I'll talk to you when my shift ends.  Oh—and ask Miss Angela to save me a plate," Michael said to Courtney.  It was July fourth, and Angela was having one of her barbecues to which she'd invited everyone she could think of.  Even Pastor Rick and Elise would be stopping by; but Michael, as always, had to work.

"She's taken care of your plate; you don't have to worry about that.  Call me when you get home.  I love you."

*"Aw,* isn't that sweet!"  Someone in the background said, but Courtney didn't turn to see who the speaker was.  By now everyone in her family, Sean's family, and everyone else's family knew she was in love, and that she and Michael were talking marriage.

"Should I say congratulations?"  Sean, who was home for a visit, asked while Courtney was peeking at the contents of several pots simmering atop Angela's stove.  She shot him a sideways glance but didn't turn around.

"Say whatever you want," she quipped, leaving the kitchen, heading toward the rear patio where most of the guests were congregating.  He followed her.

"I'm a little jealous, I'll admit it.  But you know I've always wanted you to be happy.  Are you?"  Sean sat down beside her on the concrete patio steps.

"Yes, I am.  Thank you for asking."

"And it's serious?"

"Looks like it," Sean was silent for several minutes before he stood and walked away.

Michael and Courtney were engaged the following Christmas.  After the holidays, she was anxious to have the wedding and begin their life together; but Michael was taking his time.

When the news of Courtney's engagement reached Sean, he became ill—so ill he had to take a week off from work.  When he finally returned to the office, he began making calls to business contacts back in his hometown.  Within two weeks he received a prospect so solid he resigned his position and began tying up loose ends, preparing to return home.

# Chapter Twenty-Five

"—but why not now, or next week, or next month?  We're not going anywhere; we know what we want," Courtney said to Michael, as she massaged his shoulders.  He'd escaped to her place, exhausted and in between swing shifts at the hospital; but as soon as he'd started to unwind, she waylaid him with wedding talk.

"What's the hurry, sweetheart?" he moaned.  "Are you trying to tell me you're pregnant?"

Courtney hit him, while he laughed.  "Abstinence is the most effective birth control there is.  That's another reason—Michael—" she leaned over and whispered in his ear, "aren't you tired of going home to a cold empty bed?"

Michael rolled on his back and wrapped his arms around her.  "If it was just us, you and me, we could get married tomorrow.  But you have children, and they have a father—"

Courtney sucked her teeth.  "What does *he* have to do with anything?"

"I'm going to be living with and helping to raise his kids, and he and I have never met."

She folded her arms, twisted her mouth, and stared at him.

"I need more time to adjust myself to that situation.  You know I love your kids and I want to make them happy; but as soon as the wedding's over, it's not the two of us; it will be the four of us—"

She plopped down heavily on the couch beside him.  "You're right.  I didn't think about that.  Of course, you need time," she said, then looked at the clock, and seeing his break was over, handed Michael his jacket. "Speaking of Sean, rumor has it he's moving back to town."

"That fool's been in California all this time; and now that you've found a real man, he's coming home. Don't you think it's—" Carmen said, while they lunched in the hospital cafeteria.

"I don't care. Nothing he does has anything to do with me," Courtney said, remembering how often she'd dreamed of Sean coming back for her and their children. "I don't want him. And what if I did? Where did that ever get me?"

Carmen examined her sister's face. "God, I hope that's true," she sighed and shook her head. "I'd hate to see you make—" she stopped short when she saw Courtney bristle from across the table. "Okay—okay," she lifted her hands in surrender.

When Sean moved back to town he moved into his mother's house, giving Angela the joy of taking care of him while he looked for a new place. He showered her with gifts and gratitude, something the younger Sean had rarely done. He also immersed himself in fatherhood, indulging Bryce and Cori every chance he could. For three years he'd been the daddy on the phone, who graced them with his presence four weeks a year—two weeks at Christmas and two weeks in the summer when he'd fly them to San Diego. Now he had all the time in the world for them. He was showing a sudden interest in their mother also, which Courtney dismissed as a phase, soon to pass once he started dating again.

"Let's have dinner and do some catching up," he pleaded with Courtney. It was the fourth time he'd asked her out in the month since he'd been back in town. "I feel like we don't know each other anymore. Strange considering how much we once meant to each other."

He was standing in her living room, having stopped by unannounced to take the kids for ice cream. As much as she was annoyed at him for coming over without calling, it was difficult to be angry; her kids were so excited by his surprise visit.

She looked up from her seat on the couch, computer in her lap, and frowned. *The kids are out of the room, now is a good time to get things straight.*

Before she opened her mouth, however, Cori came running into the room with a sneaker on one foot and a brown sandal on the other.

"Daddy, I want to go now," she tugged at Sean's arm.

"Cori, go and find your other sneaker. Your dad isn't going to leave you," Courtney said, and watched the child whimper back to her bedroom.

"Are you going to give me an answer?" he said, once his daughter was out of the room.

"I'll have to pass. I don't go on dates with anyone but my fiancé."

"Call it what you want; it's just dinner," Sean said, before Bryce came into the living room and stood beside him. "What are you scared of?"

"I'm not—"

"Let's go, Daddy," Cori ran back into the room, with boots on this time. She still looked a mess, her hair was fuzzy, and her sweater was buttoned wrong; but Courtney knew if she tried to further delay her outing with Sean, she'd throw a fit.

"We'll talk later," Sean said, picking up Cori and turning toward the door.

"There's nothing to talk about," Courtney replied.

Sean telephoned her later that night anyway and continued calling throughout the week, even calling her at work. Then one day he popped up at her job.

"I came by to take you to lunch, since you won't have dinner with me," he announced, standing in the reception area of the hospital administration building.

"You've wasted a trip," Courtney said, her arms folded and eyes blazing.

"Come on. Why not? I'll get you back on time. I know a place around the corner—"

"I don't want to go. That's why not," she said. "In fact, I want you to leave me alone. Date your children—not me."

"You seem angry," he raised an eyebrow and stepped back. "Am I getting to you?"

"You're getting on my nerves; that's about all," she then walked away from him. "Go away, Sean." She swiped her ID and went through the door leading to her desk, leaving him standing with his hands in his pockets.

"Can't do that," was the answer she heard before the door closed behind her.

"You're the great doctor I've been hearing so much about?" Sean said, stepping in front of Michael, while looking down at him, flaunting his two-inch height advantage. They were standing in Angela's kitchen, and Sean had walked into the house just as Courtney and Michael, who'd been her dinner guests, were about to leave.

"I'm Michael Adewele, and yes I'm currently a medical resident at the hospital, and I'm also Courtney's fiancé," Michael said, stepping around him. He'd anticipated meeting Sean McNair but was thrown off by the confrontation. "Miss Angie, thanks for dinner."

Angela smiled and nodded but watched her son.

Courtney, who'd been in another part of the house, walked into the room. She quickly grabbed her purse and stood beside Michael with the intent of nudging him toward the door.

"Where are my kids, while you're here with him?"

Courtney rolled her eyes, "They're well taken care of. Hello to you too," then turned to Michael," let's go."

"I'll call you tomorrow," Sean said to her.

"For what?" She scowled

He didn't reply as he watched them leave.

Angela looked at him once they were gone. "What's eating you? You act like you're jealous or something."

"I just don't see what's so great about him. All of you talk about him like he's some god. He looks pretty ordinary to me."

"Just because he wants to marry Courtney.  You had your chances—many of them."

"This ain't about me.  It's about some guy who's going to be living in the house with my children.  What do you or Courtney know about him anyway?"

"I know the two of them love each other.  He loves God and he loves her. I think she's found the right one this time."

"Yeah, whatever," he grimaced at his mother, grabbed his keys and stomped out the door.


"I'm getting to you; I know it."  Sean said, to Courtney over the phone the next day.

"What do you want, Sean?"  She was at work and knew she should've let his call go to voicemail.

"I want to know what makes him so great, that I'm supposed to step aside and let him have my whole life?"

"You never wanted us before—"

"I do now; and last I heard, there's no statute of limitations on fatherhood."

"That's cool.  The children are yours; I'm not."

"There's no expiration date on love either, and you loved me once; and if you'll be honest, you still do."  Sean heard the click as the line went dead.

"He claims you're still in love with him."  Michael said to Courtney as they were seated in her living room having coffee and dessert after she'd put her children to bed.  "I don't believe him, but let's wait until he's got all of this out of his system."

"No, I don't want to wait. I want us to ignore him and go on with our plans."

"I can't ignore him. He's got a stake in our future. His children will be living with us, and you two have a past relationship. How can I ignore that? We don't need to like each other, but we need to be in a place of acceptance. We're not there yet."

"Michael, I don't know what he wants or what he's trying to prove, but I want nothing to do with it. I don't want a future with him; I want him to go away. I'm happy. I'm in love with you. I know what I want."

Michael watched her: fists balled up and mouth twisted. It was always the same when they discussed the topic of Sean McNair. There was something wrong; and he wasn't going to set a date for their wedding until whatever it was, was resolved.

The next morning as he was preparing for work, he faced himself in the mirror. *God am I ready for this? Does she love me—or am I just an alternative to him? And what about her kids? Am I doing the right thing?*

He was a confident man and rarely doubted himself—until now. Courtney was pressuring him to a rush wedding to shield her from what? What was really between her and Sean? He wasn't sure and needed to be. The two of them would marry when the time was right; he refused rush into a lifetime decision, as a reaction to another man.

The engaged couple went around and around with the same debate for weeks, while Sean kept calling and turning up at random times, seemingly enjoying Courtney's discomfort.  Her impatience and badgering were starting to weigh on their relationship.


"Do you love me—really?  If you don't, just say so.  I can accept that." Courtney said to Michael, when he'd called her during his break at work a few weeks later.

"Of course, I love you; and when the time is right, we're going to get married."

"If you love me, why are you letting Sean interfere with our future?"

"I don't believe I'm doing that," Michael said, rubbing his neck, tired of having the same conversation.

"Can't you see, I just want us to be married, so all of this can end."

"I don't believe marriage is the answer to what you want solved."

"What are you talking about?"

He sighed, "Nothing.  I'll call you later."


Courtney, held the phone, knowing she was pushing Michael too hard; but Sean was pushing her, and she didn't know how else to handle it.

"Please let me in.  I want to talk."  Sean persisted, a week later, standing on Courtney's front step.

"You've said plenty lately.  I don't want to talk anymore," she said.

"I'm not trying to ruin your life.  I swear, Courtney."

Her eyes widened and she snorted, "Oh, really?"

"It's just—I have a lot of regrets about what could've and should've been. Don't you ever think about it?"

"I think about how glad I am we never got close enough to make each other really miserable," she said, arms folded.

"Please let me in.  Give me two minutes," he pushed the door gently; and after thinking about it a minute, she stepped aside.

"I'm going to be honest," he said after he'd sat down on the couch.  "I'm not happy with my life.  I've let so much of what should've mattered slip away.  My son is seven, my daughter is five, and I haven't even started being a father yet.  I can't get that time back.  All I can do is try to make up for my mistakes with the rest of the time we have until they're adults."

Courtney, who'd remained standing, cleared her throat.  "That's admirable, Sean."

"What I'm saying is—let's get back together and raise our family."

She rubbed her neck, "You make it sound so easy.  It's too late, and it wouldn't work out anyway."

"Shouldn't our children have some part in your decision?"

"Are you finished?  I'm kind of busy," she said, letting out a breath.  He stood and walked to the door.

"I'm going to give you some time to think about things, but we *will* talk again," he insisted before leaving.

*I can't believe this is happening to me,* she thought as she watched the door close.  *God, why?*

The next night when she and Michael were having dinner, she relayed to him the conversation she'd had with Sean.

"He has a point; and if he's sincere, it's valid," Michael sipped from his coffee cup. They were sitting outside having dinner on Courtney's deck.

She shook her head, "He's a liar; and even if he's changed, he had years of chances, and he chose—"

"Does what he chose in the past disqualify him going forward? Can we honestly make the claim that our pieced together family with stepfather and step siblings will be better than you and him?"

"There's no me and him and there never will be," she spat.

Michael asked quietly. "Is it up to you and me to make that decision because we're in love? Does our being in love make everything and everyone else unimportant?"

"Yes," she exclaimed, standing and nearly yelling her answer. She could give Michael a million reasons why she'd never allow Sean to destroy her life again.

Michael stood and placed his arm around her to calm her down. She always became so worked up proving her case against Sean, although he knew, she didn't have one.

"Michael don't let him do this," she begged, as she buried her face in his chest.

He didn't answer as he broke the embrace, walked her into the house, then kissed her forehead before walking out the door.

"Michael, take your time.  Marriage is a big step; the two of you haven't known each other that long.  You fell in love so hard and so fast; it just feels that way.  Don't let her pressure you.  Listen to God and to yourself," Pastor Rick advised, taking a sip of iced tea.  The two men were seated on his patio that late summer afternoon.

"Easy for you to say, but there's a problem," Michael said, lifting a can of soda.  "Sean is back in the picture and is trying to convince her he wants his family back.  How am I supposed to respond to that?"

Pastor Rick sat back in his chair.  "When his mother told me he was coming back, I suspected his reasons."

"Courtney tells me to ignore him—but, how can I?  A man has a right to raise his children if that's what he wants to do.  Who am I to stand in his way-- if he's sincere?"

"You're right," Pastor Rick nodded.  "All the more reason for you to take your time."

"Yeah?"

"My daughter has had a rough life, filled with disappointment and people who let her down.  Sean is one of those people.  I suspect she has resentment towards him she needs to deal with.  There's nothing you can do about that."

Michael sighed; hearing Pastor Rick articulate what he'd been sensing.

"Rushing into a wedding isn't going to fix it, even if she thinks it will.  All you can do is hold your ground.  It's not your fight."

"Just what is it you're saying, Michael?  Spit it out!" Courtney yelled at him as they were having dinner the following week.  "I'm ready to set the date.  Why are you back-pedaling?  Do you or don't you want to get married?  I want to show Sean and the whole world I'm done with him.  Our getting married as soon as possible will prove that."  They were in her dining room where she'd prepared a romantic candlelight dinner.  Her intent had been to create an atmosphere to talk wedding, but Michael kept changing the subject.  She was now pacing across the room while he sat at the table watching her.  "I won't let Sean have a foothold in my life—"

"We're not talking about you," Michael said, rubbing his forehead.  "We're talking about a father and his children.  If we marry—"

"If?"  She stopped.

"When—when," he added quickly, biting his lower lip, "—when we marry, I'll be good to your children, but I'm not their father.  There's more at stake than what..."

*Sean is ruining my life again, and Michael's going to step aside and help him,* Courtney thought as Michael reasoned, calmly and sensibly; it made her furious.  She balled her fists and felt her breath coming in heaves.  She was losing control—knew she needed to walk out of the room and have a minute with God.

He would've told her to be quiet—but she was beyond listening.  She opened her mouth and began to speak; by the time she'd stopped, she'd accused Michael of every offense she could think of and some she'd made up; ending the rant by breaking their engagement, then banning him from her house, church, and life.

"If you see me at the hospital, turn around and go in another direction, or I'll let everyone know what a spineless excuse of a man you are!" She screamed.

She then ran into the living room and sunk into the loveseat. Knowing she'd gone too far and regretting her words, she began sobbing, expecting Michael to come into the room to console her. She became even more distraught when she heard the front door open and close; he'd left without saying goodbye.

An hour later, she called him and apologized. He said he accepted her apology, but ended the conversation hurriedly, claiming he was running late for work.

He stopped calling her; and whenever they ran into each other at the hospital, he did as she'd instructed during their argument: turned and walked in another direction.

# Chapter Twenty-Six

"I don't know what to do.  How many times can I apologize?  I'm sorry I acted like I did, and I know it was wrong--"

"Stop whining, please," Pastor Rick said, grabbing Courtney by both of her shoulders.  "The two of you have some problems—join the club.  At least you found out now, not *after* you're married.  If Michael can't handle being married to a real woman, with real hurts, he's not worthy of you.  Do you understand?"  Once he released her, she sunk down in the chair across from his desk while he sat on the corner, facing her.

"I called him to tell him Sean is calling me every day, begging me to go out with him.  Michael says he thinks I should go.  Can you believe that?  That doesn't sound like a man who cares—does it?"

Pastor Rick stood and sighed.  "You've got to trust him, and you've got to trust the God who brought you two together.  It's the only way you're going to see things clearly.  I'd love to tell you my opinion, but it's your life and your relationship.  Sit back, take a deep breath and talk to God."

Courtney stared at him wide-eyed.  "What does *that* mean?"  You didn't answer my question."

"Where's the harm in talking to Sean and seeing what's on his mind?  Maybe this is a chance for the two of you to bury the past—"

Courtney stood, "Now you sound like Michael.  I don't have any issues with Sean –" she said, her jaws tight.

"Really? Then it can't hurt."

"Be honest—I'm not so bad.  This is a nice place, and I'm okay to look at.  I may not be your doctor, but I do have brains.  You can give me that much credit, right?"

"Give it a rest, Sean.  Thanks for dinner; it's been nice."  Courtney replied.  Sean flashed a grin as he reached for his glass of wine.

They were sitting in the dimly lit dining room of the Black Pearl, an exclusive seafood restaurant.  Their table faced a picturesque waterfall that was the focal point of the room; it cascaded peacefully, reflecting an array of colors.  It was as if Sean had selected the restaurant to match his attire that evening, a flawless combination of blues from his shirt, pants, and socks.  Courtney noted his eye for style and expensive taste came from his ex-wife Yolanda, but he'd made the most of both.

She was enjoying his company, which surprised her—and caused her to have difficulty in recalling all the things she disliked about him.  She remembered the petty disagreements and her own unmet, not to mention unrealistic, expectations.  Their chaotic past seemed to bear no connection to the handsome, suave gentleman she was with now. Her own maturity reminded her—none of their past problems were entirely his fault.

"Tell me why," Courtney said suddenly, leaning forward.

"What?" He peered down into his glass.

"You coming back to town; all the time and attention lavished on us.  You had your life and we had ours.  What is this about? Why now?"

A lump suddenly appeared in his throat, "Did I ever tell you why I married Yolanda?"

"What does that have to do with the question I just asked you? Everyone, including you, knows why you married Yolanda—"

"It wasn't money. When I was tired of her, I walked out without a dime."

Courtney raised her eyebrows and nodded.

"I married her because she wanted me to, number one, and because I thought you'd put up with it. Then I find out, once you'd adjusted to the situation and pulled yourself together, you wanted nothing to do with me—married or divorced. I'd blown it, and you were done."

"What choice did I have?"

"No question you were right. But you'd put up with so much of my crap. I mean you gave up a valuable scholarship for me and got nothing in return. You had two babies you didn't really want, because I asked you to. All the while I'm sleeping around every chance I got, and *then* I moved in with Yolanda. You said you were through with me, but you didn't act like it. I assumed you were a part of my life –like my mom, you'd just be there."

"You were wrong. We know that now."

"I can't make that same mistake with my kids. They're on the verge of living with and being raised by a stranger. How can I sit back and allow that to happen without trying to make things right between you and me? I want to try to give them the home I cheated them out of."

"My engagement, huh? That's what it took, for us to be important to you?"

"I admit, if it wasn't for your *supposed* engagement I wouldn't have come to my senses. But things happen for a reason."

"You're here and you know your presence has affected my relationship with Michael. Now what?" She asked while sipping coffee.

"I guess that's up to you." He signaled the waiter for the check before she could question him further.

He'd been the perfect date that evening; his manners flawless right up to depositing her at her front door. Courtney needed to talk with Michael to put things back into perspective.

"Hi, how are you?" She asked, when Michael answered the phone.

"Fine, and you?" Michael said in short, clipped syllables, as if speaking to a patient. She knew she'd called him in the middle of his shift at the hospital but longed to hear his voice.

"I miss y—"

"I can't talk right now."

She exhaled loudly into the receiver but received silence and the sound of the hospital paging on the other end.

"I guess I should say goodnight then—"

"Um-hmm," was all she heard before the line went dead.

It had been over a month since their argument, and Michael was still barely speaking to her. Instead of allowing the hurt to get the best of her, Courtney decided to pray. *Lord, he needs to have a talk with you...* she said during her prayer time. Before going to bed, she sent Michael a text message citing a scripture about forgiveness.

"If I'm going to lose her anyway, maybe we should make a clean break," Michael said to Pastor Rick over the phone the next day, after confessing how he'd treated Courtney when she'd called him the previous night. "She wants me to save her from Sean—but that's not my job. If she wants him and it's God's will, what am I supposed to do?"

"What do you want me to tell you, Michael?" Pastor Rick said. Seemed like he was talking with either him or Courtney daily about the same thing. "Last night you were being mean and that's wrong—I don't care what excuse you give for it. You're trying to push her away, so you won't get hurt. Is it working?" All he heard was silence in response, but knew the young man was listening.

"No, sir... it's not." Michael finally said.


"Flowers again? That fiancé of yours is really in love," Nadia, Courtney's co-worker remarked, while sniffing the fragrant bouquet.

Courtney only nodded. She would've loved if the flowers had been from Michael. They were from Sean, and he'd been sending a bouquet each week. Looking at them only reminded her of how much she missed the man she *wanted* to marry.

"Your children *must* come first." she heard her Aunt Darla's voice in her ear, from a lecture she'd received three days prior. "I know you think you're in love with that other young man, but you don't have a right to put your happiness before theirs. You made your decisions, but those children didn't bring themselves into this world. You and their father owe it to them to work things out."

She'd received the same counsel from a few of the older women at her church.  She'd tried to make the case that Sean was undeserving of another chance; but like them, Aunt Darla was unwavering.

"He goes to work every day.  You say his only bad habit is women; age and maturity will take care of that.  He loves his children.  You say he doesn't love you.  Well, you don't love him either; that makes it even.  Young people put too much stock in this love business.  Commitment and sacrifice, that's what matters in the long run.  What ya'll call love will fade out soon enough."

Courtney was starting to wonder if Sean was going to be God's choice for her after all.  She was having a difficult time convincing herself things could never work between them, although she had no reason to believe they could.


*Biophysics, Biological warfare, Biological Innova*—Courtney read through titles on the library bookshelf.  Through a gap in the column, she caught a glimpse of Michael leaning over an open book, on the counter.  She stepped from between the shelves and watched him a moment before calling his name.  It had been weeks since they'd been together.

Michael looked up and they stood facing each other.  When she started to walk toward him, a colleague of his approached and he turned away from her as though he hadn't seen her.

She stood frozen, then walked briskly past the two men out to the stairwell.  She stood at the top of the landing, leaning against the cold brick wall, staring blankly at nothing.  She wanted to head down the stairs and out the door, but her belongings were still sitting on the table.  Taking a deep breath, she moved toward the door, preparing herself. *I won't say anything to him—I'm going to get my things and go straight to the elevator...*

Before she opened the door, however, Michael walked through it, holding her purse and backpack.

"I'm sorry—" he said, handing her the purse, but holding the heavy backpack, "about everything."

"Thank you," she replied, reaching for the backpack, intending to leave once he handed it to her.

"Forgive me," he said, without releasing it. "Please."

She folded her arms, without speaking.

"I've been mean, vindictive, and stubborn. I understand if you don't speak to me. I don't know why I've acted this way; I guess I'm scared."

The two of them suddenly became aware of the noise and traffic in the busy stairwell.

Michael was also aware of how much he'd missed her large brown eyes and knew if he didn't fix things that night, he may never see them again. "Do you have some time? Can we go somewhere and talk?"

"I don't know, Michael. I don't want to give up on us, but this break-up, or whatever you want to call it, has been hard. I swear tonight I just knew—" Courtney said, shaking her head and looking down into a steaming cup of tea. "You seem tentative—unsure. I don't know if I can handle that."

They were seated opposite each other in a coffee shop they'd walked to after leaving the library.

"You're right," Michael concurred nodding slowly. "And I understand how you feel. There have been times over the past few weeks where I'd convinced myself I should give up and step aside. But when I saw you tonight, I knew I can't and I won't, unless you tell me I'm wasting my time."

"I don't know what's going to happen. Some people keep telling me I'm obligated to dump you in favor of Sean for the sake of my children. Others say marrying Sean out of obligation isn't worth it. All I know is Sean has made some bold, sweeping statements, but he's been short when it comes to any action."

"What's he waiting for?"

Courtney shrugged, "I've been more concerned about what's happening with you and me to think much about him."

Michael then reached for Courtney's hand. "I believe in prayer—and I know you do also," he said, and she nodded.

"If God wants us to walk away from each other, He'll tell us. We may not always hear from Him when we're on the right path, but He'll tell us when we're wrong. I'll be honest, He's convicted me about the way I've been treating you, but not about our relationship. I have to take that as a good sign." Michael leaned across the table and looked deeply into her eyes.

She smiled and touched his cheek with her hand. "I agree."

# Chapter Twenty-Seven

"Can I stop by?  I need to talk to you," Sean said, calling from his cellphone.  Courtney could tell by the background noise he was driving.

"It's kind of late," she said.  The kids were asleep, her schoolwork was done, and she was on her way to bed.

"I won't keep you.  It's important," he urged, giving her a sinking feeling in the pit of her stomach.  *What does he want?*

In the two weeks since she and Michael had reconciled, Sean had become a non-issue.  She'd had no contact with him; and other than the weekly bouquet of flowers sent to her job, he hadn't called her.  Courtney assumed that despite all his lofty talk, he was back in the swing of his social life and had moved on.


"What's so important?"  Courtney questioned Sean as he strode past her into the house.  She stood watching him a moment before closing the door.

He stopped abruptly in the center of the room and turned to her.  "I haven't heard from you lately."

"Were you supposed to?"  She walked around him and took a seat on the living room sofa.

"I thought we were making some in-roads," he said, still standing.

Courtney frowned, "We had a couple meals together—"

"What's happening with you and the doctor?"

"We're fine—"

"I heard you broke up."

"We've had some ups and downs—"

"Because of me?" He smirked while folding his arms.

"Not directly."

"Why haven't you set the wedding date?"

"As I said—"

"It's time for you to stop playing games—with me and with him," he said, now moving closer to where she sat. "You'll never marry him—"

"Excuse me?" She frowned, looking up while he stood over her.

"You're still in love with me; you always have been, and always will be. If you marry him, it will be a selfish thing to do. Release him so he can find a woman who loves him. You, and my children, belong to me. It's time for you to get that in your head so we can move forward."

Courtney felt her insides shift. He was looking down at her with an intensity and passion that caught her off guard. She felt cornered. Despite everything she knew to be real, a tiny voice spoke to her out of nowhere, *he finally wants me.* She broke her eyes away from his stare, which prompted him to sit down on the couch beside her. He knew her too well.

"It's been a long road for us, I know; but nothing has changed really," he said, speaking in almost a whisper. "We're not seventeen anymore; we're parents and we have responsibilities. I'm ready to honor mine. What about you?"

"Wait a minute," she declared, now standing. "You've lived your life and left us behind. Now that it's time for me to be happy, you want to step in and claim ownership?"

"It's not fair—I know. I left you with two babies, but I'm going to make it up to you," he promised, leaning back on the couch, looking up at her. "I'm going to spend the rest of my life making it up to you, but you've got to give me the chance."

She shook her head hard, as if she was trying to erase his words, then pointed at him "You've had your chances—"

"And you're being vindictive," he said, standing and facing her. "It's not up to you to make me pay for what I've done. I've paid already. I've lost precious time in my children's lives and with a woman who knows how to love me." He put his hands on both of her arms and squeezed them while gently drawing her to him.

Courtney looked in his eyes and saw the pleading—the urgency, the desire. She heard the voice again... *he wants me.* Her resolve was softening as she felt his breath on her face. When his hands moved to her waist, and their bodies touched, she broke out of the trance.

"You've got to go," she said, grasping his hands and stepping out of his grip.

"What's wrong?' he said, taking a step toward her. "You've been so distant these past few months, I can't help wanting to touch you." He reached for her again, and she felt her knees weaken; it took all her inner strength to resist surrendering to his familiar embrace. Sean's grip was tight; but sensing her resistance he released her, shoving his hands into his pockets.

"Okay, have it your way; but you need to think about what I'm saying," he walked to the door. "I've looked into your eyes, and all I see in them is me— not him."

"He got to you, huh?" Elise said the following evening, as they were having coffee and dessert. When Courtney had called her from work, saying she desperately needed to talk, Elise invited her over for dinner.

Courtney nodded. "I'm so embarrassed. What does it mean? He says it means I don't love Michael. How can that be true?"

"Let me ask you this: now that Sean's not here with those gorgeous eyes, muscles, those clothes and that great-smelling cologne—without all of that bombarding your senses, what do you feel now? That's what matters: reality, not sensuality."

"I go over everything he says: 'You love me'...'you belong to me'... 'you want me'... and I think, what's in this for me? I mean... am I really supposed to give up the man I love, for *that?*"

"Are you tempted at all?"

"Last night he looked good, and he looked at me the way I always wanted him to, and all I felt was—I wished I could go back in time and be that girl who lived her whole life around that look and those words. I even wished I could pretend I was her for the night, so we could make love and I could capture the happiness the old me never had." Courtney took a deep breath. "No—I wasn't tempted, because it was all a big lie; it was then, and it is now."

"Sounds to me like you have nothing to worry about.  You were alone with an attractive man, who you have a past relationship with.  Granted, those old flames might have started up for a moment; but it sounds like you stamped them out—"

"Yeah, but I learned something about that old saying—playing with fire..."

"Can I come and see you?  Maybe we can finish the conversation you ended so abruptly on my last visit," Sean said to Courtney on the phone a week later.  It was after midnight on the evening before Thanksgiving and the kids were staying at his brother's house

"Sean, there's only one reason a man comes to a woman's house this time of night.  I'm not interested."

"Who do you think you're talking to," he said, and she could hear crowd noise in the background.  "You and I are no strangers to late night hook ups.  What's wrong?  Scared your doctor will find out?  I won't tell.  Obviously, nothing is happening with you and him, or he'd be there."

"Good night, Sean, and don't call me anymore."  Courtney hung up, then threw on her coat and grabbed her purse.  She got to the hospital while Michael was still completing his ER rounds and waited for him at the nurses' station.

"What a surprise," he said, checking his watch twice to make sure he was seeing it right.  "It's after one in the morning.  Is this love or—"

Courtney smiled and tugged his arm, "I wanted to see you.  Can you take a break?"

"Kim," he called to another doctor in the adjacent aisle.

"I'll cover," she said, smiling at Courtney.

They walked out of the ER to the nearly empty hospital cafeteria and sat in a booth.

"What's wrong?" Michael said, stroking her hand.

Courtney shrugged. She'd run out of the house on impulse and now was unsure of how to begin to tell him what was on her mind.

"Is this about *our friend?*" Michael said, looking down as if counting her fingers.

"I haven't wanted to talk to you about this but... he's been calling me— late at night. He came over a couple weeks ago. I haven't told you and that's been bothering me."

Michael sat back in the chair and appeared to be holding his breath.

"Nothing happened," she assured him, smiling as she watched him release the breath he'd been holding.

"Then what's the problem? Are you starting to think there's something there?" he asked, sitting back, studying her.

She leaned her elbows on the table and held her head in her hands. "The past can creep up on you, out of nowhere," she said. "I found myself confronting desires I thought I'd grown out of, and I feel guilty about it. He looked at me a certain way, and everything I thought I knew about myself got fuzzy. I guess I feel the need to confess this to you."

Michael chuckled. "Thank you for your honesty, but I'd have to suspect you to be attracted to the father of your children, even if you don't admit it. It's the main reason I had to stay out of the middle of your conflict. I need to be sure I'm not the reason you and he aren't together." Courtney nodded. "Let me just say this: as much as I love you, there are women in my past—there are women in my present who—if I was in the wrong place at the wrong time, I'd struggle. We're both human," he said, stroking her cheek.

"I'm not going to see Sean again," Courtney avowed, caressing Michael's hand. "I'm done with what other people think. He's used the fact that we have children to insert himself into my life just so he can convince me to break up with you and sleep with him. I'm through wasting my time."

*Decisive at last,* Michael thought as he smiled back at her.


"I'm sorry, Dr. A: there's a man in the ER who won't say what his problem is, but he insists on speaking with you," Edith, the ER nurse, informed Michael.

"Yeah, okay," Michael said, putting the phone down, having no idea who this adult patient could be, as he'd been assigned to Pediatrics for over a year.

When he walked through the doors, he saw Sean McNair waiting for him.

"Sorry about the lie, but I didn't know how to contact you, and Courtney says you're here most of the time," Sean said; and Michael, nodding, led him to a vacant exam room.

"Yes, in fact we first met here," Michael smiled at the memory, while leaning against the exam table.

"That's cute, man, but we have a situation," Sean said, standing in the center of the room facing him.

"Really?" Michael folded his arms.

"It's time for you to step aside and end your engagement. You have no plans to marry her. Stop playing games."

Michael started laughing, his humor unaffected by the unsmiling anger etched into Sean's features.

"Sir," Michael said, standing up straight to face the taller man, "when my fiancée tells me she will not marry me, *then* the engagement is off. As of now, our plans are the same."

"Why haven't you set a date?"

"That's between us," Michael said, then checked his watch. "I'll have to cut this short. If you'd like to talk further, contact me on my day off." He headed for the door.

"I thought I could talk to you as a man. I've played enough games with women to recognize when one is being perpetrated," Sean assailed him.

Michael swung around and then let out a breath. "You know nothing about me, and by walking in here you've given me ammunition I can use against you. Fortunately, I don't need to," he then moved to the door and opened it for Sean.

Sean glared at him a moment before striding slowly to the hallway.

"I've given you a fair opportunity to claim your family—since that is what you've asserted you planned to do," Michael stated, walking Sean out of the secured area. "Your time is nearly up."

# Chapter Twenty-Eight

"I'm sorry you don't wish to see me anymore," Sean said to Courtney, as they were standing beside their vehicles in the parking lot of their children's elementary school.

He'd switched his parenting days so often in the past month, she'd gotten her wires crossed, causing them both to turn up at school on the same day. Instead of weekends, Sean was now keeping the kids three days during the week, days of his choosing, which he frequently changed. The schedule benefited Courtney, so she didn't complain about the often-last-minute changes.

"I was hoping the four of us could get away for Christmas. I've been planning a trip to Disney World as a gift."

"That's nice, but what does that have to do with me?" She said.

"I can't travel with them alone. I'll need you to come along—all expenses paid. What do you have to lose?"

"I'll think about it." she said, knowing she had no interest in leaving town without Michael. "What if Michael and I meet—"

"He's *not* invited."

"Then he and I will take them to Disney World another time," she replied, getting into her car preparing to leave the school and let him wait for the kids.

He climbed into his SUV at the same time, however, pulled in front of her, rolled down his window, and barked, "Drop them off at my place later," then drove off without waiting for an answer.

Two weeks later, Angela informed Courtney the trip was on and she would be Sean's traveling companion.

"His boss, a man named Cordoba, has a villa down there. Sean says it's fabulous: five bedrooms, a pool and Jacuzzi, and he's taking me for Christmas," Angela said, grinning.

Courtney smiled, grateful that however it had come about, Angela was happy.


"Why haven't you and Michael set a date yet?" Yolanda asked Courtney, over lunch. They'd met for a day of Christmas and baby shopping as Yolanda, now remarried, was four months' pregnant. They were dining in one of Yolanda's favorite glitzy spots; and the mother-to-be ordered everything in sight, using her pregnancy as an excuse. The table was crowded with several different entrees, and Yolanda had the entire restaurant wait staff on alert.

Courtney was eating nearly as much as Yolanda, in celebration of the fact that her kids had left for Florida with Sean and Angela, earlier that day.

"Since Sean showed up, we've been going through some changes. You know he came to town talking about how he wanted his family back—"

Yolanda threw down her fork, "Oh God, you and Michael didn't fall for that *BS*—did you?" She then burst out in hysterical laughter, unable to compose herself.

Courtney shrugged, "Michael—"

"Girl, he's got a thing going on with his boss's daughter—a Puerto Rican chick named Kiki Cordoba.  She's skinny and rich and is telling everybody he's going to be her husband; of course, *he's* saying nothing."

Courtney blinked a couple times, then started laughing also.  "Oh man," she groaned, covering her eyes.  The two of them were so loud, they drew attention from surrounding tables.

"Listen, girl, a snake can't morph into a dove," Yolanda said, wiping her eyes with the napkin, "and a gold-digger does what he does.  I learned a lot from Sean.  He's an opportunist to his core, and when a man looks like him, opportunities just pop up.  It's nothing personal."


*Perfect* Courtney thought as she and Michael danced to a nostalgic slow song, at the medical staff and residents' New Year's Eve party.  They'd both taken time off from work that week, since her kids had been in Florida, and had spent almost every minute possible together.  They'd been so wrapped up in each other, it was as if Sean had been forgotten.

"Looks like it's you and me after all," Michael whispered in her ear. "We've been fair to Sean—"

"Rumor has it—" Courtney said, speaking with her head resting on his shoulder, her eyes closed, "he's in a relationship with someone beautiful and rich." She'd been nursing that news like a jewel, waiting to present it at just the right time.

Michael laughed heartily and lifted her off her feet, so that her face met his as they kissed.  "Do you think there's any way we can get married tonight?"

"Happy New Year," Michael greeted Courtney on the phone the next morning.

"Same to you," she said. "Hold on, my kids are on the other line." It had been a strange morning for her, waking up on New Year's Day to an empty house. Even Angela was out of town that year.

She was happy, however: she and Michael had set their wedding date, and he'd told her he had a present for her.

After breakfast, he drove her east of town to a new housing development near the river. It was a gated community, and she watched with surprise as he punched in the codes for entrance. Once through, he stopped the car in front of a picturesque lot that directly faced the frozen water.

Courtney smiled as she exited the car on that frigid morning. Seeing the land dotted with snow-covered pine trees that looked out over the frozen river, she guessed that Michael was showing her their future, now that they were less than two months from their wedding.

"It's beautiful," she said as they leaned on the car, gazing over the snow-covered landscape. "I've never pictured you as a dreamer, Michael. You're always so practical."

"This is no dream. If you like it, this is where we'll live. I think it's perfect but if you don't—"

"Michael, we have a place to live."

"No. You have a house you bought for yourself. I'm buying you a new one," Michael said, still looking straight ahead.

She turned to him. "Of course, when we can afford it. The cost of this lot alone, not to mention the house to put on it—"

"What makes you think I can't afford to build you a house? I wouldn't marry you if I couldn't."

Courtney stared at him, and facts started falling into place. Michael had no student loan debt. Whatever she wanted, and wherever she wanted him to take her, he did, with no mention of cost. He dressed, lived and drove modestly; she assumed he was a man of modest means. This was the first time he'd exhibited any extravagance at all.

"You can afford this?" She asked, staring at him; he nodded.

"My school costs—will I still need to work to keep my tuition benefits?"

Michael shook his head. "Need to—no."

"Are you rich?"

"Depends on what you call rich. I have what I need. I've always had what I need. My family has concerns in oil and agriculture all over Africa. Financial resources are not an issue."

Her face went numb, and she was unsure if it was the effect of the cold December air or Michael's matter-of-fact revelation.

# Chapter Twenty-Nine

"A Valentine's Day wedding—how unoriginal," Sean said, standing in Courtney's kitchen, after she'd told him the news.  He'd dropped the kids off after having them for ten days in Florida.  She'd decided to tell him about her wedding plans then, before he heard it secondhand.

"Thanks for your well wishes," Courtney quipped, removing ground beef from her refrigerator.

"Look at me," he said, taking the meat from her, placing it on the counter, and squeezing her hand.  "Don't do this.  There's still a chance we can make it.  I know things haven't gone well so far, but don't give up so easily.  Marriage is a big step—"

Courtney snatched her hand away.  "Michael and I have taken our time; we even stepped back to think things through and listen to what you had to say.  So far you haven't said much—"

"That's because you're not listening.  All you want to hear is some wedding bells."

Courtney shook her head, turned back to the counter, and resumed cooking.

"Why are you in such a hurry?  If you'd just wait a little longer, you'll see he's not the best man for you."

She scoffed but did not turn around.

"I don't want him raising my kids.  Don't I have a say in this?"

Remaining silent, she could hear him pacing behind her.

"Since you're pushing me into a corner, how about this," he stopped. "I'll move in. We'll live as a family, the way it's supposed to be. If things work out, when we're ready, we'll get married at some point. There's no reason to rush into things the way you're determined to do with your doctor."

With the ground beef sizzling in a skillet, she turned around and looked at him.

"You'll have to be patient. The lease on my place is not up for another five months."

"I'm not co-habiting with anybody I'm not married to," she said, then turned back to the skillet.

"That's all this is about, isn't it? You want to be married. That's selfish, if you ask me. Our children need us to be together, and all you care about is a piece of paper. Why don't you think about somebody else for a change?"

"Where does Kiki fit into this?" She asked casually, as she added seasonings to the skillet.

"Who?" she heard him say, his throat sounding strained.

"Kiki—your girlfriend!" she then turned and walked around him to retrieve a pot from the opposite counter. Stepping back to the stove, she glanced at his face and saw he was flushed.

"I see my mom's been—"

"She and I don't discuss you."

"Then where—"

"It's obviously true, so what does it matter," she said.  With her sauce complete, she switched the stove to simmer and turned to him.  "Hmmm, five months would give you enough time to know if things between you and Kiki are going well.  What am I—an insurance policy—or is she?"

Sean placed his hands in his pockets and rocked back on his heels, "You knew about her all along.  Why didn't you say something?"

"I don't care who you're with.  And I never dreamed you'd try to convince me to break my engagement knowing you're in a relationship.  I didn't believe you could be that selfish."

He smiled at her.  "After all these years, shows how little you know me."

Without warning, he cupped her face in both hands and kissed her.  His eyes sparkled as he turned and walked out of the kitchen.

She stood frozen in the spot, unable to walk him to the door; amused and incensed by him at the same time.  Unsure, if she faced him, whether she'd laugh at him or grab something and strike him with it.

# Chapter Thirty

The wedding, unlike Courtney and Michael's engagement, was beautifully uncomplicated.

The wedding party was small: Carmen as the matron of honor, Jay's teenage daughters Mia and Asia were bridesmaids, Bryce the ring-bearer, and Cori the flower girl.

Earl and Natalie Brooks played parents of the bride, with an overflowing grace and pride that Courtney marveled at. Since Mary's death, her relationship with Earl had improved dramatically. He'd even apologized to her for taking out his bitterness toward Mary and Deirdra on her when she was a child.

She and her attendants were adorned in African-designed gowns and headwear, while Michael and the groomsmen were arrayed in the traditional American evening wear.

The ceremony held in the chapel was happy, light-hearted and concise. Michael hated lengthy, overblown affairs and was adamant she decline any assistance from Yolanda in planning the event.

The wedding started promptly at 2 pm, and the happy couple were in their limousine on route to the reception by three o'clock. Michael hated having to hang around posing for staged photographs.

The diversity of the guests at the reception gave Courtney a sense of the many facets of her life as she'd experienced it. There were members from her extended family, who she'd only met since Mary died; then there was Michael's family, her in-laws. They were warm and joyful people, although Michael confided to her they disapproved of her as his choice for a wife.

"They're wary of anyone outside of our culture.  In time when they see how happy we are, they'll be more accepting," Michael assured her.

Yolanda and her husband were in attendance, along with Ronnie and his twenty-year old date.

Angela and her brood took over the party, however, as they labeled themselves the bride's real family, claiming ownership because Angela had adopted her in high school.

Sean and his date, Kiki, were the most visible guests at the reception; so much so, one could have mistaken them for the happy couple.

"The only person who is supposed to wear a white gown to a wedding is the bride," Carmen hissed, watching Kiki and Sean on the dance floor.

"You have to overlook her; she needs to be noticed, like her boyfriend," Courtney laughed.

After the traditional wedding activities, Courtney and Michael found themselves mostly sitting back and watching.

"You look happy," Sean, who'd stopped Courtney as she was walking across the banquet room, said in her ear.

"So do you," Courtney replied embracing him.

"That's what I like to see," Angela's said, as she walked up behind them. "My children showing each other love.  The reason why things never worked out between the two of you is because you're family.  That's all you were ever meant to be."

When Angela left, Sean and Courtney looked at each other and smiled.

"She might have a point.  Remember when we first met, how I tried to protect you?  What happened?"

"Life, teenage hormones, dysfunction… I could go on and on." Courtney said.  Then she felt a hand around her waist.

"Ready to go, Mrs. Adewele?"  Michael said, patting Sean on the back.  "The party's in full swing, and I don't think our presence is required.  I have the limo waiting out front."

"Congratulations Michael," Sean said, as they shook hands.  Courtney and Michael then headed for the exit, saying goodbye to those they passed on their way to the door.

www.ingramcontent.com/pod-product-compliance
Lightning Source LLC
Chambersburg PA
CBHW030834110726
47900CB00006B/1877